THE EMERALD TABLET

CHRONICLES OF THE SUPERNATURAL
BOOK ONE

JM HART

First published by JMH World Publishing in 2018
This 2nd edition published in 2020 by JMH World Publishing
Copyright © JM Hart 2018
jmhartwriter.com

The Emerald Tablet:
Chronicles of The Supernatural Book One.

EPUB: 9780648558040
POD: 978-0-6485580-7-1

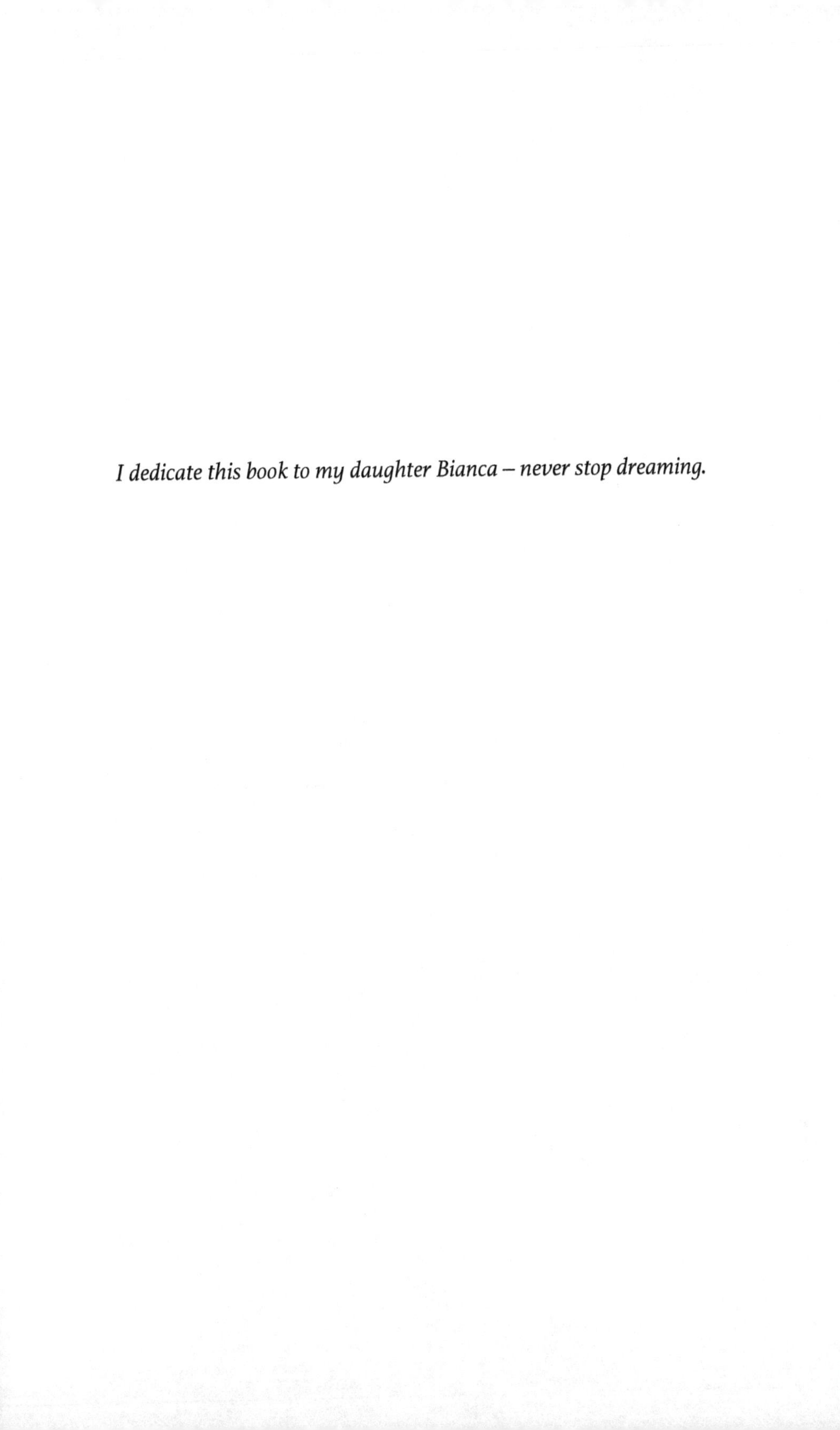

I dedicate this book to my daughter Bianca – never stop dreaming.

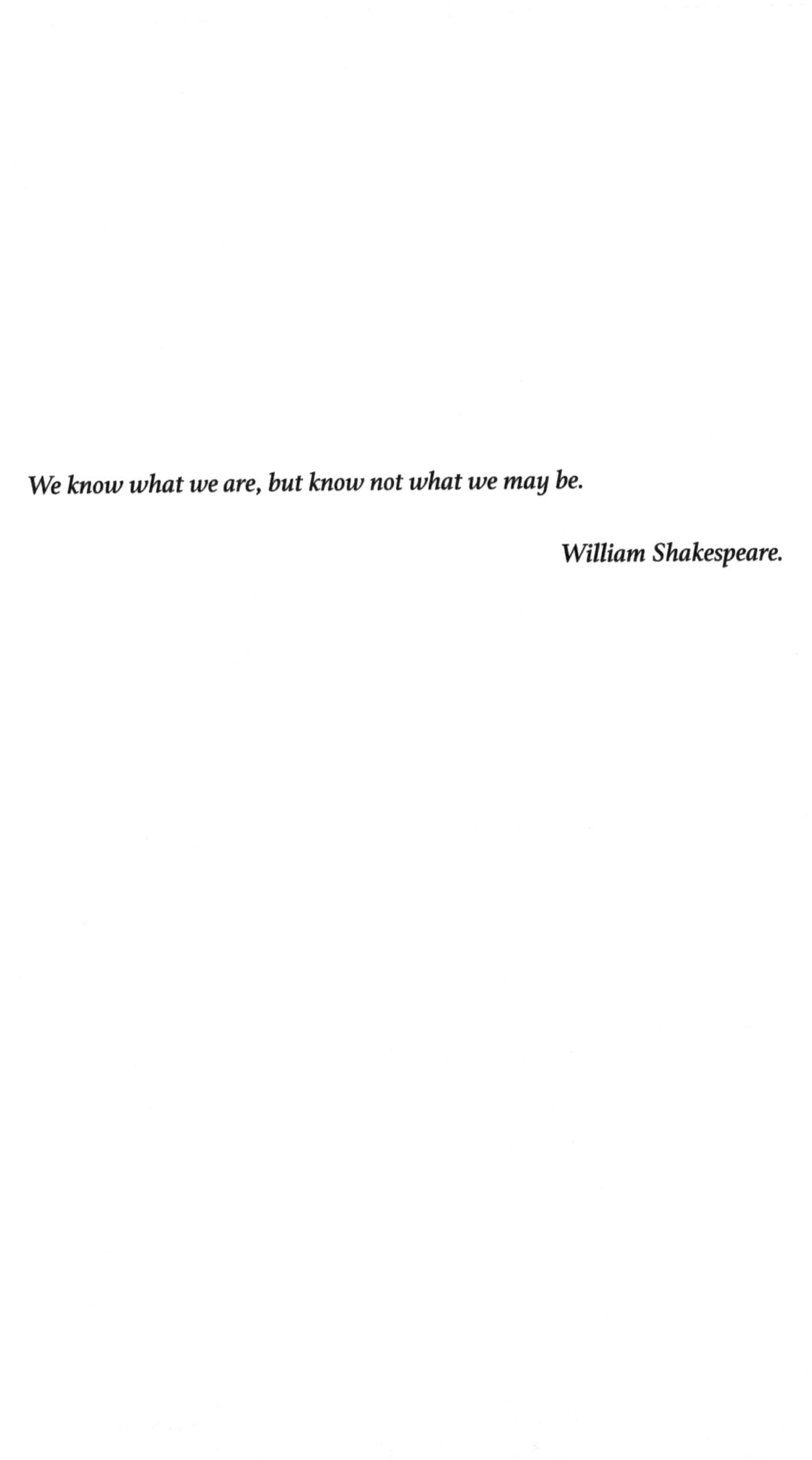

We know what we are, but know not what we may be.

William Shakespeare.

THE EMERALD TABLET: SHADOWS OF DOUBT

PART ONE

MEPHITIS PESTILENCE: SHAUN. ISRAEL

Shaun moved his legs in a scissor motion, kicking his heels rhythmically against the boulder; he felt each impact pulse down his feet to his toes. He heard the vibrations of the red string protecting the excavated sites being plucked by the same wind blowing the sand off the tips of the dunes. The area, empty of working archaeologists, was eerily quiet. Shaun imagined the sand spirits whispering, moving like ghosts in the sun's glare. Ignoring his fear he started humming, mimicking the resonance of the red string.

He'd been desperate to accompany his father on a dig such as this one, but it wasn't turning out as he'd imagined. Each time he'd begged his dad to go, he'd been told, "You're too young! When you're older; Mom needs you." His dad had promised to take him on adventures Shaun read about in books, but Shaun felt the emptiness of those promises. Sensing his mother's pain and hopelessness, he'd craved to escape the dark cloud that enveloped her.

Then, after only a few days back home in Australia after his dad had been gone for weeks, he had told him, "I believe I've found a cure for your mother; though I have to leave one more time." However this time, he'd been forced to take Shaun with him.

Shaun was wishing he was home at his mom's bedside. He closed his eyes and imagined he was resting his head on her chest. He could smell the perfumed air of her room and feel the gentle stroke of her hand on his head as she softly hummed a tune. Hours had passed since his dad and the other archaeologists had disappeared into the cave. He was in awe of his dad, but scared of him at the same time. Feeling dread creep up on him, he shivered, shifted on the boulder and pitched stones at the trucks, pretending he wasn't anxious. The red desert behind him gave him the jitters big-time. He was glad he had company, even if it was a girl: Rachel, the daughter of the head archaeologist, his dad's boss. She was sitting next to him on the boulder, chewing the ends of her long, wavy black hair. Rachel sat scanning the desert mountains that faced the distant blue haze of the Dead Sea. He followed her eyes, watching them double back to the track that was covered with sand and stone. It snaked down and around the side of the mountain, to the caves where their fathers had gone. To distract her he gave her half of his sandwich. She flattened the bread, squashing the slices together.

Earlier in the day, Shaun had seen her hiding on the back of one of the trucks. He'd spotted her peeking out from under the tarpaulin. He'd watched her as she cautiously wriggled over the side and jumped off. Seeing him, she'd frozen, knitted her eyebrows together pleadingly and put a finger up to her lips to beg him to stay silent. She must've sensed he wasn't a threat, because she'd suddenly slid under the truck like a baseball player sliding into home plate, and as soon as the archaeologists had left, she'd just as quickly — like a lizard — crawled out from under the truck and run after them.

Shaun had sprinted after her. He'd found she was taller than him, and fast, but he was faster. *She must be at least a year older,* he'd thought as he got closer; *at least eight.* She'd been wearing hiking boots and a pretty lilac floral dress that was covered with smudges of dirt. Shaun had grabbed her by the arm, and she'd jerked to a stop at the entrance to the cave. He wanted to stop her following the men. He'd been afraid she'd get lost; mostly, however, what he'd really feared was being alone in the desert.

Rachel had shaken her arm free and stared fiercely into his face.

He'd brushed his straight, sweaty dark hair out of his eyes. She'd looked back down into the mysterious cave. They could no longer hear her father or the other men. In a display of fiery anger she'd ranted and raved in her own language, waved her arms about madly, and stomped on his shoe.

She'd then suddenly stopped to size him up, tilting her head to the left, then the right and then back again, as if she was trying to work out what the image in an abstract painting was meant to be.

Shaun thought she looked at him as if there was something unusual about him. Whatever she'd been thinking passed and she smiled. "Rachel," she said with a heavy accent.

A truce. "Shaun."

Together they now waited in silence for their fathers to return. Hours had passed. At first, they hadn't noticed the time going by, because they'd quickly amused themselves, playing games as if they'd been friends forever. They'd enjoyed seeing who could jump further, run faster and throw higher. They'd taken a large piece of cardboard from a box in the truck and sat on it to race down the side of the dune. Eventually, they'd tired of climbing back up to the top. Shaun was now growing restless seeing the sky turning black.

In the valley, the nights were cold and the days hot. Shaun could feel a wind blowing in from the west and thought of how this day was a spiritual one for the locals. He could clearly hear the sound of the ram's horn calling across the land, from Metzoke Dragot, or maybe from as far afield as Ein Gedi. He loves the name, it sounds like Jedi. The wind whipped the sand against his legs. He watched Rachel jumping down from the rock, her long hair flowing behind her as she turned towards the golden sand dune. Having been perched on the boulder for so long, Shaun realized his bum was getting sore and his feet were throbbing from kicking against the rock. He stood up on the rock to scan the area, looking for any sign of his father, before he slid down to the ground.

They both shivered as the final light of the sun, and the first light of the moon was swallowed up in darkness.

Shaun noticed Rachel had become tense, and although they

didn't speak the same language, he could tell something was wrong. He felt himself shiver again, chilled by the frightening howling of the red string mixed with the distant bellow of the horn. He watched as Rachel pointed to her right, up into the distant sky, where the stars were twinkling brightly, arching off the horizon and up to the heavens. He saw the left part of the sky was empty, nothing but darkness: no stars shined, they were blanketed by a dirty haze, a sandstorm.

He and Rachel began to cough and choke, and he could feel the sand biting at his face and neck. *The dust spirits have whipped up around us. Any air that was in the valley has been squashed!* He thought.

Rachel tucked her chin into her dress to cover her mouth, and shouted to Shaun, in muffled broken English, "Quick! Come!" She reached for his hand and motioned to him to start running for the cave; they stopped just inside the mouth.

"Papa! *Papa!*" Rachel shouted into the darkness.

The wind was now blowing at their backs, pushing them forward.

Shaun dug into the pockets of his Levis, searching for his miniature blue LED light. It was a gift from his mother, she'd given it to him the last time she'd been admitted to hospital. She had pulled it out from under her pillow and pressed it into his hand and mumbled, "Turn on ... no darkness. Thoughts make merry-go-rounds. We ... thoughts control; control thoughts. She will live." He'd felt sad and embarrassed to hear the jumbled words. He hadn't understood what she had said, later his dad had explained that the medicine had taken hold and she was no longer coherent.

Shaun flicked the torch on and stepped further into the cave, feeling his throat being scratched by thick, coarse air. Cupping his hand around his mouth, he yelled as loudly as he could, "*Dad!*"

They sensed the echoes penetrating the earth and traveling under the ancient land towards Mount Zion. They waited, afraid to move.

"*Dad!*" Shaun repeated. Still no reply.

They walked a bit further in from the entrance, away from the storm, deeper into the old caves. Shaun ran his left hand along the grooved wall, then inhaled sharply and shook his hand in pain. Droplets of blood, like beads, had formed in chains across his palm.

It stung like gravel rash. Shaun rubbed the granules of sand and blood on his jeans. "The air's so gritty," he said.

Scared and alone, they crouched against the wall and waited. Shaun pointed the torch towards the ceiling, trying not to shine the light in Rachel's face. They looked at each other, wearing fake smiles to mask their fears. Outside, the storm was raging; inside the cave was deathly silent.

Rachel began to cry and whispered a prayer.

Shaun watched as her mouth moved, but couldn't understand a word she was saying. *Her eyes are emeralds.* His dad had given his mom a pair of emerald earrings, but she'd never worn them; they'd stayed a sparkle hidden inside her jewelry box.

He pulled out his Swiss army knife and started drawing in the dirt.

Rachel watched him and slowly picked up a rock to use to finish his pictures of spiral galaxies, joining them together with strong lines into the shape of a kite.

The pitch-blackness of the cave was eased by the glow of the light from his mother's torch.

The sandstorm began to pass, hard rain started to fall, and their hiding place became illuminated by quick bursts of lightning.

Shaun's concern that something was wrong increased. He knew his dad hadn't planned to be gone for so long. Early that morning, Shaun had woken to the tapping sounds of typing. He'd stayed under his bedcovers and had watched his dad on the laptop, booking the flights for tomorrow. They were to head home, back to mom. His dad had been unusually happy and excited, and while Shaun had been picking the sleep out of his eyes, his dad had come over, sat beside him and said, "After today, we'll be able to afford — and provide — all the good health your mother needs. We'll have the tablet."

Rachel moved closer to him, breaking his train of thought. He could smell her hair and see the worry on her face. Both of them were hungry, cold and tired. Bit by bit, Rachel nudged closer, until they were huddling together.

Shaun started to hum a tune his mom had sung whenever he was afraid of a thunderstorm. In the empty cave, his voice sounded delicate and shaky.

With her head on his shoulder, Rachel soon floated off into a restless sleep. Shaun was surprised he wasn't grossed out, her being a girl and all. At school, the girls were trouble, with their giggling and whispering, but Rachel seemed different.

He began to drift into sleep...

Something probed his mind — a distant sound. He surfaced to consciousness and sat wide-eyed, straining to hear. He gagged, registering a repulsive smell floating in from one of the tunnels like the smell at the garbage tip. He covered his nose and mouth, his eyes watering as the stench grew stronger.

He felt Rachel jolt as if her senses were rocked by the sickly vapors too. On the tail of the stench came the faint sound of screaming, mayhem unfolding, as the odor got closer and stronger. He heard the painful cries of men, as if from a distant battlefield, being amplified from the depths of the cave. As suddenly as the noises of suffering and torture had arisen, they ceased.

Shaun was paralyzed. He stared hard into the tunnel, squinting in an effort to penetrate the murkiness beyond the light of his torch. He bit down on his lower lip, drawing blood. He stood, and shuffled one step forward. The density of the blackness intensified, expanding like oil. It seemed to be moving towards him.

His saliva tasted metallic as if he'd been chewing his necklace and its dangling silver scorpion. He went to spit in the dirt but was stopped mid-spit by an explosion of harsh sound. Slowly he wiped his mouth. Shaun heard a corrosive shrilling within the labyrinth of tunnels. The unbearable screeches pierced his skull and reverberated in his mind. They clamped their hands tightly over their ears to block the noise that sounded like a swarm of tiny-metallic claws being dragged along the cave's walls. A message was sent to every part of his mind and body: a signal to run, to scream — anything to escape.

He saw the dense mass move like a snake towards them. He could barely move his thumb over the torch's black-rubber button to turn it off. The screeching grew louder. Rachel screamed, and Shaun quickly slapped his hand over her mouth. He saw her eyes were wide and filled with horror. He heard his heart pounding in his ears and felt fear crawling up his spine; out of the corner of his eye, he could see a shimmer of reflective light, like a flock of birds high in a sun-filled sky. That's when he saw the semi-transparent flying creatures, although he wished to God he hadn't. They had gilled necks, masses of bubbling lesions on their bat-like faces, vulturine feet, the jagged tail of a scorpion with a sharp arrow-tip, and the wings of a desolate angel. Within seconds, the faces resembling a bat's changed to a dog's snout ... the creatures were shapeshifting, constantly fluctuating and never completely forming. The air was like soup and the energy was suffocating; it had a vice-like grip around Shaun's throat.

The tiny beasts were fighting each other: pushing and shoving each other towards the entrance; tearing each other apart. They exploded from the mouth of the cave; a swarm of evil disappeared high into the dark sky. The cave fell silent. Light dancing off the walls was moving closer to them. Somebody coughed in the distance. "Who was that?" Shaun blurted out, looking at Rachel, quickly dropping the hand he had over her mouth. *She's going to cry,* he thought. *I have to protect her!* She looked how he felt: petrified.

They scurried to the other side of the cave and crouched behind a boulder. The silhouette of a man, with a backpack hanging off his shoulder, rushed past them and out into the night. He stood just beyond the entrance, coughing, "Shaun!" the man shouted. "Shaun, where are you?"

Shaun stood up and pulled at Rachel.

She wouldn't budge.

"Come on!" he whispered. "Let's go!"

Rachel didn't move; all she did was shake her head rapidly and move further out of sight.

Shaun stared at her and frowned. She shooed him away and began to cry silently, the tears marked her dirty cheeks. Their eyes met.

Despite the despair she must have been feeling, Rachel smiled.

Shaun smiled back, then turned and ran towards his father. "Dad!

Dad!" he yelled. "I'm over here!" He wrapped his arms around his dad's waist and hugged him tightly. "Where are the others?" he asked him. "What happened? You were gone for so long!"

His father pushed him aside. "Stop talking."

He looked at his father's face that was screwed up with anger and hatred; a stranger's face. "But where are the rest?" he asked again.

His dad dropped the backpack at Shaun's feet and ran over to the truck. "There was an accident," he yelled back to Shaun as he lowered the tailgate and climbed on.

Shaun was glued to the spot. He watched his dad jump off the back of the truck carrying a wooden box and rush back to the cave, where he emptied the contents on the desert floor.

"They're not coming. Now, move! Pick up the backpack and get in the Jeep!"

Recognizing the symbols marked on the box, Shaun felt he was going to wet his pants and vomit. He had such a strange feeling in his tummy he didn't know what to do. "That's dynamite!"

His dad just kept ignoring him and jamming the sticks into the cracks in the wall.

Shaun ran up to him and pulled at his belt to make him come away from the cave.

His dad slapped him hard, flinging him like a rag doll.

His face stung.

"Stop blubbering!" his father demanded as he wedged more explosives into every crack he could find. Then he set a timer.

Shaun jumped to his feet, bolted past his dad and yelled into the cave, "Rachel, get out! You have to get out!"

His dad knocked him to the ground then picked him up until they were eye to eye.

Shaun's face stung, and through his shirt he could feel his dad's fingernails. His dad's breath smelt stale and hot.

"Who the hell are you talking to?" he bellowed. "They're all gone! They're all dead!"

Shaun couldn't catch his breath. He started crying and couldn't stop. Suddenly he could see around his dad's head a cluster of parasites clashing with an invisible force field. Shaun became transfixed. *It's the tiny beasts.* He started to feel itchy all over. He wished his dad would put him back down on the ground. He could see the parasites were getting smaller as they move closer and closer to his father's head. One of them pierced the invisible force field, and the cluster streamed into his dad's left ear.

His dad, irritated, stretched his mouth so wide Shaun thought it would become unhinged. His dad became more anxious and angry, as if the parasites were urging him on.

Shaun leant back, away from his father's face. "What? The others can't be dead!" Shaun tried to pull away.

"What are you doing?" his dad yelled. He pulled him close, flipped him under his arm and used his other arm to pick up the backpack.

Shaun kicked and screamed, struggling to get down. His dad carried him to the Jeep and threw him into the back of the vehicle. Shaun heard the old Jeep grind into gear, and hung on to the seat as he looked back for Rachel. He saw the cave getting smaller and became afraid he'd lose sight of it. Then he saw Rachel emerge. As the vehicle bounced over the unsealed road, he willed Rachel to move: *Run, Rachel! Run!*

Frozen, she just stood there.

He continued watching and waiting for her to flee. He thought he saw her move away from the cave, towards him, and let his shoulders relax a bit. *She'll make it!* His dad was driving fast, and Rachel was getting further and further away. The sky was lit up by lightning, and in the distance, he thought he saw her raise her hand and wave. He raised his too, but the simple wave, the simple gesture, was lost: the cave exploded, and Rachel was no longer visible. The explosion was brighter than any of nature's fiery storms, brighter than any lightning bolt.

Shocked, Shaun allowed his hand to slowly drop. He didn't know what else to do, except cry.

"Turn around!" he heard his dad command him. "Wipe that stupid look off your face and open the luggage bag — quickly! Get the backpack! Reach in and you'll feel something wrapped up in cloth. I want you to take it out. It's heavy — be careful. But *don't* unwrap it! That's it!"

Shaun took some short, sharp breaths and felt his body jerking. He lifted an artifact out and tried to speak: "What ... what ... is ... is it?"

"Never you mind!" his dad replied. "Bury it among the clothes in the suitcase, and lock it!"

He felt the Jeep toss and turn, and twice he nearly dropped his dad's precious cargo. He did as he was told. The object was curved like a Roman chest plate covered with ancient writings and drawings. It was heavy and difficult to hold. Shaun struggled as he buried it deep in the suitcase and zipped it up. He used the back of his dirty hand to wipe the tears and snot from his face.

The Jeep screeched to a halt just outside the airport. His dad lifted the suitcase out, roughly turned Shaun around on the back seat, put the backpack over his shoulders. "Come on! Out of the car! Keep up! You're so weak it's pathetic! I've never noticed how soft you are — you're just like your mother!"

Shaun jumped out and, closing the door, spotted a leather pouch on the car floor. He picked it up and opened it slightly and saw oddly-shaped, multi-colored stones.

He pulled the straps tight and shoved the pouch deep into his pocket and followed his father. Shaun hid his feelings behind the shadows of the night and as he ran to catch up, he felt the rain upon his face merge with the tears spilling down his cheeks. Everything seemed different. He was afraid.

Once inside the airport, his dad flashed Egyptian passports. They passed through Customs unquestioned and were allowed to board the plane immediately. Shaun sat next to the window and, looking around, saw the small plane was only half full. It shook and vibrated as it screamed down the runway. The storm had become violent, lightning hammered the tarmac. The ground shook with each strike, each blast reminding Shaun of the exploding cave. Some of the passengers screamed. He could see out the side window that the ground had cracked open. *Like a sinkhole*, he thought. The plane accelerated towards the hole and the lightning illuminated the crumbling ground. *We're not going to make it, we're not going to make it!* The heavy machine's wheels were inches from the abyss below them as the plane launched into the storm. The aircraft ascended into the terrifying turbulence created by the merciless clouds of micro- beasts released less than an hour ago from the cave. *They're following us.* It sounded as if the plane was being pelted with bullets.

As Shaun gripped the seat, his knuckles turned white. Oxygen masks sprang from their sockets. The plane continued its sharp rise to the heavens. They shot through the clouds and leveled out above the storm. They removed their oxygen masks and left them dangling. Shaun leant into his dad, "I'm scared."

"Everything'll be okay now, we have the tablet," his dad assured him. "Get some sleep; you want to be fresh to see your mother when we land."

Shaun felt exhausted, confused, frightened and mistrusting. "Dad, is Mom coming home? Is she better?"

His dad didn't answer; he stared vacantly past him and out the window. Shaun shivered.

Shaun tried to sleep, but found himself tossing and turning in his seat, unable to stop thinking about Rachel...

"Wake up, boy!" he heard his dad demand. "Drink this!"

He saw his dad's eyes were black marbles — he was gone again. His dad shoved a clear plastic cup and a little yellow pill into Shaun's hands. He wanted to please his dad so he took the tablet.

Shaun fell into a deep sleep and awoke just before landing at home. He wanted to look out the window to see the beaches that stretched along the coast; he wanted to see the land of the sun and surf, his home — Australia. He felt groggy, and his body was heavy. He turned to his dad and saw him rummaging around in his backpack and wearing a different set of clothes. The couple sitting next to him unlocked their seat belts and reached up for the overhead compartments across the aisle. Shaun felt his empty stomach do a somersault and his head spun. There was no window; they were in the middle aisle, and it was six seats wide. *Where am I,* he wondered.

His dad looked at him, he heard him say something he couldn't understand as he handed over a vomit bag. *Perfect timing.* He buried his head in the waxed bag and puked. He came up for air, looked around the plane and saw it was full. That was when he realized he was on a different plane — a jumbo! He felt his dad pull him to his feet and push him into the aisle.

His head hurt. Everything was a blur as his dad kept him shuffling forward down the aisle, off the plane, and through Customs. Feeling fuzzy, and as if he was going to puke again, he tried hard to understand the Customs officer, who said to him, "Not much of a holiday for a young fella — a business trip to Dubai with your old man!" The man then handed back the two passports.

Shaun was focused on his passport, feeling confused. He fixated on its cover, the coat of arms. He ran his finger over the images of the kangaroo and emu: an Australian passport; his passport. *What happened to the Egyptian passports?* He looked up at his dad.

Noticing his perplexed look, his dad put his arm over Shaun's shoulders, as if he cared. "He's jet-lagged and misses his mom," he said to the Customs officer.

That's true, Shaun thought.

They walked out of the airport, with the backpack only, not the suitcase.

"What about the suitcase?" Shaun asked his dad.

His father opened the door of the silver taxi and blankly asked, "What suitcase, son?"

Shaun climbed into the taxi and swore he'd never trust his dad again. *Was it all a dream?* They climbed into the back of the taxi. The air was so thick you could've cut it with a knife. Neither of them said a word as they headed for home.

2

TEN YEARS LATER: CASEY. UTAH, USA

Casey was skinny and had wild curly brown hair, and a tiny gap of prosperity between his two front teeth. He was tad short for his age, but he was a bright boy and was about to use parts of his mind Einstein would have only ever dreamed about.

He was walking home from school, happy. The wind was gathering strength and the leaves started spiraling around him and were swept up into the air and across the mountain road. Thunder echoed across the valley, heavy raindrops began to slap the sealed road. Like paint flung from the brush of an angry painter, dark clouds suddenly blacked out the sun. He shivered. Something was terribly wrong — there was an atmosphere of foreboding, and a churning sensation in the pit of his stomach.

The rain multiplied, and the howling wind pushed it diagonally across the deserted road. He peered into the dense forest, towards the shortcut, thinking of how it always looked downright eerie. He decided he'd stay on the road, but an uneasy feeling crept up his spine. He shouldered his schoolbag and started jogging.

He felt his woolen school blazer become heavy because it was soaking up the rain like an old sponge. It was two sizes too big, but his mom had said he'd "grow into it". Casey knew she'd felt bad about having to buy it from the school's seconds shop, but he also knew the scholarship hadn't included the cost of his school clothes. He didn't care, not really, and especially not today, because today was his thirteenth birthday and he was officially a teen.

The wind pushed him backward, and he could no longer see the road through the heavy rain. He had to go into the woods to get home quickly. He wouldn't think about the spooky stories the other kids told; he had to get home to his mom. She was alone, and the storm looked as if it was going to get bad really fast.

Casey darted off the road down the slippery embankment and entered the woods. He distracted himself by imagining his mom baking a delicious mud cake. He held the vision within his mind, his senses filled with the smell of warm chocolate. His mouth started to water and his tummy rumbled as he pictured the warm glow of the kitchen light and cooling cake. He smiled. It was as if the clouds had opened up above and a summer sun was now shining down on him. He continued to battle the rain, feeling washed with new energy.

Ignoring the whack of the squeaking "WARNING!" sign as it banged against the barbed-wire fence post, Casey crouched down under the wire, ran through the first stand of trees and headed for the stream, which on any other day would have been placid. *The kids never mentioned a "warning" sign,* he thought, *maybe this was a bad idea.*

He seemed to have jogged for a long time before he spotted the entrance to a footbridge. Its wooden entry posts were covered with green moss that was only half- concealing the termites. *Nobody uses it regularly!* he thought. *All the stories were lies!*

Having come too far to go back, he timidly held on to the worn rope balustrade and carefully put his weight down on the first plank. He rocked back and forth to test its strength. The other side of the bridge was cloaked in sheets of rain.

He sensed something moving behind him. *What was that?* He turned around quickly, checked behind himself, and saw a little off to the right was a storm water drain; the wire mesh covering its entrance was torn away. The gap was wide enough for someone — or something — to pass through. He started to freak out, and his consciousness started to flood with a medley of schoolyard stories. He pushed his wet hair out of his eyes, as if he were able to push the images away.

He stared past the rain and into the dark tunnel, but he couldn't see beyond its entrance. He strained to hear anything above the rain. Usually Casey loved the fresh smell of rain, but not today: he smelt something metallic in the air and a terrible taste in his mouth.

The thunderclaps continued shifting; moving closer. He looked down, between the slats of wood, and checked under the bridge. Although he knew it would be impossible for a meaty claw to pull him into the depths of a beast's lair, he couldn't help looking — just in case. The bridge was old and neglected, and when he stepped forward, he heard the pillars moan. Feeling unsure, he looked for another way across. Everything looked grey and lifeless, the color had been sucked out of the day and there was no golden light, no summer sun.

The stream below was a raging body of water. Knowing he had to move, Casey held his breath while testing the next plank. He kept going, never putting both his feet on the same plank at the same time. He pushed on into the wind.

When he reached the middle of the narrow footbridge, the wind lifted the whole bridge up as if it were a sail. Casey held tight on to the side ropes. The strong gust of wind dissipated and dropped the bridge back down. Seizing the moment, he pulled himself along, feeling the old rope fraying in his hands.

The heavens released their fury on him. Hail slammed into his backpack and into his shoulders, arms and head. He let go of the ropes and raised his arm to protect his head. He imagined his nightmarish phantom was under the bridge waiting for the last sliver of light to vanish. The bridge swayed dangerously.

When the hail stopped suddenly, he reached for the rope, but the wind drove him back. He pulled his heavy blazer tight around himself and pushed on, keeping his head down. He paused and looked upstream. He heard what sounded like a hundred wild horses racing towards him, getting closer and closer. He turned to run, and slipped. Torrents of water were rushing around the bend in the river below, and in an instant, in one surge, the water shot up over the riverbanks.

Casey scrambled to his feet, immediately he knew it was too late to make any difference. He reached for the rope as a tidal wave of debris slammed into him. The bridge was torn away from the posts and dragged down into the murky water. Casey held on as he sank into the river.

Underwater, he struggled out of the harness of his school backpack and felt himself being dragged down because of his sodden blazer. He slipped his right arm out of it and then his left, and let the deadly soaked garment sink to the bottom. He breeched the water's surface and inhaled air. He used his hands to search for something — anything — and felt the velvet moss of a plank from the bridge. The current was relentlessly pulling at his body, dragging him downstream. He dug his fingers into the wooden plank as it sailed past him, but he couldn't get a firm grip. He slipped, and felt his fingernails snap back. He let go, screaming in pain, slipping further into the swirling water. The river was moving around and under his body, pulling at his legs, and the debris felt like the sharp claws of a giant lizard. "*Help!*" Casey screamed.

But nobody was there to hear. Bolts of lightning were splitting the sky, and the undertow was dragging him down. He slapped the water's surface, searching for something, anything, to hold and keep him buoyant. The flood continued violently surging down from the mountain.

Suddenly, he felt his hand brushing against a passing branch that was tangled up with rope and rungs from the bridge. He threw his arm over it and clutched on to it.

The hail returned and smacked painfully into the back of his hands. He lost his grip, the branch floated out of his reach. Casey was pulled under. He was exhausted but continued struggling up to the surface...

He thought he glimpsed a kid on the other side of the river watching him, and screamed, "*Help! Help me!*" Spotting the long thick branch of an old tree coming his way, Casey fumbled for it, used it to pull himself up, and felt hope. He searched for the kid but no one was there.

A piece of rope that was tangled around the branch and parts of the footbridge suddenly went taut, snapped, and whipped up into Casey's face, slicing open his right cheek. He let go of the branch, in surprise and exhaustion. Blood poured from his gash, but it was instantly diluted by the rain.

He used his foot to search for leverage below, and felt a rock. His foot slid on the moss, but then he managed to push himself up. He pushed again, using both feet, and lunged at the branch. Reaching for the rope, his foot slipped. His head went under, and his leg became tightly wedged between two rocks. Casey saw the light from above disappear, his heart raced as he endured the river's claws moving around his leg and latching on to his knee. He wrestled with his leg in an attempt to free his wedged foot. The rain-fueled water was getting deeper and deeper. He kept his eyes focused on the surface and struggled to escape. The light had disappeared completely; he was surrounded by darkness. *It's not fair!* he thought as he struggled. *This was supposed to be a good day! This isn't supposed to happen! It's the first day of summer, the last day of school, the best day of the year! It's my birthday damn it! This is bullshit! I'm in control of my reality! Whose crappy idea is this? Or maybe I'm supposed to die today! Righteous people come into the world and leave the world on their birthday, don't they? The stars were all lined up last night in the shape of the Star of David — it was all over the media — I can't die today, I'm not righteous!*

The desire to open his mouth and draw in a breath was overwhelming, and his lungs ached badly. *It's just not fair!* he thought. He was feeling like the comic book hero who never gets the girl because the two of them are from different worlds. *Why, damn it?* he screamed in his head.

The water seemed to rise even higher; the rock had a firm grip around his leg. He stretched his arms up in one last, desperate attempt to grapple at the water around him as if it would suddenly allow him purchase. He felt his lungs fill with unbearable pain, the pressure of the water crushing his ribs as if he were being tormented by not one, but a legion of underwater phantoms. He yelled at the darkness, *Enough! I will* not ... *die ... today!*

In a heartbeat, the hail stopped, the river went silent, he felt his chest start convulsing, and darkness slithered in. *There's no peace in drowning!*

Feeling an explosion of light deep within himself, he pushed away the darkness and let go.

THE ROAD WAS NOW covered with hailstones that looked like shiny marbles. Terry was anxious to get home to his wife, Amy. He rolled down the car window and stared out at the dark cloud that was hovering, tormenting the town. He wound the window back up, nervously gripped the steering wheel, and pulled out from the safety of the trees back on to the road. He heard the tyres crunch and slide over the ice, and he chanted, "Don't speed! Don't speed! It's okay! She's okay!" He used his left hand to wipe the windscreen, and continued carefully towards home.

The river had flooded and the road was nowhere in sight, he slowed to a stop. He prayed the bridge was in one piece underneath, and entered the flowing water. *Two weeks ago,* he thought, *the rivers and streams were barely a trickle — not even enough to quench a bird!*

Terry put his foot steady on the gas and kept the car crawling across the bridge. The water started seeping in between the door seals and pooling at his feet, he was afraid the motor would flood and stall.

Two-thirds of the way across, he spied a funnel of air dropping from the sky and spiraling out of control. "Oh, my God!" he murmured.

He accelerated out of the water, not taking his eyes off the swaying funnel, which was moving backwards and forwards gathering speed, propelling itself towards the town. *I'm not gonna make it!* he thought as he saw the funnel grow larger. He was well aware that disasters were occurring throughout the world, having vigilantly listened to the reports over the radio. *No local warnings — nothing!* he thought. Mesmerized, he watched a rooftop bouncing around in the wind, like a kite. The sky was filled with debris. The black clouds released their fury as another twister formed and started colliding with the first, creating one massive storm cell. Terry couldn't see the town any more.

The trees arching over the road were unable to withstand the force and like dead weeds were uprooted and yanked into the sky. *Coastal towns are the only places that get freak storms!*

Up ahead, something was lying on the road. He squinted, and frantically wiped the windscreen just in time to see a tree falling across the road. He planted his foot on the brake, the car screeched and spun out of control. He choked the steering wheel, terrified. The car jackknifed, Terry's head violently hit the steering wheel and the car crashed into the enormous oak...

Silence filled the car, and he slowly opened his eyes and took in his surroundings. He saw the back-left passenger door was crushed inward, and could feel the back wheel was elevated. He opened his door and tumbled out, the wind had subsided but it was still sharp and cold on his face.

He climbed over the horizontal tree trunk, opened the car boot and searched around for his emergency warning triangle, raincoat and first-aid kit. When he climbed back over the branches, he slipped, and the triangle blew away. He pulled his jacket tight around himself, kept his head down to protect his eyes, and walked to the crest of the road, occasionally looking up, searching.

Finally, he spotted something further up the road. Terry picked up his pace — the closer he got, the more he could see it looked like a body. "Hey!" he yelled. "You okay? Hello!" He didn't think whoever it was would hear him over the sounds of the howling wind as it increased in velocity. The trees started bending and snapping. He tried to run, forcing his way through the wind; he could manage no more than a slow jog. "Hey, can you hear me?" he shouted as he approached the body.

No answer. Child-sized, face down and lifeless.

He knelt beside the body, gently squeezed the shoulders, put his hand on the back, and waited to feel it rise.

Nothing.

He rolled the body on its side, and saw it was a boy. He opened the boy's mouth, and murky water escaped from it. Protecting his neck, he carefully turned the boy on to his back and checked his breathing. His other injuries were evident: a gash down his right cheek, which would warrant at least half a dozen stitches, and blood all over his left leg. Terry could feel neither a breath nor a pulse. He decided to fold his fingers together and press down on to the adolescent boy's chest, to perform CPR, but it was nothing like the rubber mannequins he'd practiced on — this real body was very fragile. Rain dripped from Terry's hair on to the boy's face, and he blinked madly to see.

No response.

"Come on, damn it!" he shouted at the body. "Come on!" He kept pumping the boy's chest: "One! Two! Three! Four!"

After what seemed like an eternity, the boy started coughing and vomiting water.

Terry quickly turned him on his right side, telling him, "That's it, good! Bring it all up!" He rubbed the boy's back and continued reassuring him until he'd stopped vomiting the oceans of water he seemed to have inhaled. "My name's Terry," he told him. "You're okay now."

The wind was getting stronger and the storm was back, building. He knew he had to get them out of there. He saw the kid's fingernails had been snapped back and the flesh underneath was exposed.

The rain stopped, and the storm became eerily quiet.

"What happened?" he asked the boy, hoping he'd hear. "Storm caught you by surprise aye? — I think the whole town's been caught out! I've never known any twister, or a storm, like it in this neck of the woods — what about you? You're okay, pal!"

The boy struggled to sit up.

"Take it easy," Terry said.

"My head hurts!" The boy announced as he tried to sit up. "The footbridge collapsed! My chest hurts! How'd you pull me from the river?" He looked at his fingers, clenched his teeth, and tried to push one of his fingernails back into place. He bent his knee and winced when he felt his torn school pants caught on his open wound.

He's hurting badly! Terry thought. "The river?" he queried. "No, I didn't pull you from the river — you're in the middle of the road, about three hundred yards from the river. I was driving. I couldn't see. Just before a tree fell in front of me, I thought I saw something on the road. I swerved to miss the tree, and the car slid out of control."

The boy stopped trying to push his fingernail back to its rightful place, and stared into Terry's eyes as if he were searching for answers but failing.

"If it hadn't fallen ..." Terry began. "That tree saved your life. I would've run over you. Someone's looking out for you, buddy — you're one hell of a lucky dude!"

The boy sat up, leant against Terry's knees. "How'd I get here, then?" he looked towards the violent river, and mumbled, "It was the light – I chose not to die – it was my choice. I did this. Did you see anybody else, another boy?"

Terry watched as the child turned his head towards the river.

"I have to — I have to get home! My mom — she — she's alone!"

"Okay," Terry said, "let's get you up. Do you think you can put any weight on that leg?"

The boy looked down at his left knee, tried to straighten it out, and replied, "Maybe — I think it's just a bit mangled."

"'Mangled', huh? Is *that* what you'd call it?" Terry said. He put his right arm under him and helped him to his feet, concerned because the boy could only stand on one leg and looked like he was going to pass out any second. "I'm gonna have to pick you up, buddy," he announced. "You cool with that?" He waited for him to register the comment.

But the boy didn't move.

"What's your name?" he asked him, feeling the rain getting harder and stinging his face as if it were tiny, sharp needles. He was now chilled to the bone. He quickly bent and scooped up the boy, just in time, as the poor fella passed out and slumped over Terry's right shoulder.

He's so heavy! he thought. *What was I thinking? This guy has to be about ninety pounds!* Bearing the boy's dead weight, he rushed back to the car, desperate to find his wife and get the boy to hospital. Each step was a struggle not to topple over as the wind pushed him from behind.

Exhausted, he sat the boy on the front passenger seat and reclined it until the boy was fully lying down. He feverishly wiped the windshield, breathing heavily as a sense of something terribly wrong came over him. He placed his right hand on the ignition, paused, and addressed the car as if it were a horse: "Okay, boy. We're gonna get one shot! You're an all-wheel drive, and we've gotta jump this tree to get out of this mess! You can do it!" He patted the dashboard and turned the key.

The car came to life.

"Good!" he exclaimed. "Good start!" He held the handbrake lever, ready to release it, and stomped down on the accelerator.

The car tried to pull away.

He released the lever.

The car hurled itself over the tree trunk on to the road, and stopped.

Amazed, he sat idling for a few seconds and then checked his passenger. Thunder clapped overhead, and he jumped. Lightning split across the blackened sky — a rip in the fabric of the universe — and he felt fear creep over his body.

Entering the town, Terry slowed the car to a crawl. He found the main street blocked and some of the buildings demolished, whereas others were untouched. Cars lay under fallen trees. Like a toothpick, a telegraph pole had snapped and was leaning, broken over the road. A frenzy of broken wires jittered across the lanes, raised up like cobras, discharging electrical sparks; Terry mounted the gutter and then swerved back to the road to avoid them. The boy he had in the passenger seat was a rag doll bouncing around.

Terry saw a few people appear along the streets. An elderly couple were weeping over a pile of rubble. He was spooked, his mouth was dry and the blood rushed around his head. He felt his heart pounding, and began to truly fear for his wife, Amy's safety. He picked up his phone, no signal. He checked the boy.

He was still breathing.

He cautiously drove on, easing the car forward over the rubble, and finally turned east towards the hospital. Leaves and twigs were caught up under the windshield wipers and were scratching against the window. He strained to see beyond them as he checked down each road to determine the safest route. The town's north-west side seemed to have taken the biggest blow, and the damage was less as he approached the hospital. "Thank God it's still standing!" he muttered. He pulled on the handbrake and jumped out of the car.

Hundreds of people, dazed and injured, were walking towards the hospital's entrance. Terry carefully picked up the boy and moved amongst the crowd as quickly as possible to the entrance. He stopped at the doorway to Emergency and looked over the sea of wounded, searching for help. He wove through the mayhem, pushing towards the front, and repeated, "Excuse me! Excuse me! I have an unconscious child! Somebody help me."

The triage nurse behind the glass window opened the side door for the next patient.

Terry slid through.

She gave him a scolding look, but checked the boy's pupils, then pulled open a curtain and said, "Lay him on that bed. What's his name?" She flashed a light in the boy's eyes, checked his pulse, and patted him down.

"I don't know," Terry answered. "I found him on the road. He wasn't breathing. I gave him CPR. He vomited water."

"Has he been in a car accident?" the nurse asked him as she placed a plastic collar around the boy's neck.

"No," Terry replied. "Well — I don't know. He was just lying in the middle of the road. I didn't see any cars."

She looked up at Terry and announced, "He'll need some stitches, at least. We'll need to check him for spinal injuries and X-ray his lungs." She pulled the stethoscope out of her ears and left them dangling around her neck. "I'll find a doctor. You'll need to stay with him. We're understaffed; relief is coming, but I need you to stay with him for now. What's your name?"

"Terry," he answered.

"Can you stay with him, Terry?" she asked.

"Okay," he replied, "but my wife ... I don't know where my wife is."

"I'm sure just as you helped this young man, someone will help your wife," the nurse assured him, and dashed out of the cubicle.

The hospital smelt and tasted like a construction site, Terry thought. He crouched down so his face was next to the boy's head, and whispered to him, "Just in case you can hear, we're in the hospital — you'll be alright." He looked at the woman lying unconscious in the bed next to the boy's. Her face and neck were blackened with bruises and her hair and clothes were caked with dirt. He thought she looked as if she'd been excavated. She had an IV line inserted in her left arm. One of the two attending nurses jabbed a needle into a narrow, orange-colored rubber tip and injected a clear fluid into the arm. The woman reacted in seconds and opened her eyes wide. She gasped for air, seized her stomach and twisted in pain, and the nurse gave her another injection into the rubber tube. The woman calmed slightly and started taking hurried shallow breaths.

That one must've been morphine, Terry guessed, watching as the attending doctor unemotionally scribbled notes on his clipboard and then hurried away to his next patient, leaving the woman in the care of two young nurses, who were now holding her right hand and speaking clearly to her to explain where she was and what had happened: "There was a storm, and you were found pinned under a cement slab. You're now safe in the hospital. Your injuries are critical. Do you understand?"

The woman made the smallest attempt to nod.

"Is there anyone you'd like us to try to get hold of?" one of the nurses asked.

The woman struggled to breathe and to speak: "My ... son. Where's ... my son?"

The other nurse held a syringe in the air, again grabbed the little rubber stopper, and injected the swirling, clear liquid into the woman.

"What's your son's number?" the other nurse asked the woman, to distract her from the pain she was feeling.

The woman made a choking sound.

Terry's heart went out to her.

She gave a cough, and blood sprayed into the oxygen mask. She moaned.

Terry saw tears fall from the corner of her left eye.

She turned her head slightly and whispered, "My son." She coughed again, and this time, more than a spray of blood was visible.

The nurse let go of her hand, moved the mask, and wiped her mouth.

The woman slightly lifted her arm, reached out to Terry, and said to him, "My son."

Terry's eyes met hers. He smiled as the nurse busied herself by placing a new oxygen mask over the patient's face, causing muffling of the words the woman was uttering: "Cay ... Casey ... my son ..." Before she slipped away, she locked eyes with Terry.

He felt a strange connection with her.

The nurses moved quickly, and the machines beeped and pinged loudly around them ... but there was nothing they could do.

Terry felt conflicted in his heart. He wanted to turn away from the misery in her eyes.

However, he held her gaze while she was dying.

He felt her fighting the pain, not knowing where her child was. *A heavy burden to die with,* he thought.

She clutched on to her last moments of life.

He believed her thoughts were only for her son. Her eyes

emptied.

He turned away from the dying woman's final moment.

The triage nurse returned with a doctor, who immediately went to work examining the boy.

"What did you say his name was?" the nurse asked Terry.

Terry pulled his eyes away from the dead woman's, and replied, "I didn't — he never told me." He looked back at the dead woman, and said, "But, it might be ... Casey. I think that might've been his mother."

The nurse followed his gaze towards the deceased woman, and closed the curtain.

The doctor turned, lowered his glasses, rubbed his tired eyes, looked at Terry, and said to him, "Why don't you get yourself a cup of coffee while we run some tests and stitch up his cheek and knee? His vitals are good; he's stable. You saved his life. He won't wake for a little while. Go and get yourself some air."

Terry rubbed the back of his neck, stared down at the springy blue-vinyl floor, thought of his wife, and prayed she was alright. Realizing he needed to try to call her again, he said to the doctor and nurses, "I'll be back in ten." He headed out of the emergency ward and came out into the ambulance bay to search for mobile-phone reception. He dialed the number, and when he heard her phone start ringing, he felt joy entwined with fear leap into his throat.

An ambulance pulled into the bay, and the sound of it drowned out the sound of the ring tone.

Terry shoved his right middle finger into his ear.

The medics jumped out of the van, opened the back door, and pulled out the gurney.

The phone stopped ringing.

The medics unfolded the gurney's wheels, secured them on the ground, clicked them into place, and asked him, "Sir! Sir! Step aside!"

Terry moved and the signal was lost. Frustrated, he wanted to scream. He was scared, hungry and cold. He stared at the gurney and then at the patient, thinking to himself, *So much pain and suffering!* He saw the person lying on the gurney was mapped with bruises similar to the dead woman's, and presumed she must have been dug out of the rubble as well. He stared at the unconscious face, and held his breath. Shocked and paralyzed, he forced himself to look closer at the bloody fingers and the black and blue arms. *She must've tried to claw her way out!* He started crying. Her long, strawberry-blonde hair was hanging lifeless, caked with blood and muck. The tube she had down her throat was taped to her cheeks and covering her face ... But he knew that face. He took her hand, and without looking up at the medics, asked them, "She's okay, yeah?" Tears trailed down his cheeks as he choked back the pain and uttered, "This is my wife. Tell me she's okay — please ..."

"Sir, are you sure this is your wife?" one of the medics asked him.

"Yes."

"You've got great timing," the medic remarked. "The big fella upstairs, he knows what he's doing at times like these — I wish he'd let us in on some of his secrets."

The other medic continued wheeling the patient into the hospital.

The other one said to him, "What's your wife's name? Sir, come with us. What's your name?"

"Terry," he replied as the automatic doors opened in front of them.

"What's your wife's name, Terry?" the medic asked him again.

"Amy," Terry answered, following the gurney and listening to the medical jargon as the medics gave the triage nurse his wife's details: "Woman; mid-thirties; pulled from rubble of house; unresponsive to sound or touch; possible fractured skull; bleeding from the head, temporal area; treated for suspected spinal injury; protruding broken left ulna and radius; lacerations to the left side of the head."

"Put her over there — number eight," the nurse instructed them.

They came to a stop, and parked her where the dead woman had been.

The ER nurse pulled the curtain behind them, blocking his view of his wife.

He caught a glance of the organized chaos as another nurse

emerged holding a folder and clicking a pen.

"Terry, is it?" she asked him.

"Yes," he replied. "How is she?"

"The doctors are examining her," the nurse answered. "I have a few questions you need to answer so we can treat her properly. Can you tell me whether there are any serious medical problems — heart? Diabetes? Epilepsy? High blood pressure?"

He answered the questions as the nurse ticked the relevant boxes and then handed him the completed consent form. He took the clipboard and signed the form.

No sooner had the doctor flung the curtain back than the bed's synthetic wheels silently moved down the corridor on the blue vinyl floor. The medics rushed Amy away, and an orderly returned the young fella to the room.

Terry saw the boy's cheek had been stitched up, and he had been changed into a white hospital gown, but he was still unconscious.

The nurse came back, and as she clicked the bed's wheel locks into place, she informed Terry that Amy was going into surgery, adding, "As soon as I know anything, I'll let you know."

Hours passed, and when Amy was finally returned, she had bandages around her head and a cast on her arm.

The same doctor who'd treated the boy said to Terry, "She has a small fracture of the temporal bone. We'll have to wait for her to regain consciousness before we can make a complete assessment. She should make a full recovery. However, the next seventy-two hours are crucial for both of these patients." He closed the curtain behind him, blocking out the chaos.

Terry sat silently in the grey plastic chair between the two, who remained deaf to the mayhem around them. He didn't know the boy, but vowed he'd look after him until his parents had been located. Resting his eyes and praying for the two patients to wake, he hoped the boy's name wasn't Casey.

The orderly came back in and placed a pink plastic bag of clothes on each of the beds. "The nurse wanted you to know ... his school shirt had been labelled. His name is Casey."

3

POSSESSION: SOPHIA. SCOTLAND

Sophia sat with Father McDonald in the church as the warm rays of the afternoon sun streamed through the stained-glass windows. She pressed her back hard into the pew, looked upwards and became transfixed as she squinted at the fragments of colored light. Breathing in the familiar smell of beeswax, she had a sense of security and peace.

"Sophia," she heard and then remembered where she was and why. She felt a cloud of depression hang over her. She'd just turned fourteen, and she felt as if she was carrying the weight of the world on her shoulders. She knew that if Father McDonald hadn't seen the angel at her birth, he might well have had her institutionalized by now — or surely sought an exorcism for her. Over the years, he'd grown to accept that angels, good and bad, are among us. Righteous souls, Ibu, spirit guides, from different cultures, with different names, all from the seed of the light, the one light of the universe, just waiting to share, to guide, but never saturate us as the darkness does. Neither Father McDonald nor Mother Catherine had chosen to share Sophia's secret with their fellow clergy, because the fear of being banished and called a heretic was still very real. Sophia was indebted to both of them for the decision they'd made.

She slowly focused her crystal-blue eyes on Father McDonald's weathered face.

"Sophia, are you feeling alright?" he prompted her gently.

"No. Father, last night I dreamed an amazing dream that felt more like a memory, and it was so sad. First I saw Casey again, the boy who drowned. Then I dreamed that deep within the ground was a burning altar in front of a fiery pit. This time, a savage flaming beast appeared. I don't know what I'm supposed to do. The dreams are frightening, they seem so real. Why did God keep me alive? Why didn't I die with my family? I've wished and prayed to die so I could be with them again."

Father McDonald slid along the hardwood pew to sit closer to her. "Sophia, you can't talk like that! There's always a reason; we just don't always know what it is. The light is with you: feel it in your heart, and feel no fear – when the time comes, only certainty can exist. The shadow of doubt will be the world's end."

Sophia contemplated his words before replying. "I also saw, in my dream, that darkness covered the days. A black cloud of evil ascended from the belly of the earth a decade ago. Then, I saw a flash of circulating blood cells; a girl with dark hair, spinning her bracelet, and next to her, an old key. People had become monsters — possessed — and were killing each other at random. Then, the images changed to a train; like a serpent moving around a mountain. The driver was on his mobile phone, yelling and screaming. All the blood was rushing to his face, and he threw the phone out the window. It was as if I was following the phone, tumbling off the edge of the cliff. Then I was back with the driver who accelerated, the train went faster and faster. It was going too fast for the curves; it derailed, tumbling over the side of the mountain. The engine dragged one carriage after the other. The engine exploded on impact. All because the driver was full of rage! Then, I was on a busy city street, and saw more blackness: evil clouds were swarming around people's heads and bodies, it looked like static noise, eating their auras, their surrounding light. Behind me, I heard a woman say, 'You have little time before the sun suffocates and the moon weeps. The rivers coursing within the soul of man will turn black. Judgement will surpass mercy, the blood of humanity.'"

"Oh, Sophia!"

She stared into his old face and could see he was in pain, searching for answers he didn't have, and she felt a tear escape from the corner of her eye.

"I'm so sorry your dreams are full of horror!" he said. He pulled her into his fragile arms and held her tight. He let go, and used his thumb to wipe her tears away. "What about the others?" he asked her. "Did you see them again?"

"Casey is nearly ready, he is happy with his adopted family. Kevin, he was in my dream," Sophia replied. "I think he too, had seen Casey drowning. Then Kevin vanished too." She involuntarily took in another deep, jagged, emotional breath, "It's time, isn't it?"

"Yes," he answered, "I think it might be time, Sophia. Father Thomas will settle in tomorrow before taking over my position, and we have the fete. We'll be free to leave soon afterwards. Go on the sleepover with your friends. Later in the evening tell Gemma's mom you're not feeling well. I'll come and get you. We'll head off then. We won't be missed until the next day. Pray to see the way, Sophia; God will show you. Try and have a bit of fun tomorrow."

"We have to leave to see the way," Sophia said, and then stared off into the distance, listening, and said, "Someone or something is coming."

THE CORRIDORS WERE SILENT, the nuns were asleep and the quarter-moon was giving no light, but still the old walls were being scaled by the shadows. Mother Catherine lay sleeping on her rickety single bed, which faced an old wooden wardrobe that contained nothing but two habits and a set of drawers. There, in her three-by-three room her rosary lay on a bedside table, on top of her Bible. Her eyelids had no movement behind them, because she didn't have any dreams.

Suddenly, she was sitting upright, wide awake. She reached for her necklace and Bible and clutched them to her chest. Feeling unnerved, frozen, she waited and felt the silence amplifying...

After a few moments, she heard Sophia's scream shattering the night and echoing down the long corridor and into her room. She jumped out of bed, pulled her robe on and ran down to Sophia. *The poor child's nightmares have become more frequent!* she thought.

When she reached for the door handle, the screaming stopped.

Father McDonald was climbing the stairs behind her, panting and moving as fast as his arthritic bones would allow.

Mother Catherine entered the room and registered the prominent smell of sage. She let her right hand fly up to her crucifix. She saw that Sophia's body was suspended above the bed, illuminated with white light. "Oh, God, have mercy upon this child! Shower her with your blessings!" she cried out, frantically rubbing the crucifix between her fingers.

Father McDonald entered the room, out of breath, and declared, "I think He already has." He stepped towards Sophia and spoke to her in a soft voice: "You're in the hands of God, Sophia: don't be afraid." He suddenly grabbed at his chest.

"Father, what's wrong?" Mother Catherine asked.

He ignored her, and his pain. His brow was covered with sweat, and some of it was dripping into his eye. He wiped it aside, and began to read from his leather-covered book: "Bless this child, O Lord ..."

Slowly, Sophia's body started to descend.

Father McDonald knelt beside the bed and continued his prayer.

Mother Catherine joined him.

The light around Sophia began to diminish, and as she descended peacefully, her body became encircled by a rainbow.

Behind them, the bedroom door swung open and Sister Clare burst into the room, glaring at Father McDonald. "What's going on here?" she exclaimed. "Why is that child screaming?"

Mother Catherine grabbed the interfering young nun by the arm, pulled her into the corridor and whispered to her, "Please keep your voice down! The child is fine. Father McDonald is with her. There's nothing you can do here."

Sister Clare was unconvinced, however, and bellowed, "What's going on? What's he doing to that girl?"

Mother Catherine drew in a slow breath, and told her, "Go back to your room and pray to be released from the bondage of your negative thoughts!"

The young nun stepped closer to Mother Catherine and uttered, "Father Thomas will hear about this!"

Mother Catherine stepped back into the room, told her "Please leave!" and closed the door.

Father McDonald remained by Sophia's bed, kneeling down and speaking in a soothing voice: "See yourself! See the energy, Sophia! Pull it back towards you, and draw in the light — all the way ... that's it! You need to want to be here."

The light swirled into Sophia's stomach; colors mingled and merged, fading and sparkling within each flicker as the light settled inside her.

"Good girl!" Father McDonald said to her. "Well done, Sophia! That's the best control you've ever shown!" His old bones creaked as he stood up. He put his hand in his coat pocket, took out a white handkerchief and used it to mop his brow.

Sophia's cheeks had turned pink, and her long blonde hair was fanned out around her head as if blown there by a sudden gust of wind. She opened her eyes, wiggled her toes and smiled at her favorite nun.

Mother Catherine stepped closer, looked down into the girl's eyes. "How are you feeling?"

"I love you," Sophia responded.

"I love you too, sweetie," Mother Catherine said. "But how are you feeling?"

Sophia smiled and answered, "I feel humbled. My body feels really heavy, but my heart feels light; strong; full of love; vibrant — a cup with an endless flow."

"Sophia —"

"I need to go outside, or at least stand," Sophia interrupted. "I need to connect with the earth, ground myself in reality." She sat up, moved slowly to the edge of the bed, touched the wooden floor, drew in a deep breath and said, "That's better."

The smell of the sage had almost vanished, and the corridors outside the room were silent.

"Mother Catherine," Sophia began, "I'm sorry." She turned her face to the floor, saddened at the memory of her vision. "He won't listen."

"Who?" Mother Catherine asked. "Who won't listen? What child says 'humbled'?" She looked at Father McDonald, inviting him to say something.

He sat next to Sophia on the edge of the bed, his weight causing the old mattress to sink.

Sophia kept her eyes cast down and announced, "Father, I had another dream. I was watching over Casey when I saw the darkness was gathering power like a storm. It now has many faces, and lives above us, like the clouds. It lives within fear; thrives in a wounded heart, in jealously, greed and rage; drifters in life who don't know where their consciousness sleeps. What does that mean: where their consciousness sleeps?"

"God will be with you always, I have no doubt," Father McDonald replied. "And I, too, am here for you always."

Mother Catherine had backed away so she was almost touching the wall, but she had an overwhelming need to know what Sophia meant. She stepped forward and moved closer to her. She spoke softly, stroked Sophia's hair gently and asked, "Who? Sophia, *who* won't listen? And won't listen to *what*?"

For some reason, Sophia couldn't answer Mother Catherine. She put her hands under her knees and stared at her own feet while swinging them across the floor. She elected to speak to Father McDonald instead, by mumbling, "I know. I'm not afraid for me, but I am afraid for you and Mother Catherine, and everyone else, because I can see, and I don't want to!" She swiftly reached for the comfort of her mother's medallion, making sure it was still under her nightshirt. Reassured, she let it go.

Mother Catherine let her hand rest atop Sophia's head. "Afraid for me? Why?" She then thought better of asking the question, and added, "No, don't answer that." She felt a chill as she pulled her robe tightly around herself, and brought herself to the present moment. "I'll get some hot chocolate, to help you sleep." She held fast to her crucifix, put aside her troubling thoughts and said, from the heart, "Sophia, have some fun tomorrow! Be a child! 'Humbled', indeed!"

Sophia started to braid her hair and smiled up at her. "You're going to rub poor Jesus right off that necklace of yours!"

THE FRESH MORNING air drifted in to Sophia's room through the open window that overlooked the grounds. The room was the same as Mother Catherine's. Sophia woke to the sounds of hammers clanging, trucks beeping and the hoisting of tents, and soon after opening her eyes she heard a slight tap at her door. "Come in." Her friends Lisa and Gemma burst into the room, jumped on her bed, and started holding hands, bouncing around like little kids excited that today was the day the three girls would be performing their ballet piece in order to raise funds for new computers in the town's library.

Sophia made a quick decision to forget about the restless night she'd had and pushed aside her feeling of impending doom. Today, she'd acknowledge only what came through her five senses and give in to being a fun-seeking teenager. She jumped up on to the old, rustic-style bed and felt it creak and moan under the strain of the girls' combined weight.

"Hey, Sophia," Gemma said to her, jumping off the bed, "I have something for you. My mom bought these jeans, and they're way too big for me I thought you'd like to try them on."

Sophia jumped off the bed and started pulling on the jeans under her nightie – her first pair of denims. She found that they felt strong and heavy.

She looked in the mirror that was mounted behind her bedroom door, seeing behind herself and into her mostly empty wardrobe. She took the brown woven belt hanging off the door, wormed it through the loops of her jeans, and fastened it tight around her waist. She flicked her braid, which was the length of her spine, out of the way and dug her hands into the jeans' front pockets. She liked the new feeling she was experiencing, having almost forgotten what it was like to wear something new.

The jeans were a tad too long and dragged on the floor. Gemma and Lisa laughed as they watched her shuffle across the room.

Reaching the open wardrobe she took out her favorite floral shirt, which Mother Catherine had rescued during a charity drive. While buttoning it up, she became aware it was a little too tight across the chest; her breasts had started to develop. *About time! I hope I get a bit more wear out of this shirt.* She loved flowers and hated the thought of abandoning it. Looking down, her feet were nowhere to be seen; so she decided to fold them up to her calf muscles. She slipped into her runners and put on a sweater because she felt an unexpected chill. "Thanks, Gem — they're great!" she declared, slapping her thighs.

"Come on, let's go!" Lisa begged, holding the bedroom door open.

The three ballerinas raced along the hallway and down the narrow stairs, exited through the kitchen door and arrived on the church lawns. There, they observed the white marquees that were lined up in three rows, piled high with goodies for sale. Cakes, toffees, flowers, handmade wooden toys and sweet-smelling soaps. The girls wove around the stalls and stopped at the Ferris wheel.

As Mother Catherine strolled among the stalls, she bumped into Gemma's mom. "Good morning, Mother Catherine!" Jillian said to her, pleased to have encountered someone she knew.

"Good morning, dear!" Mother Catherine replied. "What a wonderful day the Lord has provided for our fete!"

"How's the fundraising going this year?" Jillian queried.

Mother Catherine smiled modestly and answered, in a soft voice, "Good. Are you off to watch Gemma in the recital?"

The two started walking side by side, heading for the stage.

"Yes, I am," Jillian replied.

Three young boys who were obviously playing a game of tag came tearing around the blind corner of a stall and barreled into Mother Catherine.

She caught them and embraced them, laughing, and reminded them to be careful.

"I'm afraid this world's going to hell!" Jillian announced.

"Well, *you're* full of good cheer!" Mother Catherine said.

"Sorry," she said, looking at her fingernails, "it's just that it's all getting me down."

"Focus on sharing — and turn your telly off," Mother Catherine advised her. "All we have to do is 'love thy neighbor' and all will be right in the world. We focus on ourselves too much anyway. Was there something I can help you with?"

"Would you mind if Sophia joined the girls for a sleepover tonight? Lisa's mother has given the okay. Gemma would love it if Sophia could come too, if it's okay with you and Father McDonald — you've both raised her as if she was your own."

Mother Catherine stopped walking, looked at her, and replied, "Father McDonald said you mentioned something to him yesterday. It's fine with us."

The two arrived at the stage as the performance was about to begin.

Mother Catherine smiled when she saw that the girls were saying a prayer backstage.

"All the big stars do it," Jillian commented. "Oh, look, Father Thomas is here. He looks so young — well, compared to ... anyway, I'm just going to go and say hello to him."

Mother Catherine smiled, raised her eyebrows and said to her, "Off you go then!" She watched her give Gemma the thumbs-up and saw Gemma turn to her two friends to tell them the good news. *It's so good to see Sophia with a smile on her face,* she thought.

∼

SOPHIA FELT WONDERFUL as she, Lisa and Gemma huddled together excited about their beautiful performance. Everyone had applauded loudly over and over again as if they were professional dancers; it was the perfect end to a perfect day.

Gemma snapped a quick selfie, tied her ballet shoes together, flung them around her neck, and with a big smirk on her face, her hand on her hip, exclaimed to Sophie, "Oh, my God, Sophie, did you see that guy smiling at you?" He's a year above us at school, and more mature than any of the nerds my brother hangs with!"

"No. He wasn't looking at me, was he?" Sophia asked her.

"Here he comes!" Gemma said, linking arms with Lisa.

Nervously, Sophia announced, "I'm off. I'm going to pack my bag for tonight... I'll meet you at your mom's car!"

"What, now? No — stay!" Gemma begged her, pushing her towards the unsuspecting teenager.

Sophia pointed her eyes past his handsome face, skirted around him, and ran off to the nuns' dormitory.

"We're a row behind the blue dumpster!" Gemma yelled to her. "See you in ten!"

SOPHIA RAN UP THE back stairs, hearing her steps echo in the empty corridor. She flung her bedroom door open, tossed her ballet shoes on the bed, took off her cardigan, flipped off her sneakers, wriggled out of her leotard, and got back into her new jeans. Full of excitement she rushed to grab a hoodie from the wardrobe, pushing her feet back into her sneakers, she nearly tripped over her own feet as she reached for her backpack, which Mother Catherine seemed to have already filled with goodies. On her tiptoes, she stretched for the sleeping bag that was on top of the wardrobe, she wriggled it off with her fingers. She strapped it to her backpack; ready. She jumped when she heard a series of loud cracks and sharp claps coming from outside. Sophia held her breath, her heart raced as she mentally searched for a picture to put to the sound; she decided to stay away from the window. *It must be just cars backfiring,* she thought. *No, that's not it … I know! Fireworks. That must be it!* However, it wasn't yet completely dark — twilight was still descending — her colorful happy mental images of firecrackers started to become infiltrated with scenes from the previous night's dream. She ran from the room, eager to see the fireworks and not miss a thing. *Must be the private school boys getting up to mischief!*

Sophia's stomach turned and every atom in her body began to vibrate. The sound of people screaming grew louder. Walking from the direction of the river she saw a pale young man, barefoot, wearing a dirty pair of white jocks and a t-shirt. His long, straight, bleached hair was stuck to his dirty face, his feet were caked with mud, and his black eyes were expressionless. He held a rifle at waist height firing it randomly. Everybody in the vicinity was now running and screaming, seeking shelter. The young man wasn't taking aim at all; he looked dead, and the semi-automatic gun just kept firing.

Trying to block out her own panic she ran behind the church, towards the fete stalls and the car park behind them. Feeling as if her heart was about to rupture Sophia crouched down behind the cake stall, the last stall in the row... *Nearly there!* she thought. She'd have to sprint about fifteen yards across grass, out in the open, to get to the cars. A man carrying his crying child ran past her across the grass towards the carpark. The blue dumpster Gemma said her mother's car was parked behind was clearly visible. Her body felt strange, and she wanted to purge the adrenalin from it. Sophia could feel that her body was changing. Her atoms were now on fire, separating and joining, separating and joining; it was a scintillating feeling. She saw that the edge of her body looked pixelated, and she had to keep herself together, *literally.* She held her aura tightly in her mind, and mentally repeated to herself, *Stay connected! Stay connected! Feel the ground!* She needed to make her legs move. *I can do this.* Before losing total connection to her body, she stood up, staying low and ran out across the open space to the first row of cars. She ducked behind the blue dumpster, then scampered around it to Gemma's mother's car, and stopped. Out in the open, on the dusty gravel, just out of reach, was an abandoned pair of ballet shoes tied casually together. *They look like Gemma's,* she thought, not wanting to move and not wanting to know for sure.

The sound of gunfire was now coming from the car park, and the sky was turning black. She quickly pressed up against the back of the car and slowly peeked around the car's red tail lights. Between two cars Gemma's mother was lying on the ground, Gemma and Lisa motionless beside her. She edged forward, praying they were alive, and saw that Gemma's mother's hair was matted with blood. She slapped her hand over her mouth, squeezed it tight to stop herself from screaming and moved back behind the car. Sophia pressed her head against the cold metal of the bumper bar and cried, not noticing that the gunfire had stopped.

"Stop! Look at me!" she heard Mother Catherine scream.

Sophia spun around. She was trapped, the gunman was right behind her. Mother Catherine was behind him trying to get his attention. *No, Mother Catherine!* she whispered inside her head, taking a half step towards them. *Please, no! What are you doing? Stop! Please, stop! No! He won't listen!*

Mother Catherine was taken aback by the sound of Sophia's voice inside her head. Never having heard it before, she felt a sense of calm descend on her and a feeling of admiration for God and his creations. *You're an amazing person, Sophia!* she thought. *Can you hear me?*

Yes, I'm here! Sophia thought. What can I do? What can I do?

I love you, Sophia! Now, run! Mother Catherine replied.

Mother Catherine, no!

Mother Catherine turned her attention to the young man, and gently said to him, "You're safe. No one's going to hurt you. Please, give me your gun."

Sophia could see he was staring absently, drool hanging from the corners of his mouth. His arms looked heavy, and he swung them clumsily as he held the gun at waist height. *He's going to drop it,* she thought. She could see he was covered with a darkening grey mist that was expanding, contracting, expanding.

Mother Catherine prayed as she stepped closer to the young man.

"Protect Sophia," she began, "and forgive this young man, Lord. He knows not what he does."

Mother Catherine, move away! Sophia pleaded.

His black irises locked on the crucifix that Mother Catherine was nervously rubbing ... suddenly, he opened his eyes wide and stretched his mouth in a silent scream. His cheeks were torn apart, and a thousand bees erupted from his mouth. They flew straight at Mother Catherine, swarming around her face.

"Aaah! No! No! No! No! No! Mother Catherine!" Sophia shouted and moved towards her...

... but before she stood up, the young man lifted the gun, and the loud, frenzied buzzing of the bees was drowned out by gunfire.

Sophia saw Mother Catherine fall to the ground, her face and throat swelling up; she was in a state of anaphylactic shock.

Run, Sophia! Run! Mother Catherine mentally commanded her.

"No!" Sophia replied. "I won't leave you!" *Relax! Breathe! Just breathe!* she told herself as the gunman turned to face her. She felt the energy boiling, swirling within the pit of her stomach, and felt her atoms splitting, growing and radiating from every pore in her body.

The bees were everywhere, but none landed on Sophia.

The young man became mesmerized by the swirling vortex of light she had around her.

She began folding and unfolding the energy with her mind in order to create a barrier of space and light between them. She'd never tried doing this before. *This is way too slow!* She saw that his irises and all around his eyes were two black pools of tar, and the heavy mist around him was starting to push out from his being, causing her barrier of light to disintegrate before she could completely manifest it. She saw that the mist was made up of tiny creatures — micro-winged demons — which burst into sparks of light as they collided with her energy. They started flying in and out of the gunman's mouth, nose and grated cheeks. The dark matter was becoming dense: it pushed out violently forcing her backwards. She felt her head jolt back as her body hit the ground, she lost control of her energy, shattering the car windows and knocking the gunman off his feet. Shocked, she pushed up off the ground and crawled to Mother Catherine.

Out of nowhere, she saw Father McDonald appear next to her and grab her right arm. Suddenly he went stiff, as if he'd been tasered, and she could smell the singed hairs on his arms. As soon as he had his body under control, he lifted Sophia to her feet.

They ran down to the river and headed for a stand of trees to hide within.

The gunman was trying to stand up, when from behind, carrying a stone, Father Thomas raised his arms and slammed the stone into the back of the young man's head. Sophia turned away. When she looked back briefly, she saw that Father Thomas was taking the gun from the young man, then checking Mother Catherine, but Sophia knew he was too late: her face was now unrecognizable. She still had her hand clenched around her pendant of Jesus. Father Thomas went back to check the gunman's pulse and lowered his ear to the man's mouth, searching for any signs of life.

The gunman's mouth opened and a dark mist was expelled from it and on to Father Thomas's face.

Father Thomas backed away, coughing and choking. He held his throat as the mist entered his mouth. "We have to go back! We have to help him!" Sophia begged Father McDonald as she watched Father Thomas reach for his head and cradle it in his hands, his face twisted in pain. She reached out with her mind, connected, and heard him begging for the pain to stop — a second of it seemed like a minute, and a minute of it seemed like an hour. *He thinks he's going to die,* she thought as she felt his mind slip into darkness.

Then, as quickly as the pain had started, it stopped. Father Thomas went down on his knees, and vomited.

Sophia saw, from within his eyes, Sister Clare running to his aid and heard the sirens approach from off in the distance with his ears.

Father Thomas spat on the ground, and wiped his mouth.

"Look!" Sister Clare yelled, and pointed towards the forest.

Father Thomas followed her gaze, and saw Sophia and Father McDonald looking straight at them.

It's strange looking at myself through someone else's eyes, she thought and started to separate from Father Thomas.

"We must tell the police about Father McDonald," Sister Clare said to him.

Sophia waited — Father Thomas lost his balance and placed his fingertips on his temples. She merged back completely into his mind, scared, because he was losing consciousness and also losing control of his body. She could feel his distress, his fear, as if he was beside her in the back seat of a car while someone *else* was driving. To her it seemed as if "they" were looking out from behind his eyes together, as if his eyes were now mere windows because he had become a prisoner in his own body.

From deep within Father Thomas, Sophia heard a foreign-sounding roar of laughter, the laughter of a legion. *We're not alone,* she thought, *something else is within him.* She felt a chill ripple across his chest.

Sophia kept her thoughts as still as possible and disconnected from Father Thomas. The last thing she heard, punctuated by all-consuming laughter was, *That's right, priest: you belong to* me *now! How quickly your God abandons you!* Terrified, she wanted to scream, to explode, to get away from the evil. She quickly left him and secured herself within her own mind and body.

Father McDonald pulled her deeper into the forest, and when they came to a small hill, they settled in behind it, on their bellies, feeling like two snipers as they looked back at the church.

Father Thomas was vomiting continuously. He wiped his chin. His body slowly straightened up.

Sophia lay low in the brush, next to Father McDonald, and watched Father Thomas as he waved his fist in the air as if he were a puppet. "What happened to Father Thomas?" she whispered to Father McDonald. "Why did that gunman do that? Oh, Father, Mother Catherine: she's dead!"

"I don't know," Father McDonald replied, "I have a terrible feeling the gunman was looking for you, Sophia."

"Me?" she queried. "Why me? All these people have died because of *me*?!" She started crying uncontrollably. "No," she said, "I don't believe you: why would he want to kill me?"

"Your light. Let's get moving; it's time to leave." He lifted her up by her backpack, drawing on strength she didn't know he still had, and together they moved away from the church and travelled deeper into the woods.

4

____

KING-HIT: KEVIN. AUSTRALIA

Kevin just wanted them to stop. The sound of his parents quarreling continued late into the night. Bile rose in his throat as they yelled and screamed at each other. Each selfish word more painful than a slap in the face and the sting of each adjective lingered in his soul. He just wanted them to speak nicely to each other. *Why do they fight?* he wondered. They are both to blame, but his mom the most.

The baby cried. Love cowered in the corner. The screen door slammed. The porch light came on and Kevin moved to the window. His mother stormed down the front path clutching her cardigan. The car door creaked, tyres screeched as she sped away. *What happened? Why didn't she like the gift?* Kevin thought. *Why did she look at his dad like that? What was in the little box his dad had wrapped with care — and what's with the blue tiny esky?* Once or twice a week she left late at night with the tiny icebox and returned in the early hours of the morning, and put it away at the back of the freezer. The first time he saw it was when she had suddenly returned from the States. It contained a cold metal cylinder, locked. At first Kevin had been obsessed with getting it open, but eventually he gave up. It didn't matter anyway. What mattered was the arguing might mean she has the virus.

Earlier that day before his mother went off to work she had woken them with a jab in the rear, giving them all, including his dad, a vaccination. His dad asked, playfully — grossing Kevin out — if he could give her hers, but she said she didn't have enough. They were sworn to secrecy. Together, his little brother, Alex, and his dad cleaned the house from top to bottom, and cooked a mouth-watering dinner for his mom. It was his dad's first day off in ages. Smoke choked the neighborhood so they stayed indoors. Kevin thought his dad was pretty cool and brave, he wished he could tell him. He worked long hours fighting bushfires and saving people — their homes, and animals. That day, the fire in the mountains had been started deliberately. It had been hot and dry, and before lunch it was well over thirty-five degrees. He wanted to bail and go over to Tim's and head for the river, but he didn't want to disappoint his dad so he hung around at home. While Molly napped in her cot, his dad and his brother Alex had enjoyed cleaning the house. They laughed when his dad went sliding and fell on the polished floor while doing a *'Tom Cruise', whoever that was. Someone from the old days*, Kevin thought. Kevin had draped the sheets over the chairs pretending it was a secret club, and allowed Alex to enter with a secret password while his dad made the bed with fresh crisp sheets.

The bathroom smelt like flowers, the candle flames danced by the window. A hot summer wind came through the front door. By the time his mom came home from work and dropped her keys in the bowl on the side table by the front door next to his dad's, Molly and Alex were fast asleep. Kevin hid under the cool sheets upstairs in his room with his favorite childhood gift, a miner's light his grandfather had given him seven years ago for his eighth birthday, and it still worked. He tilted his head and steadied the light on the pages of his grandfather's collection of old *Sky & Space* magazines. He knew he could look up images online, but it just wasn't the same. It had the best old images of the stars. Kevin believed if he stared long enough at the pictures, when he slept he would dream of being in another universe, somewhere amongst the stars, a place where everything is possible. He now stared out the window and up into the dark sky wondering where his mother was going and why she was so upset. He felt heavy and sad; he didn't understand why he was feeling their emotions so strongly. His dad stood illuminated by the street lamp on the front lawn looking lost watching his mom go. Kevin looked down the street and thought he saw a car parked against the curb pull out. Molly cried. The sound drew his father into action and he turned back towards the house. Kevin ducked and dropped onto his bed. His dad was climbing the stairs to Molly's room. He looked over at Alex — his little brother was sprawled diagonally across his makeshift bed on the floor fast asleep. Kevin lay down in his bed, gazed out the window, listening to his father down the hall trying to sooth Molly back to sleep. His eyes grew heavy, the trees outside swayed and the temperature dropped slightly. Kevin pulled up the sheet, and began to drift in and out of sleep. He heard his bedroom door squeak open; light and the smell of scented candles floated into his room. Peeking out of one eye he saw his dad's silhouette standing in the doorway. To Kevin his dad looked for a moment as if he was glowing, surrounded by colored lights and he felt an overwhelming urge to hug him, and never let him go. *Why do I see these things?* He didn't understand why he saw colors around people. *One day,* he thought, *one day I will.* Alex stirred as his dad bent and kissed him on the head. He tucked Alex in before doing the same to Kevin. Kevin closed his eyes pretending to sleep, then watched his dad leave the room. He started to cry. He buried his head in the pillow wishing for sleep to take him. Eventually, exhausted just before dawn, he heard his mom come home and the familiar sounds of life returned. The pipes groaned as she turned on the shower. Kevin fell into a deep sleep to a congregation of awakening birds that sounded like an orchestra tuning up as their conductor takes the stage, the sun stretching above the horizon, dawn breaking.

"Body slam!" Alex jumped up and down on Kevin, startling him awake with a knee in his back and a wet finger in his ear.

"Get off me, shithead! For crying out loud, piss off." Kevin pushed his little brother off the bed where his head hit the bedside table. Kevin felt bad and dramatically fell out of bed and faked being hurt. Alex laughed in between sobs. "Sorry, Alex," Kevin said. "But you hurt me, little bro, not cool."

Alex liked it when Kevin called him little bro. "Dad can't find his keys, can you see them?" Alex said, tapping the side of his head.

Kevin tickled Alex. "You go finish your breakfast, count to twenty and go look in the bowl. I'll be down in a minute."

He watched Alex leave the room and go out into the hallway. He could hear Alex jump down each step as he made his way downstairs to the kitchen.

"Where are my keys, I left them here in the bowl?" he heard his dad, Daniel, say. "Callie ... did you move my keys? I've got to get to work." Then he heard, "Hey, kiddo, I told you not to play with my helmet. What if there was a fire and I had forgotten it? Go put it back. Callie, my keys!"

Kevin heard in his mom's tone that she was getting annoyed. "Why is it taking Kevin so long?" Then she yelled up the stairs. "Kevin, breakfast! Come on, we don't have all day. Holidays or not."

"WHERE'S YOUR BROTHER?" CALLIE SAID.

"Where are my keys?" Daniel said.

"Finish feeding Molly and have your coffee, I'll look for your keys," she said.

"I'm late," Daniel said, reaching for his fireman's helmet.

Alex slid off his chair and grabbed the helmet. "Can I carry it to the car for you, Daddy?" Humming, he quickly pushed his feet into his slippers not waiting for an answer, and went and waited by the open front door.

"Daddy, Daddy, your keys, your keys are here!"

Daniel turned towards his son who stood at the end of the hallway next to the side table with the keys held up high. The sun shone through the open door; Alex looked like an angel with tiny dust fairies dancing all around him. He heard Molly giggling in the kitchen while Callie made fun of a boring bowl of oats. "What was I getting so angry about?" he thought shivering. "I've got to shake this monkey."

"You're amazing," Daniel said ruffling his son's hair. "Where'd you find them?"

"In the bowl, where Kevin said. He told me to go downstairs, start eating my cereal and then count to twenty. Then he said I would carry your helmet and find your keys. So I looked and there they were, under Mommy's keys in the bowl!" Alex raised his eyebrows, shrugged his little shoulders and smiled. "How hard did you really look Daddy? Or maybe there are some naughty little angels playing tricks on you too?"

Daniel scooped him up and threw him over his shoulder leaving him dangling by his feet, laughing. Daniel saw out of the corner of his eye that Kevin had come halfway down the stairs and stopped; they shared a secret knowing smile. Kevin was a clever boy.

Callie came out of the kitchen with Molly on her hip. "Oh, she's getting heavy. Here's your lunch. I'm working late. You'll have to pick the kids up from day care and don't be late. Kevin's staying at Tim's tonight."

Daniel lowered Alex to the ground tickling his little feet. He relished the sound of his laughter. "If I'm fighting a fire, and run a little late, I'm sure they will forgive me. What do you think, champ?"

Curled up on the floor in a fetal position protecting himself from being tickled again Alex nodded in agreement. In between bursts of laughter he said, "Miss Bell ... says ... if her house is burning ... she wants you to rescue her, Daddy."

Daniel saw Kevin hadn't moved. The energy in the room quickly thickened and sounds seemed distant. Daniel didn't understand what made it change so quickly. In a controlled angry voice, that seemed like it was coming through layers of glass, Callie said suspiciously, "How do you know, Alex?"

Alex looked up at them both and shrugged. "Did I do something wrong?"

"No, sweetie," Callie said. "I just want to understand why you said that, that's all. Does Miss Bell think her house is going to catch on fire, is that why she said it?"

"No ... I don't think so. When she was brand new, I heard her whispering to Miss Poe when she saw Daddy coming through the gate."

Callie put her hand to her throat with a sigh of relief. "Oh, thank God! I thought you were becoming like your brother. That's the last thing we need right now."

Daniel's eyes widened, and he stepped forward, brushing his lips against her ear and saying in a whisper, "That was cruel; he's standing on the stairs. What are you afraid of? Are you afraid of what he will see? Maybe that's what you should ask yourself. What are you afraid he will see, Callie?" He pulled away. "I don't know what you think any more. I don't have time for this."

KEVIN STEPPED INTO full view and pushed past them into the kitchen. Before he could escape the tension and pain, his dad dropped a heavy hand on his shoulder and pulled him into a bear hug.

"I love you man, don't you ever forget it."

"I'm sorry, Kevin, that was wrong of me. I can't believe I said that. I haven't been sleeping well," his mom said, reaching out to stroke his cheek.

Kevin pulled away. "Yeah, whatever," he said walking into the kitchen, heading for the refrigerator. Chanting inside his head, *Don't cry, don't cry, it's okay, don't cry.*

Kevin watched his dad through the kitchen window, walking to his truck. Old man Pat across the road was hosing his garden.

"Morning, Pat," his dad shouted. He shouted a little louder.

"Morning, Pat!" "Morning, Daniel. Hear you guys got the upper hand on that bushfire up them mountains. Those eucalyptus trees got so much oil in them they light up like a Christmas tree, don't they."

"They sure do, Pat. Looking after Martha's roses I see."

"Yeah, just as well there aren't any water restrictions. These roses guzzle it up like a thirsty camel. Bring those kids of yours over any time, Daniel, they're always welcome here."

"Thanks, Pat. When is Martha coming home? Soon I hope?"

"Not sure. Her sister has the virus. It's so quiet without her, Daniel. This virus has got me spooked. When she gets back from her sister's, I'm thinking of hightailing it out of here. Everyone's leaving the city. The crime rate has tripled, all because of a bloody virus. Men, and women, are doing crazy things, violent things. It's frightening."

"Pat, you're welcome to join us for dinner until she gets back, you don't have to be alone."

Kevin watched them, transfixed.

"Kevin! Shut the refrigerator door and go get dressed."

Kevin jumped and spun around; his mom had scared the shit out of him. He closed the refrigerator and followed her to the stairs. On his way he passed the front door. Compelled, he opened it and stepped outside. A crow was circling the sky: *ah, ah, ahhhhhhh.*

"Hey, crow," Kevin said standing on the porch in his black and gold boxers. His dad climbed into the black Dodge four-door utility, and pulled out of the driveway. *It was a beast of a car, two more years and he could drive it,* Kevin thought and remembered when they were at his grandpa's in Queensland; he had ridden in the back while his dad spun the car in circles around the open paddock. Kevin was scared and held on tight to the roll bars, laughing and trying not to slide everywhere. That was nearly a year ago; he missed those days. Kevin came back to the present and saw old man Pat watching him and gave him a wave. Kevin suddenly felt worried about the old guy. Kevin waved again before letting the screen door slam. Kevin shivered, he had felt the warmth of the sun, but now a chill ran up his spine. Confused, he went back outside, stepped on the cool grass, and watched old man Pat, who was looking down the road and drowning Martha's flowers. Pat turned off the hose, stretched his back and tilted his head slowly towards his shoulder as if straining to hear. *Something in the air doesn't feel right*, Kevin thought. Kevin went to give old man Pat another morning salute and turn to the house when a flash of light caught his eye. An unknown car was down the street. *Who's that*, he thought. He knew everyone in his street, and this car didn't belong, but it looked familiar. He raked his memory. *Where before have I seen that car?* Old man Pat was rubbing the back of his neck starring up into the smoke-filled sky. *That's right!* A few nights ago he couldn't sleep and was staring out his window in the early morning, when he saw old man Pat putting his bin out. He had watched him, in his pajamas, shuffling down the driveway, struggling to drag the bin to the curb as quietly as possible. With the bins in position Pat glanced down the street. *Searching for the garbage truck*, Kevin thought. The streets were empty bar one car, which had its front window fogged and cigarette smoke escaping from a narrow crack. It was the same car as the one currently sitting at the end of the street. It had also been there last night, hiding in the dark. Without any lights it had pulled out from the curb after his mother had left, just before Molly had started to cry. Kevin hadn't given it another thought, but here it was, again. He tried to see the number plate; his position was no good. Kevin walked casually to the sidewalk and the car suddenly started up and did a U-turn. Pat looked at Kevin, and Kevin shrugged his shoulders turning back to the house. *Who are they and what are they up to?* Kevin wondered.

Kevin firmly pushed the front door close behind him. "Mom," Kevin shouted up the stairs. "Have you noticed that black car hanging out at the end of the street? And what's wrong with old man Pat? His shadow's got no head."

"What Kevin? I can't hear you. Come upstairs and get ready."

Kevin stood in the bathroom doorway listening to Molly and Alex giggling. His mom was annoyed. The pair of them were hiding behind a cloud of talcum powder. Alex let go of the white plastic bottle of powder. Molly wasn't ready to give up and squeezed and squealed as his mom wrestled with her. Smiling, Kevin leant against the doorframe and watched them play.

"Molly, give it to Mommy, we have to get dressed ... Ta." Through the cloud his mom saw him in the doorway. "What are you doing? Go get ready! We have to go. I am going to be late for work! Be ready and downstairs in five."

"Why bother. Hardly anyone is going to their work with the virus about. I can ride my bike. You don't have to drive me."

She looked at Kevin. "I have important work to complete. No — I'll drive you." She rushed off, dusting the powder out of her hair with Molly dangling off her hip in a cloud of white.

He hesitated and bit his lip, then quickly blurted it out. "Something is wrong with old man Pat. I don't know what, but there's something wrong."

"Kevin, not now, pleeeease. Not now! It's been ages since you ... well, you know." Their eyes momentarily locked like horns. She pulled her gaze away as if she couldn't look at him another second.

"I know what you're thinking," Kevin said. "I didn't make it up, I saw the boy drown."

"Oh God, not again, why do you lie so much? I thought you were over this. The police found nothing. *Enough.* Go get ready."

He looked down at the bathroom tiles and mumbled, "They couldn't find anything because they were looking in the wrong country."

He saw the shame, the tension in her jaw and the anger in her eyes. Sometimes when he looked into her eyes he didn't know where she was or who was looking at him. Having the police search the creek wasn't his idea. *Why doesn't she listen to me? Please help me, somebody give me back my mom. Why is she so scared?*

"But Mom ... I didn't ... grandma and grandpa ... I didn't ... I'm sorry I didn't know..." Tears started streaming down his face, it was hard to breath, he couldn't speak. *Everything was turning upside down. Why was he even mentioning this stuff; he just wanted to shut up.* Through heaving emotions he tried to hold back each wrenching sob and talk normally, but he couldn't. It was all coming out; it had been a year of holding back the pain. "I don't know why ... I didn't see. What's the point if I can't save my family?"

She stopped getting Molly's clothes out of the drawer. Crossed the room to hold him. "Oh, Kevin, is that what you think. I don't blame you."

He shrugged her off.

"What happened to your grandparents is not your fault. It was a drunk driver. There wasn't anything you could have done. You shouldn't have visions, or feel people's pain; you need to push it away. You need to be normal and have fun and adventures, like all fifteen-year-old boys. You're a good person, Kevin. Look, if you think you can ride over to Tim's without running into any of the infected — well, okay then. What worries me is there have been so many brutal bashings in the area. I'll drop your things off after I have taken Molly and Alex to childcare."

KEVIN LEANT ON Tim's dining room table with his elbows on the table-cloth cradling his face in his hands, gazing at his broken image reflecting in the crystal bowl.

"Kev, what are you looking at? Come on, move the stuff. Clear the table. This box is heavy."

Kevin snapped out of his trance and cleared the crystal bowl, books and candles off the table. "Why is it lately when I come over there is a smell of something sweet burning?"

Tim opened the lid. "Mom's been burning incense again. Thinks it will keep the house clean of the virus." He rummaged around emptying out his sister's things. "My model plane is in here some-where. I know Kath took it."

"Let's go for a swim," Kevin said.

"We can't leave until Kathy's home. She's giving me ten bucks if we stay put. We're not supposed to be in the house together alone after last time. Mom doesn't want us outside with the infected either." Tim was halfway through Kath's box of collectibles. "Here it is."

"Why, what happened last time?" Kevin was having trouble focusing.

"Don't you remember ... the pool table? Our home-made volcano? Hello! Anybody home?"

Kevin felt anxious, and sadness washed over him. Suddenly, in the pit of his stomach was a sense of urgency, an overwhelming desire to run. He knew enough, however, to know they weren't his feelings and the more he became conscious of that, it was easier to control; each time it happened he recognized it a little quicker. In the past, it had taken him days to realize they weren't his emotions. Sometimes he got lost in the darkness, but when realization dawned, *boom!* It would feel like the warmth of the sun ran through his veins, and he would be filled with excitement, as if he had received a mysterious present. A gift you could lay staring at for hours just wondering what might be inside. Then, an image would start to form in his mind. Just like now. Small, distant, a blur, slowly moving closer, and slowly coming into focus...

Tim punched him in the shoulder. "On ya."

"Piss off, what did you do that for? Sometimes you can be a real asshole," Kevin said rubbing his shoulder.

"Now you're sounding just like her."

"Who?"

"My sister! Man, you're a space cadet today. What's with you? By the way, have you seen the dude she's dating? He plays third base, big on double plays."

"You mean Nash?" Kevin said, taking Tim's model plane out of its box and sorting through the pieces. "He lives on my street; a couple of doors down. He's alright. You signing up this year?"

"Yeah, you? What's this part?" Tim asked picking a curved rectangular piece of the plane, too small to be a wing.

Kevin took the piece from Tim. Inspected it and handed it back. "It's the aileron, part of the wing. Maybe we might head off to my grandparents' property down the coast for a few weeks. It's been empty since they died in the accident. It would be a good place to get away from the infected until the virus is eradicated." Kevin looked towards the front of the house. *He didn't know if he should say anything.*

He was sick of hiding, he thought and blurted out, "I think Kathy's coming."

"Why'd you say that?"

"My mom's dad had a plane and was teaching me how to fly it before—"

"No, not the model plane bit. Why do you think we need to leave, and why do you think Kath is coming home early?"

"I ... just a feeling. She's sad," Kevin said, mostly to himself.

Before Tim could react they heard a key sliding into the lock. "Quick, help me put everything back, or I'll never see that ten bucks."

Kevin grabbed everything, putting it back into the box. "Why, what's wrong?"

"It's *her* box!"

Kevin watched Tim bolt down the hall to the closet and heave the box over his head to slide it onto the top shelf. Kathy stormed into the house seconds later, slamming the door behind her. Kevin froze and held his breath. She walked straight past him, heading in Tim's direction. He was busted for sure. Kath didn't stop. *She always wears gym workout clothes, but she never goes to the gym,* he thought. She had obviously been crying. She passed the walk-in closet, and went upstairs to her room. Tim came out of the closet and looked up the stairs before shrugging his shoulders at Kevin.

"What do you want to do now?"

Kevin ran his finger along the spine of the DVDs on the living room shelves. "Let's watch a movie. What do you feel like? What about —" Sensing something was wrong he turned around. "What's up with you?"

"I hate to say it, but I think you're right," Tim said.

Kevin raised his eyebrows. "About what?"

"She was crying."

They both stared at each uncomfortably. "Perhaps there's something we should do," Kevin said.

Tim turned on the TV and the world news headlines blurted out of the surround sound system. Terrifying images splashed across the LED screen of people running through the streets, others were being attacked by *infected*, while others watched or were looting.

"Turn it off. My mom's here," Kevin said walking to the front door.

"I didn't hear anything. Her car's not—" Before Tim could finish his sentence they heard her car pull up. The boys walked outside to meet her.

"Hi, boys," Callie said, passing Kevin his sleeping bag and backpack. "I expect you home tomorrow before dark." She kissed Kevin on the brow. "Be careful," she whispered.

"Mom, I have to tell you something. A black car —"

"Kevin, I have to go. I have important work to do. Tell me tomorrow, I'm sure it can wait."

Kevin didn't bother replying. He knew she wouldn't listen to him anyway. All she cared about was her work. Ever since she got back all she cared about was that little canister inside her *little blue esky*.

Her work shoes didn't make a sound on the driveway. "Tim, don't forget your tent. Alex is looking forward to spending some time with you boys, even if you pitch it in the garage." She waved over her head. "Say hi to your mom for me."

Kevin could see Tim busting to say some smart-ass comment. "Don't say anything."

"I'm not even thinking anything. You got a bit of lipstick there on your forehead," Tim said smirking. "Anyhooooo! So who's going to win the World Series? Cough up, how long have you been able to do that?" he said closing the door.

"Do what?"

"Why is it called the World Series, when it's only one country playing? What am I getting for Christmas? Next time, can you give me a bit more of a heads-up rather than a few seconds? Stuff the movie, let's go for a ride."

Kevin watched Tim's mouth move at a hundred miles an hour. He followed him out back to fetch his bike from the shed. Kevin waited around the side of the house where his sky blue Apollo was. He loved his bike. It was the last good thing that happened before his grandparents' accident. His mom had surprised him with it two days before she went to the USA. Tim came running out of the shed, jumping onto his bike and riding right past Kevin. "Man! Did you just skol a Red Bull or what?" Kevin asked.

~

KEVIN CLIMBED ON his bike, coasted down the deserted road catching up to Tim and overtaking. He let go of the handlebars, stretched out his arms and the fog in his head cleared. His ears popped. His mind crystallized. He could focus again. For a few seconds he dared to close his eyes, basking in the light. He felt the warmth, a surge of energy. He chuckled to himself and opened his eyes; *That's what I am,* he thought, *a solar battery*. He raised his fists up into the air, pretending to shoot bolts of light like he'd done when he was seven.

Tim caught up to ride beside him, and shouted. "What the hell are you doing, K? You look like a retard."

"Nothing," he said putting his hands back on the handlebars. Kevin flicked his gear lever and speeding off said, "Look who's the dork now! Catch me if you can!"

Kevin mounted the footpath onto the vacant block. He pedaled through the long yellow grass that slid over his legs, and pedaled even faster along the narrow, dusty path leading through the bush to the river knowing that red-bellied black snakes lay in the scrub, just out of sight. Kevin brought his bike to a sliding stop. Blocking their way was a familiar gigantic bull ant mound. They both knew the first person could ride over it before the ants poured out in frenzy: the second person would become the victim. They stared at each other, then the anthill, both with one foot on the pedal, ready. Tim broke rank first, with Kevin's front wheel inches behind. Kevin sailed over the hill standing up on the pegs. Twisting his body he looked around to see the ants pouring from the top like lava from a volcano. Feeling exhilarated, they kept pedaling, lifting their front wheels up off the ground, riding to the river.

~

GETTING A HANDFUL of brake the back tyre skidded to the side. Kevin dropped his Apollo and ran onto the small sandy patch. *You could hardly call it a beach*, he thought. He kicked off his shoes before racing through the shallows and diving into the clear refreshing water.

They swam up and down the river trying to outdo each other, played stickball at knee-deep until finally, exhausted, they just floated in the cool water. Tim was trying to rattle Kevin's cage. "Did you hear the stories about the shark that came upstream last year? Dogs were taken."

"Shut up, it did not," Kevin said, walking out of the water and plonking himself on the warm sand. "I heard someone say Shaun Grady and his thugs hang out down here."

"It did! And now you're just trying to freak me out, I've never seen him," Tim said, stretching out next to him. "You can ask Spicier. He saw it, he saw the shark." Tim scooped and patted sand to make a pillow mound.

"You make up some really good stories," Kevin said, resting his chin on his arms. "You should write a movie, especially that story about the dunny man remember! Early in the morning, before sunrise, the dunny man would sneak into backyards and collect large buckets full of a family's week's worth of shit, and if the dunny man was lucky, he would make it through a day without spilling any on himself. Tim, seriously, you should write that down. You've got a gift, man," Kevin said, laughing.

"But it's true," Tim said confused. "Ask my grandfather."

Feeling his skin burning, Kevin sat up and went back into the water to cool off. Peacefully, he floated on his back, his hearing muffled by the sloshing of the water rocking in and out of his ears. The silky water and gentle wind eased the heat of the day. Kevin stretched his arms and legs like a starfish and watched the clouds chugging across the sky as he drifted along with the current, losing track of time. He had not gone far when the feeling of the sun burning his face became overwhelming. He dived under and enjoyed the coolness of the deeper water on his face as he swam to the river's edge. He crawled into shallow water where nearly transparent shrimp swam slowly around his wrists. He kept still, resting on his elbows, watching them swim in between his fingers and over his hands.

Suddenly he felt his awareness expand and his senses heighten as if someone was standing over him, tapping him on the shoulder. He looked up, searching for what was drawing his attention away from the playful shrimp, and spotted Tim climbing up the steep bank on the other side. "Where are you going?" Kevin shouted.

Tim quickly looked over his shoulder, put a finger to his lips and pointed into the bush. He crouched low, slowly moved forward and disappeared. The cicadas' song rose to an irritating crescendo, the kookaburras laughed and the tide crept in. The little beach area was disappearing. Kevin felt sick, something was wrong; his stomach twisted in knots, his ears rang. A cold sweat emerged from every pore. *Where the hell has Tim gone?*

Kevin waited a few minutes more. The wind blew the scent of the bush in his face and the afternoon shadows started to come alive. All at once he felt cold and alone. "Shit! Where the hell is Tim?" Kevin brushed his fringe out of his eyes and scanned the area again before calling out. "Come on, where are you." His whole body seemed to buzz, vibrating with an intense concern for his friend. The trees were noisy, encouraged by the strengthening winds. He heard every sound, except Tim.

Kevin walked into the choppy water. Tiny waves driven by the wind smacked into his knees. He dropped forward and swam across. Taking fistfuls of reeds he pulled himself up the bank. He crouched low and crept into the bush. The smell of cigarette smoke was prominent. His stomach somersaulted, its contents moved upward and he vomited. His lips tingling, Kevin wiped his mouth with the back of his hand. Up ahead he heard muffled voices. The bush was so dry, with each step twigs snapped as he moved deeper into the bush. A wallaby jumped out from behind a tree and scared the crap out of him. *Something very bad is about to go down.* Still he couldn't see any sign of Tim. The voices became clearer. There were at least two.

Stealthlike, Kevin moved even closer and crouched behind a tree to listen.

"You're a retard. I'll teach you to spy on us. Grab him."

Kevin wondered if they, whoever they were, were talking about Tim. Kevin moved closer. He heard a scuffle break out. He still couldn't see anything, but a sense of urgency overcame his fear and he quickly moved forward towards the commotion.

"Hold his hands behind his back, hold him! You morons are wimps, letting this little pussy get the better of you. Hold him still."

Kevin rushed into the clearing and saw Tim spit in some guy's face. The dude pulled back his arm and punched him on the side of the head for it. Tim spun a one- eighty while the guy wiped the spit off his face. Everything seemed to be in slow motion. Tim had his back towards his assailant, facing Kevin. There were three dudes, all around seventeen to nineteen years old. At the top of his lungs, Kevin screamed, "Get off him ..." The thug lifted up his leg and kicked Tim in the back as Kevin ran forward, keeping his eyes on the unlaced runner in Tim's back. Tim's face was red, swollen, and quickly turned from a look of pain into a blank stare; he was a dead weight on a downward journey and hit the ground hard. Kevin sprinted and lunged recklessly at the thug, who mockingly raised his foot again and stomped on Tim's leg ... Kevin heard it snap. He was stunned. From outside his peripheral vision, in mid-stride, a fist collided with the side of his head. Kevin felt himself falling. *What the hell!* he thought. His left ear started to ring and was burning hot. It reminded him of a time when he had picked chilli off his plate and then accidentally rubbed his eye. *What a dumb thing to be thinking of now.* There was nothing he could do to stop himself from hitting the ground, right next to Tim.

It all happened at a snail's pace. He could only watch his assailant laugh and fist-pump the air, looking at his mates for approval, devouring their cheers. *So, there were four, not three,* Kevin thought, two he recognized from school. One was Shaun Grady, the local bully with his dumb sidekick, but he wasn't sure who the other bully was, or the one that had taken him out with the king-hit. He tasted dirt as he lay on the ground. Before his eyes completely shut, he saw an old car seat with half a dozen or so petrol bombs lined up ready to go.

SHAUN LAUGHED AS HE threw the last petrol bomb into the scrub. He watched in awe as fire raced up the face of a tree. His friends were like statues, mesmerized by his power. *I couldn't give a shit about the retards,* he thought and left them lying unconscious as he crossed the river. Stealing Kevin's Apollo bicycle Shaun pedaled as fast as possible homeward to watch the bush burn from his rooftop. Shaun felt exhilarated, full of bubbling energy. A passing fire truck wailing around the corner nearly took him out.

Shaun dropped Kevin's bike on the lawn, flung off his runners and climbed barefoot up the side drainpipe and onto the roof, dangling his legs over the edge to watch the show. He could see the firemen leap from the trucks, unwinding the hoses. Shaun could feel the wind change; the fire would be driven out of control by the arriving southerly.

5

———

THE MORNING STAR: JADE. SOUTH CAROLINA, USA

The early morning sun penetrated the heavy drapes. The memory of the warm night clung to Jade as she woke from a restless sleep. She was born in this painted weatherboard bungalow fifteen years ago. She used to love sitting outside on the front veranda during the summer reading a science journal, or people-watching. This year the temperature during the first week of autumn was high, as if it was still the middle of summer. Kicking off the blue sheet she threw her legs over the side of the bed, planting them firmly on the cool wooden floor. She closed her eyes, breathing in the morning, imagining it flowing through her soles and spreading up through her body. Over the last few weeks she had been experimenting, trying to eliminate her anxiety, and it seemed to be working.

A smell of coffee and burnt toast wafted from the kitchen. She reached for her glasses. The house was still. Jade shuffled along the hallway. The open window caught the dust dancing in the sunlight. She lost herself in the moment, twirling past the window; the lace curtain flapped and coiled itself around her. Breaking away from its gentle hold, she entered the deserted kitchen. Two lonely pieces of toast, with a thick layer of butter and speckles of charcoal sat on a plate next to a glass of juice. Jade smiled at the toast, grateful for her dad's effort. She missed her mom every day. It had been nearly a year since her mother's disappearance.

An old Indian man from her great-grandmother's tribe appeared out the front of her home more often than not. Jade could see him now through the window making himself comfortable under the tree, burning herbs in a seashell. Today she planned to escape her personal prison and act like a normal teenager. Today she had agreed to go to the beach with Ben; she hoped he would ask her to tomorrow night's beach party. It would be her first. She crunched on the burnt toast, skolled the juice and breakfast was over.

Closing the bathroom door, she ran her tongue over her just-cleaned teeth, tasting the mint flavor, and blinked a few more times making sure her contacts were in place. Her bedroom was dark and she pulled back the blinds. Her room lacked posters and the general teenage paraphernalia. There was one picture; a childhood painting, an image from her dreams of a green iron gate, with a golden padlock and a beautiful, smooth golden star in the middle of the gate — through its bars, undefined shadows could be seen. Sometimes she felt that the lock was just a lock, and at other times, like now, she felt it beckoning, crying out for her to find the key.

Breaking the magnetic pull of the image, Jade stretched her arms over her head and removed her night clothes and stepped into her bathers. She pulled on a shirt depicting the structure of an atom and a black pair of cargo shorts. She looked at herself in the mirror and sighed. *Black and black.* Her emo days were gone, but it was still hard for her to adjust. Her mom had said, "Black is only to complement, to reveal the colors in light, and enhance the patterns around you." Jade changed her shorts to a pair of white short shorts she'd never worn before. She padded into her mom's room to pick out one of her colored shirts.

She pushed the sliding door open and the smell of her mother filled her senses. For a few seconds she just stood there. Wiping away tears, she reached in and picked out a rich blue shirt. Jade tied it around her waist, exposing her belly button, feeling semi-naked. Jade grabbed her mother's handmade straw bag, which she had made with her grandmother. Just thinking of her great-grand-mother made her smile. It had always been happy days when great-gran was here. People came from miles around to be with her. Everyone was gentle, caring; they called her Great Turtle. She spoke so quietly their ears would strain to catch the pearls of wisdom. Jade thought her great-grandmother had certainly been an old turtle: slow, hard to crack, soft on the inside. To be that little bit closer to her, Jade went to her mother's jewelry box, took out Great Turtle's bracelet and fastened it firmly around her wrist. She ran her fingers gently along the etchings, feeling the notches in the aged copper. Jade stuffed a rolled- up striped towel into the bag and grabbed her hairbrush, smiling at her floating memories. Her eyes became unfocused as she brushed her long raven hair, thinking of her mother. *How many times I complained about her dragging me back to her work after school to do just one more thing; always, just one more thing.* Now Jade missed hanging around the laboratory.

Her mom had been so excited the last time they were there. The Australian undergraduate, Callie, was packing up, finished for the day. Jade's mom wanted to share her excitement, but all Jade did was pout, being difficult, demanding to go home. She didn't care what her mom was up to. She didn't want to look at specimens of organisms under the microscope, didn't care about the regenerating dying cells. Or the way the deformed structures were transforming: due to one added ingredient, the virus was being destroyed. All Jade was thinking was, *Last year it was bird flu; this year it's a new virus, which has been spreading from East Asia for nearly ten years.* There was always some virus or disaster on the horizon.

"Remember last week?" her mom had said. "You were wearing your great- gran's bracelet when you knocked your drink over and you cut yourself on the glass. You remember that day, right?"

"Whatever ..." Jade remembered saying. Jade had done every-thing she could to be as normal as possible and to forget how smart she was, but now she felt bad for being so rude. Her mom had just wanted to share.

"Do you want to know what happened?" she had continued, ignoring Jade's frustration.

"Yeah, sure, like I need a bullet in my head." She had turned away, left the lab to wait in the car. She'd listened to music, turning it up until it was blaring and posted senseless messages online. It was well over an hour before Jade had noticed the time. Her mom usually didn't keep her waiting this long; worried, Jade called her cellular phone. It went straight to message bank. *Damn! How dumb is my genius mother, forgetting to turn on her cell.* Reluctantly, Jade had gotten out of the car and went back to the lab. The building was locked. Jade walked around the unusually dark grounds to the main entrance. The compound was deserted. A good-looking security guard, a Native American, lounged behind the desk in the foyer watching television. She had tapped on the glass door; nothing, so she tapped again, he looked up and pretended not to see her. She pulled her hood down and parted her black hair to show her face. The guard's expression changed, his eyes opening wide as he pretended to see her for the first time. They checked the lab and nobody was there. The guard concerned called the police and her dad. To this day her mother has never been found. Jade still hopes one day she will come home.

Jade looked back at herself in her mother's colorful shirt. *Mom would return if she could,* Jade thought. Since the day she went missing Jade has changed, by focusing on her studies and staying out of black clothes as her mom had wanted.

The sound of a car horn brought Jade back to the present. Leaving the memories behind, she quickly caught an image of herself in the mirror. Jade stepped outside, onto the porch and into the embrace of the sun. The old Indian man watched her from under the shade of the tree. Today for some strange reason, it actually gave her comfort to see him. She boldly waved before she jumped into Ben's car and pulled on her seat belt. Ben leant over to kiss her lips, but she only offered her cheek. He was three years older. She looked sixteen and intellectually was way beyond. Graduating junior high at the age of twelve, two years before her peers was annoying; she had once tried to avoid all the attention by being an emo. Over the past year, since her mother's disappearance, she had made lots of changes, from dark withdrawn emo to stunning intel. Girls lined up for Ben's attention, but Jade wasn't one of them, and maybe that's why he found her interesting. They drove down the boulevard to the beach in silence, strongly sensing each other's physical presence.

Ben took her hand as they walked across the soft sand. The beach was filled with smells of suntan lotion, mixed with the hot food of vendors on the boardwalk. The sparkling Atlantic Ocean was the greatest attraction living at Myrtle Beach and kids reckoned that cruising the boulevard was the bomb these days. The water was forever coming closer, swallowing the sandy beach. Stretching out on her towel, Jade dug her toes deep into the cooling sand.

Ben sat on his knees to apply lotion to her back. "No thanks, I can do it," she said, sitting up.

He handed her the lotion. "Did I tell you I got the football scholarship to the University of California?"

Jade, not really listening, lay back on her stomach and twirled her bracelet around her wrist. Touching and tracing the smooth symbols, she went into a trance.

"Let's go for a swim? Jade. Jade, wake up. Have you been smoking weed or what?"

"What, no, I don't want any. I don't do drugs."

"Ha ha, you are a ditz, for an intel. Do you want to go for a swim?"

"Don't call me that. Why do jocks call intellectual people intels? What's wrong with being intellectual?" She could see behind him girls from college coming towards them. Quickly, Jade jumped to her feet. "Sure, that sounds great," she said, brushing off the sand and picking up the snorkeling gear, thrusting it into his chest. "Let's swim out past the last pier of the boardwalk and beyond the breakers."

"Aren't you going to take off your shorts?"

"No." Jade grabbed his hand and pulled him across the heating sand. Together they ran into the ocean, dropping themselves down into the tiny breakers, and molding themselves into the wet sand to pull on their flippers. The waves gently knocked them off-balance, and Ben reached for Jade as the water rushed back out to sea.

Suddenly, he jerked away and pulled his hand from her shoulder, shaking it by his side, as if he had touched a fire.

"Did you feel that?" he said.

"Feel what?" Jade looked into his eyes. "What, what's up?" she said feeling self- conscious.

"I just felt a ... zap, an electrical surge from you. I felt a current race through my whole body and I'm standing in friggin water. I feel like I should be glowing right now."

"Very funny, Ben, I bet you say that to all the girls." Jade dived into the next wave and swam out. In the silence under the water she thought, *Why am I with Ben? Am I so insecure?*

"Hey, wait up," he yelled.

Jade could hardly hear him as she dived back under the next set of waves. Beyond the breakers she cleared her snorkel, blowing water like a whale. Treading water she looked back for Ben and saw him still on shore talking to a stunning teenage girl. *Typical*, she thought, and started swimming back towards him, then stopped. She spat out the snorkel mouthpiece and argued aloud with herself: "What am I doing? I don't need this. Yes, I do. I need him to fit in with everyone." She looked around to see if anyone had heard her. She turned away from the shore and began to swim further out into the Atlantic Ocean. Ben finally caught up with her just as she dove under again. She didn't want to talk to him. She felt a sense of peace under the water and stayed there for as long as she could. Her hair floated like seaweed around her. She held it away from her mask. Her flipper dusted clouds of sand off the ocean floor. An old turtle swam below her. Up above in the distance, the surface of the water began to churn. A speedboat was approaching. Oblivious to the boat, Ben floated on the surface, face down watching Jade. Suddenly she turned towards the sky. She surfaced, cleared her snorkel, pulled the bit out of her mouth and yelled at the boat as it passed.

"Why'd you race off?" Ben asked. "And we shouldn't be so far out."

"What? It's not like you were alone for long anyway."

"Jealous are we?"

"No. Not at all."

"Maybe a little?"

"Who's the jerk in the boat?" she said.

"Maybe we should get back. We are really too far out."

"There is this massive, beautiful old turtle down there. Come, I'll show you," Jade said and chomped down on the mouthpiece.

Before she could dive under, Ben tapped her on the shoulder. "Wait. I want to tell you something. I really like you ... you're not like the other girls, you confuse me. You're smarter. You have lovely silky hair, and you have no idea how pretty you are. You have nothing to be jealous about."

"You don't know me," she said and stuffed the snorkel bit back in her mouth.

"I know enough to know I want to get to know you better. I know how old you really are too, and ..." He wanted to tell her he knew about her mother and how hard it must be for her, but he couldn't.

Jade felt exposed, naked. "And what ? What Ben? Why did you bring me here?" *What has gotten into me,* she thought. *Why do I need him to like me so much, why am I so angry?* He started to talk, but she wasn't listening.

"I know what you've been through because my dad was one of the investigators on your mom's case."

Jade couldn't believe what she was hearing. "What?"

"I saw you, at the police station," he said quickly. "Waiting for your dad. I was there sitting next to you in the waiting area. I was getting a lift home from my dad after being in the city."

Even with her flippers on, it was getting harder to tread water as Jade tried to push aside the memories of that day. She had been sitting in the waiting room staring at the floor, listening to the general commotion of the station. The smell of alcohol, vomit and antiseptic came flooding back. She had felt afraid and lost. She had counted anything and everything to keep her mind distracted. The person next to her had offered her a stick of gum.

"You had on a black pullover with a hood and black jeans, and you didn't even look up, when you took the gum, to say thank you,"

Ben went on. "Your dad came out looking exhausted. He hugged you and your hood fell down and your hair tumbled down your back. When you both turned to leave you looked me in the eye. I felt something. I asked my dad who you were and he said a sad fourteen-year-old girl who Just lost her mother. That's how I know how old you are, you're fifteen. I followed the case on and off over the year. Your mother was a brilliant scientist and you are a chip off the old block. I knew it was you when we first met at school."

Jade was uncomfortable, confused and excited all at once, not really sure how she felt. He said he always liked her, and he felt something special that day. "You knew, all this time?" Blood rushed to every pore and her entire body blushed. She clamped her jaw tight, afraid she would release a neurotic girlish squeal. She said nothing while her body moved up and down with each gentle cresting of water. "What do you think about my mom? I believe she is alive."

Ben looked like he was struggling to stay afloat. "I do too," he said. "Let's go back."

Jade looked at him, trying to work out if he was telling the truth. "Okay, but first let me show you this turtle." She dived under the water.

Jade and Ben smiled at each other behind the masks. Above, the speedboat turned back in their direction and below the turtle swam up towards them. Ben and Jade reached out to the turtle. Petite fish swam to Jade's bracelet and hung on. Ben held her other hand and they both hovered, watching. *He's going to kiss me,* she thought. *How stupid, I've got a snorkel in my mouth.* Jade laughed silently to herself. The moment couldn't last, oxygen was depleting and together they swam up to the surface. Ben was slowing his ascent trying to pull her towards him. She was out of air and had to let go of his hand. She broke the surface and the speedboat struck her from behind. Dazed, she felt a hand reaching down into the water and grabbing her. She could feel her body being dragged beside the boat like shark bait before she was yanked on board. Stars and darkness filled her vision and the last thing she could hear was Ben screaming something in the distance and gunfire over her head.

Her throat was sore, her lips were dry. Jade staggered through the mud, climbed over fallen trees, and searched for the sky. Twilight was looming as the sun dropped over some faraway horizon. The trees started spiraling around her. She was out of breath, losing consciousness, falling to the forest floor. *Where am I?* Panic and dread was turning into terror. *Why am I running?* Darkness invaded her consciousness.

She had woken to the smell of the cooling forest, not knowing where she was. Slowly she got to her feet. Her legs were unstable; as if drugged, she staggered. She reached up and touched her head — it hurt like hell, she felt nauseated, dizzy. Struggling to remember where she had been, she yelled out into the trees. *What the hell is going on!* Scared, she dropped to her knees, her head pounding. Acidic bile scorched her throat and her head felt like it was exploding with each dry-retch. She touched her head and her hair was sticky. She hugged herself, feeling cold. She sat on the mulch and drew her knees up to her chest. *What's my name? Jade. What's my address? North Myrtle Beach. Okay, at least I know who I am! What's the last thing I remember?* Jade rocked back and forth thinking. *Swimming, snorkeling, I was holding Ben's hand, that's right.*

These memories gave her little solace as she looked around at the dense forest surrounding her. *We were following a turtle.* The ocean had been warm and clear; sunlight cut through the crystal water sparkling on the ripples of soft white sandy ocean floor. She looked down at her filthy white shorts and bare feet. Feeling scared, at the same time with a sense of calmness at having regained a little control of her thoughts; the eye of a storm. Jade shivered. All sorts of scenarios were going through her mind. *Where did I get this hoody? Who dressed me; I don't remember getting out of the water let alone getting dressed.*

Jade slowly got to her feet, climbed and stumbled over rocks and up the embankment of the muddy creek. She had to fight off the panic and find a way up above the trees, to see where she was. The light disappeared. Darkness waltzed with the shadows of the trees. A wolf's howl vibrated through her bones.

THE FLOW OF LIFE WAS visible in the sway of the trees. A white deer, a doe, stood tall watching the girl. Listening and hearing the visions of the future. The deer was not the only one who was watching the girl. The forest became silent, the shadows haunting. The deer could feel something, a wolf — its heart was pounding in its chest, and it had woken to the smell of human fear. The deer watched the dark wolf drool in anticipation. It began its descent towards its prey. The deer's heart, beating strong, blossomed with mercy. The smell and sounds of the forest amplified. The girl felt the oncoming charge of the wolf and frantically looked up into the trees, searching for a place to hide. Her shoulders slumped, defeated.

The deer moved gracefully, determined to confront the snarling monster. With each moment her heart filled with certainty. Her desire to protect was stronger than the beast's desire to destroy. It raced towards the girl, watching her, unable to stop her from falling. The girl was paralyzed with fear. The deer saw into the wolf's eyes, they were red, almond-shaped pupils, with black slits swimming in a sea of yellow. It was getting closer. It traveled not alone, but accompanied by dark angels craving to please its master of death and capture more souls. The deer watched as the child confronted the darkness and saw into the eyes of the wolf, into the depths of its soul, as if searching for a sign of hope. Finding none, the girl threw her head back and screamed as darkness closed in. *Help!* Then whispered as she collapsed onto the forest floor. *Help me.* The white deer, in a flash, came up from behind and stopped directly in front of the girl as fear stole her sight and she slipped into the abyss of uncertainty and darkness.

The forest held its breath, the rivers stood still. The deer's protective aura expanded. Darkness had grown confident from the child's fear. The deer took a step towards the wolf. Clouds above began to shift. The white deer drew wisdom to her side. She had to protect the child to free the future and heal the spirit. The moon spoke, the stars joyously competed to illuminate, and the darkness fractured. The wolf calculated; the pack circled behind. The deer still dared to defy the wolves.

The deer saw the morning star pulse, watching from above and time accelerated. Thirsty spirits and captured souls fed off the starlight. Nourished, strengthened, they rose above the murky tones of darkness and the morning star descended from the heavens. The restless wolves moved from side to side looking over their shoulders and howling.

They became edgy, sensing danger as the morning light shone on them, and the shadows moved with the acceleration of time. Their leader stood firm, growling, huge teeth gleaming. The wolf focused on the deer's veins, bulging with life. The wolf lunged. Like a thunderbolt, a magnetic pulse radiated down. A burst of light from the morning star showered upon the white deer and the girl. The full force of the morning star's energy slammed into the ground, repeling the wolves back into the woods as if gravity vanished along with the darkness.

The starlight dimmed, folded within itself, again and again, getting smaller and smaller, until it became the size of a pebble and floated into the heart of the deer.

Butterflies danced upon the residual beams of light. The forest glowed; fluorescent morning dew dropped onto the undergrowth, and the flow of life continued. The deer lay down beside Jade, protecting her, giving her warmth while she was unconscious. A spark of the morning star light floated from the deer and settled, fading into Jade's old copper bracelet.

6

PROPHECY: CASEY. UTAH USA

The smell of mounds of old paper files and fresh paint was strong, but the size of the bold little man standing behind the mahogany desk was more captivating. Tiny beads of sweat traveled down the side of his face, and disappeared into the folds of fat that rested on top of his white collar. His breathing was labored, the air conditioner roared like an ascending plane accelerating for take-off. Nevertheless, tiny beads of sweat continued to pop up on the solicitor's head. He picked a handkerchief off his desk and mopped his round head and brow.

"Mr and Mrs Campbell," he said taking his seat. Fat wedged into the sides of the armchair as he wriggled and sank noisily into the leather. "Sorry about the state of my office, we are moving premises. Now, Mrs Campbell, as you know from my email, you have been invited here for the reading of your great-aunt Daisy's will."

Amy and Terry sat listening to the breathless solicitor. He read from sheets of paper that looked delicate held in his big round hands. Amy was torn between calling an ambulance, thinking the man in front of her was going to pass out any second, and trying to absorb the information he was giving her.

"What do you mean my great-aunt left everything to me? I never even met the woman," said Amy. "I didn't even know she existed. Are you sure you have the right people?"

"It is what the will states. The lavish cottage and acreage is worth a touch more than two million pounds, plus everything inside the house and on the property. The entire estate is just less than three million pounds. You may not have known your great- aunt, but it appears she seems to have known you."

"My mother told me very little about her family. She would never speak of them. She said she came from the UK to the States, met my father and they married, and that was all she ever said about her past," said Amy.

"I'm sorry, but you are the only living person from your mother's side of your family. A search was carried out in England, looking for the heirs to her estate. Your great-aunt's daughter perished in a house fire many years ago, along with her husband and their seven daughters." The solicitor sat staring at them trying to catch his breath. "I'll get myself another coffee and leave you two alone for a moment."

Amy watched the solicitor heave himself up out of the chair, pick up his handkerchief and leave the room, closing the door behind him. "Maybe we should go. We have the legal papers for Casey's adoption and his updated passport arrived two months ago," Amy said, examining the office. "There's nothing keeping us here. We've had a rough year. I know the virus has spread to the United Kingdom. Flights have been restricted, but I still think we should do it. We should try and get a flight out of here. It might be safer in a country house in England rather than here in the States. As much as I love the hills, I think we need to do something. The vaccinations don't seem to be working, I'm sure they are no more than placebos. More and more people are becoming infected, Terry. What about that woman in town yesterday? She killed her three children and her neighbor's child, too. Who could kill their own children? Once upon a time people cared, people would have filled the street with flowers of grief, but not today — not any more. I'm scared, I'm worried for Casey. What do you want to do?"

Terry stared into her blue eyes seeing the glow of vitality she felt.

"I don't know," he said rubbing his brow. "Let's forget the viral madness for a moment." He leant forward in his seat. "Let's pretend it's not even happening. What would we have done before all this? We certainly could use a vacation. I normally would have to be back at college a week before the students."

"That's if there is any college to come back to," Amy said.

Amy watched as Terry processed his thinking out loud. The concern in his words was like the soft touch of an angel wiping away her unshed tears.

"It's a long way."

"So, what do you think?" she said, breaking his train of thought.

Amy watched as his shoulders went back and he stuck out his chest. With hands on his hips, assuming an adventurous stance, he said, "Let's do it! If that's what you want, then let's do it. We can visit the cottage, or should I say," raising his index finger in emphasis, "*estate*. And you can decide what you want to do with it. It could be fun."

They sat patiently with their own thoughts, waiting for the solicitor to return. Eventually, he waddled through the door carrying a fresh cup of coffee.

"We'll travel to England in the next couple weeks. Is there any paperwork we need to take care of?" Terry asked.

"Yes, we can take care of that now. I am leaving with my family shortly, so best we do it today." The solicitor pushed papers across the polished desk towards Amy. "You need to sign here — and here. The property is now yours, Mrs Campbell. You can pick up, and sign for the keys from your great-aunt's solicitor in England."

"Casey ... you ready?" Amy yelled from the bedroom.

The rain pounded against the window. Casey glared down the darkened hall towards Amy's voice and jumped as lightning cracked deep into the night and the lights flashed on and off again. "Nearly," he yelled. His words were smothered by the sound of thunder rolling across the roof, shaking the windows and rattling his nerves.

Amy stood in the doorway of Casey's room. He had finished shoving his sneakers into the luggage bag's top mesh compartment and was scanning the room. He seemed focused on something hovering in his peripheral vision. The candle flames flickered in the absent breeze. "What do you see?" she asked.

"I'm not sure. It's an eerie glow that I can't see in the dark, only in the radiance of the moon." Casey shivered feeling rapid flutterings.

"I can't see anything. I think this storm has got us both spooked. Are you done packing?" Amy said, stepping out of the room.

"Pretty much."

Amy left Casey to finish packing and headed downstairs. She lit the candles by the front entrance. Mesmerized by the dancing flames she imagined the rich green fields of England where her mother grew up. She felt a fondness for her home in the hills of Utah and hoped one day she would return. Sheltering the flames with her hands, she said to the candle gently, "Lucky I prepared dinner before the lights went out. You wouldn't be much help."

Her brow tensed and her eyes narrowed as negative thoughts invaded her head. *The roads will be slippery,* she thought. *Terry's not home yet ...* Before she could finish her train of thought the front door opened and a surge of cold wind slapped her face and extinguished the candles, leaving her in darkness. Before she could react, Terry stepped into the house, shaking his hair leaving a pool of rainwater around him. "Terry, you're drenched!" Amy said trying to light the candles again. Then the lights came back on.

"I couldn't find my umbrella," he said, planting a wet kiss on her lips. "Or should I say, *brolly* ... ha ha. It hasn't rained since, well, you know ..."

"Don't you dare move! I'll get you a towel, and help you out of those wet clothes." Amy walked down the hall, opened the linen cupboard and fished out a towel. "The whole house is clean, packed up and we're ready to go." She closed the linen cupboard with her elbow. "I'm not going to have you make a mess. Jeepers, your shirt's sopping wet!"

Terry kicked off his shoes and pants. "I had to stop and help a young fellow and his girlfriend. His car was bogged." Terry fastened the towel around his waist. "Remember when we went parking ..."

"Dear, dear me," Amy said with a smirk. "Always the hero, you just can't help yourself."

He pulled her against his hard chest and kissed her deeply. "I love you."

"Terry, do you think our flights will be cancelled?"

"No, they're the last ones. I suppose we will have to get used to this sort of weather in England."

Reluctantly pulling away from his loving embrace, Amy said, "You'd better have a quick shower," and affectionately slapped his backside. "We only have a few hours. We have to load up the car and eat some dinner. Off you go, I'll mop this up." And she slapped him on the backside again. "Hurry up, your dinner's getting cold."

A little later, Amy and Terry finished the last drop of red wine with their last meal in Utah. Together they walked towards the stairs when the power went out for the third time.

CASEY POINTED HIS TORCH down the hallway and walked fluidly towards Amy and Terry's voices. He stopped at the top of the stairs and, in a trance-like state and without any emotion, heard himself as if in a distant room say, "It's going to get worse. I've seen into the abyss. The darkness keeps growing. Their fear of the light is diminishing. Only the power of seven can stop it. One will die to save another."

"What the hell," Terry said. "Casey, what did you say?" Terry's stomach felt like a hand had reached deep inside and was shuffling his organs around. He started climbing the stairs. "Casey, are you okay?"

Casey felt himself slowly turn away from the stairs before collapsing.

"Casey." Terry sprinted, stretching out to catch him.

Casey heard himself hit the floor like a bag of cement. Terry was on his knees beside him and held him in his arms. Gently, Terry brushed his curly hair away from his eyes and whispered in his ear. "It's okay. You're okay. Come on, where have you gone. Come on, son. Come back. All the way."

Casey could feel his eyes darting behind the thin veil of skin. He struggled to wake up, then his eyes fluttered and slowly opened. Casey felt dazed and confused. He stared into Terry's eyes for a second, then quickly pulled away and tried to rise.

"Hey, pal, take it easy, you just fainted. Go slow," Terry said.

"Yes. Sure, sorry."

"What do you have to be sorry about? Are you aware of what happened?" Amy asked, helping him stand.

"Your voice, you were asking if I was ready to go."

"That was at least an hour ago, Casey."

"I'm okay, truly. I'm a bit tired, that's all. I'll sleep on the plane."

"Maybe we shouldn't go?" Terry said.

"No!" Casey shouted. "We have to — um — I mean — we all need — look, I'm okay. Hey, let me get the bags in the car while you guys finish getting ready."

"What did you say, Casey? You were saying something before you fainted. Who are the seven? What's going to get worse?"

"I must have been sleepwalking. I think when the light went out I fell asleep while packing." Casey rushed down the stairs, worried they might sense how he really felt. He hoped he hid his feelings better than they did. *It's been nearly a year,* he thought, *and I still can't get used to seeing what people try so hard to hide.*

Casey looked back up at Terry and Amy and watched the faint aura of colors around them change from shades of red to pinks and soft oranges as they accepted his reassurance. They had no idea how much they revealed in a single breath. They were often like the lovesick teenagers he had seen at school. Bending down to pick up the bags, he hid a smile, cleared his throat and looked at Terry. "Hey, don't let me get in the way. I'll get the car packed."

"Cheeky monkey," Terry said, walking down the stairs. He held the front door open for Casey. "The rain has stopped, it's a good time to pack the car. I'll help."

"No, I can do it," Casey said. He picked up the suitcases thinking, I've stepped upon the path of a very long journey and there's no turning back. I'm finally going to see Sophia — in the flesh.

Sometimes she came and protected him at night. She surrounded him with a warm illumination. That's when he felt peaceful, and slept unaware of the negative angels that hung in the air. *Most people can't see the negative angels, the tiny viral demons, but Sophia can.*

Sophia saw them clawing over each other in her dreams, racing up through the earth like starved bats from a dark pit. She saw how people's bodies became infested and how they were encouraged by the tiny demons to be the cause of another's pain and suffering; to destroy themselves and each other. Our inner light is covered with shrouds of darkness until our soul suffocates. We feed them, we nourish them, and they will annihilate us, she had told him. They plagued him with nightmares, images of his mother in pain. Some nights Casey could hear her screams and he was filled with visions of her pleading with him to kill himself and join her. He dreamed Terry and Amy were mauled by black dogs. They would constantly try to brainwash him; showing him that Terry and Amy don't really want him, because he was strange. They would push and push. Casey would wake shaking and feel doubt slither over him. In the day, he would concentrate on others, focus on helping Amy and Terry and anyone that needed help, and the negative angels would back away. The unknown Golden Angel would move closer and in a male voice whisper softly in his ear, reaching out to him until he became emotionally aware. Reassuring about what was right, about mercy, banishing the shadows of doubt. "The tiny shapeshifting beasts know nothing else," the voice said, "but their desire to possess and destroy."

The rain drizzled and the front yard was dark. Casey, torch in his mouth, made his way to the car. He put down a bag, reaching for the door handle, but before he touched the car it beeped into life: the blinkers flashed, the interior light came on and the doors unlocked.

~

ABOVE THE CLOUDS, the flight to Denver was extremely bumpy. The flight from Denver to New York would be twice as long. Casey watched Terry pale. "You okay, Terry?" he asked.

"Ah, feeling a little sick. I think the first flight knocked me around a bit. It'll pass."

"Here, take my seat," Casey offered. "I know you'll feel heaps better by the time I get back. I need to go to the bathroom and the vacant light just flashed on."

Casey came back and took Terry's seat. He felt the energy instantly from the previous passenger. *An old fella,* he thought, *a fearful, overweight businessman. Left so much toxic negative energy it's surprising Terry didn't barf, A minute longer and he would have. It was like sitting in a pool of quicksand. First, you're a little uncomfortable and soon you become consumed by it.* Casey closed his eyes, pictured his home and remembered what it was like to be tucked in bed while his mother told him a fairytale. Slowly, the energy in the seat changed. He jolted awake, surprised he had nodded off for a few ticks, but it was worth a mint to have that brief rest. He opened his eyes and peeked at Terry. His color had returned. "Hey, swap back," Casey said.

Amy watched them dance around each other in the small space. Casey climbed over the seat and propped his pillow against the window. She smiled at him and he smiled back. She reached up and turned on her overhead light, and immersed herself in her splendid book.

He closed his eyes and drifted off, leaving Amy sheltered in a warm glow.

~

HE WOKE AS THEY finally arrived at JFK airport in New York. They disembarked and waited for their last flight to England. Casey felt the red-eye hype of the airport. There was chaos as people tried to buy tickets off those waiting for their connecting flights. Casey, Amy and Terry buzzed around, gazing into the shop windows, eventually settling in the observation lounge. Casey stood at the window, looking out at a strange sight against the beautiful backdrop of fading stars and a runway of lights — the sight of armed soldiers preventing people from running onto the tarmac was foreign.

He could see his and Amy's reflection as if they were standing amongst the stars. He smiled, thinking, *she has a good heart.* She was naturally beautiful; tall, and her long, curly hair was ruffled from the travel, but looked like it had just been styled. *People could think we are related.* His hair was a darker brown, and her curls were more ringlets, but they both had curls. He wasn't as tall, but he'd grown at least ten inches this year and working after school helping the tradies to construct the new Woodland's playground, and doing a lot of heavy lifting, had filled him out. He thought he looked more like a young man than a boy now.

"Amy, you excited?" Casey asked.

"Yes. A bit nervous. What about you?"

"Me too."

"You know what it reminds me of?" Amy said staring out at the runway. "A moment I had standing in Los Angeles airport years ago. It was so strange. I was a little younger than you at the time. It was the 2nd of September, 10.42 a.m., and we had just arrived home from a holiday on the Great Barrier Reef in Australia. The boarding time on my ticket from Australia had been the 2nd of September at 11.30 a.m. It was an eerie sensation. I had already lived the 2nd of September, it was my past. I stood silent, pressed up against a wall, while my parents waited for the luggage to come around. I watched the people and it seemed like I was standing in a corridor of time, and the world began to unfold in front of me. Sparkles of light every-where as each tiny electrifying atom of light danced around me, forming clusters, creating different shapes and densities, creating people, chairs and the turnstiles, everything. I felt like I had gone back in time to be in the future. I was from the future. I stepped away from the wall and into the stream of life that was flowing around me." Amy stopped talking and smiled at Casey. "Don't mind me. I'm just babbling."

"Why are so many people scared of flying?" Casey said.

"What?"

"I can see it." Casey watched the dense negative matter moving, growing, feeding off the light force that surrounded people, and their colorful auras were becoming clouded.

"See what?"

"They're afraid. They're afraid they are going to die. Are you?" Casey asked even though he already knew the answer.

Amy looked into Casey's eyes. "No, are you?"

"Sometimes. Do you think my mom was?"

"I don't know," Amy said, not sure where Casey was going with his thoughts. "She would be proud and grateful you lived through the storm. Delighted you can go on with your purpose in life."

"What do you mean, purpose?"

"Everyone has a purpose; we are all here for a reason. I reckon each one of us is a piece of a big puzzle trying to find where we belong. What did you mean before when you said you can see it?"

"Oh — nothing?"

"No, it's not. I see the sideways glances you give. I've seen you take a wide step around nothing as if there was something in your way. I also saw that you held onto that little kid's hoodie. You held him back, just before the car went through the red light. God knows what his mother was thinking, he should have been holding onto the pram at least. You see, I see things too that I don't talk about. But how did you know before it happened. You see something I don't, I know you do. If you ever want to talk, I am a cornfield, all ears." She watched Casey's face as his mind raced with questions he dared not ask. *He's hiding something,* she thought.

"Why aren't you scared of dying?" he asked again.

Tapping on her chest she said, "It might sound lame, but I feel a sense of peace from deep within. Like I have the support of the whole universe guiding, protecting and loving me no matter what happens."

"Not so lame." With the tiniest knowing smile, he said, "I feel like that when I think of my mom. What's the old leather book you're always reading?"

"I really don't know. It's in Aramaic. It was passed down through my family and I was told it was a book of splendor. I feel lighter when I'm sad, I feel found when I'm lost. That's why I carry it. It's my key."

"Key to what?"

"Key to whatever riddle life is sending my way. I don't know why but when I carry the book I feel good and connected."

"Connected to what?"

At that moment, a rich New York accent announced the commencement of boarding over the speakers, drowning out Casey's questions.

"That's us," Amy said.

WITH A CLICK, THE overhead luggage was secured. Terry climbed into the window seat and gazed out the small portal at the tarmac. He watched the luggage being tossed on the conveyor belt before it travelled into the belly of the plane.

"Terry!" Amy said.

"Yeah?"

With her eyebrows raised, and a sideways nod of her head, Amy indicated for him to get up and give the seat to Casey. She smiled at Casey as Terry gave a boyish look as if to say, *Do I have to?*

"Getting up," Terry said. "Right — of course, just checking all's well. Casey, my man — your seat."

Casey laughed and said, "Definitely."

The engines roared as the plane sped down the runway. Their heads were pushed back into the seat. Amy held Terry's hand and smiled at him. Casey imagined a giant hand came up from the ground, wrapped around the belly of the plane and propelled them into the electrified sky.

~

CASEY'S HEAD BANGED against the window and he woke with a fright. "Turbulence," Amy said, as the plane bounced up and down a little more. Casey rubbed his shoulder as if it was sore. "Are you okay?" Amy asked. Her arm flew up to her head as an overhead locker flung open, and handbags and jackets tumbled out falling on top of her. With her arm she knocked the stuff to the ground. The plane continued to shake violently and dropped, then levelled out. Amy had started counting. "That was the longest drop," she said, with her hand on her chest as if catching her breath. "My heart was in my mouth." She looked at Terry strangling the armrest, his knuckles white.

The air hostesses failed to conceal the worry on their faces, clutching onto their own restraints with both hands as they were jostled in their seats. Beyond Casey, Amy could see black clouds and lightning flashing outside the window.

Adrenalin raced through Amy. Casey appeared calm to her, stillness encompassing him. He reached his hand towards the navigation map on the screen imbedded in the headrest of the seat in front and placed his finger over the image of the plane.

Some people screamed, terrified, as the plane suddenly dropped again. The lights went out. A strong voice came over the intercom asking everyone to stay calm. Amy checked on Casey. He now looked feverish, beads of sweat tracking down his temple. He held his finger firmly against the screen; it was the only screen that still had power. "Sit back, Casey!" she yelled over the noise. Casey kept his finger steady on the tiny image of the plane while chaos went on around him. He was still, as if he was in a bubble, in a different time and space. The plane steadied, the people stopped screaming, and Casey collapsed back into his seat, breathless as a marathon runner, pale and exhausted. His curly mane was soaked. Amy, not sure what she had just witnessed, leant over to him and put her hand on his knee. Heat radiated from his body. "Casey, what's wrong?"

Casey rested his head against the cool window as the plane safely passed the edge of the expanding cloud of dark matter. "I'm alright, just scared, that's all. Can I have some water please, Amy?"

Amy handed him her bottled water and another bottle to Terry and they both skolled it. Casey retrieved his pillow off the floor, putting it between his head and the window. He closed his eyes and took a deep breath. "I'm okay — just need to sleep for a while. That's all."

Amy leant into Terry, kissed his cheek and whispered in his ear, "We need to drop for a lot longer, before we spin out of control. Count, each time we drop, count. But if we're going to go — enjoy the view. What else can you do?" She smiled at her husband.

The flight attendants moved through the plane offering juice, pillows and blankets and reassuring everyone the turbulence was over. Amy could see the color returning to Terry's cheeks.

Lightning cracked in the distance and Terry turned away from the window back towards Amy in wonderment. "Who are you? Where did you come from? And what did you do with my wife?"

Amy squeezed his hand, closed her eyes and tried to make sense of what just happened, if anything at all. *I am so tired,* she thought. *What did I see?* Lightning flared across the sky. Amy stood up and reached over the boys to pull down the window shade and then tightened up her seat belt. The plane hit a bump again, Terry grabbed her arm and started counting. Lightning lit up the plane once more and the thunder rumbled. The crew closed all the blinds and the plane settled down to the illusion of calm for the rest of the flight.

7

BEYOND REALITY: KEVIN. AUSTRALIA

Kevin slowly opened his eyes and gagged. Everything was blurry. The bush was saturated with the smell of smoke, burnt fur and overcooked meat. The taste and textures latched onto the back of his throat. Kevin's hand flew up to his mouth and nose. In the pit of his stomach, deep in his solar plexus, he felt animals screaming and the trees crying. He saw Tim motionless, his back lobster-red, scorched from the sun. Kevin scanned the area. They were alone.

Kevin looked past Tim, into the bush. It looked different. It was lush, brighter, practically fluorescent, and absent of smoke. Between it and Tim was a shimmering transparent wall. It looked like fluid; it moved rhythmically, rippling like the wind on the surface of a lake, or the vapors on the road on a summer's day. *It must be a mirage*, Kevin thought. He continued to scan the area. He saw the old car seat. *No petrol bombs and no teenagers, so how long has it been?* His skin was just as red as Tim's and felt like it would blister. Kevin awkwardly pushed himself into a sitting position.

"Tim. Tim!" Kevin stopped and stared at Tim's back. He searched for signs of life. Kevin held his breath, waited, afraid to move. There it was. Tim's back rose slightly with a shallow breath, and then another one. Kevin's shoulders dropped as he exhaled. He got to his feet and walked around and looked into Tim's face. He lifted Tim's eyelids — no response. He shook Tim's shoulders and still nothing. The southerly had scattered embers carelessly on both sides of the river; small pockets of fire flared up around them. Kevin heard — mixed with the crackling of the fire — a low hum, a sonic pulse resonating. Kevin turned and the lush green rainforest was still there, distorted behind the rippling wall. It was from this mirage that the sound and energy was emanating. The two landscapes were not quite worlds apart. His world was surrounded by sizzling heat and smelt like death. On the other side of the wall the world looked vibrant, tropical, fresh and rich like a cool volcanic rainforest. *It has to be a mirage,* he thought. His brain was playing tricks, protecting him. A loud crack like a stockman's whip, followed by a soft pulse, reverberated around him, reminding Kevin of a time when his granddad took him to a naval air show and from the deck of a carrier he saw a fighter plane traveling faster than the speed of sound to create a sonic shockwave over the ocean.

The wall was a veil between two worlds. Transparent liquid metal; horizontal ripples plasma-like. Kevin walked over to it. His palm open he reached out and gently touched the surface. Bolts of colored light flared from his hand and expanded along the wall. He pulled back. Arm outstretched he slowly placed his palm on the wall and again bolts of light flared. His hand, the nucleus, glowed. His mouth dropped opened in awe. The fluorescent waves of light ignited by his touch rippled and shimmered across the surface. Kevin felt euphoric — no pain, no fear. It wasn't hot or cold. It had no smell and felt just a little ... like jelly that hadn't quite set. Kevin applied pressure and his hand started to sink into the liquid. Cautiously, he pushed his arm into the wall to the depth of his shoulder and drew in a shocked breath: his sunburnt arm felt cooled instantly. He pushed a little further to penetrate its depths completely. He stopped his fingers now on the other side and he could feel cool air. He wiggled his fingers. It was nothing like the stifling humid air around him. He drew his arm out of the wall. *What the hell?* He stood there, turning his arm over and over to examine the skin. It had lost its lobster-red glow and was pale and fresh, the scorching sunburn had vanished.

Smoke suddenly filled Kevin's lungs and he had a fit of coughing and his eyes stung. The fire was now practically encircling them. Frantically, he searched for a way out, but saw only the rippling wall and its mysterious world.

"Tim, wake up. Wake up, Tim!"

Tim lay motionless, his leg badly twisted. *Crushed more like it.* Kevin searched the ground to find something, anything, to support Tim's leg. Every time he twisted his body his scorched back hurt. He found an old boot. Feeling inspired he picked up a couple of branches and tore long strips from a paperbark tree. A foreign thought jumped into his mind: *Get out and forget about Tim.* Startled, he fumbled with the boot, dropping it and just missing Tim's head.

Shit! How the hell do I do this? Okay, stop thinking, just do! Kevin dropped to his knees and quickly created a brace by winding the paperback around the two small branches to secure them to his mate's leg. His jaw was clenched tight as he was worried about hurting his friend. Mindful of his own leg starting to throb with pain, Kevin stopped. He was sympathetically feeling Tim's unavoidable pain. He ignored the sweat dripping from his brow. His fringe irritatingly clung to his face; he pushed it back with his forearm and out of his eyes. Kevin drew in a deep breath trying to calm down when a thought of his nanna emerged in his mind and a reassuring sensation enveloped him. Kevin struggled to refocus, blocking out his friend's pain. His own screaming emotions were enough. A flood of compassion, coming from Tim, washed over Kevin. Tim was aware, on some higher level, of Kevin's actions. Kevin's eyes clouded with tears as his friend's emotions embraced him and he had to wipe them away. His hands shaking, he wove a bootlace around Tim's leg brace, adding that extra bit of strength. Kevin checked the firmness of the splint, of each piece of paperbark, and finally of the snaking bootlace securing the bark. Kevin lifted Tim under the arms and dragged him towards the wall, gently placing him beside it.

"I'll go through first," he said to Tim as if he was conscious, "and make sure it's not going to vaporize us."

The air was getting thin as the fire sucked up the oxygen around them.

Kevin's eyes strained to see through the smoke and the mirage. "What is this stuff?" he said. He hoped Tim would answer. Reluctantly, he raised his right arm and softly laid his palm to the surface once again. It vibrated, light shone magically around his hand and shockwaves of colors extended out across its surface. He placed his left hand upon it and the same thing happened. With both hands poised as if to push open a door Kevin felt the coolness and pushed into it slowly. There was little resistance. He felt his fingers pass beyond the gel-like substance. His hands pierced all the way to the other side, and he clapped. He heard nothing — he did it again, not a hint of sound from the other side. He still felt relaxed, hypnotized by the sparkling lights that increased the deeper he penetrated into the wall, and the humming sound — as if the bass strings of a cello were being plucked — echoed around him. Instantly, Kevin snapped back into reality as Tim coughed. His lips looked red and swollen ... as he tried to speak the sound turned into a terrified wail. It burrowed into the very marrow of Kevin's bones. Tim stopped moving and screaming. He stared up at Kevin, searching with his swollen eyes for answers. Kevin wanted to move away from Tim's pain; instead he stepped forward towards him, took a deep breath when unexpectedly he smelt his nanna's house, lemongrass, and sage. Kevin psychically pushed back Tim's pain and fear.

"Hey, man! Welcome back," Kevin said crouching next to him. "You're pretty messed up, go slow." The smoke was getting dense, making it harder to see the oncoming flames. There was an eerie thunderous sound, like stampeding horses.

"What happened? Who were those psychos? What a pack of assholes!" Tim said. Each word sounded as if he had been to the dentist and his mouth was full of cotton.

Tim placed his palms flat on the ground determined to sit up. Slowly he began to lift his upper body, cringing in pain as his face

twisted into fear seeing his broken leg. "What happened? Blood —
what, whose ... I don't like blood especially if it's mine." He started
choking, gagging and coughing, causing more pain and he collapsed
back onto the ground and passed out.

"Tim? Tim!" Kevin slapped his face. "Tim, wake up, come on,
man!"

Tim laid still, his face wet. Tears escaped his closed eyes and he
whispered, "We need help. I can't, I can't believe you just bitch-
slapped me, K." Tim slowly opened his eyes. "Give me a hand." This
time Tim moved very slowly and sat up and stared down at his leg.
"Did you do this?" Tim said pointing at the splint. "Thanks, man,
thanks. I always thought you had a spark of decency hidden somewhere. I don't know if I would have done the same for you."

"We don't have time for you to get all ... whatever. We're about to
be cremated."

Tim, because of the pain in his leg, struggled to move. "What's
your plan? Have you seen us getting out of here in one of your
visions? Or do you see my mom crying at my funeral?"

"Don't laugh. I think we are at the edge of a parallel universe."

Tim raised his eyebrows and started to grin. He choked on the
smoke and said, "You got hit in the head, didn't you?"

"Turn around," Kevin said.

Tim craned his neck around slowly, his skin feeling like it might
tear. "No shit. Wow ... what the ... is that a mirage? Maybe we're
already dead?"

"I put my arm in," Kevin said, twisting and turning his forearm.
"Look at it," he almost shouted, "the sunburn is gone."

Tim, for a second, forgot about his pain. His mouth hung open as
he stared at Kevin's arm. "But, how, what is it? We don't know
anything about it. We can't just ..." He started coughing, "Your dad
will be here soon. Let's just sit here and wait."

"*No! He won't!* He doesn't know we're here. They will protect the
houses at the edge of the bush with a firebreak and let this burn itself
out." The roar of the fire grew louder and Kevin barely noticed they

had started shouting to be heard. "This is our only chance. I can't see any other way, we have to take it!"

Mumbling, Tim looked up towards the sky, pleading to God to save them from the inferno around them.

"What are you doing?" Kevin yelled. "This is our opportunity," and he pointed towards the wall. "We've already got an escape route. Fair dinkum, mate, you're blind sometimes. Let's drag your sorry ass over to the other side and get out of here. What other choices do we have? To stay is to die. This is going to be … an adventure. Yeah, an adventure." Sweat glistened over Kevin's youthful body which had a hint of the strong man he could become. Pain shot up Tim's leg as Kevin dragged him head-first into the coolness of the unknown substance. Instantly, they both felt soothed, calm, but Tim's leg was still on the other side and Kevin could feel Tim's pain and the heat of the fire. As each part of Tim's body passed through the invisible wall he felt renewed, he felt his body meld into the rhythm of the wall. Then the pain left, the choking smoke in his lungs cleared. He moved slowly, afraid Tim's pain would return. Fear dissolved before it could completely take over his mind. Kevin and Tim emerged from the wall and into the parallel world.

Kevin stared at what had been his sunburnt chest. They both looked back to where they had come from and watched a tsunami of fire race towards them. They instinctively braced themselves, protectively covered their heads for impact. The flames passed over them without even a warm breath upon them. Safely cocooned within the enclosure, they lowered their arms.

"*K, my leg!*" Slowly Tim stood up and put weight on his damaged leg. His knee clicked into place. The pain was non-existent, it felt fine. Kevin watched as Tim apprehensively put a little more weight on it, balancing on one leg, then he quickly removed the brace Kevin had crudely constructed. Kevin couldn't believe what he saw; Tim was completely healed. No broken bones, no blood, no sunburn and no swollen face, just dirt and dried blood.

Where are we? Kevin wondered. "We have walked through the bushes and swum in the river a trillion times and I have never seen this before." Kevin reached out towards a tree and laid his hand slowly upon the glowing trunk. He felt like he was part of it and suddenly felt himself stretch up and into the heavens. His arms stretched out wide, and his feet sank deep into the ground. He withdrew his hand. Being polite, he bowed, as if apologizing for the intrusion. Giving thanks, he stepped back and walked to the next tree. *Maybe we have never seen this because we never needed to be here before?*

"Where're you going? I don't believe this, K. The flames are right there but I can't feel them." Tim looked puzzled, suspicious, and touched the wall, which felt to him like wet jelly.

Kevin bent down into the foliage around him. He felt like he could hear it holding its breath, waiting. He touched the embellished, long drooping leaf next to him very gently. He looked even closer and was dazzled by a translucent blue insect sitting on the velvet leaf.

"What do you think this is? I've never seen anything like it." Its wings were like a cicada's, clear and fragile with fluorescent magenta veins glowing and an ethereal body of flickering silver lights. It was beautiful. Kevin leant forward to coax it onto his hand. It didn't move, so he tried to pick it up, but he couldn't touch it; his fingers tingled as they passed through the creature.

Tim screamed. Kevin's concentration shattered and he swiveled around. Flames licked the wall and a black mass of dark matter had developed, moving in a circular motion, pressing itself against the wall. It moved faster, getting stronger, expanding up the wall threatening to swallow them whole. "What the hell!" Kevin yelled. "What are you doing?"

Tim had pushed his arm through the wall, beyond the safety of their sanctuary. Flames licked at his fingers; they turned black as he screamed. The dark matter took form, latching onto Tim's arm, pulling it out of shape, wrenching at him, trying to pull him through the wall.

Kevin raced over, lunged for his friend and pulled on his other arm. He wasn't strong enough and Tim's arm slipped further into the fire and the dark swirling matter stretched it as if it was rubber, deeper into its vortex. Kevin watched shades of grey shadows flying anticlockwise within the whirlpool's black hole. Petrified and shocked as he was, he couldn't believe Tim hadn't passed out. His arm was covered in bubbling blisters. The heat and pain must have been excruciating.

Tim's face merged into the wall and his screams echoed in Kevin's head. *He's not going to last much longer and I can't hold him*, he thought. *Oh God, where can I get help? What's going on? Shit — Shit — SHIT!* Tim went limp in his arms. Kevin dug his heels in, but he was sliding and his body felt strange, suddenly sick, faint and weak.

Kevin became aware of the tiny blue insect that landed upon his shoulder and moved to the back of his neck. It burrowed into his skin and spread through his body deep to the cellular level. It injected its light into Kevin's atoms, as a bee's stinger might.

Illuminated, Kevin felt empowered and yanked hard on Tim's arm and he tumbled back in towards him. They both went flying. Kevin hit the ground, the wind knocked out of him. He stood and hunched over trying to catch his breath. Kevin felt like he was choking. He coughed and coughed and choked, until a winged ball of blue light shot out from his mouth. It hovered and looked at him before flying away. Kevin watched it disappear into the atmosphere, drew in a deep breath and whispered, "Tim, Tim ..." There was no answer. Kevin was afraid his friend was dead, toasted. He turned Tim over. Shimmering light frantically swam around Tim's body; the light was so bright Kevin had to cover his eyes. He could smell the burnt flesh, and he could hear Tim's arm sizzle, like when his dad tossed beer onto a BBQ to give the sausages that extra flavor. He dare not look. A deafening sonic buzz erupted. Then silence.

"K, Kev, what's wrong with your eyes?"

Kevin held his hands tight against his face, afraid if he let them drop he would see his friend as a ghost, talking to him from beyond.

"K, you're scaring me, show me your face."

Kevin slowly dragged his hands down his face and peeked between his fingers. He saw a hand coming towards him, touching him, trying to pull his hands away from his face. They felt clammy, cool. Not like hands that had just been consumed by flames.

"Look at me, not a mark on me," Tim said turning his arm over. "I feel great! But what the hell was that?"

Kevin looked up and down and all over Tim's body and couldn't find a mark on him. Kevin then turned his attention towards the black mass. "Can you see them?" he said to Tim. "In there, swimming within the vortex, those images, creatures with half faces." Misty bodies reached out as if to grab them, but turned to smoke, sinking down into the vortex like oil swirling in water.

Kevin stared into the darkness and knew that if Tim had been sucked back to the other side it would have consumed him forever. *What the hell?* he thought. *The life force would have been drawn out of us both. Our souls lost forever, trapped.* The whirlpool began to lose its strength and just before it completely disappeared, Kevin thought he saw a claw, the same claw that had reached up out of the murky river and grabbed hold of the curly headed boy. That was a year ago, but it felt like yesterday.

"Earth to Kev, you're babbling again. Where do you keep going, man? Stop this shit. You're scaring me now. I want to go home. I'm hungry," Tim said.

"How can you be hungry? Look around you. This is incredible — look at yourself; you were the pig on the spit. You were nearly sucked into a vortex full of God knows what! How can you be hungry?"

"You'll have to ask my gut. This is too weird for me, Kev. I have memories of my arm burning, but I have no scars. This might be right up your alley. If it's on TV I'm good, but this is real life shit."

"I hear you, man. I don't know if I should be scared or excited, but ..." Kevin's eyes squinted. He looked beyond the shimmering wall. Time had passed and the fire was out. The bush was charcoal and the sun was setting. *It's daylight saving time,* Kevin thought, *so it's got to be after eight in the evening. But how can that be, we have only been in here for ... what?* Kevin's thoughts stopped mid-sentence: *How long has it been.*

All concept of time started to elude him. "Couldn't be no more than twenty minutes surely," but the poor trees smoldered in the setting sun.

"We should go," Tim said.

"You're right, Tim. Your tummy rumbling is right on the mark, it must be way past dinner. Your sister is probably waiting to kill us. Let's walk towards home from this side, that way. We are safe a little longer, from ..." Kevin was not sure from what or whom, and whether it would be waiting for them, and walked deeper into the forest. Tiny birds of different colors — deep blue, green, red and purple — that were even smaller than finches, flew around them excited to have visitors. The luminous ferns, rich in color, glittered and appeared to be reaching out to gently touch Tim's leg.

"K — I think the plants are alive. Can you feel it?"

Kevin could feel it all right. He could hear them, too — soft harmonious sounds in his head. With each step he felt like he was walking on a sleeping giant and the trees were bowing down as he passed. He thought of a breeze, or the lack of, and then there was a wind rustling through the leaves. Kevin felt like he was a battery, charging up with every passing moment. The sun never seemed to move from directly above them, even though he couldn't actually see it. He could feel the rays shining down on him.

"K, do you think we're ...?"

"What?"

"Dead?" Tim said.

"We can't be."

"This place is strange," Tim commented, as they walked on. "I have lived here all my life and I've never seen it before. This is a rainforest. Our homes are surrounded by bush and everything is mostly dry. We look like we are on our way to Emerald City, and we've just got to find the yellow brick road. It's got to be at least twenty degrees cooler in here. I just had the shit kicked out of me and my arm was burnt to a cinder. My mom says that about Kath's cooking. I sound like my mom! This isn't normal!" Tim said.

Kevin stopped walking. "Don't freak out. Let's go back to the wall and take our chances on the other side. I'm not quite sure of our direction anymore."

"It's more like a membrane than a wall," Tim said, proud of his choice of words.

"A membrane is a wall, but not like the one that surrounds your brain because this one doesn't have a leak. God! Now I sound like my mom. Sorry," Kevin said.

"Why do you do that, why do you apologize? It was quite funny; you're a comedian in the making. This place, it feels alive."

Yeah, I hear you, Kevin thought. Everything is alive and watching every move we make. We should get out before we forget how.

"Did you say something?" asked Tim.

"No. Did I?" Kevin looked at Tim. Did he just hear my thoughts? His mind started reeling. When I was lying on the ground afraid to open my eyes I smelt the fire, and I could hear it getting close. That's when I thought of sci-fi flicks, about dimensions in time. That's when I saw an old wooden door latched and locked; hardwood reeking with sandalwood. My fingers transformed into keys and I opened it — a door to a parallel universe, a door to a place beyond the flames that is coming, as sure as eggs are eggs. Then I remembered Tim and my eyes slowly opened. What's going on?

"Whoa!" Tim's jaw dropped. "You didn't move your lips. What the hell? Fair dinkum, K, this is crazy shit. This is awesome. I heard everything," Tim said tapping his head. "In here. This is friggin awesome, dude!"

Tim to K: come in, K? Tim thought.

"Get out of my head! What the hell?" Kevin looked at Tim sideways while rubbing his head as if it hurt.

Kevin thought for a moment. *This, this is kind of cool. But let's keep moving.* In unison they raised their hands in the air, smiled, and high-fived, just like they did when they had been younger.

Finally, they found their way back and stopped at the floating protective membrane. They looked at each other then at the charcoal bushland beyond. The sun was a burnt orange, falling off the face of the earth, and making way for the grand entrance of a full moon. They moved forward together. Tim imagined a crazed pent-up cattle dog making tracks within his mind.

"Relax, man, you're scaring the shit out of me," Kevin said. The dog in his mind sat still. *That's better*, Kevin thought.

"Okay, let's do this," Tim said out loud.

The feeling of each other's fear drifted as they submerged themselves into the membrane. Kevin's eyes closed — his hands were outstretched and he relaxed into the silence of his mind. They floated not wanting to leave, not thinking, just being.

Colors engulfed Tim's mind before he left the serenity, stepping onto a burnt log. "Wow, psychedelic, amazing." He watched Kevin still floating, unmoving within the wall.

Kevin was lost and unaware Tim was beyond the wall. An image appeared before him, a deer surrounded by colored light. The sound of chanting and drums echoed in a distant corner of his mind, getting louder. The image evaporated. Kevin jolted, his arm jerked. He was being pulled away and he fought to stay. He didn't want to leave; he felt it was vital to connect. The deer was waiting for him. He felt himself exiting the embryonic state, first his hand, arm, foot, a shoulder, then half his head and chest. Tim pulled him all the way out. Kevin's shoulders slumped, his arms and limbs a dead weight, and the warmth of the dying day caught him off guard. He dropped to his knees and waited while he adjusted to the heat; it scorched the back of his throat and nose with each breath.

"You were in there for at least half an hour, just floating. You fall asleep or what? You looked like you were having a ..."

Kevin wasn't listening. Scattered black mounds paved the way to the river — swollen carcasses, they smelt like they were ready to explode, and a frenzy of flies feasted on the kangaroos. They looked as if they had been lying in the sweltering heat for days. The fire was out. Not a spot fire around or even ash or embers.

"Do you think your dad was here?"

"I don't know." Kevin rested his hands on the back of his head, confused. "How did they get it out so quick? It should be at least still smoldering."

8

PRIMAL SCREAM: SOPHIA. SCOTLAND

The forest looked misty and grey. Sophia was tired of running, tired of being alive in such a cruel world. The ground sloped to the left. It was cooler under the trees. The distant splashing sound of water running over small rocks told her a brook was close by. Sophia couldn't decide which direction it came from. Ahead, in the distance, was an abandoned cabin or an old clan dwelling. It faced east, overlooking the sloping mountainside.

Father McDonald slipped off his pack. "Stay here."

"No, I'm coming with you."

"No. Get behind the trees while I make sure no one is inside. It's still hunting season and someone could be in there."

"We haven't seen anyone for two days," she argued.

"It's best to be safe." He looked sternly into her eyes.

She cast her eyes to the ground, knowing he was right. Two days ago, after hiding from the chaos at the fete, they had munched on the lollies and chocolates that Mother Catherine had secretly packed for Gemma's slumber party. Recklessly high on sugar and over-confident, they came out of hiding looking for real food, and instead of going around the next town they walked into it.

They pretended to each other that they were on a camping trip, avoiding talking about the massacre at the fete. They craved a hearty Scottish breakfast and needed some camping gear. Traveling along back roads they had seen fewer people. Approaching the outskirts of the town they had passed a small community church alive with the songs of Solomon. The sound faded behind them as they continued on. The streets became quiet again. They passed an empty schoolyard, where a swing moved slightly in the breeze. Half a dozen or so deathly-pale faces paced the sidewalks on the other side of the road as they entered the main street of the town. A few stores were open, making it easy for her and Father McDonald to move about unnoticed. Sophia felt instantly ill with shame. Her legs went to jelly, her vision blurred. She imagined she had given the devil's puppets, the negative angels, an opportunity to see her. Sophia had to stop. She leant against the stone building to catch her breath and waited for the feeling, the ugliness, the absence of light and joy to pass. Sophia guarded her thoughts, holding onto her medallion, thinking of her sisters and better days. Father McDonald pointed out she was resting in front of a camping supplies store.

He pushed open the door to Go Outdoors. A young saleswoman was managing the deserted store. Sophia started babbling, telling the woman Father McDonald was her grandfather and they were heading for the hills until the virus consumed itself. She heard herself, felt out of balance and looked around for a chair.

"You okay?" The young woman came around the counter to help Sophia sit down.

"I'm feeling a little faint. I need to reconnect."

"What an odd thing to say," the store attendant said.

Sophia ignored the young woman and closed her eyes and thought of a tree, visualizing herself nestled into the trunk and its roots going deep into the ground, the branches stretching up and reaching for the heavens. She drew in a long deep breath, and then breathed out, repeating it a few times before opening her eyes. The store attendant handed her a glass of water and a trail mix bar.

"Feeling better? You don't have the virus, do you?" the woman asked, stepping back.

"No, no, I'm fine, really. This is good, thank you."

"No offense, but let's get you two geared up and — out of here. I don't know why I even opened up this morning. We have been closed for three days. Mr McLean, the owner, has disappeared. It was my job to open up on the weekends only. But I had to do something. My parents went to hospital during the army collections, and I haven't seen them since. I was going to go to church. I love singing but I was compelled to come here and open up."

Sophia watched her talking, as if to herself, while picking up backpacks and loading them up with packets of dried food and all the bits and pieces they could possibly need. She would have shoved in a kitchen sink if she had one. She even picked up Sophia's day-pack and stuffed it into one of the larger backpacks.

"Remember, autumn is around the corner," she said. "Don't stay up in the mountains too long. If it comes over colder than usual as it did last year, you'll end up snowed in for winter, and nobody will find you until the thaw."

The bags ready to go, she helped Father McDonald with a set of hiking poles. "You sure you're fit enough, grandpa?" Not waiting for a reply she turned to the shoe section and plucked a pair of Canadian red leather hiking boots off the shelf for Sophia.

Listening to the woman, Sophia started to feel better. She wanted to believe in her own tale: that Father McDonald was her grandfather. Sophia walked up and down the aisle in her new boots and swiveled around to her captive audience of two. "Perfect fit. Totally comfortable. I feel a bounce, and my heel is pushed forward in motion, making me want to move." Sophia thrust her foot out in a ballet pose.

Screams in the street broke into the peace of the store; like a tremor, a crevasse split open and zigzagged down Sophia's spine. Windows across the street shattered and so did the false reality Sophia had indulged in. She was fearful that this was the way it was going to always be. The screams were real enough and here she was thinking of herself. She twisted around towards the sound, craning her neck. The street seemed clear. Cars were parked against the side-walk, empty — not a soul in sight.

Sophia, Father McDonald and the store attendant moved to the shop's front window to scan the street, straining to see where the screams originated. From the direction of the church, eight, maybe twelve people came running towards them. Sophia froze; her mind went back to the fete — back to the car park — back to the shots that had exploded in her ears. The sight of Mother Catherine's swollen face, choking. *He's followed us,* she thought.

On the street with each fired shot, someone dropped in mid-stride. Car lights flashed across the street. A man switched off his car alarm, reached out for the door handle and his head exploded, blood and tissue spoiling the roof of the white Golf. Two other people made it to their vehicles and the cars roared into life, screeching out of town.

No thoughts to the fallen. Every man for himself. A mother carrying her baby in a sling across her chest ran along the sidewalk towards the camping store. Sophia could now see the gunman. It wasn't the same guy from the fete. He was older, roundish, dressed like he lived in the mountains and wore the same gear all year round. He carried two rifles — one was slung over his shoulder and he was firing the other.

Sophia felt the terror from the woman heading towards them. Sophia's knees went weak; her bladder filled with heat that spread over her body. A primal scream clawed at her throat. *Move damn it, Sophia, move!* she screamed to herself.

Sophia bolted out of the store to help the woman and her baby. Father McDonald yelled at her to stop, but it was too late. A shot was fired and the camping store window cracked, but held. Her focus was on the woman; Sophia grabbed her by the arm and guided her into the safety of the store, pushing her towards a rack of thermal jackets. Another shot was fired; the air suddenly was filled with tiny crystals. *It was like being in a snow globe.* Time moved elegantly slowly. The glass pierced Sophia's face and hands. She shut her eyes tight and screamed in pain. Father McDonald pulled her towards him. They took shelter together with the woman and baby amongst the thermal jackets.

A car exploded and the building's foundations shook. Sophia slowly opened her eyes; she could see. The panic eased. She stole a glimpse between the jackets and saw a ball of flames, black smoke billowing into the sky. The gunman was jumped on by two men from behind. They crash-tackled him to the ground, pinning him beneath them. They jumped to their feet and started kicking him. Other people joined in. The hunter had become the prey. Sophia had to turn away. Picking at the pieces of glass in her hands, she winced. Her face hurt from the tiny shards of glass embedded in her cheeks. She looked at the lady, dusted the glass off her shoulders away from the baby, and did her best to smile. "Your baby will be okay."

Father McDonald quickly picked what glass he could off Sophia's cheek and said, "Are you okay? Don't do things like that, you'll give me a heart attack. Come on, we have to go."

He looked at the store attendant. "Please help this woman and her child. I am sorry we cannot stay. We have to go. God will be with you. Bless you." Father McDonald wanted to help but he knew the only way to truly help was to follow God's lead and take care of Sophia. "Where is the delivery entrance?"

The young shop attendant pointed to the back of the store.

Father McDonald struggled to pick up the heavy backpack. Sophia saw his thin legs straining. She pretended not to notice as he mustered as much strength as he could and heaved the bag up and fumbled to fasten the waist support straps. He pulled them tight, which took some pressure off his shoulders. Sophia took charge of her backpack and sat it on the bench. She sat down to insert her arms into it and stood up feeling weak. She was more worried for Father McDonald than herself. She wasted no more time and wove between the shelved merchandise to the delivery entrance and headed into the woods.

As soon as there was enough distance between them and any town, Father McDonald sat Sophia down on her backpack while he fished through his bag for a first- aid kit. He had trouble getting the clasp to open on the little red plastic box. Sophia helped him and handed him the tweezers. He started to gently pull out embedded shards of glass. Her face cleaned, he gently laid tiny strips of tape over the wounds. Without a word, they headed deeper into the forest heading south towards England.

IT HAD TAKEN THEM two days to get here and now the guiding sun was dipping over the horizon. With the load off his back, he said, "A few fishing lessons for you, a rabbit trap here and there and we should manage quite nicely for a few weeks. Now — wait here. Don't go anywhere but if something happens to me — run."

Sophia waited behind the trees watching him struggling painfully up the small hill to the cabin. *He thinks I don't see him take his pills.* Father McDonald stopped to rub his aching hip, pulled out his worn Bible, and continued. There was no one in the cabin, she knew that, but she knew he needed to be sure. Sophia wished she could take away his pain. He placed his hand on his knee to push on up the hill. He wasn't prepared for anyone who meant them harm; there wouldn't really be anything he could do. He struggled forward, believing in God, believing in his guidance and protection. He just needed time to rest; they both needed time to rest and this small log cabin looked like the perfect place. He stopped again and pulled his pills from his pocket, catching his breath, taking a tablet to calm his heart. At the top he stopped and looked out beyond. His shoulders went back and he stood straight. His gaze swept the area admiringly. *Bless you, God, thank you for looking after him,* she thought.

Sophia waited behind the tree as Father McDonald instructed. The air was dense. An acute feeling of being watched crept over Sophia, a new and scary sensation.

Sophia remembered when she first started to control her energy and her ability to leave her body and astral travel. She would fight to overcome her desire to leave this realm and go to the next. At that time, Sister Clare spied obsessively on her and Father McDonald.

This is what it felt like now, like someone was spying on her. She missed Mother Catherine, who had protected and loved her, and wished she was back at the church, lying on the pews, gazing at the stained-glass windows.

She scanned the area, but could see nothing, so she scanned again — this time with her sixth sense and she could now feel a calm rhythmic heartbeat. Whoever it was wasn't scared of her. The energy felt gentle. A wave of fragrance reminded her of the scent of fresh lilies and the way some flower petals can float on a breeze. It had to be an animal and it had to be behind her. With a ballerina's grace she pivoted slowly, careful not to make any noise. Over her right shoulder, standing in the distance and hiding in the shadows, was a white deer. It didn't move — it just kept watching. Sophia closed her eyes with the image of the deer projected onto the back of her eyelids and stepped out of her body. Her body dropped quickly to the ground. She felt nothing. Sophia looked at Father McDonald and saw he was still laboring towards the cabin.

At ease in her spiritual body, Sophia moved silently amongst the trees. The deer's ears perked up and its nose thrust forward, smelling the air, sensing Sophia's youthful spirit. Sophia moved closer and stretched out her ethereal hand to the deer. It bowed. Sophia's hand slowly moved down its neck, over its muscular shoulder, and along its silky back. Sophia's bewilderment melted as their souls united. Sophia was in awe of the dainty ladylike energy it possessed, and the warmth of its body. She could feel the tenderness of the deer's thoughts. It was ... Sophia struggled for the right word ... *dazzled*; yes, it was dazzled at how easily Sophia had shed her skin. But Sophia was even more bewildered than the deer. She heard its thoughts, like a parent, in her heart: *You must be careful. Your youth fools you. You are truly old, and must take greater care of your physical body, or someone or something might take it.*

Sophia, finding her inner voice, said, There is nobody around. No evil dark cloud and no lost souls. Sophia felt embarrassed. But you are right. Thank you for your concern.

Come, I'll walk back with you to your body.

Together they crossed the path of fallen leaves. Sophia hugged the deer, then infused herself back into her sleeping body. She felt the heaviness of the physical world, the phenomenal limiting pressure of the five senses. She wiggled her toes and fingers before opening her eyes. The deer was licking her face with its rough tongue. Sophia wiped the sticky saliva off her face and rose to hug the deer with all her physical strength. She could no longer hear its thoughts, but still felt the essence of its celestial being.

Father McDonald was calling out: "Sophia, Sophia!" Suddenly a bright flash radiated from her locket, which had captured the sun's rays and, laser-like, shone in his direction, blinding him. He shielded his eyes as the beautiful deer stepped out from behind the sphere of light. Standing on the porch, he waved again, giving her the all-clear.

Sophia threaded her arms through the harness of her heavy back-pack, and stood up. A squirrel darted down the near-by tree trunk, startling her as it leapt into her path. She sensed the squirrel's laughter as she stumbled. The white deer didn't flinch. An eagle screamed overhead and they all glanced up. The eagle circled the air above the cabin and rose up and over the mountains. Father McDonald began to speak into the sky.

Sophia couldn't hear the words, but watched as his lips moved over the familiar passage. "He that dwells in the secret place of the most High shall abide under the shadow of the Almighty. He shall cover you with his feathers, and under his wings shall you trust: his truth shall be your shield and buckler." Sophia remembered this was from Psalm 91.

Sophia walked up the hill to stand beside Father McDonald on the porch and together they watched the eagle until it was out of sight. *I think we could call this place home for a while,* she thought. The white deer circled the cabin then walked away to the sounds of the flowing river.

"Come on. Let's get this place cleaned up," Father McDonald said, resting his arm on her shoulders.

Sophia followed him into the cabin. *It was well kept and rather modern on the inside. Obviously someone's furnished holiday cabin.* In a glance off to the left she could see a wood-burning stove in the kitchen, a small bench and hanging pots, a plastic white sink with a pump action lever and, against the wall, a kitchen table for two. It was a tiny cabin. On the right side was the living room where there was a sofa covered in dusty sheets facing an open fireplace. Off to one side of the lounge room, a narrow wooden staircase went straight up to a lofty bedroom. Under the stairs, facing the lounge room was a bathroom.

"I'm going to check under the cabin for a generator," Father McDonald said. "With this much stuff there has to be one." Father McDonald walked around the outside of the building and quickly returned, puffing, exhausted.

"That was quick. Any luck?"

"No." He walked slowly into the kitchen surveying the tiny space and finding a trapdoor under the table. Together they dragged the table away from the wall and he pulled on the metal latch. It resisted and he stopped and held his back. "I'm not as strong as I used to be." Nerve pain fired from the base of his spine to the top of his neck. "I'll be right in a minute or two."

Frightened, Sophia guided him to a chair and said. "Maybe you should rest here." Over the past week his body had visibly aged. Sophia pulled on the latch, flipping the door up, and searched the kitchen drawers, finding a working torch.

Father McDonald rose and took it from her. Slowly he climbed down the narrow stairs. He ducked, just missing banging his head against the wooden frame. "You go find yourself a bed. I'll be right," he said, as he descended.

Sophia knew there would be no arguing, and ran up the steps to the loft. There was a double bed and two singles. She picked the single that lay under the skylight and she lay down to watch the sky above for a while. Reluctantly she rose, opening the window for some fresh air.

～

THEY CLEANED THE dust off the furniture and aired the cabin, unpacked only what they needed in case they had to move quickly. They settled down the best they could. Sophia threw the sleeping bags on the beds and made up Father McDonald's to be as comfortable as possible.

The night came round quickly while they were busy cleaning and collecting wood. The generator now provided a comforting hum and, more importantly, lights. A can of hot chicken soup tasted and smelt smokey from the wood stove. Sophia cleaned their bowls and Father McDonald went and sat on the porch to read from his Bible. The outside world faded away as his warm, harmonious voice floated in through the open door. Sophia listened while boiling pots of water and pouring them into the bath. The vapors of steam rising from the surface of the water looked inviting, but she resisted the urge to climb in. "Father, come see."

Wearily he stood in the doorway and said, "You're a gem. Thank you for the bath, Sophia. It's just what I need. God bless you."

Sophia waited until Father McDonald climbed the stairs for bed. "Feeling better?" she asked.

"Totally rejuvenated."

Sophia quickly had a cold shallow bath, just enough water to wash the dirt out of her hair. Shivering, she climbed out and dried herself with the new half-size microfiber towel the storekeeper had packed. Sophia put on her second-hand dark-blue and yellow tracksuit. It looked like new and she remembered why she had packed it in the first place and started to cry. She sat on the edge of the bath and waited till her body stopped heaving. She wiped her eyes with the back of her hand and towel-dried her long hair as best she could. She felt better for the tears and better for her bath, even if it was freezing cold.

Sophia lay down on her bed and cocooned herself in the soft familiar textures of her sleeping bag. The forest was alive with sound and the cabin was dark. Stars shone through the skylight window between a few fallen leaves. There were streams of dazzling stars and four stars glowed brighter than the rest.

"You awake? Can you see the stars?" she asked Father McDonald.

"Yes."

"Do you know the names of the four stars shaped in a cross?"

"I can't see those through my window."

"Come see."

He groaned quietly as he unfolded his body and shuffled over to her bed. She made room for him to lie beside her.

"See," she said pointing into the sky.

"Marvelous, it's beautiful — Blessed are you, Lord. That's the Grand Cross, Sophia, it's very rare. There's Mars, Pluto, Jupiter and Uranus. They should be at ninety degrees from each other, I think. Throughout history, significant events like revolutions, the start and end of wars have occurred at such times. Sadly, these planets in this formation have become a symbol of pain and suffering. A great strain has fallen upon humanity, there's no denying it. It doesn't matter what happened in the past, what matters is the future. It may be a sign of great darkness, but it can also mean there is potential for even greater light. We are going to need a lot of mercy and compassion in the coming month for ourselves, and the world so it seems. The stars hold many secrets, Sophia. In the book of Matthew, astrologers from the east followed a star to Bethlehem, for the birth of Jesus."

Without taking his eyes off the stars he recited, "The Lord is my shepherd; I shall not lack. He makes me to lie down in green pastures: he leads me beside the still waters. He restores my soul: he leads me in paths of righteousness for his name's sake. Yea, though I walk through the valley of the shadow of death, I will fear no evil: for you are with me; your rod and your staff, they comfort me. You prepare a table before me in the presence of my enemies: you anoint my head with oil; my cup runs over. Surely goodness and mercy shall follow me all the days of my life: and I will dwell in the house of the Lord forever. Amen."

"Amen." Sophia didn't want to dwell on the significance of the Grand Cross. She heard and understood what Father McDonald had said, but right now she just wanted to gaze at the stars and imagine what it would be like to sail amongst them. "How do you know so much about the stars?" she said.

"I was in the navy, and many nights I prayed to God under a blanket of stars. The early seamen navigated only by the stars, believing in myths and legends. You can always find your way home if you know how to read them. Now get some sleep. God willing, tomorrow I will show you how to fish."

"I would love kippers!"

"I don't think it will be kippers."

He must have thought she was fast asleep and, careful not to wake her, he unceremoniously slid off the bed with a thud. She clenched her teeth imagining the pain rippling through his hip. He picked up his torch and headed down the stairs. He took some painkillers out of the side pocket of his backpack, and went outside. Under the light of the moon, Sophia watched as he switched on his torch and hung it from the wooden beam above. As the shadows watched, Father McDonald nestled the Bible in his two hands and read out loud into the night: "You shall not be afraid of the terror by night; nor for the arrow that flies by day: Nor of the pestilence that walks in darkness; nor of the destruction that wastes at noonday. A thousand shall fall at your side, and ten thousand at your right hand; but it shall not come near you."

He leant against a post and rested his eyes. The book fell between his knees as he drifted off to sleep. Night after night he read on the porch until the morning chased away the shadows and the world gave birth to a new day.

9

DOORWAYS TO A PARALLEL DIMENSION: SHAUN AND KEVIN. AUSTRALIA

A smoky blood-red sky covered the city. The air was thick with vermin. They were in his house, they flew around his bed and blocked out the light from his soul. Soaked with sweat, Shaun tossed and turned; flames licked at his bare skin, the heat blinding his vision as he dreamed of burning alive. Under his eyelids his eyes darted back and forth.

"RACHEL!" he screamed as loud as he could, but only a whisper escaped his lips. Out of breath, he woke, panicking, gripping the bed, his heart pounding against his ribs and tears trailing down his cheeks. He wiped his face with the filthy sheet. The images had already dissolved, the dream forgotten, but the fear remained. Shaun reached for the comfort of his mobile phone, accidentally knocking it to the floor. He shuffled into the bathroom, coughing a little. His father lay passed out on the lounge room floor, an empty bottle of whiskey still clasped in his hand. Shaun quietly stepped over his body and looked down in disgust. The desire to stomp his heel into his father's face and pay him back for the beatings and pain his mother had endured was compelling, but the thought of his mother stopped him. His foot landed on the carpet, nearly clipping the tip of his dad's nose. He walked sluggishly into the kitchen.

Shaun jerked opened the refrigerator. The light came on and his hand flew up to protect his eyes from the sudden glare. The milk was sour, the bread moldy, and the Vegemite empty. He slammed the door shut. Miserable, he went upstairs and climbed through the attic to the roof. In his boxers, he lay stretched in the early morning sun and tried to remember what it felt like to lie beside her and smell her perfumed hair.

"WHAT? WHAT THE hell do you want with me, boy?"

Shaun woke disoriented and nearly rolled into the gutter and over the edge of the roof hearing his dad's voice. Gingerly, he moved to look over the edge. There was a fireman at the door. Shaun leant a little further and slipped on a loose tile, catching himself before he went over the edge. The dude looked up, and Shaun ducked out of sight. *Shit! How could they know?* he thought. He strained to hear their words.

"I saw the bike on the lawn yesterday," Daniel said. "Do you know whose bike it is?"

"What bike? I don't know."

The fireman turned and pointed to the sky-blue bike resting on the lawn. "What about your son. Can we ask him?"

"What?"

"Is that your son's bike?"

"No. Now piss off!"

The door slammed an inch from the fireman's nose. He walked down the porch stairs turned and looked back up at the roof. Shaun lay flat trying to melt into the roof and his cheek slapped against the warm roof tile. He heard something moving beside him and twisted his neck around to see a creepy, dark flickering cloud, caught in the stream of sunlight stretched across the sky. It was like looking through a microscope at squiggles of organisms. He blinked and they were gone. His skin crawled; the atmosphere was gritty and tasted metallic. He had tasted something like it before. Suddenly he found himself falling. Instinctively, to break his fall, he pushed his hands out in front, and something sharp jabbed and sliced into his palm. He winced in pain and pushed himself up. He glared at the blood in his palm, a gash clean and straight as a surgeon's knife, right along an old forgotten scar. There was nothing on the roof that could have made a clean cut. Tiny black flickers like worms danced around his head. He waved his hands through them and they disappeared.

"What the hell?" he said. He looked back at the road. The fireman had picked up the bike, thrown it in the back of the Dodge and driven off.

"Shaun! Shaun!" his father yelled through the house.

Shaun stayed on the roof and waited for him to shut up. He felt the cool morning summer breeze dry the salty fluid from his body. Smoke rolled down from the mountains like a fog rolling in from the ocean. Shaun tuned out his father's ranting. In the distance a black streaming cloud twisted hypnotically. It reminded him of something. It felt important but still nothing came. It had been like this on and off for years. It drove him insane.

He slithered off the side of the roof and back into the house through his bedroom window. He put on his t-shirt and jeans and slipped into his runners. He opened up his top drawer and stared at the leather pouch. He felt it with his fingertips and drew in a jagged breath. It was worn and shiny from his handling, and still had the smell of a tannery. He picked it up and felt the shape of the stones, shoved it deep into his front pocket and climbed back out the window.

Tim waded into the water. "Hey, that reminds me, K. You're sleeping at mine tonight. We're not going to have to deal with your mom at all."

"Yeah, you're right".

They dove into the river and swam, using the tide to carry them across. Their bikes and clothes were gone. The bush was deathly quiet. The light was being sucked out of the day. They walked along the blackened trail and stopped where the anthill had been. "Something's not right," Kevin said. He walked on to the end of the track and stopped to look back at the charcoal trees. He didn't need to hear Tim's thoughts to feel his unease. They headed for the vacant lot; the tall grass had been burnt down to the ground. Barefoot, spiked vegetation jabbed their soles as they walked towards the empty street ahead.

KEVIN SAW TIM'S mother was in the kitchen gazing out the window. She saw them walk across the backyard and waved.

She smacked a kiss on Tim's cheek before the back door closed. "Hi, boys. Sorry I missed you both last night," she said, returning to her cooking. "I got home so late, I didn't want to wake you."

Puzzled, Tim's eyebrows hiked up towards his hairline and looked as if his mom had lost the plot. His sister walked into the kitchen and bumped hard into his shoulder. "What was that for?" Tim said, rubbing it.

"Don't you two start," his mother snapped, rinsing broccoli. "There is enough violence on the streets. If you don't have something nice to say to each other, then I'd advise you to say nothing at all."

"I'm going to my room," Kathy said. She paused just before the kitchen door closed, and beckoned to the boys to follow.

Tim's mom wiped her hands on the tea towel and opened the refrigerator. "I've made some rocky road for you guys to take tonight." She retrieved a Tupperware container and flashed it around the room.

"Kevin, your mom was looking for you. She was hoping you'll be home before dark to pitch the tent. You'll have to get a move on if you don't want to disappoint her."

Kevin finished the glass of water and put it on the edge of the sink. He gave Tim a confused look.

"Okay, Mom," Tim said. "But we're —"

Kathy launched back into the kitchen and pulled Tim out of the room before he could say anything else.

When they were out of earshot, Kathy said, "Where the hell have you been? Mom may think you were tucked in your bed last night, but I know you weren't!"

"You're crazy," Tim whispered. "What are you babbling about — you came to my room to give me a tenner this morning, so you could go out with some douchebag."

"That was yesterday, and where's your bike? I saw you from my window walking along the street. And where are your clothes?"

"What! Yesterday! What's today? So, that's why my mom was here." Kevin said. "We've lost a day. We've been gone over twenty-four hours. That's why there was no smoldering bush. I'd better get home. Grab your tent."

Kathy followed them to Tim's room, watching them scramble around for the tent, flashlight, sleeping bag and pillow. "What do you mean you've lost a day? Tim! What's going on?"

Kevin picked up his unopened backpack. His mom had packed extra things. He could tell by the way it was tied and bulging out the sides. She still treated him like a kid, which he found annoying. *But sometimes it is nice,* he admitted to himself. He felt a pang of sadness, thinking that she was trapped by her own fears. *That's the true plague,* he thought and walked out of Tim's room.

Kathy flicked the hall light on and off. "Guys? Guys?"

They stopped at the top of the stairs and turned to her.

"What now?" Tim asked.

Kath looked at them as if they were a pair of idiots. "You owe me that ten back, or I'll let the cat out the bag," she said.

"You can be a real bitch," Tim said.

"Oh, and maybe you guys are used to hanging out in your underwear, but perhaps the few neighbors left don't need to know."

"Oh, shit," Tim said, dropping his things in the hall.

They rushed back to his bedroom. Tim opened his drawers and fished out two pairs of cargo pants, one blue and one khaki and two white Bonds t-shirts. He handed Kevin a shirt and the khaki pants. Tim pulled on his sneakers and tossed a spare pair to Kevin.

Kevin's nose wrinkled in disgust and his eyes began to water. "They reek! I'm not wearing them."

Tim didn't want to part with his Nikes. "Oh, man! Okay. You so much as scuff the toes, you owe me a new pair." They grabbed their stuff and bolted down the stairs.

"Bye, Mom."

Watching the news, his mother called absently, "Aren't you forgetting something?" She heard them go into the kitchen and collect the rocky road out of the icebox. She remained in the plush leather recliner and pushed out her cheek for a kiss, not taking her attention away from the television. She was focused on the dark-haired reporter with the deep baritone voice. He was an American reporting a missing person.

"Over a year ago, Professor Ellen Freeman, a leader in genetics research, went missing from her lab and remains to this day unaccounted for. Twenty-four hours ago it was reported to police that her daughter was kidnapped. Her last known whereabouts was Myrtle Beach, South Carolina. The police are questioning the young man who reported her missing and they are trying to locate her father. They are treating the circumstances as suspicious. With the majority of the police force dealing with the violent-infected, it's unlikely there will be an extensive search conducted."

"Hey, Kevin, didn't your mom go to Carolina?" Tim's mom said.

"Yep, and she never talks about it."

Tim sat on the arm of the chair. "Wow, the girl's gone now. I reckon the father did them in. What do you think?"

"Tim! That's terrible. You have no idea what that poor family are going through. Don't be so quick to judge."

"Sorry, Mom. Let's go, K."

❧

MOST OF THE MORNING Shaun wandered around the semi-deserted city, staying away from places where people might recognize him, and he rode the trains all afternoon. *I'm just the local bully, son of the drunkard. Son of a diseased woman who died, leaving me to defend for myself against what my father had become, a drunken thief. But dad hasn't always been a drunk.* His dad had loved her so much, his spirit had died with her.

Shaun enjoyed being on trains because he didn't have to keep up an image and he mostly pretended to be asleep. Sometimes he could even believe his mother was sitting next to him. They used to travel into the city by train to see a movie before the cancer took over their lives. They would have lunch and buy a toy in the magic shop, or a book from the bookstore. He remembered walking into the grand old theatre, the walls lined with statues, his mother bought ice-cream, chocolate or popcorn, he stared at the statues wishing for them to move. They were the good times before she died. Shouts from the front of the carriage woke Shaun from his daydream. The passengers who had boarded the train at the last stop looked more than just tired. The train had only just pulled out of the station when they started arguing over who was going to get the window seat, and if the window should be open or closed. Then abruptly an old dude from across the aisle had stood up and slammed the window shut, pulverizing the guy's fingers. Shaun wasn't going to inhale the same air as those sorry-looking infected assholes any longer and jumped off at the next stop. Walking home, he picked up some groceries along the way.

He waited at the threshold of his home and listened; the house was empty. Satisfied, he hummed as he went into the kitchen and put away the bread, milk and Vegemite. He always felt better after riding the trains, but he decided he would give it a miss for a while, because more people were getting sick. *And what was with the old dude's black pupils.* He had seen shows on the TV where morons tattooed their eyeballs, but this was different somehow.

～

From his bedroom Shaun heard the front door close. His father stumbled through the house into the kitchen knocking a glass off the bench. *Drunk again,* Shaun thought, as he changed the sheets on his bed. His stomach grumbled; he was starving, but he would wait for his dad to fall asleep. Shaun opened up his sock drawer and put the leather pouch way at the back, ignoring his tummy. *Fuck him, why should I hide,* he thought, making his way to the kitchen. He quickly cooked six pieces of toast and spread butter and Vegemite on three, and peanut butter and jam on the rest. He wrapped them up in paper towels, grabbed a bottle of coke and closed the fridge door with his foot before heading up onto the roof.

He heard the toilet flushing and leant over the edge of the roof. The back door opened and his dad, half-dressed, puffing on a cigarette, dropped a bag of rubbish into the bin. Shaun worked up a mouthful of saliva and let it hang from his mouth into a strung-out spit, and sucked it back up. He did it again, letting it grow a little longer, a little thinner and a little lower before sucking it back up. He did it again til it was too thin, too long and gravity took hold: it was heading for his dad's back. His dad stepped forward and flicked his butt into the garden and the saliva splatted onto the pavement behind him. His dad looked up. Shaun had no time to move back, so he kept still, not wanting his dad to think he was frightened. *I can take a good beating,* he thought.

"You filthy bugger — you lazy good-for-nothing. Why don't you piss off?"

"Why don't you take a look at yourself, old man? I never understood what Mom saw in you. You're a clusterfuck. Weren't you supposed to be some big-shot professor? You're a pathetic fraud. You let her die."

"You ungrateful prick. I should have left you to die with your little girlfriend." He picked up the shiny lid of the garbage can and threw it up into Shaun's face. Shaun ducked and just missed being scalped, but the lid skimmed his cheek and sliced it open. Shaun dropped to his knees, holding his cheek, holding in the urge to scream with pain, because he wasn't going to give his old man the satisfaction. "Fuck, you're a dick!"

"Not so tough now are you, kiddo?" his father said, slamming the back door closed. The street was empty of all other sounds.

Shaun looked down at his hand, covered with blood. "Ah, shit." He pressed it against his face, walked to the edge of the roof and climbed over the eaves and down the drainpipe.

Kevin and Tim walked as fast as they could down the quiet street. "What are you going to tell your dad about your bike, K?"

"I'll just say I couldn't carry all this stuff. That's not going to be a problem, but something is ... I can feel my dad ... something's not right, he's worried."

"Hey, look." Tim pointed towards the row of houses.

"What?"

"On the roof over there. Some guy is on the roof."

The fading light of the sun shone on a miniature flying saucer that shot up into the sky from the back of the house, smacking hard into the dude's head. He had his back to Kevin and Tim so all they could see was a silhouette drop to his knees, going down like a bag of potatoes. They ran across the road, watching him standing at the edge of the roof, trying to steady himself before sliding dangerously down the side of the house.

"Hey man, are you okay?" Kevin called.

The guy turned around at the sound of Kevin's voice.

Kevin continued to walk across the street and Tim grabbed his arm. "Wait, K, that's the guy that kicked the shit out of me. Stuff him, let's get out of here."

"Chill, man, we can't — he's seen us, act cool."

"You okay?" Kevin walking across the lawn. He could see the blood dripping between the boy's fingers and face. Shaun pretended he didn't recognize the other two boys. However, he couldn't stop eyeballing Tim's leg. Then Shaun staggered, trying to focus on his mobile phone; he was having trouble swiping it unlocked. The sound of a car coming around the corner and stopping at the curb seemed familiar to Kevin. He turned to see it was his dad. Kevin turned back to Shaun. "You'd better go inside and get some help. Are your parents home?" Shaun grabbed Kevin's wrist with a vice-like grip and said, "No one's home, so just piss off." Then his legs buckled as he blacked out and collapsed.

"Wow." Tim looked down at Shaun's face. "His eye and cheek are already swelling. Look at that, he looks like he just went a round with Mike Tyson."

A car door slammed. "Kevin!"

"Dad." Kevin ran over to him. "Get your first-aid kit."

"What?"

"Your first-aid kit."

Daniel reached into the back of the Dodge and pulled out the green bag with a white cross on it from under the seat. "What happened?"

"He was on the roof and was hit by a piece of flying metal. His cheek's cut and it's bleeding pretty badly. He just dropped."

Daniel knelt beside Shaun and went to work checking his vitals and looking for serious injuries.

Tim tilted his head towards Kevin, half whispering, "Irony or what!"

"Kevin, sit behind Shaun's head," Daniel said. "Hold the dressing against his cheek like this. Tim, call an ambulance." Daniel handed his mobile over.

Kevin watched his dad go to work. As soon as Tim was through to the emergency operator he put the phone on speaker and Daniel took over. *Shaun didn't look so tough lying unconscious,* Kevin thought.

It took a while for the ambulance to arrive and when it did it coasted silently down the street, afraid of the infected. The ambulance staff feared being hijacked for their drugs and equipment. *Shaun was probably lucky they showed up at all.*

There was a low-pitched buzzing high above that was getting closer. Nobody else seemed to notice. Kevin felt like he wanted to run, but he dared not move. He sensed long dirty fingernails plucking at his soul. He wanted to run screaming like a lunatic from the property. The urge was becoming so great he had trouble keeping still — his whole body itched. Out of the corner of his eye he believed he saw a curtain move inside Shaun's house. Kevin kept looking straight ahead, acting as if he was watching the ambos crossing the lawn. The muscles in his eyes strained to see in his peripheral vision. Someone and something was watching them. A shadow, a dark mass inches from the ground, moving like a school of fish, curved and shifted around the side of the house, slithering out of sight. Kevin felt dryness in his throat. A heaviness he hadn't detected until now came from the house. He concentrated on holding Shaun's head, waiting for the ambo guy to take over, and soon as he did Kevin stepped back. His skin still prickled and his stomach churned. He could feel the haunting pulse of the house. He pulled his thoughts away. He was scared and wanted to run. In the back of his mind he saw a lemon tree, it grew and grew until he felt he was part of the tree and suddenly he could smell lemongrass and sage. He took in a deep breath and tried to calm down and focus on helping Shaun.

"Tim!" Kevin whispered. He tilted his head towards the house. "Someone's watching." Daniel was giving the paramedics a summary of Shaun's injury and Kevin listened to his dad speaking, sounding muffled as if he was deep underwater. The ambos crouched beside Shaun and carried out the same procedures as his dad had previously done. Kevin watched, but heard nothing. They slid Shaun onto an orange plastic board and hoisted him up onto the gurney.

"Kevin," Daniel said. "Kevin!" He put his hand on his son's shoulder and squeezed.

"Yeah ... what?"

"You okay? Why are you shouting?"

"Sorry. I'm good."

Daniel bent his face down and looked closely into Kevin's. "You up to riding in the back with your friend? If he wakes up, he will at least see a friendly face?"

"What ... yeah sure; if I have to."

Tim chuckled.

"What are you giggling about? I don't think there is anything here to be laughed at," Daniel said. "Chuck your stuff in the back with the bike and get in the car."

Surprised, Tim said, "You got Kevin's bike?"

Daniel opened the car door. "I saw it last night. I drove by this morning and it was still here so I picked it up. Is that why you three were fighting? Did Kevin come over to pick up the bike? Did you guys hit that kid?"

"You think Kevin smashed him — no way. Kevin wouldn't hurt a fly, in any case."

"I didn't think so, but had to ask."

Just before Kevin climbed into the back of the ambulance Tim ran around the front of the Dodge and purposely bumped into him and whispered in his ear: "Friendly face, ha, ha. Better you than me, K. If I see the ambulance swerving all over the road I'll know the feral cat woke and saw your friendly face, ha ha ha."

THE EMERGENCY WAITING room was packed. People were coming in and hardly anyone was going out. A mother came in carrying her young boy; his arm looked like an S-curve. He was white as a ghost and looked like he was about to upchuck. Many people were coughing, rubbing their heads, or trying to blow their noses. A pregnant teenager was crying, heaving into a plastic bag, while her caring mother held back her hair. The little boy with the broken arm was taken through the door marked Triage. A man stood up aggressively and pushed his way over to the reception's plastic anti-jump barrier and banged his fist. "Hey, what's the deal? We've been waiting for two hours and that kid gets in."

"Please sit down, sir."

Agitated, the man rubbing his head yelled at the small woman behind the barrier. "He had a broken arm!"

Both hands went up to his head as if it would burst. "I can't think straight any more. I just want to see a doctor."

"Sir, calm down and go look after your wife."

The security door to the treating area opened. Kevin could see his dad shaking the doctor's hand and together they entered the waiting area talking. He could hear his dad saying, "Okay, thanks for your help. We'll pop in tomorrow and see how he's doing. Let's go, boys," Daniel said, putting a hand on Kevin's shoulder.

The doctor walked to the vending machine and watched his coffee being dispensed.

"I've asked you nicely, sir," the lady behind the barrier said. "Now I'm going to get security."

Kevin left the emergency area through the sliding doors when, abruptly, he stopped, becoming increasingly aware of the angry man walking back to his wife. "Shit," Kevin said running back inside and nearly tripping over Tim. "*Move!*"

"K, where you going?" Tim said.

Kevin's sneakers squeaked loudly in his mind as he ran along the blue spongy linoleum floor and thought, *Why do they call them sneakers?* Security guys lazily entered the waiting room from the same door his dad had used. They were chatting casually, tucking in their shirts and hiking up their utility belts, totally blind to what was about to happen. *Shit,* Kevin thought. Everything seemed to be in slow motion again. The colors around the angry man who had been yelling at the receptionist changed to a black, oily swirl as he strode over towards his wife, who was weak with fever, her beautifully colored hijab soaked. "Stop," Kevin shouted. But it was too late. The man's face was clammy, his hair greasy. Kevin reached for him and smelt stale perspiration as he grabbed the back of the man's shirt. His wife tried to pull away as her husband snatched her arm off her chest, snapping her wrist. The woman shrieked in pain.

The man yelled back at the receptionist, "Now can we get some attention around here?"

The doctor abandoned his coffee and rushed to the woman. The security guards pushed Kevin to the floor before tackling the man to the ground. Most people sat by as if this was normal; people didn't seem to care any more. Kevin felt his dad reach down and help him up.

Daniel dusted his son off. "You okay? How did you know? What were you thinking? Let's get you out of here. Let security do their job."

Kevin doubled over and held his stomach. "I feel sick. I can still feel her pain." He ran outside and threw up on the pavement.

Daniel rubbed Kevin's back until he stopped throwing up. "I'm sorry, Kevin," Daniel said. "I don't know why this happens to you."

Kevin wiped his mouth with the ends of his shirt. "I'm okay."

Trying to lighten the mood, Tim yelled like a circus ringmaster with his arms up in the air. "Ladies and gentlemen, the quantum psycho virus has come to town!"

"I don't doubt that, Tim, but you don't have to yell it out," Daniel said. "I have been dealing with this sort of shit all week. So many guys at work have called in sick and we are running skeleton crews just like the cops. I thought being on the other side of the world had its benefits. It's been a few years since it started and I thought, given the time and distance, it might have died out, and we would have escaped it altogether, or with little casualties. Like the old bird flu."

"Anything's possible, just got to have certainty, Dad." Kevin looked away embarrassed, not knowing where the thought came from, or why he said it. It didn't feel like his. "Whatever," Kevin said, trying to cover up his confusion.

"That's what your nanna used to say. Kevin, don't ever be ashamed of your abilities, be proud. You're a good person. Tomorrow we will come back to see your mate. I don't want you guys coming into the city on your bikes. Or using the train by yourselves." They all got in the truck and he turned on the ignition. "The city is a crazy place at the moment. You don't know who is going to turn."

At the mention of his bike, Kevin felt a knot in his stomach. He was going to have to tell his dad he lost it. "My bike ..." Kevin mouthed to Tim.

"It's in the back," Tim mouthed back and thumbed over his shoulder towards the tail of the truck.

"What?" Kevin lifted his hands and shrugged his shoulders, shaking his head to imply he didn't understand.

"What are you guys going on about?" Daniel said.

"I was just telling Kevin, you have his bike in the back."

"Ah, yes. I saw it lying at the front of Shaun's and picked it up. I didn't know you knew Shaun. Hope I didn't cause you any problems. I know he is a little older than you both, but I think that boy has had a hard life. It's nice you guys have made him your friend. Just don't let him influence you to do — well, I think you know what I mean. Stay out of trouble."

TIM HELPED KEVIN grab the tent out of the truck, while Mr D lifted Kevin's bike out and propped it against the garage wall. As they walked through the garage door and into the house, Kevin called out, "Alex! You home, buddy?"

"We're up here. He's in the bath," Mrs D replied.

They dropped their stuff at the front door and climbed the stairs.

"Hi, Mom, sorry I'm late."

"Hi, Tim," Callie said ignoring Kevin. "Did you have fun last night?" Callie continued rinsing soap out of Molly's hair."

"Oh yes, thank you. Did you hear that your US professor's daughter is now missing, too?" Tim said.

Kevin held his breath as her facial muscles tensed.

"We saw it earlier at my place, on TV," Tim said.

"We're just going to pitch the tent. It won't take long and Alex can come down after he has finished his bath," Kevin said.

"Go get some dinner. I wanted you home before it was dark." She turned and looked at him. "Is that blood on your shirt?" she said lifting Molly out of the bath.

Kevin looked at his shirt.

Tim could feel the tension building; Kevin became a mess,

instantly looking guilty and ashamed. He felt sorry for him and jumped in to rescue his friend. "That's right, it's blood," Tim said. "A kid got his cheek sliced open. Then Mr D arrived and took him to the hospital. K —"

"Tim, it's Kevin, not K."

"Sorry." Kevin was holding a cloth to his face. Tim was dying inside. He wanted to rush his sentences, was starting to feel like he was lying and that he was to blame for all the shit in the world. How did she do it? Just then Kevin's dad walked in and saved them.

"The boys were genuine heroes this evening," Daniel said, lifting Alex out of the bath and wrapping him in a towel. "Kevin tried to step in and stop a man from breaking his wife's arm. He obviously foresaw it because he started charging at the man before it even happened. Well done, K."

Tim's eyes darted to Kevin's mom, to see if she would react to Kevin's dad calling him K — *go, Mr D* — but she was distracted.

"What do you mean, *foresaw*?"

You could cut the air with a knife, Tim thought, and now Mr D is going to take the tongue-lashing she had been saving for Kevin. "Let's go," Tim whispered to Kevin.

"It's too late for Alex, Kevin," his mom said. "It's nearly his bedtime."

Alex started to whine. "Oh pleeeeeeease, Mommy, pleeeeeease."

Molly copied Alex. *"Peasss, peasss."*

"Off you go, Alex," Daniel said, overruling Callie. "Get your pajamas on, and your robe and slippers."

"But it's not cold, Daddy," Alex said.

"No robe and slippers, no tent. I'll come and get you in half an hour," Daniel said.

The boys turned on their heels and made tracks outside, Alex in tow. They pitched the tent close to the house. They had so much to talk about, so the wait for Kevin's dad to fetch Alex for bed seemed like hours. They sat in the middle of the tent devouring chunks of rocky road and patiently telling Alex fart jokes.

~

"'NIGHT, BOYS, DON'T stay up all night gasbagging. You hear anything strange you get inside. You shouldn't be out here. We'll go early to the hospital, before my shift starts."

"'Night, Dad."

"'Night, Mr D."

Kevin strained his ears, listening to his father's footsteps crunching across the dry back lawn, waiting to hear him step onto the patio and into the house.

"What —"

"Shh." Kevin put up his hand to stop Tim saying another word. As soon as the outside light was turned off he said, "Now we can talk."

"What a crazy day, man. I'm never going to get to sleep. My leg was crushed! We magically survived a firestorm, ignited by that dick lying in the hospital. Now we have to go and see him tomorrow."

"Did you see him looking at your leg? He knew who we were."

"What happened yesterday, K? Where did we go? We have to go back. We have to go back and find that place. Everything was electrifying. The fluorescent colors — awesome, dude. And my leg, my leg, it just, it just healed and the sunburn vanished. What gives? And don't forget my shoulder dislocated. Man, all that shit hurt. What was that, a vortex?" Tim was nearly out of his sleeping bag, nearly on top of Kevin, and with each question, he spoke a little faster, a little more excitedly. "Everything was connected, even us. You heard my thoughts."

"I know, right. How bizarre was that, totally unbelievable!" Kevin drifted into his own thoughts and spoke contemplatively, Tim hanging on his every word. "I don't know what happened," Kevin said. "I believe it was very real, as real as it was when I saw the boy drown. The wall — it just appeared. The smell of smoke was the first thing I noticed. I then saw you, and the rest is just a blur. We needed to escape the fire — I needed to get you out of there. I couldn't see how. The fire was surrounding us. I kept looking. Then I saw what I first thought was an illusion; I was concussed from the king- hit. I got up and touched the wall. The shimmering mirage sparkled like a lake in the midday summer sun. I pushed my hand into it, and when I pulled it out, the sunburn was gone. I had no doubt, I was certain this was our way out. A door to another dimension had opened up to us and I didn't want to think about it logically, because there was no other choice."

The soft glow of the streetlight and a cluster of silhouettes swayed hypnotically across the dome of the tent. He watched Tim touch his leg and stretch it upward. He flexed his knee, making sure it still worked.

"Do you know anyone named Jade?" Kevin asked.

"Nah. Why?"

"I don't know," Kevin said, closing his eyes. "When we were leaving and we were in that, like, embryonic jelly state, before you pulled me out, I thought of the name, and I saw some other things, but I can't remember clearly."

Kevin and Tim talked and talked, throwing out one idea after another about where they could have been. Exhausted, Tim finally fell asleep mid-sentence, and Kevin crashed three ideas after. The night cooled as he slept on top of his sleeping bag and dreamed of the day's events.

10

INFECTED: CASEY. ENGLAND

Casey stretched, feeling refreshed and comfortable in the motel's feathered bed. *Now for a famous English breakfast,* he thought. He dressed and rushed downstairs to the buffet, soon sitting down to a mountain of eggs, sausages, mushrooms, potato cakes and a side plate of muffins. Terry and Amy drank their strong tea and watched him wolf it down. The motel was quiet and there were only two other couples at breakfast. Full of food, the trio headed into the lobby and waited for the solicitor.

Gary, the UK solicitor, acted like a tour guide, pointing out the sights as they drove through England into the north. Casey was glued to the window, mesmerized by the lush rolling hills and fields of yellow poppies as they headed to Amy's inherited estate. Snow might be falling in a few weeks and he shivered at the thought of the temperature pushing past zero and beyond. He loved the warmth of the sun.

The car pulled off the road onto a dirt driveway that was hidden by green hedges. Silver birch trees lined up on either side of the road and the fallen leaves were scattered by the movement of the car. He started to feel a cold sweat rush over him as they moved closer to the end of the driveway. The car stopped and Casey flung open the car door and vomited.

Amy came up beside him patting his back. Casey wiped his mouth and said, "One sausage too many."

"You're pale as a ghost!" Amy said.

He rested his hands on his hips, straightened up and drew in a deep breath. *I can do this*, he thought, *but I wish Sophia would hurry*. Running his fingers though his hair he said, "I'm okay. Check this place out, Amy. This isn't a cottage. This is a manor."

Ivy climbed the walls and arched across the entrance. The thatched roof looked old but well maintained. Casey shoved his hands deep inside his pockets, digging his nails into his leg.

"It has eighteen rooms in all," the solicitor said, "with a cellar, and a shed that was once a stable."

Terry held onto Amy's hand and said, "This is wonderful. I had no idea it would be so big, did you?"

"None, I can't believe it's ours," Amy said. "Can you smell the trees, and the grass? It smells so fresh and crisp."

"That's good old English air. My dad used to say it would put hairs on your chest. Shall we go inside?" said Gary, the solicitor.

They moved from room to room admiring the furniture and the decor. Casey walked behind Amy and Terry into the kitchen. "The smell's not as fresh in here, bit musty." *It feels like someone is here, like we're intruding,* Casey thought. The atmosphere was thick and the air stale; a shiver ran down his spine. "It's so cold, is there any heating?"

"There are six open fireplaces in the house: one downstairs in the living room, another in the library, one in the master bedroom and two in the double bedrooms," Gary announced. "Amy, your great-aunt only used a small part of the cottage. The story is that once the arthritis clamped around her fragile bones she settled into the down-stairs rooms. Nobody has lived upstairs for at least five years." He kept talking as he walked out of the house. The trio followed. "A cleaner used to come once a week and her son chopped the wood. The woodpile is big enough to keep you warm for two winters. Some-times you will be snowed in. There is a snowmobile out in the shed.

Do you have any questions?" Gary's shoes crunched on the gravel as he turned around to face the road. "Oh, and you can get general supplies at the wee town about twenty miles south, that way," he said, "and the ocean is that way."

"All of this is mine. You sure?"

"Yes, ma'am, everything in the buildings and every bit of the land from the beginning of the drive to the fences in the back paddock. From time to time you'll see some fine Shetland ponies grazing. They're not yours; they belong to the family two paddocks south, but with this virus, they have left them to roam just in case, well, you know ... Oh, one more thing: there's an old Jaguar, a Jeep SUV, and a Bonneville in the shed. The keys are in the library desk drawer. Now, if you have no more questions I'll take my leave. My family are heeding the Queen's advice and seeking safe harbor in the countryside, as are you. Until, well, I am sure you know as much as I. Good luck and God bless".

"What's a Bonneville?" Casey asked, glad to be outside. He watched as the man smiled and bounced on the spot.

"What's a Bonneville? Young man, you haven't lived till you've been on a Bonneville. It's a classic Triumph motorcycle. I'm sure you'll take a shine to it, if your dad can pull himself away from it, because I'm sure he will fall in love with it. Maybe he'll teach you how to ride it one day."

Terry, Amy and Casey looked at each other, but no one spoke.

"Right then, I'll be off." He opened the car door and climbed in, fastening his seat belt.

"When is the cleaner due?" Terry asked him through the window.

"I gave her a tinkle, no reply. There's no cell phone reception here by the way; you need to use the landline. Her number and address is on the library desk. He waved calling, "Cheerio, God bless," as he hurriedly drove the vehicle around the garden and headed down the drive, leaving the trio, gobsmacked, on the steps of their new home.

~

OVER THE PAST few weeks, settling in the house had been fun. It was a little cold but a place Casey felt he could call home. His room was awesome, huge with four double-sized in-built bunk beds, a writing desk and a window seat that looked out over the moors.

He saw Terry reverse the SUV out of the shed ready to head into town for supplies. Casey grabbed a light jacket before he ran downstairs to join him.

Standing out front of the manor, Casey looked over at the birch trees towards the quiet road while Amy was saying goodbye. She pecked them both on the cheek.

"We'll be back soon," Terry said.

Terry scooped up Amy, kissing her passionately. Casey felt a little awkward as he leant against the car and stared up into the gloomy sky. *Will they ever get over each other?* he wondered. It was kind of sick that they were still mad for each other.

"I know, just be careful," Amy said patting Terry on the arm. "Have you got the list? Get two months' worth and — don't ask me why two months." Amy raised her hand to block any protests. "I feel a crescendo; the human race can't go on like this forever. Something's got to give." With a sudden change in tone, like the cat that got the cream, and a smile in her eyes, she said, "Oh, one more thing." She pushed her hand into the pocket of her slacks and pulled out a second list. This one was a smaller piece of paper. "I nearly forgot. Can you also get me these things?" She handed the list to Terry.

Casey sensed she was up to something. He watched the colors change around her, from the electric blue covering her throat, to swirling yellows and oranges, and shifting to peaches and pink. Her aura became a blaze of pastels that flowed out to Terry. Casey walked around the front of the SUV to the passenger side smiling, giving them some space.

Terry looked down at the list and started reading out loud. "Night light, nappies and safari wall decal ..." He looked up at her, confused. "Casey doesn't need a night light, he's practically a man." Nearly inaudible, he said, "Incontinence?"

Casey shook his head, trying not to listen. He couldn't help thinking about this morning's media update; they had had a fleeting satellite connection and the broadcast was really an update of death. Few people found compassion and nursed their loved ones. Many people were abandoned to the crumbling city hospital systems. The infected, the possessed, roamed the streets, terrorizing everyone who didn't have the sense to stay indoors. Images of abandoned, feral children filled the screen. The reporter said parents who feared being murdered in the night would strap their infected children to beds. Once-infected people didn't seem to really recover; they were merely shells of their former selves, empty puppets waiting for the puppeteers of hell to claim them.

Terry had said, "Mass suicides are making Jonestown in the 70s look minuscule. Thousands are dying weekly. They believe God has abandoned them, or that God is calling them home and so are taking their own lives. No country has been left untouched. One infected man in particular claimed to be the soul of Christ and persuaded four thousand *uninfected* men, women and children to poison themselves together while online. And, of course, the media hounds latch onto these stories and broadcast their latest opinion poll: to suicide or not to suicide. The Children of the Stars cult believed suicide was necessary for their final transition and they needed to shed the human form to go back to their place among the stars; they believed their forefathers, the aliens, brought the plague to stimulate them to transcend this world."

"Suicide is never the answer. Love is," Amy had said.

Casey, Terry and Amy were shocked at the reporter's lack of empathy, the three of them had stood transfixed in front of the screen.

"God help them all," Terry had said.

Casey noticed his thoughts straying again, and snapped back to the present.

"How long have you had the problem?" Terry was asking Amy. She shook her head and put her finger to Terry's lips.

"Shh."

"Of course, it's a personal matter and I shouldn't bring it up in front of Casey. It might embarrass the lad."

"Terry! You're killing me!" Casey said.

Amy looked down at the ground. "I was thinking of making this place more homely." She looked up and expanded her arms and swept her surroundings. "I like the idea of staying here more and more. Everything is so green and alive. You can apply for a teaching job here if the schools reopen ... I shouldn't say if, but *when*. I think it might be a good place to raise a child."

Terry looked at Casey and back at Amy. "I'd hardly call him a child."

"Don't look at me," Casey said, leaning against the front fender. Casey knew what Amy was trying to say and couldn't believe someone as intelligent as Terry could be so thick. Casey chuckled to himself, shaking his head in disbelief.

Terry looked back at Amy, feeling like he was missing something. Then she took his hand and placed it on her tummy and the penny finally dropped. Wide-eyed and with a grin from ear to ear he said, "Are you sure?"

Amy tilted her head to the side, looked him in the eyes and smiled. "Yes! I'm sure. That second list is for the baby store."

Terry picked her up and spun her around and around then safely delivered her back onto solid ground. "How far?"

"Nearly three months," she said, holding on to steady herself. "You'd better head off and get the supplies. Last week the old women were nattering in the general store, saying the army was going from town to town taking food and killing infected."

Terry kissed Amy rapidly on the cheeks. He lost his footing, and slid on the grass, catching himself before falling. They were both giddy, laughing with joy.

"Congratulations, guys." Casey gave Amy a hug and Terry a manly pat on the back.

"Thank you," Amy said hugging Casey back. "You will make a wonderful big brother. You have a lot of pestering to look forward to."

"Funny, Amy, funny. Sometimes you guys are so lame. Come on, Terry," Casey said, dragging him towards the SUV.

Terry gave Amy one last hug and kiss. "I can't believe we're going to finally have a baby." Then he remembered the world had gone to hell and maybe a baby wasn't such a good idea at all.

It took fifteen minutes to get into town and park in front of the general store. There were three other cars in the lot, and two cats ducking into the dumpster for scraps, but not a person in sight. Casey pushed open the store door. The female store clerk behind the counter didn't register Casey or Terry's presence. Her long, starved face was cast down.

"What's she fixated on?" Casey stepped up to the counter to take a closer look. There was nothing to see but a pair of dirty brown shoes. The woman's aura was dirty brown too. Flickers of dust like micro-metal shavings swarmed around her head. Casey backed away and said softly, "She's infected."

"Let's get what we need and get out of here," Terry said, touching Casey on the elbow, guiding him away from her. Terry ripped the supply list in half and quickly they gathered the items and met back at the front of the store.

Terry was finished first and could see Casey coming up the central aisle. "I'll leave the money on the counter. Go straight out and load up the car."

Casey pushed his trolley out to the parking lot. He hauled the bag of rice and buckets of chocolate and vanilla protein powder into the rear of the SUV. He packed in the dried potato mix, dried eggs, flour and cans of tuna and vegetables. He made room for Terry's load and helped him pack it in. Casey closed the back hatch. "We have everything on the list. Except for the live chicken ... that might be difficult!"

The baby store was on the corner at the other end of the deserted street. Terry parked the car so it was front forward, ready to leave town. Terry admired the buildings, finding in them a special charm.

The old, stone heritage cottages were probably part of an earlier estate.

"One of these days," Terry said, looking left and right as if on a busy city street, "I am going to dig into the town's history. This would be a nice place to raise a child. Not too far from the sea, far enough away from the city, and close enough to the hills. Weather's getting extremely overcast and damp; I think a storm's coming."

"I think it might always look like this," Casey said.

Terry pushed the door open. The tiny wind-charm above the door jingled. With one hand on the door he paused, preventing Casey from entering. "Hello, you open, hello?" No one came to greet them. Warily he moved in and Casey followed. Together they walked among the shelves.

"Hey, look at this, Terry." A playful smile stretched across Casey's face, as he held up a strap-on pair of breasts. "Male breast feeding."

"Funny!" Terry said laughing. "Actually, not a bad idea, you could use them too. One size fits all, right."

Casey looked horrified and quickly put them back.

"Very chic for a small town," Terry said. "Where's the owner. Hello! Hello!" Terry was becoming uneasy. "Something's not right. Casey, stay with me." Terry moved towards the back of the store. The sign on the door said, Staff Only.

Casey could see what Terry was about to do and said, "Don't open it."

"I have to."

"Don't. Let's leave the money on the counter like before."

"I have to. Stay behind me." Terry pushed the door open and it banged against something on the floor. He stuck his head through the crack and peered into the darkness. The smell was the first thing to hit them. He held his breath and waited for his eyes to adjust. Exhaling, he pushed harder against the door. "A woman lying on the ground is preventing the door from opening." Terry angled his hip into the gap to squeeze through but hearing a deep growl fill the room, he stopped moving.

"Was that a wild dog?"

Terry withdrew his hip and stuck in his head only.

"What are you doing?"

"I count four sets of yellow eyes in the darkness. I think the woman is dead," Terry said looking back at Casey.

He quickly pulled the door closed and reached for the bookshelves. Terry heaved at the metal shelving, packed with the latest baby books, and began to drag it across the floor.

"Help me, quickly. Get on the other side and push."

Casey directed all his energy to the bookshelf. He felt an electric sensation between his eyes. He started imagining the bookshelf moving, then placed both hands flat against the shelf to give the impression of physically pushing it. Books fell to the floor and the shelf scraped across the painted concrete floor.

"I told you not to open it. Let's take what Amy needs and get out of here." They loaded the back seat with the baby essentials.

"Jump in," Terry said.

"Wait. One more thing." Casey ran to the back of the store and slid to a halt at the pile of books. He rummaged through the heap. The wild dogs were sniffing under the door, gnawing, scratching and banging against it; the shelf wobbled, more books and wooden toys fell, hitting him on the head. The shelf had become lighter, easier to move. Casey scattered the books across the floor until he found the one he was looking for, then sprinted to the exit, grabbing a stuffed bear on his way out. He climbed into the idling SUV and tossed the book and the bear on top of the supplies on the back seat.

Terry looked over his shoulder to see what Casey had thought to be so vital. "Twins! A book about twins? No, you've got to be kidding me? You're not serious ... really, you think?"

"Just in case. Amy will be fine. I'll help. I can clean the house and do the washing while you change the dirty diapers."

"Thanks, pal. Two ... seriously?"

~

As they drove home Casey stared vacantly out the car window. The sky was absent of life, no birds darting up from the hedges, the road deserted. The SUV turned into the driveway and Casey jumped out to open the gate, securing the latch once Terry was through and then jumped back in the car. They pulled up in front of the house. "Don't leave it here, drive straight into the shed," Casey said looking back over his shoulder at the main road.

Terry held onto the steering wheel and took a long look at Casey. "What is it, what aren't you saying?"

Casey shifted in his seat. "It ... it just doesn't feel right. We need to move it. Trust me."

Terry had come to love Casey like he was his own. "You okay? We will be okay. This virus will blow over, right? We're pretty isolated. The winter should bury it. It will be our first winter here." Terry didn't give Casey time to answer. "Forget I asked." He couldn't imagine the burden Casey carried. "That reminds me we have to find that leak in the basement. Something's got to be causing the rot up into the kitchen."

"I'm good. Just wish I could do more," Casey said.

"You are helping just fine. Don't put so much pressure on yourself." Terry turned off the ignition and jumped out.

Casey still had his seat belt on as Terry opened his door. "What are you doing?"

"It's about time I taught you how to drive. Don't you think?"

"For real!" He didn't need a second invitation. He unbuckled his seat belt and climbed over to the driver's side.

"Okay," Terry said, a little nervous. "The ignition is ..." The car roared into life. "Okay, so you know how to start the car. The brake is on your left and the accelerator is on your right. This lever is the transmission. Put the gear into D, for drive, release the handbrake and the car should start rolling forward. Slowly, push down on the accelerator."

The car bunny-hopped forward until Casey found the right pressure on the pedal. "Now turn the wheel to the right, towards the driveway. Go down to the gate and then I'll get you to stop and back it up to the house."

"This is awesome." Casey was sliding the stick into drive and pressing on the accelerator.

"You're doing good. You can speed up just a little. Feel that kick; that means it's going up a gear. If it was a manual, you would have had to change the gear using a clutch pedal."

The car crawled along the dirt road towards the gate. Casey felt like he was moving faster than he actually was. It felt good, he wanted to keep going, out onto the road, but he knew they had to get back to the house, now wasn't the time.

"Okay, foot off the accelerator and ease your foot onto the brake. Now shift the gear into R and look into this mirror," Terry said, pointing to the one in the middle of the front windscreen. Make sure nothing and nobody is behind you. Arm over the back of the seat, foot off brake, and slowly accelerate."

Again the car jerked and beeped like a truck as it moved backwards towards the tree line. Moments like these, Casey forgot everything troubling. *Terry will be a great dad*, he thought.

"Okay, foot off the accelerator, slowly brake, bring the car to a stop, pull on the handbrake and put the car in P. Leave it running, jump out and I'll park it in the shed." Terry maneuvered the SUV into the garage, put it in park and pulled on the handbrake. He reached to turn the ignition off, but it was already in the off position.

Casey stood just outside the shed and waited for Terry to pop the back open to get the stuff out. The car was idling in the garage. He was taking too long. Casey ran up to Terry's window. "What's up?"

"The ignition, it's already off. It's in the off position."

Casey's heart started to pound, he quickly touched the car and it stopped idling. "Must have been a delayed reaction," he said.

11

ILLUSIONS: KEVIN. AUSTRALIA

Callie dropped the coffee pod into the machine, opened the blinds and wiped away her tears. The smell of fresh coffee was relaxing. She could see the tent, drooping with moisture. She knew Kevin lay sleeping, safe.

"Morning," Daniel said.

Callie didn't respond. She didn't want Daniel to know she had been crying. She took a sip of coffee.

"Why won't you go back to the research lab?" he asked. "You're better than a mobile pathologist. Why won't you talk to me?" Daniel was getting tired of the bickering and secrets. "What are you running from?"

Callie kept staring out the window and into the yard, watching the stillness of the morning. "Stop. Just stop," she said. "You wouldn't understand. No more, Daniel. Don't bring it up again." Callie put her cup in the sink and, without so much as a glimpse in his direction, walked out into the backyard. The morning smelt of the recent fires and a haze smothered the city. People weren't bothering as much about getting to work. Everyone was either afraid of catching the virus or becoming a victim of someone who had. *If only she could synthesize the formula,* she thought.

Callie pulled the tent peg that kept the front peak taut and let it collapse onto the boys. They kept sleeping. She put it back into place and unzipped the mesh screen. *A two-man tent used to be a lot bigger,* she thought, gently nudging Kevin. "Time to wake up. You've got fifteen minutes before your dad heads off." Kevin stirred, grumbling, pulling the sleeping bag over his head.

Tim stretched, rubbing his eyes. "Good morning, Mrs D, isn't it great to be alive!"

With a look of bewilderment, Callie said, "Morning, Tim, it sure is. See you boys in the kitchen, in ten." Callie let the flap drop and walked back towards the house. *That boy is always happy;* she thought shaking her head and smirking. *Whatever he's on I want some.*

Upstairs in his bedroom, Kevin finished changing his clothes. He slipped into his Nikes while Tim rumbled with Alex on the floor.

"I wish you were my brother, Tim. You always play with me when you come over."

"Yeah, but that's because I have a sister and she never likes to rumble with me."

"Who does she like to rumble with?" Alex asked.

"She likes to rumble with her —"

Kevin kicked Tim in the leg before he could finish. "Good to go?" Kevin asked.

"Guys, downstairs, I'm going to be late for work," Daniel yelled from the foot of the stairs.

Alex held onto Tim's leg and slid across the polished floor as Tim walked down the hall to the stairs.

"Alex — get up!" Callie snapped as she walked across the hall into Molly's bedroom.

Alex jumped to his feet and slipped on his socks, he lost his balance, falling, tilting forward over the edge of the stairs when Kevin reached out and grabbed him from behind. "Alex! Be careful."

"Thanks, K. I'm glad you're my big brother."

"I wouldn't swap you for Tim's sister."

"Guys, come on!" Daniel yelled again.

Kevin yelled downstairs to his dad. "If it's too much trouble, Dad, we don't have to go. We can wait till he comes out of hospital?"

"Come on, guys, I don't think he is going to get many visitors, do you?"

"Um — no, I suppose not." Kevin looked at Tim and shrugged.

They walked down the stairs as if going to a funeral and slowly climbed into the Dodge. Daniel took off as soon as they were buckled up.

"Where is everyone?" Tim said. "Was there an evacuation nobody told us about last night or what."

Brown smog nuzzled against the grey sky making it seem as if it was late in the afternoon. The morning traffic was practically non-existent. The peak hour traffic had reduced by ninety per cent and all the cars seemed to have congregated in the hospital parking lot.

"Why are all these people sleeping in their cars, Dad?"

"I don't know, Kevin. Let me find a place to park around the back at the service entrance and we can find another way in."

Kevin was feeling agitated and itchy. They walked along the service road past a stinking garbage truck. "Do you think it's going to rain?"

Daniel looked up into the sky. "I don't know. It's dark but that doesn't look like a rain cloud. It looks more like a metallic dust storm; it reminds me of iron shavings."

"You mean the ones that we used in science to show the magnetic pulling and repelling forces?" Kevin said.

"Yeah, yeah, I do, I did that when I was at school too. It's good to know some things don't change."

"So that's where Kevin gets his nerdiness from," Tim said. "Like father, like son. I thought it was his mom. Not that you're not smart, Mr. D — it's just that she developed medicine, experimented on blood and stuff. Um, I think I should stop talking now."

"Good idea. She's a geneticist, Tim," Daniel said.

The hospital lawns generally would be littered with med students enjoying a coffee and fresh air before heading back in to finish, or start, a twelve-hour shift. Makeshift tents to treat the infected were lined up across the lawn with military precision. The trio entered the hospital from a side entrance and took the fire stairs up to the ward. "Why does Shaun get a bed when there are so many sick people outside, Mr D? It doesn't seem right."

"They're all infected, quarantined."

"Kevin, you're being quiet."

"I'm okay, Dad."

SHAUN LAY WITH his back to the door, staring out the hospital double-glazed window. He heard the door open and didn't move, didn't care who it was or why; probably a social worker. He just wanted everyone to get off his case. The last time he was in the hospital was to say goodbye to his mom, but he hadn't been able to do it. She had looked so scary, he was frightened. He didn't want to say goodbye, he wanted her to come home. Now he lay in the same hospital. The nurses had probably called his dad and his dad probably ignored the call; no surprise there. The nurse said he could go home once an adult signed for his discharge otherwise he would have to go with child services. Shaun could see the intruder's reflection in the window. She was a stout woman with a no-nonsense attitude, sitting with a clipboard on her knee and asking him questions. He refused to turn or answer.

"The police have been past your home and your father seems to be out. You're under eighteen and we can't let you go home alone."

"Get out, leave me alone!" Shaun picked up the plastic cup of water and threw it at the woman. She ducked as if she had done this a million times.

"Being rude and yelling will get you nowhere. If you haven't noticed, there are a lot of sick people and no one is going to pay any particular attention to you. So let's stop wasting each other's time and get this over with."

~

Kevin watched his dad poke his head around the door on the first floor and then quickly close it. Kevin caught a glimpse and it looked like Central Station. His dad did the same thing on every floor until they reached the fifth. Daniel opened the door, poked his head around then yanked it open wide. The floor was empty. They walked towards a nurses' station.

"What's your friend's last name," Daniel asked, scanning the patient board. "Is it Grady?"

"You know more than me. We hardly know the guy."

"Why would you lend your bike to someone you hardly know? There's his name." Daniel pointed at the nurses' whiteboard and read Shaun's room and bed number.

"Let's just get this visit over with. This place gives me the creeps," Tim said. "Are we in the psych ward? What's with all the yelling? Maybe I should go wait in the car?"

Daniel put one hand on Tim's shoulder and one hand on Kevin's and ushered them down the hall. Kevin realized they were heading in the right direction as soon as he recognized it was Shaun yelling obscenities.

"What the hell!" Daniel said, letting go of the boys' shoulders. He extended his stride, moving faster towards the commotion. He pushed open the door to Shaun's room. "What's going on in here?"

"You know this boy?"

"Well, no, but my boy does." The three boys stared at each other. Tim couldn't help feeling a sense of satisfaction seeing Shaun all banged up.

Shaun saw them as his ticket out of the place. "Hi, guys. Glad you could make it. I was hoping you would swing by."

Kevin glanced at Tim, wondering what Shaun was up to.

"Sorry, I missed your name," Daniel said to the social worker.

"I didn't say. This boy needs an adult to sign for his release and we can't get hold of his parents. Not that I'm surprised. There is a multitude of homeless children right across the city. I don't know why I get up and go to work each day. Nobody else seems to bother."

Daniel was taken back by this woman's lack of compassion. He moved closer and spoke with a soft tone. "His mother died, and I think his father is having a rough time with it," he said.

Kevin didn't know much about Shaun and he was surprised that his dad did.

"A lot of people are dying if you haven't noticed," the woman said in a matter-of-fact way.

Daniel stepped closer to Shaun and examined the stitches in his cheek as he spoke to the social worker. "I saw his dad only yesterday. We had a bit of a catch-up on his porch."

Why would he be talking to Shaun's dad? Kevin thought.

"Well, sir, maybe you can help out on this one. I have an extensive list of displaced kids. It seems that a side effect of the virus is to abandon your children. I thank God I don't have any."

"I don't need nobody's help," Shaun said. "I'll take the train."

"Don't be stupid, boy. You have a broken cheekbone, eight stitches in your face and you can barely see out of that swollen eye. Ludicrous!"

"My dad must have worked last night. He's probably asleep. He sometimes turns off his phone. No need to get twisted about it." Shaun swung his feet over the edge of the bed.

Daniel realized Shaun was trying to make excuses for his dad, who was no doubt home passed out drunk. "That's fine, give me your pen."

"What? What's fine, Dad?" It registered to Kevin what his dad was doing. "No. He can call his own dad. His dad will come sooner or later."

"No, Kevin, it's okay. We'll drop him off," Daniel said and took the social worker's plastic clipboard and signed the documents.

She put the documents and clipboard into a folder, snapped it closed and marched out of the room.

Shaun was out of bed. Groggy, he grabbed his bloody shirt and jeans out of the pink hospital bag. He dropped the gown to the floor and pulled on his smelly clothes. He hadn't even finished buttoning up his jeans as he went for the door.

"Where do you think you're going?" Daniel said.

"Home."

"I said I'll take you and I will. Kevin, help your friend get his stuff together. I'll call work and let them know I'll be late."

"Okay." Kevin looked around the room to see what could be Shaun's stuff. He watched him shove a wallet and phone in his back pocket; a leather pouch went into his front pocket along with a set of keys. He had no shoes, and there wasn't anything else in the room.

THE THREE BOYS AND Daniel walked back to the car, avoiding the chaos at the front entrance.

"How did it happen?" Daniel asked Shaun.

Shaun stared straight ahead out the windshield. "I dunno, I don't remember."

"Kevin and Tim said you were on the roof. Were you?"

"Dunno."

"They said you were struck by a piece of metal."

"They talk too much. What are you, a cop? No, that's right, you're a firey."

"Were you watching me the other day from the roof? How do you know what I do for a crust?"

Shaun didn't answer. He sat in the front of the Dodge next to Daniel, pretending to be asleep. "This is your place, right," Daniel said, turning off the engine.

"Yeah. I'm all right, I don't need an escort." He jumped out of the car and ran to the front door before Daniel could take off his seat belt. He fished his key out of his pocket and let himself in. He leant inside the door, suggesting he was talking to someone — popped back out and gave an all-okay wave. He flipped the bird and quickly shut the door.

Shaun walked around the house, seeing if the coast was clear. He was alone. He went to his bedroom and emptied his pockets onto his bed, then went into the bathroom, closing the door behind him.

He tried to avoid looking in the mirror. He was feeling frustrated and wanted to punch himself in the face for being so weak, and instantly struck out at his reflection, smashing the glass. He looked at his father's razor, transfixed. Shaun turned on the shower, stepped in fully clothed and sat on the floor. He buried his head in his knees and cried. The salt of his tears stung. The bite of the cold water pelting hard against his head and cheeks hurt. He imagined he was in a nuclear decontamination shower. He peeled off his jeans, stamped out of his underwear and yanked his wet shirt over his head. His skin quickly turned red from the battering of the cold water. He lost track of time as he continued to inflict pain upon himself. Eventually, his body went numb. He reached up to the soap holder, and pulled himself up. The cracked vanity mirror distorted his image and he refused to look at himself as he left the bathroom sopping wet, grabbing a clean towel from the hall cupboard. Shaun wrapped the towel around his hips and shook his head like a dog, splashing water onto the walls. Emotionally exhausted, he went into his room and locked the door before collapsing on his bed.

Daniel leant out the car window. "I'll see you boys tonight. Stay out of trouble. I'd prefer it if you steered clear of the Grady's for a bit."

"Gladly," Kevin and Tim said in unison and waved Daniel goodbye. As usual, old man Pat was pretending to concentrate on watering his wife's flowers, but Kevin saw that his eyes kept drifting down the road, staring at the same parked black car. He waved to the old guy, who didn't wave back. Kevin's Apollo was still propped up against the garage. "Hop on. We can get your stuff later," Kevin said climbing on his bike.

"Why don't we take your dad's dirt motorbike?"

"Old man Pat's watching and it's not a dirt bike. It's a BMW GS."

"That means squat to me."

"It's an on-road off-road motorbike. You have to have a license to ride it. Dirt bikes you don't. I don't think I could ride it anyway. I would need to use the gutter or a rock to get on and off. Knowing my luck, I'd drop it and not be able to lift it back up."

"You're the luckiest dude I know. You thinketh and so be it. Like your pushbike ... and what about the ice-cream van last summer? Whenever you were craving an ice- cream, it pulled into whatever street we were on, turning on its scary clown music."

"That was summer. The guy was driving down all the streets."

"Well, what about when you wanted to fly your grandpa's plane? Your mom had that research assistant summer-thingy in the US, and you were shipped off to the farm. He let you help with the crop dusting. You got to fly the plane, K."

Tim climbed on the seat and Kevin pedaled standing up, ignoring Tim's constant chatter. The bike wobbled with the extra weight as they entered the street. Kevin steadied the bike, just missing the side mirror of a parked car.

"Go to mine," Tim shouted. "I'll take Kath's old bike. She won't miss it. I'm starved and have to pee anyway."

For the whole time, riding to Tim's place, old man Pat was the only person Kevin saw. He steered the Apollo into Tim's driveway. Tim and Kevin jumped off the bike and raced into the house, using the bathroom and getting a quick feed.

Heading down to the river, the hot sun bored through the dense cluster of clouds. The anthill remained flattened; the stench of rotting kangaroos and wombats harbored a frenzy of flies. Kevin slowly cycled along the dirt road as if it was a cemetery. There was an eerie absence of sound: no crickets, no birds, and even the usual few lizards and slithering brown snakes were gone. Kevin coasted on one pedal, ready to dismount and drop his bike on the sandy embankment. The tide was out and Kevin felt a sense of foreboding. He stopped and took off his shoes, tying the laces together and flinging them over his shoulder. He pushed his bike downstream along the edge of the river.

"Where are you going?" asked Tim following Kevin.

"I'm looking for a good place to cross." The river narrowed and turned a corner. "Remember that time we walked down here and found those guys growing weed; we kept walking, pretending we didn't see them?"

"We were lucky they didn't shoot us. Shit, it's humid. It's not even summer yet."

Kevin stopped where the river offered a sandbank. He bent down to pick up his bike and hoisted it onto his shoulder.

"What are you doing now?" asked Tim.

"I'm taking the Apollo with me. I'm not leaving it behind this time."

Tim looked at his sister's bike, contemplating if it was worth the effort. He came to the conclusion that it was better to carry it than have her pissed at him. He followed Kevin and waded through the shallow water. They helped each other lift the bikes up the embankment and climbed up themselves. They sat amongst the ashes and pulled on their runners. They silently walked back up the river.

"There, the remains of the burnt-out car." Tim dropped Kath's bike on its side.

Kevin kicked down the Apollo's stand, and slowly moved around towards where the veil between the two worlds had been. He scanned for the shimmer of the wall. The passageway, or membrane — whatever it was —wasn't there.

"Where do you think it went, K?"

"I don't know. We didn't imagine it. Your leg is a reminder that it was real. Did you see how Grady looked at you? He thought he was hallucinating."

Tim rubbed his leg, remembering the pain, afraid it might come back.

"I was lying here," Kevin said. "I could hear the animals and feel the trees. I was scared, man. I could hear the roar of the fire, like rolling thunder. I opened my eyes and first saw you. Beyond you, there it was: rich, lush ferns, green and vibrant. Tree trunks hung with moss, some so tall I couldn't see where they ended. Then I felt the heat of the fire, looked back at you and started shitting myself bigtime."

Tim stretched out on the ground on his stomach.

"What are you doing?" Kevin said.

"I want to lie down and recreate what happened," Tim said.

"Don't be weird. Get up and let's go, there's nothing here." Kevin started to walk to his bike. *It happened right here! It really was here.*

Tim got up and dusted the ashes off his cargo pants. "Seriously, I think you're the one who created it."

"You've seen too many sci-fi flicks," Kevin scoffed.

Tim pulled Kevin's arm. "Shh. Get down."

They both crouched, listening. They heard voices moving towards them. There wasn't much left of anything to hide behind, so they kept still.

Kevin whispered. "Let's get up. We haven't done anything wrong."

"You're crazy. What if it's Grady and his thugs?"

"It sounds like a couple of men," Kevin whispered. "Come on, they're going to want to know why we're hiding." Kevin stood up, wrestling Tim to his feet. Kevin could see the badge of a fire investigation team on the side of each of their blue shirts. Regardless of the uniform, Kevin knew he had made a mistake. These guys were up to something; they didn't fit with the uniform.

"It's the investigation team," Tim said.

"Tim, something's not right. I've met all the guys at Dad's station. I don't know these guys." Kevin couldn't quite put his finger on it. They didn't have any equipment with them for a start. He saw the two men climb up the embankment and wave at the two boys. They looked European, perhaps Italian, Greek, or maybe Russian, he thought. One was older with short, cropped hair and was taller than the other, who was younger. They were both buffed to the max. Kevin's mind reeled with images from the old mafia movies his grandpa used to watch.

"Hi son, what's your name? What are you doing out here," the older taller man asked.

"Nothing much."

Tim, nodding as if he knew, said, "You must be interested in figuring out how the fire started?" He looked at Kevin who cleared his throat, and Tim got the message to keep his mouth shut.

"Yeah, smart kid." The old guy spoke with a strong accent. "Do you know how the fire started?" he asked, while the other man walked to stand by Kevin and Tim. "Is that your blue bike, son?"

"Who wants to know?" Kevin asked.

"Is that your bike?" the older man said to Tim.

Kevin just walked over to his bike and climbed on casually; Tim mirrored Kevin's movements.

"What's your name, son?" the younger guy asked. His biceps seemed to prevent him from being able to straighten his arms. He held them at an angle.

"Why? Who wants to know?" Kevin asked.

"You're a rude little prick, aren't you? Where do you live?" The old guy stepped forward.

"Down the road," Kevin said, rocking his front wheel back and forwards. Suddenly, coming up through the handlebars Kevin felt a low pulse, a soft hum and could smell sage and lemongrass. He had a metallic taste in his mouth and could hear a scrunching or a slow-tearing Velcro sound.

"Don't get smart, boy. I'll ask you again — what's your name?"

"Look, we didn't start no fires," said Tim.

Kevin frowned at Tim to keep quiet.

"I didn't ask you if you started them, and I don't care."

Kevin's sense of smell heightened and the aroma of dead animals turned his stomach. These men weren't here to investigate the fires, he realized.

"I think you know what we want. I think you both know," he said, looking from one to the other, and then began to undo his buckle. The older guy looked at his partner.

"*Vremaya dlya distsipliny. What you think?*"

"What does that mean?" Tim asked.

"It's Russian; it means it's time for a good whipping. It might jolt your memories."

"You can't do that?" Tim said.

Yes, they can, Kevin thought.

"What's your mother's name?" he said to Kevin.

That's when Kevin started to feel his body changing, becoming lighter. He could feel every atom in his body become alive and all fear evaporated. He felt a strong sense of urgency and was certain of his movements, confident, buzzing, alive. He was again feeling like a solar battery soaking up the sun, feeling its rays energize him, pulsating through his being and he thought, *the universe provides.* Rippling liquid waves appeared behind the older man, suspended in mid-air over the embankment, growing wider and stretching. Kevin's skin tingled. A window, instead of a wall, was opening, a tear in the atmosphere into the parallel world. Kevin felt the coolness of its vapors radiating towards him; his hair puffed out a little. "I know what you want," Kevin said. The older guy had removed his belt and wrapped it around his fist. "See over there, where the burnt-out car is?" He pointed behind Tim, leading them away from the window.

The oldest walked up and stuck his face in Kevin's. "What is it that you think we want?"

"You're looking for how the fire started — right?" Kevin said, playing dumb. "Go check it out, over here." Kevin pedaled over and behind the old car and said, "Come and see." Tim followed Kevin's lead and lapped the car.

The older man reached out for Kevin and missed. He walked over to the burnt-out car, saying, "Get off the bikes!"

Kevin snuck a sideways glance at Tim and nodded. Tim nodded in reply and they pushed down hard on the pedals and took off, riding straight off the edge of the embankment into the shimmering vapors and disappearing. Skidding to a stop and sliding the bike around to face the wall, Kevin saw the guy stumble on the edge of the embankment.

"What the hell!" The youngest and closest of the two men gave chase. He halted at the edge of the river, nearly falling in.

He looked surprised, as if expecting to see Kevin and Tim bogged in the water below.

The older guy came up behind him and called out. "Stupid move, boys. I was told you had your dead mother's brains."

Looking up and down and across the river, the fake fire investigators searched for Kevin and Tim.

"How come they can't see us, K?" Tim whispered.

"Shh! Why do you always ask me everything? I don't know!"

Tim raised his eyebrows and smiled. "Because you usually do know."

"What the hell are those metallic things flying around their heads? Look, it's trailing them like a veil of flies," Kevin said.

"I don't know, a commercial for hay fever. What did they say about your mom?"

"I don't know! Stop asking me all these questions, and how do they know my mom? I think maybe they've been following us. Did you notice the car parked down the road from old man Pat's?"

"The black hummer with the scratches along its side. Yeah, I've seen it at school too. I thought it was that new guy's dad's. The one who started a year ago just after your nanna and pops — well, yeah, I've seen it around."

Kevin watched the men, who were in arm's reach. He wanted to jump them. He was getting pissed off having to hide all the time. He stepped back into the vapor, it felt like silky satin. He calmed down. The feeling reminded him of the edging on Molly's blanket and the fresh new clean-baby smell. His body relaxed and he felt neurons firing in his head, the infinite sparks of life being shared by the embryonic window; nourishing effervescence of light raced through his body, sparks of colors ignited around him, flaring brightly. Tim pulled him back just before he stepped out and into the older guy. He was bigger than any bully at school.

He looks like a gym junkie, K, not a good idea. They probably spot each other when they aren't chasing kids, Tim thought to him.

Kevin was feeling fearless within his parallel world. Hearing Tim's thoughts again, they high-fived and smiled at each other. They kept watching to see if the men sensed their presence.

The shorter, younger man was wearing a bulky smartwatch and

he was sweating like a turkey on Christmas day. Kevin was focused on wanting to know how they knew his mom and why they thought she was dead. There was so much about her he didn't know. She was the hardest person to read. She had said to his dad that it was her "fault", because she had kept her family name. Maybe, just maybe they had killed nanna, thinking she was Mom. But why?

"They're not here," the old guy said. "Shit!" He jumped down the embankment into the river and walked across, following Kevin and Tim's tracks, heading downstream. A crow on the other side cawed and a kookaburra sitting on a burnt limb laughed raucously. The younger guy picked up a rock and threw it high. It missed the bird and ricocheted off the side of a tree just missing his own head. He turned around and threaded his belt through the loops of his pants. He looked back to where the boys went airborne.

"Where did they go? That has to be her kid. Best to call it in."

The short man picked up the squeaking radio to mutter a few words in another language and then hung it off his belt.

"Let's get out of here and get some extra hands."

"Yeah, piss off," Tim said. Gym junkie stopped and looked back across the river right at Tim. Tim froze, his eyes widening — his eyebrows raised and he held his breath. The man turned away. Kevin watched Tim's shoulders drop as he let out a sigh of relief.

"They can't see us, Tim. It's just a coincidence."

"There is no such thing as coincidence. My mom says it's just God remaining anonymous."

"No way. My nanna said that too!"

SHAUN BACKED AWAY from the track. He saw the gorillas chasing Kevin and Tim over the embankment and saw them and their bikes disappearing into thin air. The men were heading back in his direction. Shaun ducked behind a charcoal tree waiting for them to pass. He followed the goons to the entrance of the track where a black hummer was parked. They sat talking with the windows down. A hungry, stray German Shepherd, sniffing around for scraps, leapt up and rested its big front paws on the open window. The driver, the tall guy, pulled away from the drooling, panting dog. The other guy freaked out and quickly extended his arm that held a gun with a silencer, and fired. The dog dropped. The driver jumped out of the car, screaming.

"What the hell? It's all over me. You stupid idiot!" He walked around to the back of the car and popped the boot. He wiped himself down with a greasy rag.

"Sorry, boss. It had that look ..." He backed away from the bigger dude. "It had that rabies look, like the animals in the labs, the infected ones. Hey, man, it was seriously fucked-up shit."

"I should shoot you dead! But I can't be bothered cleaning up your sorry ass."

"Why do you reckon we haven't caught this bug? Shit, we've had enough exposure."

"Who said we're not infected?"

Shaun watched them get back in the car. Once the car took off he ran back to the river looking for Kevin and his sidekick, to see if they had returned from wherever they had gone. He walked across the river to where they had disappeared and waited. His head hurt badly and daylight was fading. He eventually passed out from the pain and dehydration and did not stir even as the moon sank and the sun rose.

12

ASTRAL TRAVEL: SOPHIA. SCOTLAND

Morning light streamed into the cabin, settling across Sophia's bed. She woke with the warmth and the brightness of the sun on her face. She opened her eyes and a bird hopped across the skylight and flew into the sky. Sophia rolled over in her sleeping bag. Father McDonald wasn't in bed. She unzipped her sleeping bag, padded across the room to her backpack. She emptied the contents onto her bed, separating the clean from the dirty clothes. Sophia dressed in her second new pair of jeans before she stuffed the dirty items back into the backpack and carried it downstairs for washing. She looked around the cabin. Father McDonald wasn't on the couch, in the kitchen, or the bathroom. She dropped the bag on the floor by the bathroom and stepped towards the open door and into a patch of streaming sunlight. Instantly, she felt the warmth under her feet rise up into her body. She stopped reaching for the door handle, closed her eyes and breathed in the light.

The door squeaked as she stepped outside. Mindful of the noise, she let it go softly and tiptoed across the porch. At the end of the porch on a wooden bench next to a box of kindling Father McDonald sat sleeping. Sophia picked up his fallen Bible, placed it neatly next to him and went back inside. She busied herself in the kitchen making breakfast: a can of corned beef and powdered eggs. The external and internal silence felt great. Nobody's voice in her head but her own; nobody's thoughts or fears coursed through her space. There was no one except her and Father McDonald. *Thank you, God, for the calmness, the lull in my mind,* she thought. Sophia looked beyond the window, into the blue sky, and said, "How you manage hearing the thoughts and prayers of every man, woman and child, I can never begin to imagine. But that's what makes you God. Give my family a big hug with your endless loving mercy. I'm sorry for not wanting to be *me*; it was just hard to find me, to separate from others. Thank you for giving us a place to rest." She stood on tiptoe reaching for the plates in the cupboard high above the sink.

The smell of the food wafted out the kitchen window, waking Father McDonald. "Breakfast," Sophia said, holding two plates. She watched as he pushed his glasses up the bridge of his nose, cleared his throat and slowly unfolded his stiffened joints to heave himself off the bench. He stood stretching, looking out into the distance. Sophia followed his gaze. Between the trees, she could see rolling hills, and suddenly had the impression they had to walk across those hills into England.

"It's a beautiful morning. God bless you."

Sophia sat on the bench placing the two plates beside her. Father McDonald cast his face to the sky. "God send your angels that govern this day to guide the souls of this earth, to seek within their hearts the door to your eternal light. Give them the strength to battle against the virus and fight for their spirit. Many souls in the past few years have been lost to your enemy. I pray you help keep Sophia safe so she may fulfil her purpose. Help us to walk the path of light. Thank you for restoring our soul with the creation of this glorious day. Amen."

"Amen."

Sophia saw the white deer walk into the clearing with the sun shining brightly behind it. "Good morning to you, too," she said and Father McDonald saluted the deer with his Bible in hand.

～

THE WATER LAPPED around her bare feet. She waited for the tug on her line, for the fish to bite. Fresh water from the mountains flowed down into the river, creating the sound of gentle splashing over rocks. It was blissful. Occasionally an eagle cried above, music to Sophia's ears. From time to time she jerked the fishing line. The hook sported a piece of stale bread. She laughed, as the tiny fish seemed to prefer nibbling on her toes. Two weeks had passed and every day was bright and sunny. Grey clouds circled at night and lightning lit the distant horizon, but every day was beautiful.

Sophia tied her reel to a rock and pressed it into the ground so she didn't need to hold it. She saw the white deer drinking at the water's edge across the lake. She watched until it went back into the woods. Sophia sat next to the rock and reel and daydreamed of living a hot summer's day in a small town in an average house on a street full of kids.

The town generator blew. There were no fans or air conditioning. Screen doors slammed as children rushed onto the streets heading for the lake. She imagined jumping on a pushbike of her very own and riding where the sun would be so hot the tyres nearly stick to the tar and sweat would be dripping from her armpits. A place where there was a lake, with people of all ages camping on top of rocks that overhung the fresh crystal-clear water, shaded by willow trees.

"Pull up ya shorts, Dave," one of the women would yell.

She imagined turning away, shocked at the unclad nannas with the wobbly arms. Sophia smiled to herself, thinking how her friend Gemma might be inclined to stand high up on the edge of the cliff where other kids were throwing themselves into the water, laughing and calling down to Sophia, encouraging her to climb up onto the overhanging rock to join in on the fun. Sophia could see herself huffing and puffing, her nostrils burning with each breath, as she reached her friend. Flies would buzz loudly around her head; she might frantically wave one away as it tried to settle onto the side of her mouth, swatting at it and accidentally slapping herself in the face. Gemma would be in stitches of laughter to Sophia's great delight.

"Jump, I dare you," Gemma would say.

"No, you go first."

Sophia started to feel her pale skin turning lobster red. Not caring how high up it was, yearning to be in the cool crystal-clear water below, she scanned the water for an empty patch, nearly impossible with most of the town out swimming. Finally, she finds a spot, bends her knees, throws her arms back and dives over the edge. For a moment, she would be free. Splashing into the silky ripples of the river, submerging into silence, Sophia would feel alive, refreshed, and cool, as if pulled just in time from the wicked witch's oven. She continued to daydream, imagining she was floating endlessly under the water, watching big and small fish darting around her legs. Her lungs would eventually push against her ribs, craving oxygen. She wished she could gulp water and extract oxygen just like the fish. Holding her nose, closing her eyes, and seeing her heartbeat getting slower, until giving in and pushing off the bottom of the lake, swimming up through the sun's rays and breaking the surface with her ears popping, her lungs drinking up the air, and nothing would have changed: the sky is still blue, the women would still sit chatting at the river's edge and kids laugh and jump off the rocks. Floating on her back, until she gazed upon a blanket of stars.

In the distance, Father McDonald was calling, pulling her back into reality, back to the cabin by the lake, back to sitting by the rock and fishing line.

"Sophia! Sophia, you alright? Dear God, let her be okay."

Hearing the panic in his voice, she yelled back, "Sorry, sorry. I was just daydreaming." She lifted her rock and gave the line a tug and smiled at the fading image. *One day,* she thought, *I will live on a street with other children in a regular house and have a normal teenage life.*

Sophia looked over her shoulder and saw Father McDonald walking down the embankment.

"What are you smiling about? I am so happy to see you smiling. It lights up your face so beautifully," he said, carefully lowering himself to sit beside her.

"Oh, nothing really. Daydream, that's all," she said and tugged on the line again. "The fish aren't biting today. Not the bread, although they nibble on my toes a lot. It tickles."

"We have some rabbit stew left over," Father McDonald said. "I know it's not your favorite but it's better than going hungry, right?" Her appetite had improved since she had been up in the mountains. She had color in her cheeks.

Sophia smiled at Father McDonald. "Rabbit stew will be good." She felt calm. She had been working on controlling her communication with Casey over the past week. The more inner peace she felt the more she was able to stay in her own body while connecting to the universe, as if she was holding the front door open but not stepping over the threshold. *The white deer would be pleased,* she thought.

Sophia liked the routine they had settled into. Together they would have breakfast; she would tidy while Father McDonald prayed. Afterwards, they would check the traps and fish. In the afternoon, they would both sit quietly on the porch. Father McDonald would pray while Sophia meditated and connected with the oneness of the universe, then Casey. Monday was laundry day. Friday night to Saturday night the world felt lighter. Sophia didn't understand why, it just did. It felt like God's eye was keeping a close watch and pushing the shadows of the dark creatures back. In a couple of weeks, if they could avoid getting the virus or killed by someone who had it, Sophia and Casey would finally meet. She was certain of it. He made her smile; he made her feel good about herself. Her heart skipped a beat when she felt him reach out for her.

God knows why she was so taken by his wild, bushy curls; the teeth of a comb would drop off in fear of being pulled through his mane. She had never known anyone like him before. He controlled his thoughts. Unlike the kids at school, his thoughts had an angelic afterglow of light.

She really hadn't paid much attention at school. Didn't really try too hard; she just wanted the annoying kids to stop shouting and the teachers to stop thinking bad ugly thoughts about them. They gave her a heavy heart and her head was bombarded with their complaining voices. Sophia had believed that she too was bad, because like attracts like, until she realized that she was just like a radio, a receiver, and needed to learn to change the channel or turn down the volume. The past few weeks, her reflections on the past showed her how she had been self-absorbed, always thinking about what she had wanted, and what she didn't have. She never tried to understand the pain of others; she just didn't want to feel pain. She didn't know how to help anyone. She hadn't been able to say anything because people already thought she was weird, living with the nuns. Luckily she had her two friends and they didn't believe she was strange. She had only taken up ballet to please Mother Catherine and now, Gemma, Lisa and Mother Catherine were all gone. How easy it would be to lie down and die; so much harder to truly live. She decided it was right to want to live and she would continue to learn to control the influx of other people's thoughts and help whoever God sent to her, instead of running. First, she must help change whatever has been done to create such evil entities on Earth and do it before there is nobody left and she never hears another's thought again. But she didn't know how to help.

Yesterday, meditating, she had seen pictures in her mind of people as colored silhouettes, their physical bodies surrounded by red, then expanding away from the body and changing to orange, yellow, green, blue, indigo and violet, then lastly, white, just like a rainbow. Golden light was at the center of their being and each golden spark was thousands of tiny atoms. Within the atoms was deeper light, sparks of positive and negative energy: at the heart was the neutron that balanced the two forces, the residence of the soul, and this was where the battle took place inside each infected soul. The positive energy was sparks of white light, and the negative energy was sparks of metallic grey laced with black. The black was multiplying, consuming the white light. In the vision in her mind, each silhouette had been surrounded by darkness, but still the core sparkled, reflecting all the differently colored particles of light. Every atom vibrated, busy with the light. A backdrop of darkness surrounded the body, but it couldn't penetrate the protective rainbow shell. Slowly, a dark spot would grow and an atom was swallowed by the negative force, metastasizing like a cancer spreading throughout the cells, spreading throughout the body, destroying the light. The colors melted away, the shell became jagged until the body was unrecognizable, no distinction of form, just one with the darkness that had surrounded him.

Sophia had wanted to break away from the meditation, to wake up and stare into the blue sky, but then more bodies and more souls appeared, flickering like candles being snuffed out one by one. Sophia had pulled back from the visions, felt the ground beneath her and opened her eyes, leaving the images to disappear into the back of her mind. She remembered the feeling of the tiny fish nibbling at her toes while she recalled the images that haunted her inner world.

Sophia knew time was running out and people were being used like puppets, being fed negative thoughts and feelings, until they would kill one another — and if they didn't, they would end up falling on their own sword. Her dreams showed her the negative energy hiding inside flesh disguised as a virus, but she pushed away the images and thought of a daisy, a big bright beaming daisy, a chain of giant daisies, and her sisters joyfully dancing in a garden where flowers surrounded them and trees bore succulent fruit. A protective cloak of light tightened around Sophia and her medallion was illuminated under her shirt. She shifted a little, being released from the images, and she hugged her knees. Father McDonald wrapped his arm around her shoulders in comfort. Sophia was grateful for the gift of sight and accepted her destiny.

The deer stood on the other side of the river. Father McDonald saw the deer watching and bow her head to Sophia. "Come, let's get some of that rabbit stew," she said.

They walked, helping each other, back up to the cabin, accompanied by the smell of pine and fresh mulch. Each step scrunched the dry leaves and amplified the silence of the woods. Father McDonald longed to give her ease from her visions, but he could not; it was for her to shoulder alone. It weighed heavily upon him that a child had to carry such painful burdens, but she must fulfil her purpose if she was to be free. They passed the pine tree where the rabbit furs hung. "Tomorrow I think we can make you that pair of moccasins," Father McDonald said as they stepped up together onto the porch.

AN EAGLE CIRCLED high above the cabin while the afternoon birds chirped, jumping along the veranda collecting breadcrumbs. The clanging of the dishes was homely. Sophia stepped out of the cabin drying her hands on a tea towel. Father McDonald pulled out his Bible and randomly opened it.

"Read out loud, Father, please." Sophia hung the tea towel on the rail to dry and stood gazing into the valley.

Father McDonald smiled at her and cleared his throat before he began. "He that dwells in the secret place of the most High shall abide under the shadow of the Almighty. I will say of the LORD, He is my refuge and my fortress: my God; in him will I trust. Surely he shall deliver you from the snare of the fowler, and from the deadly pestilence. He shall cover you with his feathers, and under his wings shalt you trust: his truth shall be your shield and buckler. You shall not be afraid for the terror by night; nor for the arrow that flies by day: Nor for the pestilence that walks in darkness; nor for the destruction that wastes at noonday. A thousand shall fall at your side, and ten thousand at your right hand; but it shall not come near you. Only with your eyes shall you behold and see the reward of the wicked. Because you have made the Lord, who is my refuge, even the most High, your habitation; There shall no evil befall you, neither shall any plague come near your dwelling. For he shall give his angels charge over you, to keep you in all thy ways. They shall bear you up in their hands, lest you dash your foot against a stone. You shall tread upon the lion and adder: the young lion and the serpent shall you trample under feet. Because he has set his love upon me, therefore will I deliver him: I will set him on high, because he has known my name. He shall call upon me, and I will answer him: I will be with him in trouble; I will deliver him, and honor him. With long life will I satisfy him, and show him my salvation. Amen." Father McDonald stopped reading and looked into Sophia's blue eyes and smiled.

"Amen," she said. "Casey's on the other side of those hills."

"I think they could be the Cheviot Hills," said Father McDonald, "which are on the border between Scotland and England. If that's the case, the ocean is to our south-east. When we leave here, we might head in that direction. What do you think?"

"I'm not sure, Father," Sophia said. She sat on the deck and folded her legs lotus-style, preparing for meditation. "It's hard not to want to stay here."

She closed her eyes, listening to Father McDonald's voice reading words of strength and protection, and called out to Casey. All afternoon she felt him sleeping, popping in and out of her aura; like a cat he brushed past her but recoiled before he actually latched onto her energy. He was gentle as a petal falling on her face. Ripples of love and compassion fanned out from his aura into hers before he jerked back into his own space and time. Again she called out to him. The sound of Father McDonald's voice was fading as she travelled towards Casey, sensing his energy. Excited, she saw him sitting in a darkened lounge room, lightly furnished. The windows had been boarded up, otherwise the sun would have beautifully filled the room.

The overhead lights were on and Casey was sitting at a computer studying the contents on the screen. White noise burst out of the speakers as she came closer. He turned and examined the room. She hadn't been in this room before. It looked cozy with an open fireplace and a sofa you might lose yourself in, she thought.

He kept turning from left to right; she sensed the hairs rising on the back of his neck. "Soph— Sophia, is that you? I can't see you."

Sophia was manifesting as a shimmer in front of the boarded-up window. Millions of scintillating particles of light started to band together and a ghost of a person materialized. It was Sophia. He smiled. "You look radiant, but faint. Your projections are getting weaker," he said, concerned. "Are you okay?"

She could hear his voice in her mind echoing in space. "I'm better than ever," she said. "I'm trying to project without leaving my body, so it's not left vulnerable for a hostile takeover, so to speak, ha ha ha."

"You look more like a hologram," he said.

"You might want to shut down the computer, before the hard drive fries. Where're Amy and Terry?"

"They're boarding the windows in the rooms upstairs."

"How are you guys holding up?"

"Good, considering. Thankfully, we don't have the virus which is the major plus. Are you still up north?"

"Yes. I think we're just a few days away. But I don't believe that it will be easy."

"We can travel to the next town," Casey said. "That's it, though. There are roadblocks on the main road heading north. South, we managed to get a few miles inland before the next roadblock. We've been able go east to the coast and we traveled as far as the Holy Island. Somewhere near a place called Berwick-upon-Tweed the military had a blockade and it was lucky we were in the Jeep; we heard gunfire and quickly headed into the scrub and turned back."

"We have to go to Israel," Sophia said. Her energy pulsed with light.

"What, where?"

"Israel. Jerusalem, I think."

"We can't get into Scotland. You can't get into England. How on earth do you think we can get to the Middle East. And it's not on my bucket list." Casey knew there was a greater purpose in what was going on between them. He wanted to imagine that they were just a guy and a girl having a long-distance relationship.

"Why Israel?" he asked.

"I don't know yet. I'm not sure if it is Israel. I hear an angry man say *dovesti zhenshchinu* and see the Middle East. I keep dreaming of a bracelet and a green gate with a star on it. Show me something," Sophia said.

"Like what?"

"Turning the lights off and on, you choose."

"Okay, well, flickering the lights, we can't do. Terry has boarded up the windows and he thinks there is a problem with the generator every time I practice."

The computer screen started to flicker with white noise. The radio started hissing and a lonely voice came to life broadcasting the latest counting of the dead. They both stared at the radio, and Casey quickly turned it off as if feeling sorry for having a little fun when there were so many people dying.

"Don't stop," Sophia said. "What else? Pick something up." She could see his eyebrows knot together as he focused on the cushion on the lounge. It moved a little, his body trembled; the cushion started wobbling and fell off the lounge.

"Now pick it up," Sophia encouraged. "Go on, Casey, lift it up, You can do so much more than that. But the key is, you need to believe you can; you can control it, rather than it controlling you. You need to clear your mind of any doubts. It's when you think you can't that you won't. Believe you can and you will."

Casey looked up, rubbed his eyes, then brushed his wet palms on his knees, took in a deep breath, and slowly breathed out, channeling energy towards the pillow. Sophia watched the phenomena of energy swirling through the air like liquid towards the cushion, pushing it down. "Lift it, you're squashing it. Flip it like a pancake. Close your eyes and imagine the pillow rising," she said.

Casey sliced into the air with his hand, as if scooping, and the pillow suddenly went straight up and hit the ceiling. It rebounded into the side table knocking the lamp off. The twirling liquid zapped into nothingness.

He rubbed his forehead and pushed back his long curls, revealing his handsome face. "I know ... follow me," he said, and opened the door to the kitchen.

She watched him stare hard towards the barn. An engine roared into life and a Jeep started backing out on its own. Casey was vibrating, buckling under the power of the energy, his hands outstretched as if holding a giant ball and pulling it towards himself. It was too much; he had to stop. He dropped his arms cutting the connection. The Jeep ceased and the kitchen door slammed closed.

"You okay?" Sophia asked, floating closer to him.

From upstairs they could hear movement, tools clanged and banged hard on the upper floor. "Casey, are you okay down there?" Amy called over the railing.

"All good," he called back.

"You're flickering," Casey said to Sophia. "Don't go."

"Are you really okay?" she asked.

"Yes, just tired," he said, moving back into the lounge room. He bent down, picked up the lamp and placed it back on the wooden table. He fluffed the cushion and laid it on the lounge. "What about you?" he said avoiding eye contact.

"I have to go. I am still connected to my physical body. I'm using the body's energy and it is tiring. I've been eating so much, but this uses up tremendous amounts of energy. I wanted to tell you about the gunman in the last town we got supplies from, and the deer in the forest. Next time."

"What gunman? Maybe I can give you a boost?" Casey said scratching his head.

"No, not today. You're exhausted and you need to get better control of the energy. Even though you're tired you're liable to blow me into infinity and I'll never find my way back," she said and smiled.

He blurted out, "How are we going to get to Israel?"

It was too late to answer him. She could feel the link stretching. Saw in his eyes the light around her flickering. She slowly disappeared. She started to travel; it felt like she was hanging onto the end of a stretched elastic band that recoiled sharply back into her body. She landed hard. Her aura contracted, the vibration was painful. Her legs had cramped with pins and needles. Her neck had stiffened as if it was locked in place. Father McDonald was still reading and she concentrated on the sound of his voice as she settled back into her body, returning all on her own. She was pleased how far she had come in such a short time. At the realization she started to cry. Tears trailed down her cheeks: it was still really emotionally exhausting.

FATHER MCDONALD SAT on the bench behind Sophia, watching her body sway slightly. A bird sat on the edge of the plate in Sophia's lap picking off crumbs. More and more birds came and dared to sit close on the rail of the veranda. Some collected in nearby trees, chirping like a group of theater-goers, chatting and getting comfortable before the show started. He thought about Mother Catherine and how she would find his reference amusing. He missed her, her fussing and good intent. He leant back against the wall of the cabin and continued praying for the world's redemption and Sophia's protection as she settled in to her body. He saw her tears and his heart cried with her. He kept reading until her hand went up and wiped her face. She looked at him and her eyes didn't look troubled, they sparkled.

"You okay?" He closed his book and held his dear friend in the palm of his hand. He leant forward and pushed off the bench.

"Starved," she said. Carefully, Sophia lifted one leg at a time, grimacing from the pins and needles. The bird stealing the crumbs off her plate flew away.

"Stay there, I'll get you a cup of tea and a sandwich." He felt just as stiff as Sophia, having not moved the whole two hours she had been gone, so it took him a little longer to get moving again. They sat on the porch eating their sandwiches and drinking the hot tea until the sun disappeared over the horizon.

"Where are you, Casey?" Amy called from upstairs. "You've been catnapping all day. Come up here and help."

He had sunk into the couch and refused to think of getting up.

"Casey!"

He grabbed the nearest pillow and pushed it against his ear to block out the sound. He was so tired today; he was feeling unmotivated and a little embarrassed. He wondered if Sophia knew he had been showing off. How stupid he'd been to move the Jeep. He seemed like the guys at the gym who tried to impress girls; he never thought himself to be like that. He had preferred track and cycling, being out in the sun. *When the virus has gone and everything is normal I might become a cyclist like Lance Armstrong, without the drugs.* He wondered if he too would be cheating, just by being himself: if people knew he could generate energy and channel it where and when he liked, maybe they'd think he might be using it to make the bicycle go faster. But he wouldn't cheat, because if they caught him they could claim unfair advantage. *But if it came out,* he thought, *that would be the least of his worries.* He would be ashamed and shipped off to some CIA laboratory to be studied. Casey drifted back to sleep to dream he was racing the last mile of the Tour de France when he was suddenly whacked in the face by the pillow. In his mind he fell off his bike just before the finish line and everyone passed him. He was left bleeding on the side of the road watching, nursing his pride.

"Up," Amy said. "Now, unless you're sick — get up! You can't lie around daydreaming all the time. It's difficult for everyone. You can't get out and do things you would like to do, I get it. But you can't lie around doing nothing. Up."

Casey caught the pillow before she planted another playful blow to his head. "And let's not mention how you guys have dragged me across the world away from everything I have ever known."

"Is that what you think?" Amy's eyebrows lifted slightly, looking him straight in the eyes. "Really ... is that what you think, is that how you feel?" She looked concerned, and her shoulders slumped.

Casey saw the pain in her eyes. "No. I'm sorry. That's not ... that was lousy. I shouldn't have said that. It's not how I feel. I just feel, I don't know, I feel trapped. I sometimes feel impatient, like there is something more I should be doing. But I am so scared of whatever it is. I'm afraid of something I am not even aware of. It's like I have eaten something sour and my mouth feels like velvet. I miss my mom and being a kid. I don't feel like a kid any more. I am only fourteen, and I feel forty." Casey swallowed his emotions. "It's like there is a battle somewhere and I need to go and be part of it."

"*Go?* Go where."

"I don't know. Wherever the battle is. But I can't even see the enemy that we are supposed to be fighting. It makes me feel useless, which pisses me off. I feel frustrated."

"Really, we understand precisely. We are living amongst great darkness. We're bound to sense the heaviness and confusion as the world battles the virus. If we start thinking bad thoughts, then that's all we are going to have. We have to create our own reality and ride through this storm. There is no Noah's Ark, or Moses parting the waters. The messiah hasn't arrived, it's up to you," she said pointing to her head. "The greatest battle is within you, Casey. It all starts in here."

"What about getting a boat? We can make it to the ocean."

"Then what? Where would we go?"

"What about Israel?"

"What? Why Israel?"

"Forget it. I don't know what I'm thinking," Casey said, pushing his hair off his brow and letting out a deep sigh.

He knew Amy was aware that he was struggling, wrestling on the inside, but he wasn't going to share any more.

"There're two ways to Israel. You could sail into the North Sea, down to the English Channel, out into the Celtic Sea past France and down around Spain to get to the Mediterranean Sea and up to Israel. But none of us knows anything about sailing and ocean currents. We could also consider driving the Channel Tunnel to France, across Austria, until finally going through Turkey and Syria. Who in their right mind would want to do that? It would take considerable time and planning under normal conditions. We can't drive for more than an hour, Casey, before we are turned back by the army, and we are hindered by the infected. Besides all that, you would have to have a pretty compelling reason to embark on a journey that just might kill you. But, having said that, that's how you can get to Israel, logistically. Oh, and you can also fly, but we would be shot down." Amy turned on her heel and headed for the stairs. "Now, are you coming? Terry could use those growing muscles of yours."

Casey moaned at the prospect of physical labor and followed Amy. He grappled for the banister and hoisted himself up, one stair at a time.

～

GLAD THE DAY WAS over, Casey stretched out in bed, hearing Amy and Terry arguing in their bedroom. The air grilles in the walls filtered sound like an intricate cochlear system. The staff in the past must have had a field day with gossip.

"I'm worried about Casey," Amy was saying. "I'm not sure if he is handling this as well as I thought he was."

"How is he supposed to handle it?" Terry said. "I am having trouble and he is just a boy. I wanted to scream every time there was a report of a tsunami. Every time I saw reporters focusing like leeches on the faces of crying people as they walked amongst the debris searching for survivors, screaming out their loved ones' names, hoping somehow they were alive. Or the earthquakes in California and Japan. The volcano eruptions in Italy and Hawaii. How are any of us supposed to cope? Then there is this goddamn virus. We're being crushed like ants. How is he meant to be coping, Amy? Tell me that?"

"Why are you yelling at me? What? Are we supposed to just give up and die?"

"No, I didn't say that —"

"Well, you might as well have. I'm going downstairs to read my book," she yelled.

Casey pulled the pillow around his ears and focused on the chest of drawers. His eyebrows knitted together as the drawers slid across the floor, screeching like a nail dragged down a chalkboard; it sent a chill down his spine, his body shivered. Casey released the pressure on the pillow, comfortable now he was no longer unintentionally eavesdropping. He had never heard them arguing before and it was toxic. He sensed the cause was the dark cloud hanging above the house, manipulating them, feeding off their anger. He closed his eyes, wandering into sleep thinking about Sophia, hoping she would hurry. *Is she real or is she a ghost? She better be real, or they're all going to die.*

13

———

INTERDIMENSIONAL TRAVEL: KEVIN.
AUSTRALIA

Comfortable the men weren't coming back, Kevin soaked up his surroundings. The air was cooler in this parallel world, it looked alive, smelt fresh like after a summer storm. He felt safe. He wasn't tired or frightened; his body was relaxed and energized. *Where are we?*

"You're in my head again," Tim said.

Kevin ignored Tim and said, "It's the same place as before, but it's different somehow. It's in a different spot, too. We were on the other side of the burnt-out car."

"I'm telling you, man, you created it."

"Really, wake up! That's ridiculous. Can't you be serious for once? Sometimes I wonder how we became friends."

"Don't put shit on me. We're friends because nobody else would be your friend. Since the first day of school you've been weird; you'd put your parka on before it started raining. You knew when the school bullies were coming and walked the other way. You've known the answers all your life. You'd stand up before the principal even walked in the room. Everyone said that when you saw a kid drown in the river, you were looking for attention. The cops and all the people

172

searching found nothing, no such kid. But for some reason, I believed you. That's why we are friends. That and you like baseball.

"Look at this place, K. It's magical and you created it. No one can see us behind this wall, this waterfall of ... rippling jelly. It's so smooth, and it moves like silk. It's endless. It flows down into the earth, but it doesn't pool, and it's not wet. We are in a cocoon of electrifying energy. This is an image through the lens of a slow shutter. The colors are so transparent and vibrant it's like going into a 3D gaming zone. Man, what I would give to be able to create another world." A bug landed on the back of Tim's hand and he turned it over and over again as he spoke. He touched the tiny transparent wings, giving himself an electric shock.

"I didn't create it."

"Sure you did."

"No. I've just opened a doorway, like some portal." A little blue-winged bug flew above Kevin's head and was quickly joined by another and another. Kevin felt the ground move under his feet and he quickly jumped back.

"A door to where?" Tim asked.

"I don't know," Kevin said, looking at his feet. "The ground smells like earth. The dirt looks rich and moist and the air is filled with aroma. An electric-blue sky can be seen between those giant trees. We can still see the river and the burnt forest, but we can't smell it, or feel it. It's sort of familiar but I get the impression we are far away. It is neither hot nor cold. As magical as this is, it's not reality."

"Yes, it is, because we're here, we're in it," said Tim.

"You can hear my voice inside your head. How is that reality?"

"It belongs in here in this reality. Not out there. How many times have we heard in science that we only use a small percentage of our brains? Maybe it is reality here in this world and in our world too, but we don't know how to access it. We don't know how to jump a level, we can't search for the cheats, this isn't Halo. You have to stop running from yourself, K."

Kevin jumped back. The tree roots had slightly lifted up out of the ground as if shifting position, making themselves more comfortable, nearly knocking Kevin off his feet.

The petite blue-winged creature flew off the back of Tim's hand and landed on the massive tree trunk. Tim's gaze raced up the side of the tree and watched the canopy shake like a wet dog. Birds went flying, as if woken abruptly from an afternoon slumber, squawking loudly, and then peacefully settled back in the foliage as the tree completed its stretch. The roots burrowed back deep into the soil and everything went still for a few seconds.

Kevin looked off into the distance, deep into the forest. He saw a white deer staring at him. Kevin detected the deer before he saw it. Gentleness radiated from the creature, overshadowing everything else. Its surrounding light shone, beckoning him, and he started walking towards it, moving deeper into the foreign world away from the window that led the way home. Tim followed.

"I've seen this deer before," Kevin said. "When we were in the wall, in transition, the first time ... when we were leaving, remember? Moments before you pulled me out, I saw the deer and felt it calling. Remember I told you."

The foliage thickened; iridescent colors bloomed. The blue bugs continued to fly around their heads. Kevin noticed one sat on his shoulder and one was on Tim's crown. The forest would open up — virtually stepping aside for the deer to pass — and then close in behind them. Kevin and Tim were filled with wonder and continued to follow the deer deeper into the forest. The glowing blue creatures flew over and around the deer, settling on its back, taking the form of a human-like fairy, with a set of massive blue transparent wings and elfish ears. You could see its veins the wings were so thin. Kevin was worried that a strong wind would cause them to tear.

They're stronger than they look.

That wasn't Tim, Kevin thought.

No, not me, bro. Do you think it's the deer?

Kevin didn't respond, just waited. But no more was said and their attention was captured by a translucent, pink crystal waterfall, channeled along thirteen streams that pooled together into a sparkling lagoon. A garden surrounded the body of water. Soft voices came from no particular direction, drifting upon the air like a song. The white deer gently stepped off the grass and onto the water. The boys stood at the edge and watched, wondering if they should attempt to follow, wondering if they would sink.

Come, said a voice inside their minds.

Kevin stretched his leg out; his foot hovered over the water. "Here goes!" He didn't plunge straight down like he expected. The water gently lapped at his shoes. It was a weird sensation: his body felt like his blood was carbonated, he felt elated and bubbling with joy. They both followed the deer, experiencing a sensory overload as they walked.

"*It's like I've been shaken like a soda bottle and the lid has just popped off,*" *Tim said aloud. This isn't anything like walking on a waterbed. Where do you think we are going? Maybe we are dead for real this time.*

The blue-winged creature riding upon the deer disappeared into a hundred sparks of flickering light. The deer's long muscular legs disappeared behind the waterfall and into a cave. Kevin was right behind and he was bone-dry. The cave was lit with purple and white crystals. Fifteen feet ahead was the exit, as wide as a bus, and beyond that a row of swaying willow trees. The forest continued sliding back for them to pass. Kevin, looking up, noticed shining stars and a glowing moon in the daytime sky. *How bizarre,* he thought, *this is so cool.*

"LOOK," TIM SAID. "It's the wall. We're back where we started."

Kevin soaked up the details of the outer world, making comparisons in his mind. "No, we can't be, look, the trees, they're not burnt. That place isn't home."

Exposed creek-bed rocks and fallen branches covered in moss lay outside the wall and the sky was filled with looming dark clouds. A howl penetrated the rippling liquid membrane. "I think it's Earth," Kevin said. "Maybe we're in a different place."

Kevin looked at Tim. "Can you hear that? Wolves."

The deer turned around and came up behind Kevin, nudging him forward into the wall. He stepped closer scrutinizing the shapes in the dry creek bed; nestled against a fallen tree was a body. The deer nudged him again. The wolf howled louder, closer. "Okay, I get it," he said to the deer. Kevin didn't need to be nudged a third time and stepped into the space between his new world and the next and melted into the bliss. He could stay there forever. The cry of the wolf was louder again, as if right behind him. A sense of urgency sparked every cell in his body and he stepped out. To his credit, Tim was right there by his side. "Stay close," Kevin said.

The drone of annoying insects filled the air. Kevin crouched beside the body and said, "Hello, can you hear me?" The body curled up in a ball, a hooded jacket pulled down over the head, concealing the person's face. The deer came over and nudged at the ball, inciting a moan. The head slowly, as if too heavy, tilted back and the hood fell away. It was a girl. She opened her eyes and saw the boys.

"Hey, you okay?" Kevin asked.

Confused, she tried to scramble to her bare feet, slipping in the mud.

"It's okay," Kevin said. "We're not going to hurt you."

She sat with her back against the log, holding her knees tight against her chest. She looked scared and confused.

"Who are you?" she said. Her hands went straight up to her head as if trying to stop it from exploding. "Oh, my head kills. I think I have a cranial fracture."

"What? You're bleeding," Tim said.

Her long, raven-black hair covered her face as she tried to push herself up. She was weak and dizzy. She sat on her heels and rested for a moment. "Where are we?"

"I don't know," Kevin said. *She's beautiful*, he thought and felt a little uncomfortable, and shifted his feet amongst the fallen leaves. "Who are you?"

"Jade. Who are you and what do you mean, you don't know?" she said, trying to stand up again.

"Hi, Jade. Nice name," Tim said.

"What's he mumbling for?"

"You can talk directly to me, you know. I'm standing right here. Fair dinkum."

"You're a foreigner. You speak funny. Where are you from?" she asked.

Her hair was dirty, caked with blood. Her clothes were filthy and her face, too, but Kevin didn't see any of that.

"K, the deer has gone."

Something's moving in the shadows of the trees, stalking us ... Kevin heard the bay of the wolf and sensed it getting closer, and that's when he saw a black paw, the size of a lion's, step out from beyond the trees behind the girl, growling. Saliva dripped from its sharp teeth, its lips pulled back in a snarl and it snapped its teeth together.

"Don't move."

"We're dead!" Tim mumbled. "What do we do, should we run?"

In a voice that sounded deep and foreign to Tim, Kevin said, "I don't know."

"Why do you always say you don't know? Of course you do, you always know."

"But I don't," Kevin said.

"K, open the door."

"What?" Kevin couldn't take his eyes off the saliva dripping from the wolf's sharp teeth.

"Oh my God, I have been rescued by a pair of retards," Jade said. "If we run, it will get the slowest of us."

"K, open the door!"

The wolf took a step forward.

"Now, K."

Open the door, Kevin said to himself. *I can open the doorway. I don't create the world, but I can access it.* But how, he just didn't know how. Kevin remembered the electric pulse and how the colors resonated with his touch. He imagined the shimmering mirage was before him and it began to manifest into reality. Doubt crept in, and it disappeared. *What shall I do? Nothing? Maybe it's just not going to happen this time, maybe we are all going to die,* and with that thought, Kevin started to feel sick in his stomach. He closed and opened his eyes quickly, as if he had dirt in them, and felt his mind hush. His face started to tingle; he was breathing rapidly, looking deep into the wolf's eyes. Sweat trickled down his spine. His stomach was in knots. A vapor, a ripple, a mirage the size of a basketball grew as transparent liquid waves expanded, flowing up and down hypnotically, between them and the menacing wolf.

"K, have you done it? Stop messing around, we have to go now!" Tim said.

"It isn't big enough for any of us to enter. When it is, we have to step forward, towards the wolf. I'll tell you when."

The wolf began its run, leapt over the fallen tree and lunged.

At the last second, the hole expanded. "Now!" Kevin and Tim jumped, pulling Jade with them through the silky membrane. They all flinched as the wolf howled and snapped its jaws. *It can't see us, but it can still taste our scent in the air.*

JADE FELT KEVIN reach in and pull her out of the embryonic state to the other side and instantly she was aware of the change of environment. Her mouth and eyes were wide as she scanned the area from left to right. "This is incredible. This is too much." Jade held her breath and brushed herself off. *Everything is so bright and colorful, it's like a painting.* She felt as if she was being cleaned somehow, on the inside. The beauty of the scintillating purple and emerald-green trees made her weep. The pain of the past year came flooding up and was washed away, healed. It reminded her of the gate with the star. She tried to blink the tears away and saw Great Turtle. Her great-grandmother was holding a seashell full of smoldering sage and was fanning the smoke into the air with a white feather. Then she was gone. Jade's tears of sorrow were replaced with tears of joy; she felt like she was home. Her headache cleared, her pain had gone and the tears stopped. *My body feels so alive!* "Where are we? No, let me guess," she said smiling and biting her lip at the same time.

Tim looked at Kevin. "She wants to guess. This should be interesting."

"I know, don't tell me. This is so abstruse."

"It's what?" Kevin said, taking his eyes off the wolf and looking at Jade.

"You know," Tim said, lifting his shoulders to his ears. "Abstruse."

"Who are you kidding? You've got no idea what that means."

"Guys, are you in a relationship or what? It means puzzling, heavy, incomprehensible. Capeesh? Now let me think." She held up her finger to hush them. "We have completed a quantum jump into a parallel world. This is colossal." Jade spun around looking back at the wolf. "It can't touch us, it can't see us, and it looks like it can't hear or smell us any more. How long have you guys been able to do this? Is this some sort of experiment?" Jade was full of excitement and wonder at the expanding possibilities, her mind racing. Suddenly the joy in her face turned solemn. "Are we dead?"

"Why do you think you're dead?" Kevin asked.

"I thought we were dead too," Tim interjected.

"I saw Great Turtle — my great-grandmother was known as Great Turtle. She's dead. She is in the spirit world."

"We're not dead," Kevin said.

"Then we are in a *quantum* time and space, a parallel universe, perhaps." Jade lit up like a Christmas tree. "I feel like the menorah on the eighth day of Hanukkah. This," she said, twirling around with her arms open, "my mother would have a field day with. Look at these plants. They appear to be soulful and alive." Gently, she brought her hand up under a soft leaf that was twice her hand size and touched it.

"That's one way to express it," Kevin said.

"How did you find this place?" she asked, letting the leaf down slowly. How did you open the passageway? I have so many questions."

"I think, first — first we should get home." Nervous, Kevin cleared his throat. "I think my mom might be able to help. She can come across as a real cranky person, but I feel we need her."

"Will she drive me home?" Jade asked.

"Sure," Kevin said.

"Okay, let's go see the dragon lady." Jade walked slowly, tilting her head back, gazing high up into the giant trees. "This is marvelous, absolutely marvelous," she said. "How many places have you been to?"

"Wait till you see the crystal cave."

"I'm lost as it is," Kevin said. "But to answer your question, this is the second time. Well, third, including now."

Kevin dropped behind and listened to Tim and Jade talking. She seemed intrigued and confused all at once by what they were saying.

Kevin allowed his thoughts to drift back to the day the boy drowned, wondering if he had opened a doorway then, and hadn't realized it. He remembered the details clearly: riding his bike around the block testing the brakes, he had gone off-road down the track to the river. *I stopped to adjust the front end by placing the wheel between my legs and aligning the handlebars. When I found a cherry protein bar in my pocket, I ate it. What next, what next? I leant my bike on a tree near the river and took a leak.* He had looked into the river and watched the ripples on the surface floating in to the shore. Hypnotized by the rhythm he had taken off his shirt, and shallow-dived into the tiny waves, swimming underwater and holding his breath as long as he possibly could. He had surfaced and that's when he saw the boy upstream on a wooden bridge as it collapsed. Kevin had seen the boy clawing at the wood as it plummeted into the raging water. He could see the torrents as if they had been rushing his way but they never arrived. He had dived under, searching for the boy, thinking, *Nothing makes sense; there was no bridge.*

Breathless, he had surfaced into calm waters and the small sandy inlet before him. His bike had been leaning against the tree were he had left it. Quickly picking up his things, he had expected the water to still rise up behind him and over the sand and flood way beyond the trees. He had taken off on his bike, and waited. Nothing had happened, he had waited a little longer, but still nothing had happened. Balancing the bike between his legs, he had put his shirt on, then ridden off back to the river. Standing on the pedals he had craned his neck trying to see as much as possible before he actually got there.

Nothing ... the river had been sleepy, gently lapping against the sandy shore.

He had listened for the roar of the torrents of water, but there was no sound, except for some cicadas chirruping. He had propped his bike against the same tree and walked to the water's edge; nothing. He had jumped back onto his bike and coasted up along the river to where he thought he had seen the boy. There had been no bridge, no raging rapids, and no boy. He wasn't sure what he had actually seen, but the boy was real and his fear was real. Kevin had felt him gasping for air, his lungs being crushed.

What the hell! Kevin had thought, speeding home. His parents had called the police and they had found nothing and said he was crying wolf. *Maybe when I dove under the water, I arrived in a different time and place.* Abruptly, Kevin remembered there was someone else watching the boy drown, a pale girl with blonde hair watching from the other side.

Kevin didn't realize Tim and Jade had stopped walking. He would like to experiment with opening and closing the doorway like Jade has suggested. But how to start?

"He does this often. Earth to Kevin, Earth to Kevin." Tim stopped in front of Kevin, so that his friend crashed right into him.

"Sorry, man, you said something?"

"No, but I think you did, K," Tim said tapping the side of his head.

Kevin's face went red; he let his hair flop over his left eye. "Oh, shit, how embarrassing."

"We can still hear you," Jade said. "This is —" Quickly she tried to think of a word to dumb it down for them. It was hard to think of something simple.

"No way! You didn't just say 'dumb it down'?" Kevin looked askance.

"You can hear me?" Jade was shocked and even more excited than before. "This is phenomenal!"

Eyebrows raised, together the boys said, "Yep."

"This just keeps getting better and better." She reached behind and pulled her shorts out of her butt. "Give me a pair of cargoes any day," she said red-faced.

Kevin couldn't help watching as she tied her hair back, and wiped her face on her shirt. *She is simply beautiful.*

"Okay, stop there. We need some protocol here, guys. Like mind your thoughts."

Jade wasn't sure about these two, but they seemed harmless enough. Tim's sort of funny. Kevin has a crop of hair he's forever pushing out of his eyes or flipping to the side. If it bothers him that much, why doesn't he get a haircut? He's mysteriously amazing. Not too talkative, but he thinks a lot. He looks down at the ground most of the time as if lost in his own emotions. But he looks strong, muscular, athletic, and has a warm smile. "You know who you look like?" *she said to Kevin.* "River Phoenix."

"Seriously, who's checking out whom now?" Kevin said. "We heard all your thoughts just then."

"Who's he?" Tim asked.

"An actor from long ago who allegedly died of a drug overdose."

"Great! So Kevin looks like an actor who is on drugs."

"No, that's not what I meant. My mom and I watched a movie he was in, and she said he was a promising actor, very handsome in a rugged way. She had a crush on him when she was young."

"Nice save — I think," Tim said.

"When you said my name back there," she said to Kevin, "you said it as if you knew me."

"I had a vision of a deer and heard your name."

"A vision of a deer, and you heard my name. You're messing with me, right? This isn't real. I'm dreaming, aren't I? Great Turtle would have loved you. You had a vision." Jade laughed merrily.

"It's true. The deer led us to you," Kevin said.

"What happened to the boy who drowned? Did they ever find him?"

"No, and I don't want to talk about it."

"Then you'd better not think about it," she said.

The trio reached the cave and walked through it. Jade was entranced by the flickering crystals embedded in the walls. "I would love to take some samples but it feels inappropriate, the whole place seems to be breathing."

Together they emerged from behind the waterfall. Jade was in love with everything she saw. "A pink waterfall." She put her hand out and chuckled before putting her lips to the tiny pool in her palm. It tasted so sweet and clean, she just didn't know how to describe it. The water glided down the back of her throat and into the pit of her empty stomach; it felt like there were microscopic love butterflies gently calming and caressing her internals. "I feel so relaxed," she said. "This is so wonderful. It looks like a colorful painting done with cream, icing sugar, coconut and jelly. I just want to eat it all."

Tim turned to look back at her. "First, you want to take samples, and then you think it's like a painting, and now you want to eat everything."

"Come on, we have to move," Kevin said, "time is ticking on. We need to find where we started from. It can't be far now."

"Hello!" Tim said. "There's the wall and our bikes." He pointed into the distance. The trees and leaves parted, creating a path for them. "Why couldn't you have created that an hour ago?"

"Stop saying that. I didn't create anything."

Wow, I don't want to leave. I want to stay, Jade thought.

"That's how I feel, too," Kevin said.

THE EMERALD TABLET: IMMERSION

PART TWO

14

METATRON: CASEY. ENGLAND

Casey sat on a fallen branch, scanning the silver birch trees. They hid him and the house from the road. He rubbed his palms on his denim jeans and cleared his mind, trying to connect to Sophia, when from between the trees a sandy-colored Labrador stepped into view. "Here girl." The dog ran straight to him and licked him on the face. Casey shuffled the leaves at his feet for a stick. He picked one up, placed it across his knee and snapped it in two. He threw the longest piece of the stick into the air and obediently the dog fetched. Casey threw it again and again the dog retrieved it. "No more, girl. I need to think." The dog kept pushing the stick with her nose. "No, I need to focus on my friend Sophia. Go home." The dog picked up the stick and again dropped it at Casey's feet. He eyed the dog, and then the stick. He began to visualize it lifting off the ground — and it lifted. Not very high, but it hovered. He flicked his head to the side, making his curls bounce, and the stick went sailing up into the air. Like a rubber band it retracted, smacking him in the face. "Shit!" He dabbed under his eye. He tried again. He connected with the stick and imagined it soaring through the air, then flicked his head up and to the side. The stick flew into the bushes. The Labrador bounded after it. Casey's head hurt; he rubbed his temples, the pain was minimal, but an electric sensation above his eyes travelled down his face and his lips became itchy.

Out of the woods came the dog, drooling with the stick in its mouth.

"Yuk, I'm not touching that."

"Casey, you want to come and help me?"

Casey looked over his shoulder. Terry was hanging out the back door. He turned to the dog and with a slight movement of his eyes and a tilt of his head, he lifted the stick and tossed it into the air. "Fetch," he said. The stray Labrador mirrored Casey and tilted his head. Casey glanced over his shoulder at Terry. "Sure, Terry, give me a sec," he yelled back. He picked up the stick with his hand this time, and tossed it towards the hedges and the dog started to lumber after it. The ground vibrated. The Labrador stood still and began to howl.

"What is it, girl?" Through the narrow parting in the trees, a series of army trucks shot past in a blur of camouflage-green. "It's starting, girl. It's the virus. Hell's circus has come to town. Come on, girl, you look like you could use some water." Casey headed over to Terry at the house.

"Who's your friend?" Terry asked.

"She came out of the trees." Casey turned on the tap and the dog lapped it up. He jerked his head to the road. "Where do you think they're heading?"

"Town, probably."

Terry rested his hand on Casey's shoulder. "Come on. Come give me a hand downstairs. Maybe give her something to eat first. She's looking a little thin. Give her a couple of powdered eggs and the sausages left from last night."

"Wait here, girl," Casey said.

The dog sat, its tail dusting the ground.

The kitchen was freshly painted. It was looking new except for the moldy section that grew up the side of the wall.

"Where's Amy?" Casey continued to mix the egg powder and water in a bowl.

"In the cellar."

"What are you guys doing down there, anyway? And isn't it called a basement?"

"Sorting through her great-aunt's old treasures. Some of the things are actually amazing. I have a hunch that the dampness in the kitchen wall began down there."

Casey took the bowl out to the dog. "I'll meet you downstairs."

At the sight of the bowl the dog stood, a whimper escaped its mouth and saliva hung from the corner. It tapped its paw, wanting to step forward, then barked. Casey put the bowl on the grass and the dog buried her head in it. "That will keep you going for a while."

"Terry! Do you want me to bring the toolbox?" he yelled.

"Why are you shouting?"

"Ha ha. I thought you had already gone downstairs."

The stairs creaked as Terry descended ahead of Casey and the light bulb swung overhead. Amy was sitting on one of the many trunks, absorbed in unpacking another. Terry looked as though his heart fluttered when he looked at Amy. Casey knew she was his touchstone in life: they would fall apart without each other.

The air was thick and moist in the cellar. "You shouldn't be down here in your condition," Terry said.

"Ah!" Amy jumped off the trunk, arm up ready for attack. "Don't creep up on me! You guys here to do some real work or just scare the hell out of me?"

"Okay, no need for sarcasm, madam. What's with the kung fu moves?" Terry said, chopping the dust with his hands.

"He's right, Amy. Mold would be thriving in this atmosphere and it's not good for your lungs."

"It's not good for any of our lungs," Terry said. "Why don't you pick which trunk you want to go through next and we will lug it upstairs to the sunroom for you?"

"Well, I don't know. It's a lot of work for you."

"We'll have to cart the stuff upstairs that you want to throw out or sell. You might as well sort it out up there," Terry said.

"Who are we going to sell it to? There's hardly anyone around," Casey said.

"Don't be so negative, okay. I'm finishing this one now. It's full of beautiful old clothes. Turn-of-the-century stuff. You can take those old trunks against the far wall, behind the stairs, over there." She pointed. "Those ones are also ready to go."

Casey moved over to the trunks. Examining them, he could feel the energy of the past saturating the wood.

Casey sat next to Amy on the leather chest that smelt like a worn saddle.

"The room was filled with priceless memories," she said. "Think of the people who must have worn these clothes years and years ago. The dinner parties, balls, formal courting. How romantic it must have been."

Casey saw her aura expanding, as she imagined her family's past.

"Did you see the cot, Terry? It's to die for. It's so old — and that desk chair, look how worn that seat is."

"Yep, a lot of backsides have been in that chair. Maybe your great-uncle, with a pipe in one hand and a whiskey in the other, spinning the odd yarn to guests," Terry said.

"You're mocking me? You know, all of this stuff should really go upstairs. The air down here will damage it eventually. I'm surprised it's not already covered in mold. God knows how it has survived."

Three trunks were stacked up high against the wall. "We are going to need a ladder. I'll get it," Casey said, mounting the stairs two at time.

The back door slammed and the dog stood at attention, wagging its tail. "You still here? Don't you have a home? Isn't there someone missing you, girl?" Casey asked. "Come on, then."

They both stopped a few steps from the barn and the dog growled. "What's the matter, girl. Afraid of a few rats?"

The decaying wooden door hung unevenly with one corner wedged into the grass. "It will need to be fixed, girl, but not right now." Casey gave it a couple of good yanks and it opened. Instantly, he saw the ladder hiked up on the side wall. He reached up to unhook it, but lost his grip, the ladder crashed to the floor, landing a hair's breadth away from the dog. "Sorry girl, I — what the hell!" A black mist of tiny insects, like a thousand fruit flies, swarmed down from the rafters and encircled him. He coughed and choked. They went up his nostrils and down the back of his throat. Pain exploded in Casey's head. He grabbed his hair and doubled over gagging, vomiting up his lunch. His body was on fire, his head hammering. Tiny claws dug into the sinus cavities up his nose, the fastest route to the brain. His ears and nose bled. "Oh, God!" He released an agonized scream as his eyes turned black like swirling pools of oil. His mouth stretched wide, his jaw unhinged, and the black vileness travelled to his brain.

Casey fought for control. The barn came alive with projectiles and the dog ran.

An explosion of intense blinding light filled the barn and everything stopped in mid-air and collapsed to the ground. A figure, which stood three times the size of a man, emerged from the center of the light. It had three sets of wings unfolding behind him: from his shoulder blades, from the middle of his spine, and a set from just below his waist. They sparkled with trails of misty light. The lower right wing gracefully extended and swooped down, catching Casey and rolling him up, squeezing him tight, pressing out his last breath until all the devil's vermin was expelled from his body, freeing Casey from the virus. The heavenly being held him tight until the demons were crushed and vaporized.

Casey felt no pain as his bones were crushed. The angel's touch was gentle, its illumination was blinding. He couldn't look into its face, his eyelids sealed tight and in Casey's mind's eye he saw a rainbow enclosing them. In a partially conscious state, in that feeling of being between sleep and wakefulness, just before the sensation of falling, Casey saw his mom. No oxygen left in his body, he smiled back at his mom while the wings unfolded two at a time, lowering Casey to the dusty floor of the old barn. He heard the dog move. Casey imagined it was listening, tilting its head to the left and to the right. The dog barked in the distance, running to the house. Casey, not breathing, moved towards his mother.

The angel gently laid down Casey's head. "Metatron, my name is Metatron."

THE BARKING ECHOED into the house and down the stairs. Terry and Amy looked at each other for a second, then together they ran for the stairs. "Casey," Amy yelled. The sound of the step splintering under her foot was like bones breaking to Terry. She lost her balance. Reaching for him, she felt her fingers skim his shirt. Terry stretched out to catch her but missed and Amy fell over the edge of the stairs landing on the hard dirt floor.

"Amy!" He raced back downstairs.

The wind knocked out of her, she struggled to breathe. She spoke between breaths. "I'm ... okay. It's ... Casey. I know it ... go!" She pulled herself up awkwardly.

Terry ran up and outside. The dog headed in the direction of the barn.

"Oh no, dear God, no," Terry mumbled. Casey was on the ground with blood coming out of his nose. Terry's mouth went dry, his heart raced. The horror of the first time he'd seen Casey lying motionless came flooding back and he was afraid. Terry got down on his knees and placed his hand on the boy's chest — nothing; he put his ear to his mouth — nothing. A tear escaped from the corner of Terry's eye and dripped onto Casey's neck. Terry waited to feel the warmth of his breath — nothing.

"Terry. What's happening, what's wrong with him?" Out of breath, Amy crouched opposite him.

Terry ignored Amy's quivering voice and began resuscitation. *Compressions, one breath, compressions, another breath, compressions, another breath, ...* He kept repeating the mantra inside his head.

The sound of Casey coughing and choking was bliss. Terry turned him on his side. Casey coughed up blood and spat.

Amy brushed his hair out of his eyes. "What happened?"

Casey looked pasty; exhausted, he managed to push out a smile.

He watched them fuss over him. He lifted his head up. Amy gently pushed it back down and moved his hair out of his eyes.

"Don't try to get up, wait a few minutes," she said. "Think it's about time you had a haircut, mister. You're a mangy poodle." Amy's attention was drawn to the lofty heights of the barn. "I never noticed how much light there was in here. I bet the rafters would be filled with secrets."

Casey lifted himself to his elbows and slowly sat up, breathing deeply. His chest expanded, filling with air, triggering a fit of coughing.

"Take it easy, pal," Terry said crouched beside him.

Once the coughing stopped he took in a couple of deliberately short breaths. His body wasn't satisfied, and independently took in consecutive rapid shallow breaths. He looked as if he had bottled up the tears of a lifetime and breathed out in a heavy sigh.

"My mouth tastes terrible." He snorted back blood from his nose and spat. "I feel like I have just gone twelve rounds in the boxing ring." He massaged his cheeks and said, "My jaw's stiff, and my ear is throbbing."

"And you don't remember what happened? You gave us a hell of a fright!" Amy said.

"I'm not sure. I opened the door, grabbed the ladder, then my head exploded.

After that, I don't remember."

Terry held out his hand and Casey looked up. "Ready to stand, pal?"

"Yeah, yeah sure." He steadied himself against Terry. He wanted to just hug him and bury his head into Terry's chest and sob. But he couldn't; he was supposed to be grown-up now. He had had hairy armpits for the past year, and his voice had matured. *Then why do I feel like a terrorized little kid?* he mused. They both helped him walk back to the house and into the kitchen. The dog followed, settling in to sit by the door.

$\sim$

"WELL, GOOD MORNING," Amy said, a little too chirpy, turning off the computer screen. "You slept well. Grab yourself a bowl of cereal and come downstairs when you're ready. I'm off to sort out those last few items. We're going to have a great garage sale when the world gets back on its feet."

"What are you doing on the computer that you don't want me to see, Amy?"

"Nothing. Nothing really."

She looked embarrassed, avoiding his eyes as she glanced out the window.

"What am I doing? This isn't like me," she said and looked him in the eyes. "I was just watching the online news. It feels like we are cocooned out here and I want it to stay that way. I want to protect you from the chaos out there." She flicked her head towards the window.

"You can't protect me, not really."

"But we have to keep trying. I saw you with my book the other night."

"Which one?"

"Don't play dumb, you're no good at it," she said, pulling her long hair into a scruffy ponytail. "My grandfather's leather book of splendor."

"Sorry, I should have asked."

"I don't mind. I don't own it, I'm just the caretaker. You're welcome to meditate on it anytime. I know you speak Aramaic too."

Casey laughed. "I know, right. And I feel something, I really do — I don't know how come. When I hold it, when I open it, I become transfixed on the letters. I'm pulled into its energy, I don't know how to describe it. My body relaxes, I feel calm. It's like somewhere inside me a treasure box is flung open and sparkling sapphires, rubies, emeralds and diamonds radiate through my body. I feel illuminated in gold dust, and my eyes are filled with a scintillating light. I feel close to God — to all things, as if the universe is cradling me."

"Wow. That's amazing! Were your parents religious?"

"No, I haven't even been baptized."

"Have you ever read the Bible, Torah, or Qur'an?"

"I read the Bible a little when we were in the hospital. There was nothing else to read."

"I think God has his eye on you, Casey."

"There's something else though."

"What's that? You can tell me anything, Casey, honestly."

He paused. Should I tell her about the experience of drowning in the river, or about my ability to see auras, or that I can move objects with my mind? Can she help me? God, I wish she could. But she has enough just surviving, and now the pregnancy. I'm not her kid, I'm not her responsibility. Sophia will help me."

"Casey, what is it?"

"Um, nothing. Let's just finish watching the news together."

He turned the computer screen on. Amy watched him sit on the side of the old table, dressed in denim jeans and a white t-shirt. "That shirt is getting too tight around the arms for you." She patted his leg, letting him know everything was okay.

On the screen, the reporter standing in the middle of a street tried to make an announcement, while looters ran around in the background. The tall buildings blocked the sun casting a grey haze across the reporter's face. "The USA has closed its borders," he said. "All planes have been grounded and the airports have been closed. Cruise ships are being denied the right to dock for supplies. The death toll has tripled and is rising. We are annihilating ourselves. Who said we would *nuke* ourselves, blow ourselves to smithereens? Forget about the threat from other countries, the battle is within each and every one of us. What is the government doing? Where is the vaccination we were promised? Where has Professor Ellen Freeman and her promising vaccine gone? Has all this madness been an engagement in biological warfare? These are the questions on everyone's —"

The reporter ducked. Gunfire filled the streets; looters were shooting shopfront windows and setting rubbish bins alight. The reporter composed himself and pushed his earpiece into his ear. "It has just been reported that the National Guard will now close New York City. I have been advised to stop broadcasting and leave the area immediately but —" His shirt puffed with a breath of air before it changed to crimson. He seized his stomach, looked into the camera, and painfully stated, "I've been shot." The cameraman swung around to where the shots had been fired from, and through the lens the world was eyeballing the smoking barrel of a gun.

Violently, the gun was pulled back, turned around and the butt of the gun was smashed against the camera's optics, cracking the glass as the soldier yelled, "SHUT THAT DOWN, SHUT THAT DOWN — NOW!" The screen went blank.

Amy had her hand at her throat. "God help them; help them all."

"You just saw what they did, Amy. Why would you say that?" Casey, not waiting for an answer, left the room.

CASEY SAT ALONE ON the back step in the morning sun, shuffling his cereal around with his spoon. *The soy milk still tastes like cardboard.* He looked up to see the Labrador running out of the barn.

"Hey, girl, are you hungry? I've got a half-eaten bowl of cereal with your name on it." He left the bowl on the step and went inside, down to the basement.

"Morning, pal," Terry said. "You up for this?"

"Sure, lay it on me." Casey's throat was sore and his head felt a little light. But otherwise, he felt fine.

They both lifted the top trunk down and could see the mold on its back. Amy inspected each one, dragging her hand along the surface as if stroking an elegant stallion. "If you guys could take both of these upstairs, that would be good."

"Terry, what's this?" Casey asked.

"Its mold. It's also along this support beam. The wall is stone. Something has to be causing the dampness. Casey, help me with this last trunk." Together they shuffled it away from the wall, exposing a hole. A few select stones were missing, which had created an opening the size of a small dog.

"That's the biggest rat hole I've ever seen," Amy said, trying to lighten the tension that had suddenly entered the basement. "Pass me the torch, Amy," Terry said, putting his hand out behind him.

"Can you see anything?" Casey asked.

Terry was lying face down on the dirt floor peering into the hole. "It looks like there might be a chamber beyond the wall, a tunnel maybe. I've read there are tunnels all around here that were used for walking secretively between different properties, like lords meeting their mistresses, or hiding loot from thieves. The Cleeves Cove cave system is north-west of here. Shh, I can hear dripping."

"You're the only one talking, sweetie."

Amy and Casey smirked at each other, shook their heads and rolled their eyes. They crowded around Terry, trying to get a look. "We'll have to make the entrance wider. Wide enough for us to crawl through and take a good look."

"I'm not crawling anywhere," Amy said, losing interest. "I'm happy with the trunks. You two can go crawling through a maze of tunnels, but I'm going to go make us some lunch."

"I'm feeling a little tired," Casey said. "I wouldn't mind some downtime."

"I can smell the forest, how come I smell the forest? Can you smell my room? It's got a musty smell. That old-grandma smell," Casey said.

"Don't freak, okay?" Sophia whispered.

"Okay, but why would I freak?"

"I can't smell your room, because you are visiting me this time. You came here, you came to me. This is really good, Casey, but you can't leave your body unprotected. You're a flame to moths, and you don't want the kind of moths that are fluttering around the world at the moment."

"This feels terrific. If I look down, I can't see my body. It's like I am awake within my sleeping self."

"You are really changing, Casey. This is the last time we will be able to communicate for a while. We're moving on — it's time for me to leave the cabin. Next time we talk it will be in the flesh."

"You remind me of Amy. Your confidence — she has such confidence that this virus will blow over and everything will be okay. You even look a little like her, you know."

"Her thinking is resilient, mine is not so." Sophia's tone deepened. "Casey, I have wanted to be with my family, and the only time I can do that is when I am asleep or astral traveling. Astral travel isn't the healthiest thing, living in this reality. I have been selfish and have wanted to die. Amy is selfless and tough. I am learning to be strong."

"Do you still want to die?"

"My best friends were gunned down. Mother Catherine, who I loved as if she was my own mother, died a painful death to save me. But no, I don't want to die."

"There's a lot to live for Sophia. I'm your friend. The universe wants us here for a reason. It wants us to want to live. I was saved from the flood and you were saved from the fire. We have to keep going. I know things are pretty crazy. We went into town last week to get supplies for the next few months: buckets of protein powder, tinned food, a whole bunch of stuff, and we saw some infected people."

"How're the headaches?"

"Pretty good. The more I practice, the less it hurts. I can move things as long as they're not too heavy, otherwise I get a killer headache. It's actually starting to be fun."

"Learn to reverse the energy flow."

"What do you mean?"

"Instead of projecting your energy onto an external object, use it to propel yourself. Use the Earth's gravity to your advantage; like the opposite pole of a magnet. Flip yourself between the two to draw things near, or propel. Imagine you can create your own flying carpet."

"Flying carpet, that sounds a little nuts."

"Well, maybe not a flying carpet. Jet streams of energy from the soles of your feet, like a rocket, might be more like it. You can do it. The question is: do you want to do it? You're fading. Casey?"

"I can feel myself awakening, I can hear Amy and Terry talking. Bye, Sophia. I'll be waiting. I hope you're real. God, I hope you're real."

15

____

FRENZY OF FLIES: JADE. AUSTRALIA

It was time to leave the parallel world and Jade shuffled as close as possible to the membrane and placed her hand against it, feeling the coolness. It reminded her of her mother's lab, the agar jelly she would find in a petri dish. When Jade was younger, she had loved to watch the bacteria multiply. *The wall is moving, it's a living energy. It feels thin and pliable,* she was thinking as she felt the pulsing, magnetic field. She pushed her arm through until her fingertips could feel the breeze on the other side.

"Come on, let's go." Tim went through, then Jade and Kevin followed behind.

Jade put her hand to her mouth as soon as she was on the other side. "What's that stench?" A frenzy of flies buzzed around swollen carcasses. "The poor things, they're kangaroos. Where are we?"

"Back in everyday reality," Tim said, "where everything has about one per cent of the color of the other world we just left."

Jade looked around at the burnt landscape. It looked like shades of grey in comparison to where they had been.

Tim babbled on in her ear, his shoulders slumped. "It's where people don't give a shit about each other, and the almighty plague is upon us. It's depressing actually."

"No, I mean what country?"

"Australia," Kevin said. "Where do you think you are?"

"Home. Myrtle Beach."

"You live in a resort at the Gold Coast?"

Jade looked at Tim as if he had two heads. "No. I don't even know where the Gold Coast is," she snapped.

"You're from the States, aren't you? You don't live around here at all," Kevin said. "We just walked from one end of the world to the other, didn't we?"

"I must be still drugged. I must be ... still in the cabin in the woods!" *That's right, I was kidnapped and woke up feeling cold. There was a black hooded jacket over a chair in the corner. I took it and ran.* She touched her head — no cuts, no pain, but there was dried blood matted in her hair, a bruise on her arm and a needle mark. "You got a cell I can use?" she asked, rubbing her arms.

"You mean a mobile. Nah, sorry," Kevin said.

Thrusting her head forward and raising her voice, she said, "Everyone has a phone!"

"Then where's yours?" Tim said.

"Look, there's no point standing around arguing. Let's get back to my place and you can use my mom's phone."

Jade started scratching, feeling tiny pricks against her skin, and her stomach somersaulted. It was nerves. The atmosphere between them had changed. They no longer had an internal dialogue. *The effects of the quantum world were wearing off.* The day had become gloomy.

"We had mobiles, but our parents snatched them because we ran up a hefty bill of twelve hundred bucks. We use prepaid now and never have any credit. Can only receive calls, so what's the point in carrying them around?" Kevin explained.

"I couldn't live without mine," Jade said.

"Let me guess," Tim said. "You're one of those girls always texting her friend who is standing right next to her, and posting online what she had for breakfast, and how beautiful her hair smelt with the new shampoo Mommy bought from some flash department store."

"No! I use it for research, watching university lectures on YouTube and I can calculate mathematical formulas with it."

"We have to cross the river. At this time of the day it's only about knee-deep," Kevin said. The sky was filled with the same grey clouds and the air was suffocating, with the same humidity that the boys experienced before they had disappeared.

"Is it always this hot in Australia?"

"It's hot, but not usually at this time of year. Queensland wears that crown," Kevin said.

"What happened here?"

"There was a fire a few days ago; some assholes with petrol bombs. They stole our bikes and left us for dead," Tim said.

"And that's when the wall first appeared," Kevin said.

The guys pushed their bikes over the flat anthill, yards away from where Shaun had been waiting for them two days ago. They came out of the bush and a dead dog lay in the gutter. Its head looked like an exploding watermelon and it had begun to rot.

"This place gives me the creeps. Why do you hang out here?"

"It's not normally like this," Kevin said.

They silently continued on. Not a single car passed by, and only one kid coasted down the street on his board.

"Where is everyone?" Jade asked.

"The virus," Kevin said.

"It hasn't hit this bad at home — well, it didn't appear to be this bad. We always seem to have some massacre happening anyway, some degraded moron taking innocent lives. Maybe we have been infected for years and it's like bamboo." She stopped and put her hand over her mouth. She couldn't believe her own attitude. "That was very obnoxious of me."

"Ob — what? and what's bamboo got to do with anything?" Tim said.

"Nasty, I was being really nasty." She rolled her eyes. "Bamboo is invasive; it proliferates above and underground — seen and unseen — spreading to unwanted areas. It's tough to eradicate, like a nasty virus spreading unseen through our bodies. Lucky your name only has three letters," she said to Tim. "Oh, sorry, that was nasty too." She pressed her fingers against her head as if it hurt.

"It's been pretty crazy lately," Kevin said, looking sideways at her, confused at the sudden change. "We thought the virus would pass us by, but it hasn't, it has created millions of psychopaths."

"In the emergency waiting area last night, we watched a man break his wife's arm so she could see a doctor. Kevin foresaw it, and charged at the man. He was too late and copped a backhand."

Jade looked at Kevin, trying to see his face. He tilted his head, letting his fringe drop into his eyes, and looking down at the road. He stepped up his pace and stared at the road ahead. He reminded her of the way she had been before her mom went missing. She'd always tried to hide behind her hair, in case someone saw how she really felt.

"Hey, retards, yeah you! I want to talk to you."

Kevin looked up. Across the street Shaun swung his legs over the side of the roof.

"Why are you walking in the middle of the road? Who's the girl? She looks pretty messed up."

"Run," Tim said.

They bolted down the road and around the corner, turning off at Stewart Avenue. Along Kevin's street red and blue lights reflected off the windows and he could see a police car parked out front of his house. Kevin went to run inside, but stopped. Suddenly he was filled with dread. He became worried for his family; he was scared something had happened. It brought back the memories when his grandparents died.

Kevin and Tim stood shoulder to shoulder. "Shit, dude, what the hell's going on?"

Kevin focused and searched inside the house with his mind, feeling for the emotions. "It's about us. Your mom is in there too, she's crying. Kath's pissed off and she's holding Molly who is crying. Let's go."

"It's about us?" Tim said. "I feel like Tom Sawyer and Huck Finn."

Jade looked at Kevin suspiciously. "Why would you think you are in trouble?"

The trio walked up the porch. Kevin watched Jade let her hair down to cover her face as he opened the front door. Everything happened so quickly. Alex ran to him and wrapped his arms around his legs. His mother started yelling at him. He looked at his dad who was showing a school photo of Kevin and Tim. The scent of sage and lemongrass wafted past him, he felt relieved. *Nanna is here.*

Tim's mother was on the sofa with a box of tissues. She jumped up for joy at the sight of him. The tissues fell off her lap as she raced over to Tim and held him tight. His faced was buried in her chest and Kevin thought Tim would suffocate if she didn't let him go soon.

Nobody had noticed the barefoot girl beside him. Kevin was worried Jade would run. He could sense her hiding, peeking into the room, watching his mother yelling at him. He was embarrassed, his face turned red. She was rough and squeezed his shoulders demanding to know where they had been. Kevin had never known her to touch him aggressively, but supposed it was as close to a hug as he was going to get.

As soon as the boys walked in, Molly had settled down. Kath gently placed her in the playpen and laid the bunny rug over her before making her way to her brother. She pulled him from her mother's clutches and pretended to be glad to see him. She hugged him, and whispered in his ear. Tim's mother pulled him back into a bear hug as soon as Kath let go. Crying and thanking God for returning her son.

Tim's voice was muffled as he yelled, "Ma, I can't breathe."

Kevin tried to wriggle out of his mother's grip, but she wasn't letting go yet. Daniel stepped in between Kevin and Callie and hugged him. Kevin wanted to collapse into his arms and cry. He wished his dad would never let him go. *Keep it together,* he said to himself, feeling his body ready to drop. He stepped back and looked up at his dad and quietly said, "We found a girl. She's at the front door and won't come into the room."

"What?" Daniel looked up, saw Jade and was at her side in a few strides. He looked back at Kevin, then guided Jade gently into the room.

Everyone looked at Jade as she entered the room, concerned at her appearance. "Where have you boys been?" the policeman asked, quickly moving to Jade. "And is that blood in your hair?" He pulled a pair of gloves from his pocket and examined her head. "There doesn't seem to be any wounds. Did these boys hurt you?"

Jade just kept staring at Kevin's mom, and his mom looked at Kevin with a dumbfounded expression, then she looked at Jade, confused. *What are they both thinking?* Kevin wondered.

"But how the ...?" Callie walked over to Jade and pushed her hair away from her face. Kevin watched Jade stare at his mother, her eyes filling with tears. His mom pulled Jade into a reassuring embrace and comforted her. He himself hadn't felt that from her in a very long time.

Kath leant in between Tim and Kevin and said as loud as she dared, "You've been gone for nearly three days."

Kevin and Tim didn't understand what was happening, but they both knew the police had to go. "We're scared to walk the streets with so many psychos wandering around," Tim said, drawing their attention. "So we went bush. That's when we found Jade. She had fallen down an embankment. It was getting dark and we were lost so we made camp. The next day we started out together when the sun came up and kept walking; we were going in circles and extremely thirsty. I thought I was going to have to drink my own urine. Luckily, we found the fire trail, though home was still far away and it was getting dark. We had to stop for the night for fear of getting lost again."

Kevin looked at the adults, wondering if they thought Tim believable. What was the part about drinking his urine? He is mind-blowingly nuts.

Kath spoke first. "So why did you take the bikes?"

"That's not important," Tim said.

"That doesn't make sense," Kath said.

"Now you two, stop your bickering," Tim's mom said.

Kevin wondered why the hell Tim was making up a story. He

looked at his friend and raised his hands slightly as if to say, what gives?

Daniel cleared his throat and shook the officer's hands. "Well, mate, it looks like all is accounted for and then some. My wife obviously knows the girl. We'll see she gets home safely."

The policeman pulled his leather gloves from his pocket and turned to Kevin and Tim. "You guys are right to stay off the streets. The infected are outnumbering us these days, but stay close to home. Don't go hiking till this is over," he said, tilting his head towards the street.

Daniel and the policeman walked out of the room. "I'll be off then. A word of advice — The army will be moving tomorrow and there will be roadblocks in all capital cities to prevent people from leaving. Sixty-mile perimeter north, south, east and west and the docks are staying closed. Most people won't even know they have been boxed in. Orders are, shoot to kill. You didn't hear it from me."

"Seriously, that bad, huh?" Daniel said.

The policeman pulled out his sunglasses. "Well, it's happening. All the action at the moment is over at the hospital, which you're probably well aware of. So many people infected. It's crazy."

"Any sign of a vaccine?"

"No. No vaccine, no antivirals, and antibiotics are useless. The suicides are the worst. Heartbreaking — whole families sometimes. The world is going to hell. This job is getting harder every day. I am tired of meeting people when they are having the worst day of their lives. I'm glad it has turned out well on this occasion. You take good care of yours, keep your boy on a leash for a while. I think it's time I put in for some leave, if you know what I mean."

"Thanks, officer."

"Call me Bill." They shook hands again.

Kevin wondered when his mom would let go of Jade, then Callie pulled back and held her at arm's-length. Jade started sobbing.

"Jade, how did you get here? You're safe. It will be alright." Callie pulled her back into her arms.

A waterfall of long, black hair fell forward and hid Jade's face from him. Kevin watched his mom protectively putting her arms around Jade again. *How did his mother know her name, and how does Jade know my mom?* He had so many questions. He went over to Tim. Before he could say anything Tim's mom shuffled him out of the room and to the front door.

"Home with you, boy," she said.

"You stink," Kath was saying as she passed Kevin. "Where have you been? I don't believe a word of your story."

Tim blurted out. "Ah, we were really helping Shaun. Mr D said to steer clear of Shaun. That's why we didn't say anything."

Kevin didn't know what to do or say. What the hell was Tim up to now?

"Who?" Tim's mom asked.

"Shaun, a friend of ours."

"Yeah, right," Kath said. "Since when has Shaun Grady been a friend of yours?" She placed her hands on her hips. She cocked her head and raised her eyebrows, daring him to answer.

Daniel walked over and tilted Kevin's head slightly back so their eyes met. He couldn't look away. "Is that true? You should have called. We were worried. Don't ever do that again — is Shaun alright?"

Kath looked confused as she watched Daniel speak to the guys as if he knew what they were babbling on about.

"He, his head ..." Kevin wasn't as quick as Tim in coming up with compelling stories and felt uncomfortable. "Shaun's head was hurting pretty badly and he didn't want to go back to hospital. We stayed until his dad came home. I thought Tim called his mom and she called you guys."

"That's right," Tim said, grinning at Kath. "But I thought Kevin called you, Mr D, and you called my mom."

Kevin tried to keep his emotions under control and he knew his dad was doing the same, knowing they were playing him. He was just as confused as everyone else about Callie and Jade. Kevin felt something was going on; he sensed it, and he knew someone would have to explain eventually. Right now, he was grateful they didn't question him any more.

"Is there anything else you want to tell us?" Daniel said.

"Sorry," Kevin said. Daniel gave him a look of disbelief.

"Come on, Tim, let's get you into a bath."

"I'm fifteen, Mom. I don't do baths."

Callie let go of Jade, but kept her close to her side as she said to Tim's mom, "Sally, if you like you are welcome to join us for dinner. Kath has the magic touch with Molly."

Kevin looked at Molly sleeping soundly in her playpen.

"Thanks, but we'd better head off. Don't want to be out after dark. The storm clouds look nasty. Lord knows we need rain, but those clouds don't look ordinary. I'm just glad the boys are back." Callie followed them to the front door. Moths were dancing around the porch light.

"By the way love, the smell of the lemongrass and sage," Sally said. "Very humbling, nice choice under the circumstances."

Callie smiled and nodded in thanks, waving and closing the door behind them.

Tim shoved his head around the doorframe and shouted to Kevin, "Call me," then quickly pulled his head out of the way of the closing door.

"I don't have any aroma oils in the house. I'm assuming that's what she meant." Callie shook her head in confusion. "Anyway, Daniel, can you get dinner ready for Molly and Alex. We can have dinner and talk once the little ones have gone to bed. Kevin, go shower. You can use the main bathroom and Jade can use my en suite."

Kevin and Daniel looked at each other, not knowing what was going on or why she was being so nice. They both replied, "Sure."

Kevin looked at his mom fussing over Jade. How does she know Jade's name? I didn't tell her? Jade hasn't spoken. He was aware that his mom's behavior had nothing to do with him. He walked upstairs to his bedroom to get a fresh set of clothes when there was a knock on his door.

"Kevin, can Jade borrow a shirt and your green cargoes, please," his mother asked.

"Sure." Jade stood behind his mom and it was difficult for him to make eye contact with her. Her head was lowered, her eyes were swollen from crying. "Is Jade alright?"

"She'll be fine," Callie said.

"Mom, how do you know her name?" He passed her some clothing.

"Get yourself cleaned up and then we'll make our own pizzas and chat." She closed the door.

He heard his mom say, "Let me get this straight. You were swimming, knocked out, drugged and kidnapped? And you're wearing short shorts? That's not like you, Jade."

16

PESTILENCE'S FUSION: SOPHIA. SCOTLAND

The time had come to travel south. Hiding in the highlands and meditating was over, although it had given Sophia and Casey time to connect while the universe aligned the stars. The essence of the forest was comforting, the sound and the freshness of the stream healing, and the view of the valley from the cabin was enlightening, but it was time to go. They were lucky to have stumbled upon it. Father McDonald and Sophia said their goodbyes and the eagle circled above them as they walked out of the forest.

Worn denim jeans, a beard, messy hair, a black t-shirt and a sports coat helped to disguise Father McDonald. He no longer wore his collar. He carried his Bible in his inner-left breast pocket. The days were still warm, the evenings cool, but summer had begun to fade. Ten o'clock at night and the sun had finally settled over Scotland. Depression hung over the city of Glasgow. Under the darkness of night they entered the town, and took a seat in the corner booth of a small cafe, keeping their heads low.

They watched the television, seeing angry protesters in London demanding the fall of the monarchy. The next images were angry protesters in Rome surrounding the Vatican, demanding the removal of the Pope. From his balcony he appealed to the people before him to help each other, to love their neighbor, and promised they would find peace. They ignored his pleas, demanding he perform a public exorcism, claiming their loved ones were possessed by the devil. He tried to reassure them, advising them to stay in their homes and not to travel; the government would find a vaccine. Ceremoniously he released two white doves, the sign of peace, and the crowd went silent as the birds took flight. Then suddenly a burst of cheering rose from St Peter's Square as a crow swooped in and attacked the dove, dislodged white feathers drifting on the wind. A seagull joined the crow to attack the second dove. The cheers grew louder as the doves started to fall and the crow continued to peck at the Vatican's symbol of peace.

Horrified, Sophia and Father McDonald continued watching images from across the world of people lining up outside the churches, synagogues and mosques. "The people claim their loved ones who have been infected have become possessed by demons," the reporter announced from behind the safety of his desk, then broadcast the next set of horrific images across the screen. Home-made bombs hurtled through the air, exploding on the White House lawn.

Father McDonald looked over at Sophia. Tears were streaming down her face.

"Let's leave here," he said, holding his hand out to her.

They shuffled out of the booth as a picture of a younger Father McDonald and a young Sophia was splashed across the TV screen. The reporter accused Father McDonald of being a pedophile who had kidnapped Sophia, a young orphan girl, after shooting his parishioners.

They were both horrified and hurried from the cafe. The streets had become scary, so they looked for another place to eat and hide. The last cafe had stolen a little more of their light, and Sophia could see Father McDonald was weakening. They moved on, looking for a decent place that was open. They walked down dark narrow back streets that stank of urine and alcohol. Sophia kept away from the building walls, staying in the middle of the roads afraid of what might reach out of the shadows. A light was switched on up ahead, revealing three steps to a back door. They looked for a place to hide. Sophia stumbled over a pair of legs; the owner didn't flinch, not a sound. Sophia picked herself up. The door opened beneath the light: a silhouette, then a tall man emerged carrying a bag of trash, cigarette dangling from his mouth. He put down the garbage, inhaled on the cigarette and as he puffed, the smoke floated up to the light and the moths. He looked down into the alley, stepping in their direction.

Ducking behind a dumpster wasn't an option. Father McDonald's legs were liable to snap, so they kept walking. The man watched them go by. Father McDonald's hands were casually stuffed into his pockets and Sophia's hoodie was pulled up over her head. They kept their heads down, and cautiously passed him by.

"Hey, you two," the tall man said in a thick Scottish accent. "It looks like you could use a good meal. Come on in." He chucked his smoke to the ground and ground at it with his heel. He pulled the door open and held it for them.

The duo looked at each other, as if having a conversation only they could hear.

"Thank you," Father McDonald said. They walked into a kitchen, entering the back of a cafe. "You and the wee hen can sit here." The man showed them to an empty table away from the others; no TV screen, low lighting and hardly anyone was in the place. Perfect.

"I'll be back." He came back with a coffee, a milkshake, hot fish and chips, toasted club sandwiches and a bottle of water.

"Thank you," Sophia said, pushing her sleeves up to her elbows.

"You're welcome, hen. It's a slow night, what can I say? It's mayhem out there. Where are you two headed? Trying to get out of the city, or did you just come down from them hills?" He couldn't help looking at Sophia. Strange young lady, he thought. Her eyes were constantly looking past him and over his shoulder as if he had something on his back. He turned and looked behind him, but there was nothing. She looked above his head and he too looked upwards. But there was nothing.

"We're heading south," Father McDonald said.

"What's south, that's not north? This whole country is about to be put to sleep and under lock and key."

"Why are you open? Why aren't you leaving?" Sophia asked.

"No point running, hen. The virus is everywhere. No purpose in leaving. What do you keep looking at, young lady? You're giving me the creeps. You're making my skin crawl."

"Seeing if you have the virus."

"You can tell?" He took a step forward and looked her square in the face.

"Yes," she said.

He glanced at Father McDonald. They didn't look like a pair of hustlers. "Well! Let's have it." Feeling uneasy, his heart started to race. His stomach boiled and churned, as if he had eaten a bucket of hot peppers. He was scared; he didn't want to be one of the infected. Last week he was elbow-deep mopping up the blood of his dear brother, an infected. They had shared the restaurant for twenty-five years and his brother had never missed a day, not even when his kid was being born. Last Wednesday, he didn't show. He didn't answer his home phone or his mobile. So, for the first time, Joe had closed up shop, went to his brother's house and banged on his door. Silence. He checked around the back, took the spare key from the top ledge and let himself in. The old black-and-white checked linoleum floor was now red and black. A bloody axe by his brother's side and a gun in his hand. His baby brother had removed his wife's head before shooting his son and biting down on the barrel of the gun.

"No. No, you don't have the virus," Sophia said and smiled.

He dropped to his knees; his hands clasped in prayer, he raised them to the ceiling. "Thank God!"

"Do you want to know why?"

"Sophia!" Father McDonald warned.

"Sure, maybe I can prevent someone else from getting it. Maybe it's my blood type or something."

"That's why. Because you think of others first, and you think that there is good in everyone. Last year you were in a motorbike accident, weren't you? Drunken joy riders lost control and cut you off. Your leg was crushed between your bike and their car. You freed yourself and, dragging your crushed leg along the road, around to the other side of the car, you checked on the others. The driver was breathing. You smelt fumes, but you didn't stop. You reached up, opened his door and dragged him out. Seconds later, the car exploded, scorching your face. You lost your leg. You have a prosthesis attached to your knee, and still you don't hold a grudge. You believe there is a reason for everything. I could go on, but I think you get the message." She smiled gently. He was standing with his mouth open in amazement. He wasn't sure what to say or do; everything she said was correct.

"Who are you, a psychic? What's my past got to do with me not catching the virus?"

"The virus affects the brain. It is a small evil parasite that feeds off negative thoughts. When we get angry or scared, we create a different energy. They feed on fear, rage, pride, jealousy, envy and anger. Simple."

"The Evil Eye. That's why I wear this," he said, pointing to the string around his wrist. "My mother put it on me when I was a wee 'un and every time it fell off she would put a new one on. I continued to put it on after my bar mitzvah. I always wear my watch over it. I made the choice to keep wearing it even though we stopped going to the synagogue. My mother was asked to leave because she refused to stop studying her father's way of teaching, which was reserved for men over forty. She told me it was what her dad's father taught him, and he taught her, and they had continued to study even after they left Israel. The string is a protection, a reminder to be good — not to judge others or bring shame upon them, and to look towards God for guidance. Treat others how you would like to be treated, she always said. 'Life is too short.' So I always wear the red string. Wait, I have some for you." He pushed his way through the swinging door and they watched it move back and forth. Within a few swings he emerged with a tiny packet. He opened it up, mumbled a blessing, and tied it to Sophia's left wrist. He did the same for Father McDonald. He then held their hands together and prayed.

"Thank you, you're very kind," Father McDonald said. "God bless you."

"If you like, you can stay the night here."

"Thank you, but we don't want to put you to any trouble."

"Shouldn't you be telling someone in authority what you know about the virus?"

"It won't save people from themselves," Father McDonald said. "The authorities will just think she is a crazy young girl, some religious nut and lock us both up. I've learnt to let God guide Sophia — as much as I've wanted to end her pain and confusion."

People in the restaurant were looking at them suspiciously — or was it his paranoia? "Wrap that up and bring it with us," Father McDonald said.

Sophia unfolded a napkin and wrapped her unfinished sandwich, sucked back the rest of her milkshake, and stuffed her hot chips into the empty waxed cardboard cup, putting it under her jacket.

"How much do we owe you?"

"Nothing. It's on me. Call me Joe."

"Thanks, Joe, and may God bless you. Come on, Sophia."

They flipped up the hoods on their jackets and stuffed their hands in their pockets. They stepped out of the cafe to hide amongst the very thing that was seeking them out in the dead of the night: the dark, swarming invisible mist. It moved amongst the motorists, floating through open car windows, circulating amongst the passengers, up nostrils and into open mouths. Sophia watched in horror. Families began to argue as the virus impregnated their bodies, spreading across the brain, killing off neurons and consuming their souls.

Cars suddenly screeched to a stop, drivers and passengers jumped out yelling obscenities. Sophia and Father McDonald hid in the shadows. The brawl escalated, affecting oncoming traffic. Another car screeched to a halt. Men and women jumped out of their vehicles and randomly started beating into each other. Bystanders watched; some seemed to enjoy the violence. A few horrified people looked down at their shoes and walked briskly away. No white flags were raised, no sirens wailed.

"Maybe we should go back to Joe's and wait till morning. It's harder to see the swarm in the dark. We can leave at first light?" Sophia said.

"Agreed. Let's go." They headed back to Joe's cafe, but the sign said "closed". Sophia and Father McDonald turned to leave when Joe flicked on the lights.

"I figured you might come back. It's a little rough out there. It smells a hell of a lot worse than usual. I have an apartment upstairs, come." They followed Joe into the back of the cafe, up an old narrow staircase that led into his apartment above.

"May I use the bathroom, please?" Sophia asked.

"Second door on the left, hen."

"You can sleep on the couch if that is okay. I'll make up a bed on the floor for your granddaughter. She is very gifted," Joe said as Sophia closed the bathroom door.

"Sophia is very blessed. The couch is more than enough, thank you."

BEFORE FIRST LIGHT, they delicately walked downstairs trying to avoid any squeaky steps, careful not to wake Joe. They wanted to evade any offer for them to stay for breakfast. Father McDonald left a thank-you note and promised to keep him in their prayers. The bell on the front door jingled when the door opened and they closed it behind them. The street was quiet and an early morning fog was lifting. A few yards away a crow was walking over a dead body, a victim of the night. The crow behaved as if inspecting the carcass before purchase. Another crow landed on the dead man. The two crows cawed at Sophia and Father McDonald's approach, making their claim, eyeballing them. The empty street intensified the noise of the birds. Father McDonald couldn't walk past the body. He stopped, shooed away the birds and prayed for the man's soul. He took his Bible out and opened the book randomly. Sophia stood next to him with her hands by her side. "The word of the Lord came again unto me, saying, Son of man, set your face against the Ammonites, and prophesy against them; And say unto the Ammonites, Hear the word of the Lord God; Thus says the Lord God; Because you said, Aha, against my sanctuary, when it was profaned; and against the land of Israel ..."

A light began to glow around the body and the crows took flight. An ethereal body slowly, painfully, separated from the man's physical being, crouching on one knee and ripping itself away from the body. Sophia, feeling the man's pain, allowed her aura to expand and her energy to feed his soul with her light. The spirit of the man broke free from the chains of his physical body and his spiritual essence stood tall. He looked back at his body lying in the street, beaten, bloody, discarded. He turned to Father McDonald and nodded thanks and floated into the sky.

They watched him ascend, his soul sparkling like a million stars. It soared up into the gorgeous colors of the morning sky. Suddenly, a swarm of blackness appeared from behind the buildings and descended on the man's ascending soul. She felt the pain of the man's soul, as they dominated it, pulling it apart, fighting each other for a piece of its light until his spiritual essence was completely absorbed.

"Oh God, don't let them see us. Quick, Sophia, help me with the body."

Sophia broke away from the feelings of pain and helped prop the body up off the road next to the storm water drain, where they wriggled under it to hide between it and the gutter, praying the corpse would restrict their light.

The demonic entities had finished devouring the soul and Sophia peered through a gap near the man's armpit, watching the swarm hover. The mass was turning, searching below, and began to unite: the winged entities were imp-like, forming, defragmenting, reforming, shapeshifting until they became one giant monster with the head of a bat, the torso of a man with leathery wings, claw feet, and a long, sharp, jagged scorpion tail. It was a giant of a beast. It dropped from the sky onto the street and the impact rumbled like thunder through the ground; the buildings shifted and windows exploded as cracks opened wide along the street and the road collapsed, creating a sinkhole.

Sophia and Father McDonald lay under the dead man's body not daring to move. Sophia held onto her necklace, her precious family heirloom, for courage. She squeezed her eyes tight and imagined being at home, when she began to feel a gentle summer breeze ruffle her favorite dress. Then she saw the wind touch the tip of the tall blades of grass; she feasted on the familiar fields and flowing river, the place she called home. She felt at peace and took a deep breath and breathed in the beauty of the day.

Father McDonald, too, felt a breeze, a gagging stench, as the beast sniffed and snorted at the dead man's body.

Sophia kept focusing on the gentle breeze in the fields and her image was getting stronger, panoramic. She felt her hair whipping across her face, the wind building around her, bursting with energy, changing to gale-force. Suddenly her hair and her clothes froze. Her state was shifting: flashing between the fields and lying under the dead body. The states merged into one existence and storm clouds from the fields appeared in the sky above the beast and lightning flared. The wind intensified. Debris went flying as a twister developed and traveled towards Sophia and Father McDonald; Sophia had become the eye of the storm. Her inner storm, which had been building up and up, exploded from her solar plexus and the two storm cells emerged and blasted the demon into a million pieces again, back into its weaker viral state. It was scattered in every direction for miles and miles. The ferocious storm lasted less than half a minute then the wind disappeared leaving a few leaves floating in its wake. Father McDonald and Sophia rolled out from under the body and staggered to their feet.

Sophia held her head, feeling groggy and unsteady. "I don't drink alcohol, except for a sip from the chalice, and I certainly never will if this is what it feels like. Maybe, if this ever ends, I can teach teenagers how to get high on light. I can start up a club." Sophia rapidly blinked, trying to clear the fog from her eyes. "Focus! What am I thinking, what was I doing?" Her vision was blurry and her ears were ringing. She waited for her blood pressure to return to normal as she harvested her energy. Father McDonald put his arm around her, to steady her on her feet. She felt the warmth of his body and looked up at his lanky frame. He was old and fragile, but nevertheless a tower of strength to her. "We have to run," she said, pulling at his arm weakly, "before they regroup and come looking for us."

The sound of a horn blasted from the alley. A four-door blue sedan sped around the corner, heading straight at them. Sophia jumped out of the way as the car braked and the tyres screeched while the car turned in an arc and came to a stop beside them.

The passenger side window rolled down and the driver leant across and shouted, "I had a dream! Get in." He looked in his rear-vision mirror. "You did all this?"

Sophia smiled at Joe. "Not all of it."

"Get in."

Without further hesitation they jumped in the car. They raced along the streets as fast as Joe dared, dodging abandoned or burnt-out cars for about five minutes until he finally slowed down. "Heck, what happened last night?"

"Thanks, Joe. What was your dream?" Sophia asked, rummaging in her backpack. She opened a paper bag and pulled out a white sage stick. She broke off a piece and handed it to Joe.

"In my dream we were cooking in your family's bed and breakfast and you were laughing and shimmying in the kitchen. The next scene was I had to get up and leave Glasgow immediately to find you both. So I did. What's this?"

"It's white sage and it will help keep you free of negative energies. If you are going to stay with us, you are going to need it for protection from the dead and the living."

"The dead?" Joe started chewing.

"We'd better tell you our story," Father McDonald said. "You need to know what you are getting into. You might recognize me if I shaved off my beard and got a haircut," Father McDonald said. "My name is

Ian McDonald. I am a minister of the church and this is Sophia. Her family died years ago and she has been under my care ever since."

"No need to shave, I recognized you both. Didn't know where from. After a while I remembered watching the tube. I was about to turn it off, had my finger on the button when your wee smiling face popped on the screen. Yesterday I recognized Sophia first when she smiled. She didn't look like she was being held against her will, and you, sir, didn't come across as anything but a God-fearing man."

Sophia sat back in her seat and closed her eyes. She visualized a reflective sphere around the vehicle, a cocoon of emerald-green, purple, yellow, orange, blue and, of course, a soft touch of red for vitality — a seamless mirror. Anyone or anything that looked at them would see no more than a reflection of themselves. Good would see good, and evil would see evil.

They had been driving for a while and were entering the center of the waking city of Edinburgh. Sophia leant her head against the window, watching people with half-open eyes. They walked without purpose along the sidewalk like zombies. No hint of emotion, just moving machines, religiously following a well-worn path. There was a man with a briefcase in his hand, his eyes hidden behind black, police, frameless glasses. He reminded Sophia of some of the characters in an old classic movie, *The Invasion of the Body Snatchers*.

Joe wanted to put his foot down and hightail it out of there, but he knew it would only attract attention. He held the steering wheel tight, gripping and un-gripping. Rubbing his sweaty palms on the leg of his pants and mopping the perspiration from the side of his face onto his shoulder, he looked into the rear-vision mirror at Sophia. "Can you see if they've got the virus?"

She wondered about telling him. *Is ignorance best? Maybe not.* "Yes."

"Are there many?" Joe asked.

"They're all infected, Joe. Their souls are hanging by a thread to their body. The demonic entities can't take up a hundred per cent residence because the body will perish. A fragment of the soul is trapped, tethered to the body while it's used as the devil's puppet."

"What does it look like? Oh, my god, did you see that guy's face at the lights? It just transformed and snarled like a monster as we passed. Why aren't they attacking? Why are they still driving?"

"Robotic behavior. They can't see us, they can only see a reflection of themselves. The virus looks like a grey cloud filled with tiny metallic flies. They are passing in and out of people's noses, mouths, eyes and ears. Some latch on and hang off the body."

Father McDonald scratched the side of his head, his skin crawled. He wanted to run and dive into a body of water. He rubbed his back against the car seat feeling uncomfortable at the image conjured by Sophia's description. He pulled his Bible from his jacket pocket and prayed.

Joe ducked down a side street before realizing it was a bad idea. A few feet away he saw three men in suits attacking a woman lying next to a Vespa bike. He wanted to jump out and help. He slowed. The men stopped, as if listening, and turned towards them. Satisfied there was no one there, they leant over the woman. One man unhinged his mouth, covered the woman's bloody lips and sucked. Her cheeks collapsed. The other man pushed him aside and did the same thing. They seemed to grow taller, wider. Finished, they picked up their briefcases, and started moving closer to the car. Moving purposely towards them, running. Joe put the car in reverse and swung back out into the main street.

"Calm down, Joe, don't speed, it will be okay. They can't really see us. They're not sure what they see," Sophia said.

Father McDonald stopped praying and made eye contact with Joe. "God is with us. Just don't panic."

The stream of cars thinned out and they slowly made their way out of the city. It seemed like a lifetime to Joe. Sophia gave him a fresh piece of sage and he shoved the dried head into his mouth and chewed. He opened the window to clear the car of his stale perspiration.

"Let me drive for a while," Father McDonald said.

"No, it's okay. I need to drive," Joe said.

"That reminds me," Father McDonald said, "of when I was a kid and we were driving to the seaside, a place called Saltcoats, for a holiday and my dad ..."

Sophia tuned out, having heard the story a hundred times, and closed her eyes. "Casey, can you hear me?" she whispered in her mind, then a little louder. But there was no answer.

17

S = K LOG W: JADE. AUSTRALIA

"Where's your dad, how did you get here?" Callie asked. Kevin pushed his ear against the door trying to hear a little clearer. His dad walked up the stairs with Molly asleep in his arms.

"Psst, what are you doing?" Daniel whispered.

Startled, Kevin jolted back from the door. His face turned red. He lifted up his shoulders and dropped them.

"Get away from the door. Give them some privacy." Daniel slapped Kevin gently on the side of the head. Kevin's hair flicked up and dropped back into place. "Go downstairs and watch your brother." Daniel disappeared into Molly's room. He turned on the rotating light which cast a production of colored ponies on the walls and into the hallway.

Kevin tiptoed past the room, dodging the odd squeaky floorboard. He stopped at the first step and looked back down the hall to his mother's room. He was resisting the urge to go back and listen when his dad came out of Molly's room.

"You're not — seriously?" his dad said.

"What?"

"You know what, eavesdropping, that's what," he whispered.

Kevin pushed his hand up over his forehead, running his fingers through his hair and feeling the softness of his hair. He was frustrated he didn't know what was going on and what Jade might say. Kevin started down the stairs with Daniel on his tail. Once out of earshot of Molly's room, Daniel probed Kevin.

Daniel pulled out an assortment of ingredients for their pizzas. "Start grating," he said, handing Kevin the cheese.

"So, Kevin, what's her name? And what did you mean, you found the girl?"

Alex ran into the kitchen and pulled at Kevin's arm. Kevin shook him off, and continued grating the cheese.

"Alex, what did we say about running in the house? Go back and come in again. Without running!" Daniel said.

"Sorry, Daddy." Alex spun around and slid on his socks across the kitchen floor and out of the room, but re-entered the kitchen slowly, marching up to Kevin again. He stamped his feet and said, "Come play with me. Come on, come play with me. I'm at level five, about to fight the evil monster. Come on, it's on pause." Alex had his hands in Kevin's back pockets. He tugged and tugged. "Come on."

"Okay, okay," Kevin said, grateful that Alex was being a pest. "Dad?"

"Go on. We can talk when your mother is ready. But first, what's her name?"

"Jade." Kevin went into the living room and plonked himself on the floor next to Alex. He watched Alex battle the animated monster, but his mind was miles away.

~

"WHAT HAPPENED TO you? How do you know Kevin? I have so many questions, Jade. But you look like you need a warm shower right now," Callie said, turning on the light in her en suite.

Jade followed her into the bathroom with the pile of Kevin's clothes. Callie hung a fresh towel on the rail for her.

Jade sat on the edge of the bath and massaged her feet on the bamboo mat. Jade had had sleepless nights thinking of all the questions she would ask Callie if she ever had the opportunity. In a barely audible voice, not making eye contact, she asked, "Where did you go that night? Why didn't you come and see me? You were the last person to see my mom, and you ran." Jade pushed her hair back behind her ears and looked up at Callie. She raised her voice. "You came to our home and ate at our table. I thought you were more than just another one of my mom's post-grad charity cases. I thought you were my mom's friend, my friend, but you just left us." Jade's face contorted in anger and resentment. She stood up, grabbed her shoes and headed for the door. She stopped at the bathroom threshold and said, "Within hours of her going missing, you were on a plane, and out of the country! Where were —" Jade's throat tensed with anger and she couldn't speak. She choked on tears and confusion and she felt suffocated with emotions. The room started to spin. Jade believed that Callie knew something about her mom's disappearance. "Why won't you tell me?"

"I'm sorry, Jade, I'm so sorry. I had to think about my own family, my own life. There are people that wouldn't hesitate to hurt my family, or kill you if they thought your mother had shared her knowledge with me."

"Did she?" Jade asked.

"They would have taken me too. It has haunted me. Believe me, I regret it every day."

Jade stood still, flecks of silver light dancing behind her eyes. She no longer paid attention to what Callie was saying; she had cheated herself, allowing anger to control her. Behind her eyes, Jade's inner night sky was filled with diamonds splashing across her consciousness. She had an overwhelming sensation to just drop into infinity, endless space. Her legs and body felt heavy. Spots swam before her eyes. She knew logically what was happening, and it was controllable in her mind, but still her body was reacting, which made her even angrier. She fumbled for the edge of the bath and dropped her head into her hands.

"Jade, you okay. Just breathe. Where's your puffer?"

"I lost it."

"Wait there." Callie ran into her bedroom, and Jade could hear her opening and closing drawers before returning with a Ventolin puffer. Callie shook the puffer so it was ready if Jade needed a dose. "Relax, Jade, it's a panic attack, it will pass — breathe in slowly, 1 ... 2 ... 3. Breathe out to the count of three." Callie spoke while Jade struggled to regain her composure.

The room was blacked out. Jade couldn't see the bamboo mat under her feet, but she could still feel it and hear Callie's voice. Her body felt like it was going in slow motion. Jade focused on the feeling of her chest rising and expanding as she followed Callie's instructions.

"That's it, relax, and breathing in slowly 1, 2, 3, and out again, slowly 1, 2, 3 ... I see you found your bracelet. Your mom had me searching high and low for that. It must really be important, she was ropeable."

The darkness started to evaporate. The light of the room appeared behind her eyelids. She blinked until she was able to see and the flickers of light disappeared. Jade looked down nervously at the bracelet and twirled it around her wrist. Callie kept speaking. Jade began to relax, tracing the patterns with her fingers.

"It reminds me of a turtle shell," Callie said, watching Jade relax as she focused on the bracelet.

"It was my great-grandmother's. People called her Great Turtle. But you know that, don't you?"

"Where's your dad, Jade?"

Jade wasn't sure what she should say. She didn't want to lie because she just wasn't good at it, and she was tired, so tired. She just wanted to get clean and crawl into her bed. She didn't know what to say, or how Callie was going to react to being told that Kevin had the ability to create a hole in the universe. *Should I just say it: by the way, Kevin possesses the ability to apply the laws of quantum physics and step into a parallel universe. He has journeyed beyond reality as we know it; across time and space where he found me at the mercy of the wilderness. Somehow, I don't think she's going to warm to the idea.* "I was kidnapped and Kevin found me. I don't know what happened."

"I saw on the news that you were missing. But how did you get here, to Australia?"

It felt strange to say it, but there was nothing else that came to mind. Jade always had the answers, but this time she was lost. "I just don't know what happened."

"Are you saying ... the kidnappers, brought you here? Where's your dad?"

"At home looking for me, I guess. I don't know how I got here."

"All planes have been grounded, Jade. In every country around the world." Callie's eyebrows knotted together; confused. "But how ... perhaps the military, your mom thought her research was being monitored. They're the only planes that would get clearance to fly. But why would they bring you here? How did you escape them? And what do you mean, Kevin found you? Where did he find you?"

"Look, I'm tired, Callie, and hungry. You haven't answered any of my questions. All I can tell you is this: I was swimming on Myrtle Beach with Ben," she said, looking at Callie. If Callie was interested in the slightest about her being out with a boy, she wasn't showing it. "I surfaced, and I was hit from behind."

"Jade, that's terrible!" Callie started to check her head and found no wounds. Her beautiful black hair had clumps of coagulated blood, but no visible injury.

"Then, next thing I remember," Jade said, pulling away from Callie, "is that I woke up to the sound of men talking. It was muffled; my head was splitting and I was loaded up with narcotics. Comparatively, my ability to walk was very compromised. My neurons were cross-wired. I crumbled like a piano accordion and passed out. I woke again; I don't know how much time had passed. I was alone in a cabin on a makeshift bed, hooked up to an IV. They had taken my blood and kept me drugged up. I pulled the IV line out and after a while was able to get myself up off the bed. I suppose they thought the drugs were enough to keep me restrained, but I managed to get outside. It was daylight and I just started staggering and running and running till I passed out. I regained consciousness and started moving; it was getting dark and I passed out again. The rest is just a blur. I was lying in the woods when Kevin and Tim helped me. I regained consciousness, startled by the guys. They looked harmless enough, so I allowed them to help me up and then they brought me here. That's all my mind can recall right now. It's probably blocking stuff to protect me." Jade stared at Callie, waiting to see what she accepted.

Callie searched Jade's eyes looking for answers. It was like a stand-off between them. Callie was unable to see beyond Jade's shattered appearance. This was a child, but it was Jade, and she wasn't an average girl. If it had been anyone else, she would not have believed her. "They took your blood, do you know why?"

"No, but logically I would have to assume there would be a connection to my mom."

"Oh, sweetie, maybe we should take you to the hospital, get you checked out. We might find a strand of hair or skin under your nails; you know that might be all it takes to track your kidnappers."

"No, that's not necessary; I don't think there would be anything of significance. I just want to be clean, I stink. I just want to wash this all away." She caught a glimpse of herself in the vanity mirror and quickly turned away.

"The hospital is packed," Callie said. "Not really a healthy place to be right now anyway. Jump in the shower and we can bag your clothes for analysis later if we need to. You feel okay, right, besides the anxiety and vertigo? You must be so tired, and your dad must be frantic. We'll call him when you're ready. Maybe Kevin can fill in some of the blanks and explain how he found you, and where he found you?"

"How long have I been missing?" Jade said, dropping the soiled jacket on the clean bathroom floor.

"Seven days," Callie said, checking the needle marks along Jade's arm. God knows what they'd put into her veins.

"Seven days? I feel like it has only been a day or two, three tops."

Callie got up from the toilet seat and made her way into the bedroom.

"Don't leave. I feel irrational. I'm afraid the world will drop out from under me again. I know it's not real. Am I really here, Callie?"

"I won't leave," Callie said. "Yes you're really here. I'm going to sit on the edge of the bed and think."

"Okay. Keep talking, so I can hear your voice." Jade shouted over the splashing water of the shower. "Tell me about my mom's research." The water felt so refreshing. She lost herself in the rhythm of the spray massaging her body. The water turned red and swirled down the drain at her feet. She sat on the floor with the soap, and rubbed her hair until the water ran clear. Grateful for the fresh apple-smelling shampoo, she vigorously rewashed her hair before combing conditioner through with her fingers. She could no longer hear Callie. A light film of steam was building and, using her index finger, Jade drew on the wet glass: $S = k \log W$, and then a shape of a circle with a square around it. Her stomach started rumbling, snapping her out of her zoned out thinking. Jade hadn't noticed the door had been slightly closed. She strained to listen and heard Callie softly singing 'Songbird', a song Jade's mother had once loved to sing. Ever since her mother left it always made her cry. She rinsed off the conditioner and turned off the water, pulled down the towel from the rail and wrapped it around her. Quickly she dried herself and pulled on Kevin's cargoes and t-shirt. She tugged a comb through the tangles in her hair. She felt around her head for any sign of the laceration ... nothing. She shook her head in amazement at the speed of healing within the parallel world. Grabbing her hair, she twisted it into a bun at the back of her neck.

Callie was sitting on a deep-blue bedspread that had half a dozen white daisies embroidered across it. She stared at the ceiling as if something was written on it and she was trying to process its meaning. Jade stepped into the room. The coolness of the floor reminded her of home and the last time she rose from her own bed; she had floated down the hall to the smell of burnt toast.

Callie's window was open and the nylon curtains gently flapped. A tree blocked the bigger view beyond the window, but the sound and the smell of the evening was still homely amongst all the chaos.

"Callie?" Jade looked around the room. On top of a tall, white chest of drawers, a digital picture frame was scrolling images of crystal clear waters, laughing children, memories of happier days. "Callie?"

Startled out of her own deliberations, Callie quickly turned around, looking over her shoulder, wiping away tears, and smiling. "That's better, that's the Jade I know. Who on earth were you trying to impress with those short shorts? You're a beautiful girl. It's good to see you out of black." Clenching her tissue in one hand, Callie picked up her mobile and started to call Jade's dad. Jade was taken aback that Callie had his number.

"Hi, yeah, she's out of the shower. I'll just put her on." She handed the phone to Jade. Surprised, Jade stared at the phone and then back at her. *She must have already spoken to her dad while I was in the shower.*

"Dad?"

"Thank God you're safe! I couldn't believe it when Callie called. I'm unable to imagine what you have been through."

"Dad ..."

"What happened?

"Dad ..."

"I'm sorry, you must be traumatized."

"Dad! I'm okay, confused, I don't know what happened. It's hard to believe I'm in Australia. I was at the beach —"

"What were you doing out with a boy? He claimed you were knocked by a speedboat and dragged on board. The police thought that you had drowned and that Ben was making it up. There were no other witnesses."

"Okay — but I'm not dead." As soon as it was out of her mouth she knew it was stupid. "I think it's got to do with Mom. I really believe she is still alive, Dad."

"Honey, I'm so glad to hear your voice. I don't know how I'm going to get to you, or how to get you home."

"I can stay here with Callie. Is the old Indian still keeping watch?"

"We talked this morning. He asked me to go with him into the hills. He said he must keep me safe because we are family and you will one day return with your mother. Why did you ask about the old fellow?"

"I don't know. An image of him jumped into my mind when Callie handed me the phone. Don't go back to work, Dad. Wait until a vaccine has been developed. Go with the Indian."

"Your mother and Callie were so close. If she hadn't vanished they would have succeeded by now, I know it."

"What?" Jade let her hair out to drop over her face to hide the fresh tears. "Dad, what did the Indian say about Mom?"

"Don't worry about that, he's just hopeful."

"I need to go eat something. I don't remember the last time I ate. I am losing perspective."

"Lucky you're not driving."

"Dad, that seriously was a dysfunctional attempt at a joke."

"I love you, little Raven Wings."

Her great-grandmother named her Raven Wings when she was born. She believed Jade would be like the raven that appears when there is sickness and disaster, bearing gifts of healing upon its wings for all those who desired to be healed. The memory of Great Turtle telling her the tale over and over again was exploding inside her and she just wanted to run into her dad's arms and cry. No one had called her Raven Wings since Great Turtle's death.

"I love you too, Dad," she said, hiding her emotions.

"Call me every day, and listen to Callie. She has been the one person I have been able to talk to since your mother disappeared. She understands what we are going through."

Jade looked over at Callie, ashamed of her own previous assessment. "Okay, Dad, till tomorrow." Jade pushed the end button and handed Callie back her phone.

"You and Mom were working on the vaccine." Jade put the mobile phone down on the bedside table and said, "Why didn't you tell me?"

"I don't know what you are talking about. Let's get something to eat."

"Tell me!"

"It's not going to happen! You need to trust me when I say I don't know anything about a vaccine." Callie put her hand gently on Jade's shoulder, guiding her towards the bedroom door and out into the hallway. Arms across her chest, Jade reluctantly let Callie maneuver her. They peeked in on Molly. The yellow glow of the hall light shone through the crack and streamed across Molly's cot. Ponies were dancing across the walls, a change table sat under the window and stuffed toys filled the shelves. Baby animals hung from a mobile above the cot, swaying in a gentle breeze. Callie closed the window and Jade stepped further into the room. Molly was on her stomach with her knees curled up to her chest as if she was trying to crawl in her sleep. They both quietly left the room, closing the door.

Walking on the stairs behind Callie, Jade casually rubbed the back of her head still expecting to feel a gash, but it was completely gone. Her legs felt heavy, but her mind was racing with questions. A quantum jump through time and space from one side of the world within minutes, involving a high level of physicality, and days had passed, not to mention the healing of her wounds once she had gone through the membrane. She started to feel rejuvenated, light, and endless possibilities flooded her mind.

WHAT ARE THEY DOING *up there*, Kevin wondered. It was dark outside. At least an hour had passed since Jade and his mom went upstairs. Alex had stopped slaying dragons on his Xbox and had crashed on the lounge. Daniel was about to lift him up when Callie and Jade came into the living room. They both looked like they had been crying. Daniel looked at Kevin. Kevin's eyes widened and his chin tucked in, as if to say, *Don't look at me, I don't know.* Through semi-clenched lips he huffed a sigh, the air blowing his fringe. He prepared himself for a battle with his mom. He had no idea what Jade had said, but he didn't think his mom was going to like any of it. Did she tell her about the parallel world? And it was his fault that they were in there. Does she know that they were lying about being at Shaun's? He was freaking out; he was going to burst not knowing. He could see her mouth opening, she was going to speak. Fire, like with Alex's monster, was going to come out of her mouth and turn him to ash.

"Kevin," she said.

He waited, it seemed like forever; a siren went off in the night as if alerting him to the impending doom about to fall upon him. Okay, snap out of it, he told himself. *I've been hanging with Tim a little too long.* He took in a deep breath, closed his eyes and searched the space to gauge their emotional state.

"Kevin, stop it," his mother said.

He quickly opened his eyes, pretending he had momentarily drifted into sleep.

"Take Jade into the kitchen and show her how we make pizzas."

Kevin was confused. His dad saw it on his face, and said, "You're in for a treat, Jade. Kevin scatters cheese like nobody else."

Kevin smiled. *What* was his dad raving about?

"Daniel, can you help me with Alex?"

"Sure."

Kevin and Jade walked into the kitchen. Kevin scratched his head and said, "Okay, grab a pizza tray, then take what you like," indicating the prepared ingredients on the bench.

"I hope you're going to wash your hands before touching the food," she said.

He looked down at his hands and said, "Why? They're clean."

"You just scratched your head. Do you have any idea the number of germs that can be packed onto a pinhead?" Jade followed Kevin and picked up the tray: the dough was already laid out on it. Kevin leant close into her space and quietly asked, "What did you tell her? How do you know my mom?"

Jade looked down at the ingredients and scooped up a spoonful of tomato paste spreading it over her base.

"Well?" he demanded.

"Do you have any avocado?" she asked, teasing him.

"Forget the avocado. How do you know my mom and what did you tell her?"

"Who, the dragon lady? Ha ha. I told her I don't know how I got here and you and Tim found me in the bush. She'll probably ask you where exactly."

"That's it, nothing else?" he asked.

"Nothing else that involves you."

"How do you and my mom know each other?"

"She stayed with us while she was assisting my mother with genetic research. My mom was researching free radical cell mitosis, primarily a mutant cell multiples by division and destroys the organs. She believes she found a way to reverse and stop the destructive cells. Come to think of it, if that was the case, then they may have been able to ..." Jade went off into deep thoughts on how the theory could be a vaccine, for the virus.

Kevin watched her and could feel her intense emotional journey of discovery as she tilted her head to one side, her eyes squinting, circling the ceiling as if finding ideas and searching for answers. She was like an astronaut, floating into the unknown regions of space, seeking the unknown, believing something else was there, just beyond her reach. *So this is what I look like to Tim.* "Earth to Jade, Earth to Jade, come in, Jade." She looked back down at the tomato paste so he nudged her and she nearly lost her balance.

"What did you do that for?"

"You were off with the fairies. You're the missing girl! Your mom went missing and now you. But you're here. What happened, why were you in the forest? And my mom stayed with you in the US, right?"

"Yes. As soon as my mom went missing, your mom packed her bags and was off on a flight home. She left before we even got home from the police station."

Kevin reached for the mushroom and the tomato, spreading them around his pizza before smothering it with three types of cheese. Jade robotically followed his actions, shuffling along the bench. He pulled the metal handle of the oven, the heat shooting out; he instantly pulled his head back and banged into Jade's.

"Shit! That hurt," she said.

"Oh — really sorry."

Jade slid her pizza on the bottom shelf and said, "Now it's my turn to ask a question. How do you do it? How do you access a parallel world? Will you show me?"

"I don't know how I do it. I think I just slipped into it."

"If you like, I can help you work out how to do it. We can treat it like a scientific problem. That way, you will have a method to follow in the future, or a documented procedure to share with the world."

"Jade, I'm trying not to use my — gifts. It freaks out my mom."

"Why, that doesn't sound like your mom."

"I don't know what happened over there, but when she got back here, she was different and things went from bad to worse at sonic speed. My grandparents died in a car accident when coming to visit us, she quit her research and she has been fighting with my dad ... and hiding."

"What do you mean, *hiding*?"

"She doesn't let me see her emotions, unless it's her anger."

"What do you mean, see emotions? You mean facial expressions and body language?"

"No, I see them in colors around the person. I feel them in the pit of my stomach, and taste the pain in my throat. I feel your excitement right now, and I feel your confusion and sadness when you think of your mom, and your hope of finding her alive. I feel the anxiety you're always pushing away. You're afraid the room will start to spin and you will faint. You think I can help you find your mom, but I can't."

"Wow! That's incredible. That makes me feel —"

"Vulnerable and uncomfortable," he said.

"You're freaking me out." She stepped back. *Okay Jade, pull yourself together; what are the facts, let's get the facts.* "Were you always able to sense others' feelings and thoughts? Or only since you were in the parallel space?"

He could feel her deliberately regrouping and adopting a new stance. "Always," he said. "I've tried to shut it down, push it away, pretend it's not happening. Hiding away."

"Hiding — that's what you just said about your mom. You have an amazing ability to know what someone else is feeling."

Kevin and Jade were at the bench talking, their backs to the door, when Daniel cleared his throat and said, "So, you're Ellen's daughter." He held out his hand to shake hers.

Quickly Kevin jumped in and said, "Dad, I think she's got OCD. You might have to wash your hands first."

Jade elbowed Kevin in the ribs and shook Daniel's hand.

"I wish it could have been under pleasanter circumstances," Daniel said. "Callie spoke highly of your mother."

"Are we going to leave, like the policeman suggested?" Kevin asked.

"I don't think so. Where would we go?"

18

CELESTIAL WARRIORS: SOPHIA. SCOTLAND

Joe hit a bump in the road, startling Sophia from her waking dream. She blinked and pinched herself, making sure she was back in the car. She dipped her neck to the left, and then the right, to stretch it. Fields of poppies sailed past as Joe picked up speed before coming to a sudden stop. Up ahead was an abandoned military blockade.

"We're not going anywhere along this road," Joe said.

Abandoned cars led up to a tall, electric fence. Hanging off the fence were dozens of jittering bodies. How they were still alive, Sophia couldn't begin to imagine.

"Bless these souls that hang before me," Joe said.

"Amen," said Father McDonald.

Joe reversed the car, swinging it around. He turned down a side road and pulled over.

"Where are we?" Sophia asked.

"We're past Paisley, heading south-west."

"We have to be on the east coast," she said, unbuckling her seat belt and leaning her arms on the back of the front seats. The sky was a hive of activity and growing darker. The light of the sun was hidden behind the iron-colored clouds.

"We tried, we can't get through. I had to turn around. We are being pushed in this direction," Joe said.

"Then we should keep moving," Father McDonald said, "in the direction God is guiding you. You asked him to bless the souls that belonged to those bodies; he will also bless you for asking. Don't be reactive, trust in the light."

Joe twirled the red string around his wrist and counted the seven knots his brother had tied. It was starting to look a little frayed. He reached for the light switch.

"No, don't turn them on." Sophia nearly jumped over the seat to turn them off herself.

Joe felt her urgency. His skin crawled with fear. He felt himself fraying like his red string. The clouds merged together and it was hard to see the road in front of them.

"Drive," Father McDonald said, pulling off the handbrake.

"I can't." Joe was feeling melancholy and extremely tired. "No, I have to sleep now." His eyes started to close; his arms dropped from the steering wheel.

"Yes, you can!" Sophia said and pinched him at the base of his neck. Joe jumped in pain, his eyes opened and he stared with a blank face. The horror of the bodies hanging from the gate flashed in front of his face, along with his brother's body and all the images of death that the media shared: it was overwhelming.

"No, I need to sleep."

The skies grew even darker; the howling wind was rocking the car. "We have to go. If you don't we are going to die, Joe. God sent you to help us. You must push aside the lingering negative images. The demonic angels have also heard your prayers for blessings for those poor souls. They are now searching for you; they heard your tears, Joe. God believes in you and they know it."

Sophia placed her hand on the back of his neck. His mind filled with images of his mother putting his first red string around his tiny chubby wrist, the sweetness of his first kiss, his first love, and how alive he felt. He saw the memory of his brother's wedding day. He saw the images of hellos and goodbyes, and the smiles from the people who came and went from his restaurant. Sophia withdrew her hand gently; the images faded, but his feelings remained high. "Connect to those feelings, Joe."

He put the car into gear and drove blindly into the darkness.

Sophia sat back against the seat, closed her eyes and imagined a tether, like a leash to a dog, and left her body. She only went up a short distance, stopping just outside and hovering over the roof of the car. It was too dangerous to venture further, she would be noticed. She couldn't move beyond the fragile protective shell. She flipped over onto her back and looked up. Above, in the sky, angels — bad and good — battled, armed with bolts of lightning. The lights were diminishing as celestial warriors were beaten and the devil's horde absorbed their essences. There was one angel that grew brighter; it had three sets of wings and wielded a sword, its breath fire like a dragon. Its enemies were reduced to ash and the substance floated from the sky to land on the windscreen.

Joe turned on the wipers and Father McDonald prayed from Ephesians 6:10-18. "Wherefore take unto you the whole armor of God that ye may be able to withstand in the evil day, and having done all, to stand. Stand therefore, having your loins girt about with truth, and having on the breastplate of righteousness; And your feet shod with the preparation of the gospel of peace; Above all, taking the shield of faith, wherewith ye shall be able to quench all the fiery darts of the wicked. And take the helmet of salvation, and the sword of the Spirit, which is the word of God: Praying always with all prayer and supplication in the Spirit, and watching thereunto with all perseverance and supplication for all saints."

"Amen," Joe said, and started mumbling his own prayer. "Ana beko'ach gedulat yeminecha tatir tzrua. Kabel rinat amecha sagevenu taharenu nora ..."

Joe glanced into the rear-vision mirror. Sophia's body was still and upright and tears dripped from her chin. Her spiritual body, outside, could no longer endure the visions of the battle. She was starting to feel the hand of darkness grappling for her heart and soul. She had forgotten why she came out here and slipped back into her physical body, ignoring the pain of her ethereal body retracting. Before opening her eyes or entirely merging back into herself, she said, "Take the next turn."

"Left or right?" Joe said. She didn't answer.

"You'll know it when you get there," Father McDonald said.

"I can't see shit! Sorry, Father." Up ahead, he saw a pinprick of light and wondered if it was real or just his imagination. "Can you see that?"

"See what, Joe?" Father McDonald asked.

"That light? It's growing." He thought he heard his mother calling his name from deep within his head. He watched the speck get bigger and bigger until a form appeared, with three sets of wings slowly unfolding, surrounded by divine light. "Can you see it now? It's right in front of us."

Father McDonald was in a cold sweat as he sat forward, pressing hard against the dashboard, straining to see; his palms left damp imprints that quickly faded. "I see nothing, Joe."

He was so close Joe could see the definition in the angel's anatomy and its youthful face. Joe was afraid he was going to hit it, crash and kill them all. After driving in pitch black, the light was so blinding. He had to close his eyes. He yanked the steering wheel, turning sharply to the right, the car sliding and swerving. He corrected and opened his eyes and the sky was its usual pale grey, and the sun was shining somewhere. He slammed on the brakes.

"I told you, Joe, you would know," Sophia said.

"Can we pull over for a wee bit, hen?" Joe asks.

"That's a good idea."

"There is a tiny bit of forest about five minutes ahead. A cluster of trees of sorts. I'll pull up over there and hide the car." They went off road, squeezing between the hazel and mountain ash trees. They got out of the car and stretched their legs. Sophia was a little unsteady, but quickly came good. Father McDonald put his hands to his lower back and stretched backwards, cracking arthritic bones, while Joe stretched his arms up and down. They looked like a bunch of friends limbering up to do calisthenics. Under any other circumstance it would be funny.

"I think I know this place, it's a wooded glen. We're near Dusk Water, not far from the coast," Joe said. "When my brother and I were young lads we used to imagine we were smugglers; our ship anchored off the coast, we would row ashore to find a hiding place for our loot, which would be Cleeves Cove caves. There are a couple of entrances to a natural cave system that has been the location of a few myths." Joe started walking off, exploring the area.

Sophia followed him, Father McDonald trailing behind both of them with his hands on his hips, occasionally stopping to take in deep breaths of fresh air. Further into the woods, they heard a waterfall and the terrain became very damp and mossy. It was also very lovely. Sophia helped Father McDonald while he jumped over green rocks and climbed over fallen, velvety trees. Wild foliage and large trees like hazel and mountain ash. A large rock loomed above the cave's opening.

"This is awesome," Joe said. "This is the place where my childhood ghost stories began. Who figured I'd be taking refuge here one day?" He helped Father McDonald up into the entrance of the cave where he sat down to rest, clutching his chest.

"What's wrong?" Sophia crouched beside him and wrapped her arm around him.

"I need my backpack, my heart pills."

"I'll go." Joe rushed off. He swiftly jumped down over the trees and rocks and up the other side of the glen. In a short time, he was back with three backpacks.

"There in the side pocket," Father McDonald said.

Sophia fished them out and gave him the bottle. His hand was trembling, and he couldn't get the lid off. Sophia took the bottle from him and pushed a pill into the palm of his hand. He swallowed; they all waited. His color started to return and he said, "Just a few months ago, I carried you into the church and laid you down on the very pew you were born on, and today I can hardly lift up my own arm. I have aged a hundred years over the last few weeks."

"You'll be right, old man," Joe said patting him on the back. "You just need to catch your breath, and let those pills work their magic." Joe waited till Father McDonald stopped sweating and his body had relaxed.

Sophia was wiping his brow with the sleeve of her jacket. "How's the pain?" she asked.

"Just about gone, and so are my pills," he said.

"I'm going to have a wee stickybeak inside the cave, if you two are okay with that?" Joe said.

Father McDonald opened his eyes and nodded his approval and closed them again.

Joe pulled out his torch. "I won't be gone very long. Will you both be alright?"

"We'll be fine," Sophia said.

"There's some chocolate fudge protein bars in the front pocket of my pack. Help yourself." Joe walked into the limestone cave, leaving Sophia and Father McDonald to rest for a while.

The cave was cold and smelt damp. It opened up into a larger musty chamber. The further he penetrated, the more the air became stagnant. Joe took one of the tunnels branching off the main chamber that led east, further away from the coast. This is what he imagined as a kid. He stopped to lay his hand on the rock face, feeling for its heartbeat. There were more passageways branching to the left and right, but he went straight ahead, then took the second left for twenty-five yards. It started to curve and the air became sour, his eyes watering. He covered his mouth, and imagined a gutted animal that had come in to die. A real exploration of the caves would have to wait for another time, when his brother could be with him. Then he remembered the blood on the kitchen floor. His brother was dead. Lots of people were dead, and more people were going to die. He was on borrowed time; there was no later.

All of a sudden he felt claustrophobic. He had only been gone about ten minutes but it felt like an hour. He started to make his way back to the main entrance. He stopped at a junction and now couldn't recall if he had gone left or right. He stood looking down each tunnel trying to decide which way to go. Making choices wasn't his strongest trait: there were always too many variables, too many choices to weigh, so his brother, a man of action, had usually taken care of the decisions while he Joe did the hard yakka. He chose the passage on the left, but it soon became colder and unfamiliar. Joe quickly turned around and went back the way he came, moving towards the right. He arrived back at the same point and without hesitation took the right passage, and it wasn't long till he could see it opening onto the main chamber. He could see the light from outside and the silhouette of Father McDonald leaning against the cave wall, and Sophia standing at the opening tossing something into the scrub. Sophia turned towards him and he couldn't see her face; she had a glow about her. "I thought you had gotten lost." she said. "Father McDonald was exhausted so he's drifted into a deep sleep."

Joe sat down beside them and pulled out a peppermint chocolate protein bar from his backpack. He tried to rip it open, rustling the wrapper and making a considerable amount of noise. His big hands were searching for a good place to pinch the sides and pull it open, with no luck. He smacked it down on his knee hard and the bar popped out the other end. "Do you want a bite?" He offered the bar to Sophia.

"No, I'm good," she said. "I've just been enjoying an apple. I hope you don't mind?"

"No, not at all." He nodded towards Father McDonald. "Is he okay?"

"I hope so." She sat down next to the priest and wrapped her arms around her legs, resting her chin on her knees. Joe sat against the opposite wall of the entrance, and waited with Sophia for Father McDonald to wake.

$\sim$

"TELL ME AGAIN ABOUT your red string," Sophia said.

She watched Joe look down at his wrist and start running his finger underneath it. She copied him, twirling the knots between her fingers; it was soft and she found the motion relaxing.

"It was wound around the tomb of Rachel, the matriarch," Joe said, "for her protection and blessings. For me, it is a reminder to treat people how I would like to be treated. Not to bully or judge. To forget about jealousy, because it's poisonous and makes you old and bitter. It keeps me positive. We all have negativity, we all need to duck and weave from the evil glances of others. It's also a constant reminder of my mother, my childhood, and how important it is to try and see the good in the chaos around us, especially in times like these."

Sophia watched his face change with each thought. He actually believed in what he was saying, she realized. The energy around him changed: he had started with bright vibrant shades of earthy colors and now they were softening, becoming cool blue and violet. The dominant color in the central part of his being was a glowing green. It moved like a turning crystal in the sunlight. She wondered what it would be like if what he said was true. She fiddled with her red string and wished it would come true. All the dark angels would starve and flee; they would choke and burn in hell because of the mass consciousness sending out good thoughts and desires. The world would light up like a Christmas tree every day. *Could it be that simple?*

"What you have to do is have certainty," Joe said.

"Certainty in what?" she asked.

"In whatever it is you're doing. Like how you said I would know which way to turn, back there. You had certainty; you didn't doubt it for a minute, did you?"

"Well, no."

"That's what you have to feel. That feeling where there is no possibility for anything else, no room for doubt. You have to have certainty and go for it. I had doubt and glimpsed your reflection in the rear-vision mirror. You were struggling internally and at that moment I had certainty in you."

"They should teach us this at school," Sophia said.

"Something is guiding you beyond my vision. There's something that surrounds you, a magic that floats just out of my sight, Sophia."

She saw his energy change and his muscles tense.

The sound of a couple of larrikins screeching and laughing across the paddocks could be heard through the forest canopy. Joe stopped. "They must have seen the car."

Sophia could hear the slamming of doors and the jabber about who might own the vehicle, and where they were. A dark cloud hung above them, masked by the trees but Sophia could sense it. She woke Father McDonald. "We have to go."

Father McDonald was dazed, unsure of where he was. Joe was suddenly by his side, supporting him and picking up his pack, tossing it over his shoulder and his own bag over the other.

Sophia could hear the sounds of the hooligans getting closer. "We have to go."

Father McDonald's face looked worn and old and her heart was breaking; this was too much for him. She held back her tears as she flung her backpack over her shoulder. She had forgotten how heavy it was. She locked her arm with Father McDonald's and Joe supported him on the other side. They hung onto him while he took a moment to balance himself. His Bible fell out of his pocket. He pointed at it and Joe gracefully — for a big fellow — scooped it up and put it inside Father McDonald's coat pocket for him. Sophia was worried. The only place to hide was inside the caves.

Joe took the lead, remembering the turns he made the first time he was there. They could hear the sound of the gang entering the caves behind them.

They yelled, "Here we come, ready or not," and laughed.

Sophia turned, faced the last passageway, and focused on blocking the entrance by unfolding her energy. She felt it traveling around her body from the center of her being, down her shoulders — like sand running down her arms — and into her hands. She projected the energy outwards until it touched the walls and ceiling, creating a mirror image of the cave wall.

Sophia, Joe and Father McDonald walked deeper into the caves, then stopped to listen. They heard the fading sounds of yelling and laughing. Sophia, holding onto Father McDonald's arm, wondered who was guiding whom. She didn't know any more, but she had to protect him. He was the only one left who knew her family; *he* was her family. Sophia missed Mother Catherine and she wanted to cry remembering all she had lost in such a short time. She felt angry at God for taking her friends and family, she was angry for the pain and suffering Father McDonald was going through. She had never dared before to be mad at God. She lifted her left hand up to push strands of hair behind her ears and wiped at her eyes, and noticed the red string on her wrist. Suddenly she felt old, as if she had been fighting a battle that spanned many lifetimes, and she felt that the image she treasured of running through the streets with other kids on a hot summer's day was a mirage, an illusion. Sophia hadn't realized she was still fixed to the one spot and that they were both shining their torches at her.

"Sophia, what ya doing? We have to keep moving, hen."

Father McDonald turned off his torch and placed it in his pocket. He looped his arm tighter around hers and patted her hand. He started to tell her favorite story.

"On a fresh Saturday afternoon," he began, "before the end of autumn, amongst the fallen leaves, beside the lake, your mom and dad laid down a checked red and blue rug. Your sisters set out the contents of a picnic basket; they were all excited, and you stood a few steps back from the blanket, just out of their reach, taking off your diaper and clothes. You were wriggling out of your diaper when your sisters, who were supposed to be keeping an eye on you, noticed you had stripped. They yelled at you to stop. Sure enough as soon as everyone was watching, you started to run butt-naked across the fields, laughing. I was fishing one last time before the lake froze for the winter, and had a bird's-eye view of your devilish behavior. You were hysterical with laughter. Your sisters gave chase and you ducked down, hiding in the long green grass. You burrowed under the fallen leaves, waiting for your sisters. You popped up with splayed fingers in front of your face and roared like a lion. Quickly, you ducked back down and covered your eyes with your tiny hands, thinking no one could see you. Your sisters hid in the grass around you and when you jumped up you couldn't see them, so when they sprang up from the tall grass you fell over backwards in fright. You started crying and they were laughing; you slowly stopped crying and started laughing a little too. Your big sister scooped you up in her arms and carried you back to the rug."

Sophia couldn't help visualizing the images even though she had no memory of that day, but he had told her the story so many times, it was easy to see it in her mind's eye. She suddenly realized she had lost track of time listening to the tale as well as her sense of direction, it seemed. She searched back along the tunnels in her mind and waited. The young hooligans were lost and had given up their pursuit.

"We should go back now," Joe said.

"No," Father McDonald said, "we have to keep going."

"We can't, we don't know where we are going." Joe's voice was filled with panic. "We'll end up dying down here."

"I had a dream, a terrible dream," said Father McDonald.

Sophia looked at both men and wondered why adults freaked out so much. "We have to keep walking and you are to guide us, Joe," she said.

"This is suicide," he replied.

Sophia watched Father McDonald walk up close to Joe. She tried to peek inside Father McDonald's mind, inside his unique room, to quickly search in his grand old library amongst the polished shelves for the dream he had mentioned. But it was locked and she could only see a hardwood door with a shiny new lock. She felt suddenly ashamed and pulled out, but not soon enough. He turned towards her as if sensing what she was doing. He frowned with disapproval; she looked away, avoiding eye contact, but sensed he was also pleased that she was still practicing using her gifts. She looked back, watching the two men and wondered if she should have a peek inside Joe's head. She pushed the thought away as quickly as it had come. She trusted Father McDonald, and even though he seemed to have aged terribly, he was strong mentally and spiritually. He showed little fear and there was no doubt in his eyes. She had followed him this far and he had protected her.

"We should turn off our torches, save the batteries," she said. "That will give us a few days with light so we don't end up in total darkness all the time."

Joe looked at her and back at Father McDonald. "A few days?"

"No doubt," she said. He was such a big cuddly bear she just wanted to wrap her arms around him.

"Oh God, what have I gotten myself into?" He looked up at the dark blank roof of the cave and back at her. "You're special, I'll give you that, but hen, you're mighty cheeky." Sophia watched him turn to Father McDonald to say, "If death wasn't walking the streets, I wouldn't stay, I have to tell you, I would hightail it out of here. We're not prepared for a hike through these caves."

"We're prepared enough, the best we could ever be," Father McDonald said.

Sophia fumbled with her torch and Joe caught her smile before she found the off button. "We love you, Joe," she said.

"Remind me never to play cards with you," he replied.

They had to take a minute for their eyes to adjust to the light of one torch; darkness suddenly seemed a little closer.

"How am I supposed to know which way to go? Shit!"

Sophia couldn't see much and stayed close to Father McDonald. They continued walking, the air cooling the deeper into the tunnels they went, turning down different passageways. It seemed hours had passed when Father McDonald stopped reciting from the scriptures and suggested they take a rest. They crouched by the wall shining the torch at the roof and shared protein bars and some water. Joe kept checking his watch, afraid he would lose track of time.

"It's still daylight," Joe said, aiming the torch at his watch, "but down here I suppose it doesn't matter. I wonder what the stars would be like tonight. I can just imagine them now."

Sophia watched him tilt his head up as if he had a sweeping view of the sky. This was their second day travelling south-east through the musty caverns. They were exhausted and covered in sweat. The rations Joe had brought were ample: the protein bars were chocolate, mint, cherry and orange flavors, but they were now running out of water.

Sophia was wondering how they were going to get to Israel. She wondered about Kevin and Jade and how they were going to meet. Sophia didn't have the answers; no pictures flashed across her mind, except for images of flames and everything burning; a wall of scorching heat. She closed her eyes and started to fall into a dreamless sleep when she unexpectedly jolted awake as a chill raced up her spine and instantly she was worried for Casey.

19

DOORMAN FOR DEATH: SHAUN. AUSTRALIA

Shaun sat on the roof, dangling his legs over the gutter, and watched the flashing police lights leave Kevin's place, only to stop in the next street. It had been days since he had seen the two retards disappear into thin air. He had waited for them to reappear after those other jerks had killed that poor German Shepherd dog. He was surprised to find he had slept through the night in the bush and had missed any reappearance of Kevin and Tim. His cheek had been throbbing so he had left his hiding spot and headed home for the comfort of his own bed and a couple of painkillers. He wasn't anxious about them; they were complete losers, but he couldn't help being curious. He was surprised to see them a little while ago walking down the middle of the street with the barefoot girl. Where had they been and who was she? Mostly he wondered, *Why do I care?* People were just disappearing, and he wished his dad would disappear. He could hear him inside the house and could smell his cigarette smoke.

"Shaun, is that you up there? Come here, I want to show you something."

Shaun looked over the side, thinking about climbing down and hightailing it out of there, but he didn't feel like wandering the streets tonight, or riding the trains. He looked over his shoulder at the solid

249

mass of cloud boiling up over the horizon; it moved like a flock of birds rising up from the ocean and migrating towards the city. He climbed down off the roof back through the attic. His dad was standing at the bottom of the stairs holding an old photo album.

"Have you seen this picture of your mother? She's just your age."

Shaun cautiously went down the stairs looking for a hidden agenda. His dad was drunk as usual, but his words weren't as slurred. "No, I haven't," he said.

"Well, come on, boy, why you walking so slow? Take a look." He sat on the bottom step and moved across for his son to sit beside him. "Look how happy she is."

Shaun was afraid to move and he worried about his choice of words, in case they were taken the wrong way. He scratched his groin and rubbed his eyes. "She looks pleased." She was at the beach and had star-jumped off a grassy embankment; she was in mid-air, her toes pointing down towards the white sand.

"This was the first time we met," his dad said. "I was on holidays from university, and had just got back from an archaeology field trip to Peru. The last thing I wanted to see was more sand. My friend dragged me along saying it would be good for me. He was right. I met your mother, and she was the best thing in my life. I took the photo on an old instant camera, and we shook it to help it dry. I told her about Peru and she said she wanted to see the Nazca Lines." He turned the picture over and written in her handwriting was her name and phone number, with a smiley face drawn inside a flower. "I called her that very night."

His dad flicked through the album, stopping occasionally. Shaun was thinking his dad had forgotten that he was there beside him. They both looked down at his mother's ruby complexion; she was exaggerating her baby bump and laughing. His father had stopped talking. Emotions had got the better of them both. Shaun used his shoulder to casually wipe his eye, stretching, pretending he was tired. His dad slammed the album closed, and rubbed his chin before picking up the bottle by his feet and taking a long drink. He rocked a little on his heels and walked away.

Shaun sat on the step, contemplating his options. He could go to his room and lock the door before his dad started turning from a sad drunk to a violent drunk, although a locked door hadn't stopped him in the past. He moved the pouch in his pocket and could feel the different shapes of the stones digging into his thigh. He stood and put his hand in his pocket, felt the stones, and decided to go out. He had a shower and went into his room to dress in jeans and t-shirt and grabbed a lightweight hoodie. He went back into the bathroom to fish the pouch of touchstones from his dirty pants. His dad was still in the lounge room, sitting in his mother's recliner. During her last few days at home she had slept sitting up in it, because she had been unable to lie down comfortably. It was looking old and tattered, but his dad wouldn't give it up. He never washed it and believed it still smelt like her. But it didn't; it smelt of smoke and alcohol. His dad's wallet was sitting on the side table next to an empty bottle.

"You want another drink?"

His dad lifted his finger and wagged it knowingly, slowly nodding his approval. Shaun picked up the empty bottle and with a little sleight of hand scooped up the wallet. He threw the empty bottle into the trash and plucked the plastic cards from the wallet. He chose a bottle of wine from the rack, then skillfully put the bottle and wallet back on the side table and pocketed the cigarettes.

"Get a glass and I'll give you a drop."

"No, I'm good."

"You think? Too good to drink with your old man? I doubt that. Ever since you were conceived, death follows you. You're nothing but a doorman for death. You could start a euthanasia business, you wouldn't have any costs, but you're so ignorant you probably don't even know what the word means. I've heard you screaming out your little girlfriend's name at night. *Rachel, Rachel.* I should have left you there to be buried in the explosion with her."

It all came back and hit him like a giant wave. He was looking over the back seat of the Jeep, they were moving away from the caves and the mountains heading towards the Judean Desert. She stood in front of the cave as the charges his dad had laid exploded behind her.

Rachel, he thought, Rachel. He couldn't feel his legs, he couldn't feel his body; his mind assaulted him with forgotten images. The drugged flight, his mother lying in hospital not getting any better like his dad had promised. He remembered whispering in her ear, telling her what his dad had done, and when she was an angel she had to look after Rachel. Shaun wanted to explode with anger, he wanted to cry, he wanted to run, but he was stuck with his father's smirking face.

"Don't tell me you had forgotten about your little girlfriend? You're useless. You can't be my son. You don't have an ounce of my brains or balls."

Shaun's fists clenched, then opened and closed again. He screamed like a wounded animal. "You're a murderer; you're not my father. You're a failure. Mom must be in hell. Fuck you, you son of a bitch. Even in heaven she would be in pain, seeing what you have become. I told her what you did. She never would have stayed with you, never." The bottle of wine beside his dad came hurtling towards him. Shaun ducked; it smashed into the wall and the LED screen.

"You're pathetic. Who the hell do you see every time you look in the mirror? Piss off, retard," his dad said.

Overwhelmed by his memories, Shaun didn't have to be told twice. He took off, slamming the front door behind him. He went to the nearest auto-teller machine, swiped his dad's card, punched in the PIN, withdrew five hundred dollars cash and headed for the train station. He couldn't get the images out of his mind. Feelings he didn't even know existed were coursing through his veins. He stepped onto the platform where a cold, sharp southerly wind blew.

Shaun felt a little spooked. The platform was deserted and vomit had dried and crusted on the only seat. There was one train scheduled to arrive in seven minutes. He walked to the end of the platform and leant his back against the brick wall. He felt for the cigarettes in his top pocket, pulled out the lighter and tapped out a smoke. He worked the lighter, then stared at the flame. The veins in his neck bulged as he screamed into the night. He slid down the wall and cried for the first time since his mother died. He thought he heard someone walking along the platform, so he wiped his eyes, spat in front of him and turned to look but there was no one else around. He lit his smoke, inhaled deeply and coughed up his guts. As soon as he stopped, he inhaled again. He drew on the cigarette as if he was drawing in the breath of life. He looked down at his hands, thinking that they were dirty; with the smoke dangling from his lips, he started rubbing them against his pants. He tossed the cigarette butt, and watched the red tip glow upon the tracks. The arriving train lights could be seen approaching the station. Shaun kept looking at the butt, wondering if he had time to jump, jump down and stamp on it, time — but it didn't matter really if he had time. It would be quick like the explosion, quick like it was for Rachel. He stepped forward over the yellow security line, everything was in slow motion. The train hurried forward sucking him towards it; the train slowed, losing its hold. It came to a complete stop. The doors opened right in front of him.

No one was in the annex stepping off so he stepped aboard, grabbing hold of the cold metal pole. It was covered with smudged handprints and gum, and he recoiled in disgust. He screwed up his nose and eyes and held his breath. A bum was camped out on the lower deck, and the stale air and the aroma of fresh urine assaulted his senses. Whoosh. The automatic doors sealed behind him. The train screeched, labored, then jerked twice as it pulled away from the station. The train rocked, picking up speed and he maneuvered towards the connecting carriage door. He couldn't believe his karma. His dad was pulling him way down, emotionally he was beginning to unravel, and when he wrenched at the connecting door lever, he found the door was locked. He let his head drop and bang hard against the window. He pushed off the door and walked through the top carriage to the other side, and this time the door was unlocked.

A nervous, fat greasy-looking man, wearing a suit with runners, clutched a briefcase in his lap. He was watching Shaun's every movement through the reflection in the window. *At least he doesn't smell, and it's better than being alone.* Shaun ignored him, walked to the back of the carriage and stretched his legs up onto the seat. He pulled his hoodie over his eyes, folded his arms across his chest and slouched down. He drifted into a restless sleep, dreaming of flying demonic angels and fire. He felt a soft whisper behind him and woke in a sweat. The train had jerked him awake as it stopped and started at a station. He read the station's name off a bench; he was a few stops away from the city. He wiped the sweat off his face with his sleeve, and closed his eyes.

The sound of the rushing wind alerted Shaun to the fact someone had just come through the connecting doors. He kept low, his eyes closed, listening to a group of teenagers walking in the lower carriage. There was a loud bang. It sounded like something or someone hitting at the windows. The noise stopped. Shaun looked up and could see the fat guy in his seat up ahead and that his shoulders and head were shaking. He then heard the first footfall on the steps leading up to the top level. The train came to the next station, the signs and building flashing past. The train didn't stop. There were three hooded guys coming up the stairs and one was banging a metal baseball bat on the rail.

"Well, looky here," the guy with the bat said, pointing it at the fat man.

Shaun kept low, knowing what these guys were capable of doing. Their tormenting and teasing had begun. The big guy was scared out of his mind. They pulled his briefcase off his lap, rummaged through the contents and tossed it about the train. Shaun heard them slap the guy on the side of his head. Yelled at him to cough up and dig into his back pocket, and hand over his wallet. Shaun had treated others the same. He knew the fat guy would be pissing himself in shock. He moved slowly, fearfully, and then the guy with the bat laid it down onto the man's shaking shoulder. He gripped the bat with both hands and yelled, "Home run!" The window became painted abstract red. Shaun kept low, avoiding being seen; he rolled off the seat and onto the floor, listening.

The assailants pulled off the guy's watch and Nikes. They dug into his pockets, pulling out his phone. Shaun kept as quiet as possible. The gang started to turn, leaving the way they had come. Shaun panicked as his mobile start to vibrate.

The train was pulling into Kings Cross station. Shaun was ready to leap out of hiding and throw himself down the stairs and out the door. He could see their feet heading towards him. His phone had stopped. They kept coming. They were talking amongst themselves.

"Try him again," one of them said.

Everything seemed to be muffled and in slow motion. Shaun held his breath; they had stopped halfway down the stairs and the last guy was swinging on the rails inches away from Shaun's head. The train jerked to a stop and they jumped down and off, onto the platform. He still couldn't see them, but he waited till the last minute before jumping up and off the train. He pulled his hood up, dug his hands into his pocket and headed in what he thought was the opposite direction. He hid amongst the few people waiting to get on the train when he thought he heard his name being called. He ignored it and kept walking, picking up his pace. He didn't understand what had gotten into him and why he was afraid of his own shadow. The world had become crazier than he was. His phone started to vibrate; he pulled it out of his pocket to see it was his mate Kyle. "Where the fuck have you been?" he said into the phone.

"Where you at, man?" Kyle said.

"Just got into the city."

"Same, dude."

"Stop shouting into the phone, you asshole." Then Shaun realized he could hear his name being called from somewhere behind him. The three hooded silhouettes were coming towards him; the guys from the train. One had his hands dug into his pockets. *This is it,* Shaun thought, *some dude coming for revenge.* As he watched, the guy removed his hand from his pocket and he saw the shape of a gun.

"Look what we found." It was his mate, Kyle, shouting and waving the gun above his head.

Commuters kept their heads down, getting on the train and out of sight. Shaun looked at his phone and pushed "end". His friends looked and acted differently from usual. They were more violent than he could remember, and it had only been a week at most. Or had he become weak.

"Hey, mate, where have you been?" Kyle said.

"Around. Had an awesome fist-fight in the city last week, had to spend a few hours in hospital. The other dude was pretty fucked. You should have been there, man."

"Yeah, what you score?"

Shaun reached into his pocket and pulled out the wad of money he had taken out of his dad's account and waved it in the air.

"Alright, Let's party," Kyle said.

"Who's that?" Shaun asked, nodding towards the third guy.

"That's Homer."

Shaun didn't recognize the guy at first. He wasn't wearing his school baseball jacket, which he practically wore everywhere as a status symbol. *He's the state's star baseball player, headed for the big league in the US. Shit, he's even dating the retard's sister.*

Kyle chattered on. "He's got the virus and has come over to the dark side, and I think he likes it. He has one hell of a swing, man, and has found swinging at things other than balls to be more fun." As if on cue, Homer picked up the bat and swung at the ticket booth and started to beat the shit out of it. Kyle and his offsider started cheering him on and laughing as he became more enraged with each swing. Shaun started walking.

"Hey, wait up," Kyle yelled.

They followed Shaun like a pack of wild pit bull dogs, attacking and frightening people randomly.

The flashing neon lights of the city looked different, they no longer seemed real to Shaun. The menacing and minor crimes — like smashing some geek's headlights so he can't drive home, or getting drunk and picking fights, the things he generally saw and liked to do — were somehow different: there was no order to the crime he was seeing. There were guys smoking ice on the street and the little discretion prostitutes may have had was gone. There was a sense of something forbidding. Shaun felt sick. The image of a burning lion deep within a cave haunted him, waiting to drag him to hell. Relieved, Shaun saw there was no bouncer on the door of Frankie's Laboratory and they walked straight into the bar. Fluorescent lights strobed the wall and the DJ was kicking ass. The waitresses came over with a tray of syringes and injected shots of mixed alcohol into their open mouths.

Shaun's head soon started to spin and he needed fresh air, so he got up and went outside, with Kyle and the others following him. *Why do they keep following?* he wondered, and accidentally bumped into a hooker. He stepped back, nearly apologizing, but blurted out, "What the fuck! Move your skanky ass."

Kyle walked up to the woman and stuck his face into her breast and asked how much for her to get on her knees. "Pay the lady," he said to Shaun, not waiting for her to reply.

Shaun didn't recognize these guys. They've become hard-core. They're not just a bunch of idiot teenagers any more. I need to get home.

"Yeah, great idea, Kyle. What about you two?" Shaun said. "Are up for a blow job? My shout."

"Shit, yeah," Homer said.

Shaun pulled out a couple of hundred and stuffed it between her breasts. She led them into the alley and Shaun lit a smoke.

"You're not coming," Kyle said.

"I'll join in after I have this smoke." Shaun dragged on his cigarette and waited till they were deep in the shadows. He turned the corner and walked away. He threw his butt into the gutter and crossed the road, slipped into an alley on the other side and waited. A pack of drunken girls walked past him and he pushed himself into the wall. They were tormenting an old guy who had become too friendly. They pushed him to the ground and started kicking him while people just walked on by. The virus had taken over the city. Shaun realized he had created enough negativity to fester in his aura to be able to hide in the darkness. He saw his mates come out of the shadows, looking up and down the road. They were crossing the road, heading in his direction.

They stopped to watch the girls beating the guy. Amused, Kyle said, "Let me help you, ladies," and pulled out the gun. He had a crazed look on his face and his eyes were blacker than the night. Kyle lowered the gun into the old man's face. The man held up his hands, begging for his life. Kyle fired. The girls cheered and welcomed him and his mate into their fold. They walked off, slinking into the nearest bar together.

Shaun waited for the prostitute who had given his mates a blow job to come out of the shadows, but she never did. He started to make his way back to the station, then a loud explosion lit up the streets. People ran towards the sound, excited. He kept moving through the back streets, keeping just inside the shadows. A fire truck pulled up in front of a burning skyscraper and Shaun couldn't help being entranced by the flames. People started pushing the firemen out of the way, wanting the building to burn. The spectators soon became violent, yanking the hoses from them. One police car showed up. The officers had no chance of getting out of the vehicle, because the crowd descended upon them and began rocking the car, flipping it onto its back. Then someone hurled a petrol bomb. The firefighters hosed the people away from the police vehicle and dragged the cops to safety. The crowd booed. Windows on the upper levels of the skyscraper exploded, and people were drawn to look up and cheer as shards of glass pelted down. Shaun saw that the police and firemen were searching for a place to hide and were heading in his direction. Stepping backwards down the laneway, watching the chaos, he managed to trip over his own feet. *Stuff this,* he thought, and started running to the train station.

There was one train waiting at the platform, so he ran at the security wire cyclone fence, jumped up, climbed over it, and bolted to the train. The carriage he entered was empty. He stared through the window as the train pulled out of the station. Red and orange flames licked the walls of the tall buildings. Shaun's thirst for fire had been quenched, perhaps gone forever. In that moment, watching the city burn, he felt no desire, he felt lost. The city that held happy memories of his mother was burning.

~

THE WINE WAS dripping down the wall when he realized Shaun had stolen his cigarettes. He slowly pushed himself out of the recliner and went into the kitchen for another pack and another bottle of wine. Before plugging in the old fan, he used his shirt to wipe away the red wine from around the socket. He liked the feeling of the breeze on his skin as he dropped back into the recliner. He uncorked the bottle of wine, took a long drink, then opened the packet of smokes. He cupped his hands around the lighter's flame, protecting it from the fan, and dragged deeply on the cigarette before sitting back and slowly blowing out the smoke. His wrist dropped onto the armrest, the cigarette dangling between his fingers, as he smiled at the wedding picture hanging on the wall behind the fan: his beautiful wife, her beautiful smile. He closed his eyes, capturing the image. The smoke continued to burn and slipped from his fingers, falling as he was sinking into a deep sleep.

The old fan shuddered back and forth over the smoldering cigarette and his slumbering body. The wine trailed down from behind the picture and over the edge of the power point into the sockets. A blue spark flared and ran up the cable into the fan's motor. It ignited into flames which instantly enveloped the nylon curtains.

JADE AND KEVIN were in the warm kitchen, gazing every few seconds through the thick glass door at their pizza. Callie, having put Alex to bed, walked in behind his dad.

"I think you have some explaining to do," she said.

Kevin felt like a trapped mouse not knowing which way to turn. He looked at Jade and recalled what she had said. *She's just going to ask you where and how you found me.* "About what?" he said, trying to act in control in front of Jade.

"Really, you're going to play that game. About what? You're kidding, right? You have been gone for three days, not three hours. That's seventy-two hours, Kevin! And you come home with a young kidnapped girl who lives on the other side of the world. And you have the audacity, to say *about what*?"

Kevin's face grew hotter with each word she spoke. He looked at his dad and he looked just as angry as she was. He hoped his voice wouldn't quiver as he answered. "Tim ... Tim and I were down at the river. We found her lying there, in the bush. She looked like she was dead. We went over to see if she was, and she opened her eyes. We helped her up, then a rabid-looking dog tried to attack us, and we ran. I told Jade you guys would help her get home. I didn't know who she was or where she was from."

"Where was Shaun?" his dad asked.

"This was after we left his place," Kevin said.

"Come on, I want you to show us," his mom said.

"Let them eat first, Cal."

"Make it quick."

"What's the rush, Cal? They can show us in the morning. We won't see much in the dark anyway."

She picked up the phone, ignoring him. Kevin tried to listen to his mom on the phone while he pulled the pizzas out of the oven, but he couldn't catch what she was saying. They ate the hot pizza straight off the tray. They only had time to eat four pieces before there was a knock at the door. Kevin jumped up, but his mother blocked him and walked to the door herself. "You finish up," she said, and opened the door. "Thanks for coming back."

Kevin thought it was the cops and he didn't want to lie to the cops. *They're going to see straight through me.* "He's in the kitchen," she said.

He wiped his mouth with the back of his hands and then slid his hands down his pants into his pockets. His shoulders slumped and relaxed as Tim walked in with his mom and sister.

"What gives, K?" Tim said, taking a slice of his pizza.

"Don't know."

"Yes, you do, you always do."

"Shh, not now," Kevin said.

"Molly and Alex are upstairs sleeping. Alex is on the recliner in Molly's room. Kath and Jade can sleep in Alex's room across from

Kevin's. Molly's generally a good sleeper, although lately she has been a bit restless. You will just have to check on Alex once or twice."

Kevin watched his mom give instructions to Tim's mom and when she took a breath his dad dared to interrupt.

"The kids will be fine. They're sound asleep."

She glanced at his dad and continued speaking to Tim's mom. "Did Kath bring some clothes for Jade? And the boys can sleep in Kevin's room when we get back and you should take the guest room." Callie looked at Kevin. "Put your shoes on."

Tim followed. "Where are we going?"

"She wants to see where we found Jade."

"She knows."

"All she knows is we found her in the bush. We thought she was dead, and we helped her up and brought her here."

KEVIN WAITED FOR his dad to get the car out of the garage. The night was thick with smoke and he could see a glow over the city. His mom jumped in the front seat with a large dolphin torch while Tim and Jade climbed in the back with him.

Kevin took them the long way round. They weren't going to be able to drive through the vacant lot to the other side. Daniel put the lights on high beam as they came to a trail leading into the bush. They saw a dead dog lying by the road.

"Was that the dog you were talking about?" his mother asked.

"I don't know. It's hard to tell." He didn't want to look at the poor dog and it seemed everyone else felt the same, except his mom. She pulled a pair of latex gloves out of the glove compartment and jumped out of the truck to examine the carcass.

"Bullet," she said to Daniel.

They all got out of the car and circled the dog.

"Which way? Kevin, Tim, which way?" Callie asked.

Kevin saw the determination in her face and started to sense her urgency. Her guard was coming down and she was afraid, looking for something. She was desperate, hoping to find it, but outwardly showed a mask of authority. Kevin was starting to sense her true feelings and she threw a look at him, as if she felt him rummaging around inside her emotions.

He looked down and said, "This way." They came to the anthill. "We would normally have to run together over it," he said and looked at Tim. Tim looked like he was having the time of his life; just another big adventure. Jade was quiet and hanging back, but he kept an eye on her. The river was close and they could hear movements in the bush, the nocturnal animals returning to the area. "Over there, on the other side of the river," Kevin said, and watched his mom sweep the area with her torch. Fish darted away from the light.

"Are there any buildings around here?" she asked.

"No, not that I know of," Kevin said.

Daniel agreed with Kevin. "There was an old shed over the other side that gave access for the submarine cables. But it's derelict and it wouldn't be standing after the fire last week."

Kevin looked at his mother. She was thinking and searching the other side as far as the light from the torch would travel. She hoped to find something, something she had lost, something that was very important, but Kevin couldn't see anything. What could she have lost down here? Her face turned down in disappointment that she hadn't found what she was looking for.

Kevin saw her pain and said, "We can come back tomorrow and have a better look. I can show you how to get over the other side without having to swim across." She looked at him and for the first time since his grandparents died he felt a connection with her.

"Sounds like a good idea," Daniel said.

"Hang on. We can wade across now the crocs are sleeping," Tim said.

"What planet are you from?" Daniel asked. "There are no crocs here. He is just trying to scare you," he said to Jade. Daniel gave Tim a gentle brush up the back of his head.

"I suppose you're right," Callie said.

THE TRAIN PULLED into the deserted station. While it was still moving Shaun jumped off and started running home. Passing Kevin's house, he slowed to a jog; the garage door was open and he could see Kevin's bike propped up against the far wall, next to a jerrycan. He stood, thinking of knocking on the door to ask permission to borrow the bike. *Maybe they will let me.* He turned away, walked to the end of the street and turned the corner. For the second time in his life Shaun was immobilized with fear: his house, his home, was burning. He snapped himself out of it and as he started running, the front windows exploded. He ignored the heat, dug into his pocket and grabbed his key. The door was swollen and, no matter how much he tried, it wouldn't open.

Shaun rushed around the back of the house trying to find a way in, calling out to his dad. Shaun searched the backyard hoping his dad had stumbled out the back door. He screamed, "*Dad! Dad!*" ... no one came. Not a neighbor stirred. He was alone and screaming at the top of his lungs for help. He tripped, got back up and ran towards the drainpipe and started climbing. It was hot and he could smell his skin burning. He kept climbing.

KEVIN HEADED BACK to his dad's Dodge following the glow of torch-light as they swept across the dirt path. Hoisting himself up into the car he heard a cry for help. It sounded as if it was a street away on the other side of the vacant lot. It would take ten minutes to drive around. Daniel started running; Kevin jumped down and chased after him, with Tim following close on his heels.

"House fire," Daniel yelled to the boys.

Daniel, Kevin and Tim entered the street and could see flames over the top of the houses. Kevin knew the fire wasn't too far away, just around the next corner. They entered the next street and saw Shaun's house engulfed with flames.

Kevin saw Shaun in pain, rushing up the pipe, trying to avoid the flames.

"Get down," Daniel yelled. "Kevin, get the hose and aim it at Shaun and the pipe."

Shaun kept climbing; Daniel ran up to the house and wrapped his shirt around his hands and started to climb after him.

SHAUN SUDDENLY FELT someone hit his leg from behind, gripping his calf muscle and pulling him down. He hoped it was his dad. He looked down and saw Kevin's dad. Shaun's hands slipped and he found himself falling. It wasn't a long fall, but it seemed to Shaun to go on forever; he started to think of how many times he had fallen off the roof over the years. His back hit the ground and he couldn't catch his breath. He let himself drift, hoping he was dead, then he could see his mom and Rachel and tell them how sorry he was that he couldn't save either of them.

He passed out.

THEY COULDN'T HEAR any emergency vehicles. *Nobody was coming,* Kevin thought. He held the hose pointed at the house, feeling uneasy, his skin crawling. The air was getting thicker and he could feel mosquitoes biting at his neck. Even in the face of so much smoke they were determined to attack. "What are we going to do, Dad?" Kevin said, slapping at the bugs on his neck. "Shaun's dad must be in there."

"Something is terribly wrong, K. Look at that glow on the horizon. It's the city burning."

"Dad, we have to leave."

"I'm with you, K."

His mom pulled up, yanking on the handbrake, the Dodge screeching to a stop. She leapt from the truck with the first-aid bag,

Jade close on her heels. They both went to Shaun. Jade watched him and Tim hose down the house using the neighbor's hose.

She looked around the street and he could see her noticing the empty houses, where no lights flickered and no curtains were drawn back.

"Where is everyone?" she said.

Shaun started to come around, trying to sit up, mumbling as Callie nursed his burnt hands.

"Shh, just relax. You're safe now," she said.

Shaun collapsed back onto the ground while Callie finished wrapping cold wet bandages around his burnt hands.

"You right to walk?" Callie asked.

"Sure. What about my dad?"

Nobody said anything.

"He's probably at the pub," Shaun said to them.

Callie and Jade helped him into the back of the Dodge.

"You're probably concussed," Jade said, putting on his seat belt for him. The boys jumped into the open back tray.

Daniel drove home. No one spoke as they pulled into the garage. Kevin stayed seated in the back watching the lowering of the electronic garage door locking out the world.

20

ECHOES OF THE DEAD: CASEY. ENGLAND

"I'm going to make that rat's hole a hell of a lot bigger." Terry stood, dusting off the dirt, then picked up the mallet. Casey still lay on his belly, waving the torch through the opening. "You might want to move?" Terry suggested.

"What?" Casey turned and looked at Terry with the mallet, and sprang to his feet.

Terry swung, smashing the stone wall of the basement. It buckled. He swung again, a few stones dislodging and dropping to the ground. He cleared an opening wide enough for them to explore what was beyond the basement.

Casey ran upstairs for a second torch while Terry peered into the space beyond the wall. Running back down the stairs he nearly tripped on the last step, but managed to save himself from falling. They stepped through the hole into a chamber with two tunnels. Water was dripping down the wall rhythmically, pooling near their feet. Flickering, like fireflies, darted at the edge of the torch beams. They both shivered. In the corners, beyond the light, Casey caught a glimpse of a sudden movement. Terry turned to Casey knowing they had both sensed something, but neither knew what to say or do and chose to follow the beams of light.

Terry started off towards the tunnels, with Casey reluctantly following. Walking backwards to point the torch at the entrance Terry had made, he swept the light across the wall: *rats, just rats*. He turned, bumping into Terry.

"Where do you think this goes?" Terry said, stopping at the mouth to one of the two tunnels.

"Have no idea." Up on the wall near Terry's head, Casey saw an old hook with a bucket and a wooden baton fixed on the wall next to it. "What's that?"

"It's probably for tar. You'd dip the baton, then hit two pieces of flint together and ... let there be light."

"You missed your calling, you know that, don't you," Casey said. "Can we try it?"

"I don't think it would work," Terry said.

The light penetrated further into the tunnel, startling the rats out of the darkness. They rushed over and around Casey's feet. Terry jumped back, knocking into Casey and they both nearly fell on top of the rats.

Casey said with a slight smirk, "Just rats, Terry, just rats."

Terry held onto Casey's arms, acting as if he was helping him. "You right, pal?"

Casey decided to go along with him. "Yeah. A bit freaked, you?"

"I wasn't expecting them, that's all," Terry said, hiking up his pants.

The walls were cold and wet and getting narrower. The sound of bones crunching under their feet was like seashells. "Terry, we should go back."

"Just a little further. I felt a breeze, this has to lead to somewhere," Terry said.

Casey touched the cave wall, his fingertips slipping into tiny indents that made the wall look like a giant sea sponge. Something splashed on him from above and he flipped his torch quickly upward. Within a split second his imagination took over and he saw saliva dripping from the fangs of a rabid bat, but the light revealed nothing more than an empty cavity. He could see Terry was getting ahead of him. He moved quickly to catch up. The tunnel widened into another chamber with more passages branching off.

Terry had stopped and was nervously scanning the walls. Shining the light as far down the tunnels as possible, while trying to hide his own apprehension, he said, "This is just going to keep going."

A stale smell, a metallic taste, sat heavy in Casey's mouth and irritated his nose. The sound of the dripping from the passageway became louder in his mind. There were pieces of wood and a jug protruding up from the ground.

"Alright," Terry said, looking over his shoulder. "I think you're right. I think for now this is far enough. We'll probably get lost if we go any further."

"This is a little freaky," Casey said. "Do you think we're still on the property?"

"Na, don't believe so." Terry turned around, thinking, looking left and right, then back at the jug. "Look at this old thing. Maybe it's still full of rum. What do you think, matey?"

Terry picked up a piece of the wood and started digging around the jug. He picked it up and shook it — empty. Under the jug, a bone was half buried, and he pulled and wiggled it until it came free.

"That doesn't look like a rat's bone to me," Casey said.

"Maybe it's not, maybe it's human," Terry said jokingly. He handed the bone to Casey. Casey looked at it; he didn't want Terry to think he was scared, because he wasn't treating him like a kid any more most of the time. But Casey hesitated, pushing his long curls up off his brow and out of his eyes. He rubbed his hands on his shirt. He knew he shouldn't doubt his feelings, but he wanted to go along with Terry, who was trying to be playful, a big kid.

Arm extended, ready to grab the bone, Casey dropped his arm to his side. "You know, on second thoughts, I'll pass. We should go back and check on Amy," he said, scratching his ear.

"Go on, it won't bite," Terry said, shoving it forward. "Take it."

"It could be diseased, or something," Casey said.

"What are you afraid of?" Terry playfully thrust it forward like a sword. Casey quickly sucked in his stomach, hoping it wouldn't touch him. Terry continued his banter, pushing it into the boy's chest. Casey seized the bone with both hands, trying to push it away, his body was instantly paralyzed and pain raced up his arm, into his shoulder. The sound of a young woman screaming filled his head, along with the image of her arm being ripped out of its socket. Casey's stomach exploded with pain, as she was kicked. The pressure on his lower back was horrific. He tried to move, heat crawled up his spine and he felt like his insides were going to drop to the floor.

Casey could barely hear or see Terry yelling at him to let go. He couldn't feel him wrestling with the bone, prying at his fingers, one by one until he let go. At that moment, Casey's body folded, dropped to the ground, and he grabbed his stomach and curled into a ball, crying.

Terry threw the bone away and it cracked as it hit the wall. "What the hell?"

He crouched down beside Casey and held him in his arms. Casey could hear him whispering like he had the first day he had found him lying on the road, reassuring him he was safe. He could see Terry's alarm and confusion. Casey was scared and skittish as if someone was there waiting, waiting to deliver another blow to his abdomen. He held tight onto Terry, hiding in his aura, not wanting to let go.

The feeling of being inside the woman's body was dissipating. He had never been so aware of how his own body felt until he couldn't feel it. He was grateful it had stopped. He was petrified, nervous, violated, and afraid it would start again. He slowly sat up with the distinct taste of blood in his mouth.

He watched Terry's hand lift to his own face, rubbing his eyebrows, concerned. He was trying to comprehend what had happened.

Terry brought his hand back down and patted Casey gently on his back, and asked him if he was all right. "What happened pal?"

Casey's torch was lying on the ground, shining down the right-hand tunnel; he thought he saw something move. He turned away and looked at Terry. He didn't know what to tell him. *He probably thinks I'm crazy anyway. That's not fair, Terry's not like that, he has always been there for me. What the heck.* "It belonged to a young servant girl, the bone. Her arm was dislocated, ripped out of its socket. She was malnourished, her bones were frail. She was beaten and kicked to death because she was pregnant with her master's child." Casey watched Terry's jaw drop. He didn't blink but he shivered, and Casey could see his Adam's apple bobbing as he swallowed.

Terry looked back towards the bone, then back at Casey, and studied his face. "How, how do you know this?"

"I don't know. It has never happened like that before."

"What *has* happened before?"

"You know, how like, when we were getting supplies at the baby store and I told you not to open the storage door. You did and the wolves were — well, you know. And then like, the book I gave you."

"I thought you were just having a lend with the book, and I thought you must have heard something in the storage room that made you cautious. I don't know much about this sort of stuff. Sorry, pal, Amy will know what to say. Hang on, does that mean we are really having twins? Never mind, I don't want to know."

Casey could see Terry was confused, but he didn't see any look of sneering judgement that an adult has when they think a kid is lying. He could see the worry in his eyes, his teeth clenched, thinking hard. Terry hauled him to his feet and dusted him off and Casey felt the man's strength and his need to protect Casey. He had never known his father, but he imagined him to be just like Terry. If Terry could've carried him, without embarrassing Casey, he would have. Instead, he looked down at Casey's feet making sure they were both planted firmly on the ground.

"Let's get you out of here to die another day."

Casey had to smile. "You think you're funny, don't you?"

"Uh huh. You right to walk?"

"Yeah." He held Terry's gaze, then at the corner of his eye he saw movement coming from the left passage and his eyes opened wide.

"What?" Terry said.

Casey leant closer and whispered. Terry bent down to hear. "We're not alone."

"The servant girl?" Terry whispered.

"No, don't turn, let's just go."

Terry picked up Casey's torch and handed it to him. Scared, they both acted as casually as possible, walking back the way they had come, trying to be rational and not run. Ducking through the entrance, back into the basement, they quickly dragged the old trunks across the floor and stacked them against the opening. They moved at a fast pace and raced up the stairs to the kitchen, locking the door behind them.

AMY WAS SITTING IN the sunroom on a daybed. Even though the windows were boarded up, her head was tilted towards them, as if the sun was shining and warming her face. Sensing she was no longer alone, she opened her eyes. It took her a moment to focus and they stood silently. She looked to Casey like someone had just walked over her grave. Casey started to feel sick, bile rising into his throat. He felt himself go pale and gagged.

Amy jumped up. "Sit down," she said. She pulled him towards her and sat him down on the edge of the daybed.

His foot struck her book. He nearly tripped, accidentally kicking it open. "Sorry," he said as he continued to gag.

"Lean forward, put your elbows on your knees and your head in your hands, take slow breaths."

Casey did as she suggested. As he cast his eyes down they locked with the different letters of the open book. His mouth tasted of blood and he coughed violently, needing to spit. Amy passed him a tissue and he wiped his mouth, expecting it to be red with blood, so he was surprised when it wasn't.

"What happened to you guys, Terry?" She breathed out slowly as if she had been holding her breath. "Guys, someone has to let me in," she said.

Terry fetched two glasses of water, gave one to Casey and sat beside him. Amy was pacing the room. "What happened, what's wrong? Are both of you going to just sit there and say nothing? I know something's not right."

Terry sat back against the sofa to lift his head towards the ceiling and then dropped it down, stretching it and rubbing his neck. "You'd better sit down," he said. He then proceeded to describe the events as best he could, although it sounded strange. Casey spoke up to explain what he had experienced and Amy's faced was mapped with confusion. She stood and paced up and down the room trying to comprehend what Terry had said. "Casey! You had a vision of a young woman's *death* by touching a bone that was centuries old?"

She looks worried. Casey could see her thinking, while he sat quietly on the lounge studying her face wondering what she was going to do. Surely they weren't going to keep him around once the twins were born; he was too creepy. They were probably regretting adopting him, and once the world got back to normal they would almost certainly send him to boarding school. Out of the corner of his eye, Casey saw a mist of energy move from the shadows and float into the hallway and up the stairs. The floorboard at the top of the landing sighed under some phantom weight, and they all looked in that direction, waiting, but there was only silence. Different smells wafted into the room, some pleasant, some not so. Amy looked like she was trying to focus on something that was hovering just out of sight. When the wind stirred outside, the windows behind the boards began to rattle.

"It's a tornado!" Terry yelled.

"They don't have tornadoes here!" Amy yelled back. The sound got louder as if a thousand pebbles were being pelted against the house.

Casey and Terry were on their feet and Amy was coming towards them. Casey witnessed the room fill with apparitions. Making a run for it, Amy scooped up her book from near Casey's feet and a circle of light radiated from the book, concealing them. Amy, Terry and Casey disappeared, becoming ghosts. Huddled together in the gentle whirlwind they saw people forming silhouettes, then colorful auras, and clothing from different time periods, moving around as if they belonged. A young woman sat in the side chair across the room and a man opposite her was smoking a pipe, the smell of tobacco filling the room. They talked and laughed casually.

"That couple are from the photo in the basement," Amy whispered.

Some of the ghosts look confused and lost, Casey thought. An old man kept repeating his movements, taking a book off the shelf and putting it back, taking it off the shelf and putting it back. A woman in a long black maid's dress with a white cotton apron walked into the room, seized the doorknob and walked backwards and closed the door. The door flung open by itself. The maid again walked into the room, seized the door handle, and walked backwards out of the room to close it.

"Those ones are just memories," he said pointing to the bookcase. "The people that keep repeating themselves are emotional memories. There is no stream of consciousness," he said.

"How do you know that?" Amy said.

He spoke in a low voice so as not to attract attention. "It took me a while to work it out, but after the river and my mom I thought I was a complete basket case. Take the flight over, for instance. You felt sick, right?" He looked at Terry, desperate for him to understand. "What you felt was the emotional memory of the person in that seat on the flight before you. It was his fear, his emotional energy he left behind. Like an imprint of a sweaty palm on a bench, or footprints in the sand. You're sensitive, Terry; receptive to other people's feelings. See that one by the kitchen doorway, not moving; the one with a beard and a frown, well that one is a lost soul, and he thinks he's still alive."

The windows stopped rattling, the projectiles against the house had ceased, and the apparitions flickered in and out, like a lost signal, a fading hologram. "The thing I don't understand is why I haven't seen my mom." Suddenly the room seemed vast as the apparitions vacated the space and went back into their reality. Casey stepped forward and the surrounding light disappeared. He looked back at Terry and Amy, scanning for a hint of what they might be thinking.

"They're gone but ..." Terry said, "... it feels like they're still here."

"I feel it too," Amy said.

"That's because they are, we just can't see them any more. They're in between the two worlds, ours and beyond."

"What two worlds?" Terry asked, following Casey into the kitchen.

Casey went to the back door and called for the dog. She didn't come. He called again, she still didn't come. The ground was littered with insects and they were embedded in the door.

Terry knocked them off the door and brushed them back outside. Casey and Terry circled the property, checking the house for damage while calling for the dog.

"She probably sensed the storm and took off for shelter," Terry said. "She'll come back. Don't worry about the dog. She will be all right."

They stepped into the kitchen and Amy pulled her cardigan tight, as if a chill had passed over her body. "Close the door, Casey. We can't go anywhere, we have to stay here."

The thought of staying was terrifying to Casey, but the idea of leaving was worse. There was no hiding.

"Who's hungry?" Terry said.

Casey watched Terry rub his hands together and pull out pots and pans. Cooking was Terry's way of dealing with stress. The conversation about what had happened and what they saw was over. To be fair, they were handling it better than any adult he could think of. But he still didn't know what they thought about him being able to see beyond this world. He wanted to show them what else he could do. How he controlled the flow of energy, whether it was the lights, Amy's hairdryer, the stove or the car.

Amy stood next to the old wood-burning fireplace and watched Terry get the gas stove going. She moved towards him and held his arms softly, and turned off the gas. "I couldn't think of eating now. I can't believe what I just saw. We have to talk and Casey —"

She sat at the old wooden kitchen table and studied her fingers and nails. Terry hadn't moved. She turned to Casey. "What else do you see?" she asked him. "Do we survive this?"

Casey saw her eyes glaze over. "Amy, you're scaring me." He had never seen her look vacant, but Terry had and was scared too. Terry sat beside Amy to slowly rub her back. Casey leant against the sink and crossed his arms.

With tenderness, Terry said to Amy, "Look at me. Look at me, Amy."

She didn't take her eyes off Casey and said, in a robotic tone, "I know you can see things, Casey, and I want you to talk to me, I do. I want to help you make sense of what is happening to you. But the truth is, I don't really understand. It is so overwhelming, I don't know how to help you."

Casey had never seen Amy as anything but a tower of strength. He searched within himself for the right words to lift her from this dark place she inhabited. She moved slowly, like she was caught in mud, and it was encasing her. What could he say? He opened his mouth and let the first thing come out. "People have died and people are going to die. Maybe we all die tomorrow, I don't know. What I know is my friend Sophia is real and she is coming. Whatever happens, it will be the right thing."

Amy tumbled into the black hole. She said condescendingly, with a slight tilt of her head, "Your friend Sophia is a figment of your imagination. You conjured her up after your mother died so you wouldn't be alone. I get it. At best, after today your friend Sophia may be a ghost. I'll give you that."

Casey had wondered about it himself from time to time, thinking maybe Sophia was a ghost, or part of his own creation. "She is real, Amy. I thought that you of all people believed me."

"I believe you are emotionally sensitive and caring. Like when you took hold of that little kid's hoodie, seconds before he stepped in front of the car. His mother should have been holding his hand, and you knew that, and that's why you held him back. No other reason. Not that you saw the car before it came, or that he was about to step in front of the car, but that you were aware he was not being cared for by his mother, because you were missing your mom, and you are emotionally sensitive."

"I can't believe you, Amy. That's a load of crap, and you know it!" Casey's head started to hurt, his throat felt tight. His hands gripped his head, trying to stop the pain. "So that's what you thought," he yelled. "And you pity me." Shocked, Casey felt his energy as a river that dragged him to its murky depths which then surged up and pumped through his veins. The kitchen lights started to flicker and the bulb overhead blew. Amy and Terry jumped out of the way as the shards of glass fell on the table.

Casey pulled the back door open and ran outside.

"Casey, stop," Terry yelled after him. "Casey, where are you going? Come back.

Amy, stay inside and shut the door behind me."

Terry saw Casey pass the barn and as he did the car and motorbike roared into life. Terry, confused, didn't know if he should stop and turn them off, or keep chasing Casey into the woods.

Tears blurring his vision, Casey tripped. He never realized Amy pitied him. All this time she was just humoring him. He couldn't believe it. He screamed and released his anger into the forest. The crows took flight and sticks and leaves started swirling around his feet, moving up and outward. The debris around him spiraled faster and faster. He didn't see how dangerous and out of control his behavior had become. A bad smell hung in the forest, the same smell that was in the house, but Casey was blind to his environment as he pushed his energy further and further away from him. He pounded his fist into the trunk of a tree and a shock wave vibrated into the ground, lifting the soil. It rocked fear into Casey.

Terry watched amazed at the growing force and chaos. He was worried Casey was going to get hurt unless he got himself under control. "Casey!" he called out. Terry hid behind his forearm, protecting his head and face and pushed through Casey's personal cyclone.

Casey faced Terry. A flying branch hit Terry on the side of the head, knocking him down. Casey heard the dog bark in the distance and everything went still, hovered in mid-air, and dropped. Casey felt electrified and exhausted. Then his senses focused on Terry and, horrified, he ran to Terry's side. He had never lost control in this way before, never hurt anyone. He had never wielded such power. He had felt detached and it terrified him. He bent over and brought up his lunch. Sophia was right — he had more power than he ever would have believed and he couldn't handle such power. He wiped his mouth and slid down by Terry's side and started crying. Terry wasn't moving. "I'm so sorry, Terry, please, Terry, I am so sorry. Please, please wake up." The dog and Amy came running.

"I am so sorry, Amy. Please wake him up." Amy was quick to act. She checked his breathing, running her hands along the top of his head. "He's got a bit of a gash just above his ear."

Casey sniffed back the tears, and nodded.

Amy resumed checking Terry's body from head to toe. "He'll be alright, Casey," she said. "He'll have a big lump on his head and a massive headache, but he will be okay. I'm sorry about before," she said. "You are my first child, and you're hardly a child. I have only had a year to get to know you and how to be a parent. I love you, Casey. This is very new to me and I handled it poorly. I am frightened, and I am sorry I hurt you. I saw what you just did and we will help you. You will learn to control it, or shut it down." Amy wrapped her arms around him and he dropped his head onto her shoulder and cried.

All the pain over the past year came flooding back. Terry started to stir and sit up. He gently placed his hand on Casey's arm. Casey felt the touch and lifted his head from Amy's shoulder to see Terry smiling at him.

"My head feels like it's being squeezed like a ripe tomato. And since I'm the one that was knocked out here, what about saving some of that loving for me?" Terry said in a mock-dejected voice. Casey let go of Amy and threw himself at Terry.

The dog started to bark at the sky. They followed its gaze and saw the dense metallic cloud that appeared to be made up of tiny winged creatures swarming, moving like a snake with purpose, towards them.

They hadn't noticed the sky turning charcoal, or that everything around them had darkened into shadows. An intense sickly smell was getting stronger.

"This isn't good," Casey said. "I think I attracted them."

Amy and Terry in unison asked, "How?"

Casey and Amy helped Terry to his feet. "Negative energy. I think it's the virus." They started running back towards the house, the dog leading the way. The beastly swarm came closer. The air thickened.

Inside, Terry dragged the table across the floor to jam it against the closed door. All the windows simultaneously started to rattle, and the wind whistled between the cracks. There was a crashing sound in the living room. Casey ran towards it and as he stepped into the living room, the boards against the windows moaned and distorted, bowed and splintered, yielding to the force of the wind. The windows erupted, the boards went flying. The stench magnified, and the swarm entered the room. It stopped, searching; it rippled like the movement of wind on the surface of a lake. It banked left towards Casey; it wasn't random they were heading straight for him. Amy grabbed his arm and dragged him back into the kitchen. Terry was right behind them, leaping down the basement stairs. The dog, thinking way ahead of them, barked at where the hole had been blocked.

"You're right, what choice do we have?" Terry said to the dog.

"Give me a hand, Casey." Terry's head pounded, trying to push the cases away to uncover the hole.

Casey placed his hands against the stack and closed his eyes, pushing with his mind. He heard Terry say "on the count of three".

"One, two —"

He put a little of his energy into his shoulder ready to push, but Terry never said three. Casey's eyes flew open, fearing the worst, and saw Terry standing clear of the suitcases. They had already moved and the hole was clearly visible.

Amy and Terry were quiet and still.

"Ah, good, good," Terry finally managed to say.

Terry picked up the torches and they moved into the tunnel. "Can you put them back across the hole from this side?" Terry asked.

"Maybe, yes." He again imagined in his mind the hole and the bricks that had filled it, and the cases piled high in front of it. Just the way it was when they first found it. He opened his eyes. He couldn't tell if the trunks were against the wall or not, because the cavity had been filled. They were entombed.

21

———————

THE TALKING STICK: JADE. AUSTRALIA

The house was quiet when Jade crept out of Alex's room careful not to wake Kath and tiptoed into the hallway. She could see the light under Callie and Daniel's door as she moved towards Kevin's room. She stopped to listen.

"We have to go. We have to leave the city," Callie said. "If we can't find Shaun's family, we will have to take him with us. His hands will need to be cared for."

"Where do you want to go?"

"Saddleback Mountain. There is enough space, it has solar power, back-up generator, batteries — everything we need. My parents' belongings are there, including dad's light plane, a Piper Cherokee 6-300. Nothing has been touched."

Jade could hear Callie blowing her nose as if she had been crying. Feeling guilty about listening, she started to moved away.

"I have to tell you something about Ellen."

Jade was immediately glued to the spot.

"Ellen said, 'Hide. An ingredient has disappeared. I have failed.' Daniel, when she said it, I knew she was talking to me, telling me to run, to get out of the country and that's what I did, I ran. I watched them force her from the lab. She asked them where they were taking

280

her and one of the two men, who had Russian-sounding accents, pulled her violently by the hair and pushed her towards the stairwell door. They were only inches away from the door to the bio unit where I was hiding and I held my breath. The man was telling her to stop asking questions, she would have plenty of time to finish her research. They opened the door and pushed her into the stairwell.

That's when I ran. I wanted to go to her family, to the authorities. Instinctively, I knew I should run and not look back. I took what she had been working on and ran. I felt like I abandoned them. I also think whoever took Ellen killed my parents and have been looking for me ever since."

Jade started to cry silently.

"Why would you think that?"

"I never changed my passport from my maiden name. My mail still went to their place and my parents died a week after I returned. I think they, whoever *they* are, have been looking for me and I believe they have found us."

Jade backed away from the door and leant against the wall, trying to decide what to do next. She wiped her face with the bottom of her shirt before opening Kevin's bedroom door.

Jade pushed him gently, but Kevin was dead tired and didn't wake. She tried again and he woke with a start, nearly falling out of bed. Tim snored on, stretched out on the floor under the closed window. The full moon shone into the room, bathing them in the reflected light of the sun. The unity of the movements of the worlds fascinated her and she became absorbed in the essence of the moment, trying to forget what Callie had said.

"Jade, what are you doing?" Kevin said. She didn't answer. He waved his hand in front of her, casting a shadow across her face, as if he thought she might be sleepwalking.

"Stop doing that," she said. Jade watched him lean across to his side table and turn on the light. Kevin rubbed his eyes, waiting for them to adjust.

"How do you do it? I have to know," she said.

"Do what?" he said, sitting up and throwing his legs over the edge of the bed. He didn't have a shirt on and Jade admired his muscle definition.

"You work out?" she asked casually.

Kevin looked down at his chest. Looking self-conscious, he grabbed the shirt lying at the bottom of the bed and put it on.

"You have the body of an athlete. You should figure out what sports you like best. You will excel at whatever you choose. Anyway," she said, sitting and making herself comfortable on the floor in front of him, "you have to tell me how you do it."

"I don't know, Jade. It just happens."

"Nothing in this world just happens. We create our own reality; we are the cause of our lives. Let's say the thing just happens to you. Is it happening now? No. So there has to be certain criteria, a particular state or energy force that creates it. It's like the story about a mother seeing her child stuck under a car and she is miraculously able to lift the car. There is an energy force that comes from within her that enables her to do this. She is in a different state of being. What state of being is your body in when you are able to step through time?"

"I wouldn't say that I step through time. I don't know where it is; it's not here, but it is. It's like running through the cavity between the inner and outer walls of a house," Kevin said, scratching his shoulder.

Jade twirled the ends of her hair and started running the soft end up and down her cheek like a paintbrush. "A corridor, perhaps. It didn't look like Earth, although it also did, just more vibrant. The colors were radiant and I saw Great Turtle."

"You saw what? A turtle?"

"My great-grandmother. So it can't be just out of your imagination. It has to have an existence in time and space. It seemed to be parallel to this reality. Tell me what your state was each time it happened." Jade studied him carefully.

Kevin looked deep into her eyes and he saw a flicker of light. "Do you wear contacts?" he asked. "I can see the light reflecting off the right side."

Reactively her hand shot up to her eyes. Wearing contacts was one of the changes she had made since her mother went missing, substituting the chunky black- rimmed glasses for them. "Yes, I do," she said feeling a little defensive.

"Are they uncomfortable?" he asked, mindful of Tim, asleep nearby.

"Not as uncomfortable as being teased for being intelligent. The glasses attracted negative attention. Now tell me, what was your physiological state when you created an opening and stepped out of our time and space?"

Kevin tilted his head slightly to the side nearly resting it on his shoulder. The ceiling was absent of answers. "There was always urgency. Trying to avoid something, to prevent a disaster occurring. I am still trying to work this out myself. What you heard me thinking about in, what shall we call it ... Kevin's world?"

"That's too egotistical even for you, K," Tim said sitting up. "Having a midnight powwow without me, are you. Who has the talking stick?"

"Go back to sleep. Don't mind him," Kevin said, looking at Jade.

"Actually, that may be very perceptive of him. Why did you say that: powwow and talking stick?"

"It's the first thing that came to me. I thought I could smell wood burning, which reminded me of a campfire," Tim explained.

"I am part Native American on my mother's side, my traditional name is Raven Wings. My great-grandmother, Great Turtle, was a medicine woman, a spiritual healer and could talk to the spirits in the afterlife. I had never seen proof of this until we disappeared in front of that wolf, into another dimension, where I saw Great Turtle watching us."

"Can we call you Raven Wings?" Tim asked.

Jade stuck her neck out and eyeballed Tim. "No!" she said firmly and turned to Kevin. "Tell me what state you were in when you opened the doorway."

"When I saw that boy drowning, nothing was happening to anyone. I was alone."

"Why were you there?"

"I wanted to swim and keep swimming."

He does that," said Tim. "He will jump in the pool at school and lap swim for over an hour and he will do the same at the river."

"Do you get into a rhythm?

"Yes, it's peaceful in the water."

"Do you swim when unhappy or upset, or when you're happy, excited?"

"Both, I've seen it happen." Tim's eyes widened, understanding. He knew why Kevin swam so much. "He is slow, swimming for ages, when he has a fight with his mom."

"Shut up, Tim." Kevin frowned at his friend.

"Let him speak," Jade said.

Tim stood up and paced in front of the window as if he was solving a riddle.

"Okay, Sherlock, lay it on us," Jade said.

"When he is excited, he swims like a rocket and splashes a hell of a lot, like a man possessed."

"So, K — Can I call you K?"

"Sure."

"What were you thinking about before you went to the river?"

"This is stupid." Kevin felt reluctant to admit he had been crying, and wanted his nanna to come back, and wanted his mother to hug him again.

"Come on. Look at this scientifically, an experiment."

"I wanted to see my nanna, I missed her."

"That's right! Soon after his mother returned from the USA, they were killed in a car accident on the way to his place."

"Tim, shut up!" Kevin growled.

"I know about your grandparents and I'm sorry," Jade said. "That was a bad time for us all. So you were upset, wanted to see your nanna and went for a swim. You dived into the river, but when you surfaced you saw a boy fall off a footbridge where usually there was no bridge. No footbridge ever existed where you swim, right. I think you dived into, and surfaced, in his time and space, becoming a witness. Did you go on the internet to search for the details?" Jade was getting excited and leant her body forward waiting for his answer.

"Yes, and there were no missing persons or death-by-drowning reports. There were weather anomalies across the world that day. Nature had a seizure. There was nothing I could find, the virus had washed up on our shores and the authorities thought my mind was infected."

Jade looked solemn, remembering her experience of that day, seven days after her mother went missing. "We are all connected." She reached up and pulled Kevin's pillow off his bed and lay on the floor with her legs resting on it. "Who's the pebble?"

"What pebble," Tim asked.

"The cause of all these effects. Everything starts in the Middle East."

"I thought you were a geek with a sci-fi brain," Tim said. "Thought you would believe in the Big Bang theory."

"I do, but who created the big bang, the one sonic clap, the one pebble. We are all connected: six degrees of separation." Jade had gone off into a spiral of thinking, believing there was something in front of her she wasn't seeing.

"When was the next time you stepped out of this reality?"

"Last week there was a fire."

"There was more than a fire, K," Tim said. "It was a scorcher of a day and we went for a swim; all good. I heard something on the other side of the creek, so I went to check it out. There was a bunch of drop-kicks smoking and I hid behind a tree but one of them saw me and the next thing I knew was a fist ramming into my face and a foot stomped on my leg, hard, breaking it in two places."

Jade looked at his leg. "Impossible," she said.

"I know, right. We were burnt to a cinder from the sun when we came round and the whole place was ablaze. Kevin here made a splint for my leg while I was unconscious then dragged me to the edge of this wall. I kept passing out."

"When Tim didn't come back," Kevin interrupted, "I went to find him and saw Shaun and his mates beating up on Tim. They saw me and I was knocked out with a king-hit. Before I hit the ground, I saw the petrol bombs lined up, so I know Shaun and his mates set the bush alight and left us there to fry. I regained consciousness and before I opened my eyes, I could smell burning sage. My nanna used to burn sage and lemongrass. Then I saw the wall and couldn't see if Tim was breathing, or was it the other way round? I don't remember. The wall was a massive ripple of energy and I could see through it. It went to somewhere not part of this existence, but there was nowhere else for us to go, we would have died. Once we penetrated the wall's membrane and we were on the other side, Tim's leg was healed and the sunburn vanished. The fire engulfed us and we didn't feel a thing."

Jade sat mesmerized by the story. "You were healed? That's why, as soon as I stepped into the parallel universe, the atmosphere was calming and I didn't feel dizzy and my head stopped hurting. So when was the next time?" she asked.

"We were at the same place looking for the wall and couldn't find it. A couple of morons came around trying to pass themselves off as fire investigators. We knew they weren't and I freaked. That's when I saw a ripple, like a mirage. It wasn't in the same place as before, and this time we rode our bike into the rippling wall. We skidded around to face the men and it was evident they couldn't see us. They gave chase, but they couldn't see the wall, they couldn't see us, or hear us. I know they couldn't hear because this one didn't shut up," he said, thumbing towards Tim. "The rest you know."

"I think those guys have been looking for your mom. Your mom thinks they might be the ones who kidnapped my mom. She said tomorrow we are leaving for Saddleback Mountain. Okay, I want you to trust me," Jade said, jumping to her feet.

"Wait, what, how do you know this?" Kevin asked.

"I heard your mom and dad talking as I snuck past their room. Come on, don't lose focus."

None of them felt tired. Kevin focused on the floor and noticed shadows moving quickly across the floor as if a full moon had moved into mid-heaven.

Jade stood behind Kevin and said, "Tim stand beside me." Tim rolled himself over the bed nearly hitting Kevin in the head with his ankle. Jokingly, Tim massaged Kevin's shoulders as if getting him loosened up for a boxing match.

"Stop it." Kevin slapped at Tim's hands.

Jade ignored Tim and focused on Kevin. "Now, close your eyes, and I want you to think about that day when you could smell the sage, and the fire was raging around you. How did it feel seeing Tim lying still beside you? What thoughts were going through your head?"

"This is sick," Kevin said.

"Relax, K." Jade watched Kevin's jaw tighten and flex, his breathing increasing. "How loud was the roar of the fire? How power-less did you feel?"

"You're making me feel like crap," Kevin said.

Jade fired off the questions. Kevin was feeling more and more helpless, wondering how he was going to get her to stop, when a hum, a low pulse and the sound of the rustling wind like slow-tearing Velcro entered into the room.

"What the hell?" Tim said.

"Shh," said Jade.

The scent of sage and lemongrass drifted past them. A metallic ripple of energy was forming in front of Kevin. A wall between two worlds. "Okay, Kevin, this is just a memory. You are safe in your bedroom with Tim standing right behind you and I'm standing next to Tim. Now open your eyes."

Tim couldn't hold himself back and blurted out mockingly. "He *loves* me." And held his hands to his heart and dropped onto the bed.

Jade whacked him on the side of the arm and he dropped the child's play. The three of them stared at the spot, as big as a basket-ball, shimmering in mid-air, a window in time. It wasn't a major opening, not like the other times. The energy flickered, folded into itself and disappeared.

"Awesome, K," Tim said.

"Alright," Jade said. "Now we know how you can create it. Next we need to see if you can choose your destination."

"What do you mean?" Tim said.

"She means, can we go anywhere within the universe?"

"Well, I was really thinking a little smaller, like how about this planet first," Jade said, tying her hair into a bun and sticking a pencil off Kevin's desk into it. "Like maybe we could go to my place. Maybe we could go back in time before my mom was kidnapped and warn her. There are so many possibilities."

"I don't think we can mess with time. I don't believe we should play around with this, we don't know what effect it has," Kevin said.

Kevin's bedroom door squeaked open and Daniel popped his head into the room. "Guys, it's been a long day. It's after one o'clock so get some sleep. Jade, back to Alex's room. It's going to be a big day tomorrow and we need to get up early."

Jade, embarrassed, scrambled out of the room, ducking under Daniel's arm. Tim jumped back onto his makeshift bed under the window. Daniel smiled at Kevin. "Lights out," and started to close the door. Jade was halfway down the hall when Daniel said to Kevin, "Can you guys smell that?"

Holding onto the door handle of Alex's room, Jade whispered. "Sage." She smiled and walked into the bedroom, gently letting the door click closed behind her.

KEVIN WAS SURPRISED he had slept so well. He lay still listening to the sounds of the morning when he felt his dad's big hand stroking his cheek softly and he swatted at it as if it was a fly, but his dad pulled his hand away quickly and Kevin smacked himself in the face instead. Tim opened his eyes just in time to see the impact and started rolling about with laughter. He was lucky he was already on the floor. Kevin threw himself out of bed and landed on top of him, and started punching him playfully in the ribs.

Daniel smiled, watching them for a second. Life almost seemed normal again. Then the smile fell from his face and he said, "Okay, you two, I need you to help me pack the car." The boys stopped wrestling.

"Where are we going?" He looked at Tim and back to his dad.

"We are all going. Tim, your mom and sister will come too, as well as Shaun and Jade."

"Where are we going?"

Daniel didn't need to answer. Kevin answered his own question. "Nanna and pop's, right? How did you convince Mom?"

"It was her idea. Now come on, get dressed and meet me downstairs."

THE DOOR TO THE garage was open. Tim recognized his hiking pack amongst the bags already lined up to be crammed into the cars. "Fair dinkum, nobody tells me anything," he muttered to himself.

"Your mom and Kath, about an hour ago, packed up a few things, and locked up your house," Daniel said.

"But what about my things?" Tim asked.

"Your mom knows what you need," Daniel said.

"No, there are things I want that she can't know because I don't know, so I know there're things that she doesn't know I want. I have to go to the house." Tim walked quickly away from Daniel to the front door and ran for home.

"Tim, get back here. Kevin, go get him."

Kevin chased, but didn't catch Tim before he reached home. He ran around the backyard, dug the spare key up from under the rock, and unlocked the back door leading into the kitchen.

"What are you doing?" Kevin yelled.

"Wait there. Hang on," Tim said.

Kevin looked around at the quiet street. He got a creepy feeling they were being watched. Across the road, Shaun's mates and Kath's boyfriend were coming out of a house. Tim stepped from the kitchen to see Kath's boyfriend swing his bat; the metal smashed the window of the car in the driveway. Kevin pulled Tim out of sight as he reappeared, awkwardly stuffing an old photo into his Velcro wallet. Jumping the neighbors' fence, Tim's shoelace caught in a crack, pulling his shoe off. Together they unlatched the runners and sprinted back to Kevin's.

"What was all that about?" Kevin asked, walking into his house.

"Nothing."

"Yes, it was. What gives?"

"It's a photo of my dad holding me when I was born. All right? Now shut up about it."

"Chill. It's all good. Don't sweat it."

Kevin followed the smell of pancakes. Jade was cooking with Alex's help. Molly played with her breakfast, dipping her jam toast into a bowl of rice cereal. She seemed to really enjoy sucking the cereal off the toast. His mom was sitting at the table applying a fresh dressing to Shaun's burnt hands. Shaun became agitated as soon as Kevin walked into the room and his mother looked up at him. Neither of them spoke.

She raised her eyebrows and Kevin shrugged his shoulders. They hadn't communicated like this since — he couldn't remember the last time. She tilted her head towards Jade and he nodded in agreement.

"Jade?"

Jade turned away from the stove and looked at Callie.

"Can you make Kevin a stack with lemon and honey to share with Tim, please?" Callie looked back at Kevin. "I'll call you when they're ready." She then nodded in the direction of the garage. Kevin knew what she meant. She wanted him to help pack the car. He said nothing and left the room. He was excited his mom was back, but afraid she would turn again. He decided he would be cautious in her presence; she was still the dragon lady.

IT HADN'T TAKEN long to pack up the two cars and be on their way. Tim looked like he had been crying. Kevin focused on the carnage out his window. His dad was in the second car with Tim's mom Sally, Kath, Alex and Shaun. Kevin was with his mom in the Dodge with Tim, Jade and Molly. Their car was out front. His mom steered around abandoned vehicles, tail lights flashing on and off. She turned off the main road, towards the coast, driving through the national park along the winding roads hidden under richly-scented vegetation. As they emerged out into the open, they could see the ocean on their left and as they rose to the top of a hill, Kevin could see the black cloud that hung over the city of Wollongong up ahead. His mom and dad stopped for Alex to use the bathroom at the lookout that was a jumping-off spot for hang gliders. Kevin could see the road winding below.

Thirty minutes later they entered the city and his mom slowed the car to a crawl. Tim said in a flat voice, "Look at that guy."

Kevin leant across to see out Tim's window.

"He looks like a zombie, without the blood drooling from his mouth. Why are they so pale?" Tim asked.

"I don't know," Kevin said.

"They probably don't sleep much any more," Jade replied. "Maybe they are low in iron, barely eat and just — keep wandering the streets, trying to remember what it is that they're supposed to do."

"It's so quiet, nobody is talking," Callie said. "There is no connection between anybody."

"Check out his pants, that guy's too, they look ..." Tim hesitated, searching for the right word.

"Soiled," said Jade.

Callie turned down a side street, away from the coast and towards Saddleback Mountain, some forty miles further south. The street was dark and looked cold. A shiver ran over Kevin's body. "What the hell?" A winged giant of a beast hovered before them, eating. The banging of the car's brakes as Callie tried to stop had no comparison with the crunching of bones and the horrific image of the little clumps of hair caught between the beast's bloody teeth. It slowly flapped bat-like wings while a scorpion's tail flicked wildly behind it, lancing into people on the streets. The town was its buffet. Each claw had a person skewered and ready to eat. Over the building tops the grotesque heads of two more beasts could be seen. This one was the biggest and stood at least four storys high.

Callie threw the car into reverse and took the side street they had just passed. Kevin, Tim and Jade swung around to look behind. Molly started crying. He saw his dad enter the side street, closing in behind them. Kevin flung around to see out his side window, leaning his head back to look up and felt the demon looking straight at him. He quickly pulled away from the window. The blood drained from his face, a chill filled his chest and warmth suddenly filled his bladder. Uncomfortable, unable to prevent himself from rubbernecking, he watched the beast swallow a man's bloody torso. His body became heavy with pain and dread. Suddenly, the creature's head and body exploded into a thousand tiny versions of itself: it became an angry swarm, and headed in their direction. Molly screamed louder.

Callie yelled, "Guys, face the front." The car jerked to the right, then to the left and the swarm, like a malicious pyroclastic cloud, raced up behind them. They didn't have a chance.

Jade's world spun, vertigo invading her senses. She slowly turned around to look at Kevin in the back seat and slapped his leg for attention. She was short of breath, pretending to be calm. "How do you feel now, K?"

Screwed, is the first thing that came to his mind. Kevin knew what she was hinting at: where, where to, where to go? Then the image of the long driveway leading up to his nanna's home came into focus. *Of course.* He hadn't consciously done this before but he had to believe it was possible. He felt the black wolf start to circle and doubt found a voice laughing in his mind. He pushed it away, blocked it out, and listened to Molly wailing; the sound fueled his desire to succeed, to create a safe place for them all. He looked over his shoulder, making sure his dad was following close behind. The cloud, the shapeshifting beast, the swarm — whatever it was — was close and moving up and over his dad's car. Kevin saw his dad violently swerve his car from side to side in an attempt to shake it off.

"Call your mom, Tim," Kevin said, "and tell her to put it on speaker." The sound of the phone ringing was a strange sense of normalcy.

"Dad."

"K, not now."

"Dad, shake that thing off, you have to get closer, bumper to bumper. Or you won't be able to follow. I'm not —" The reception was lost. Kevin had no choice but to focus on the road out front, where translucent waves, a mirage, started to appear.

"What now?" Callie shouted. She butted her nose up against the windscreen and saw a sinkhole was opening, growing, in front of them. She started to slow and search for another way. Molly's screaming filled her head. Callie glanced into the rear-vision mirror. "Kevin! Quieten her down."

"No! Go straight for it!" Jade said. She leant over the gearstick and grabbed Callie's leg, pushing it down onto the accelerator.

"What? Stop it! Don't be foolish, we'll all die."

Tim pulled faces at Molly in vain. She couldn't be distracted. He looked behind him to see where his mom and Daniel were. They were still trying to shake the swarm. "Come on, K, you can do it."

Kevin was breaking out in a sweat and his face became red, his eyes sparked. There was no time for the car to brake or swerve. This time his mom would have no choice but to floor it, and hope they could jump the sinkhole. The car went straight up and hovered over and into the mirage. Kevin felt Jade's vertigo and anxiety vanish. He heard Molly stop crying and Tim's panic dissolve. Everything went quiet. They should have been alarmed, but they only felt peace.

They all thought they were on their way to the pearly gates, soon to see a bright light. The nose of the car tilted downward. They braced for impact, the world came alive, and the car dived into the dirt and gravel. Its back wheels thumbed the ground and the car slid out of control, sliding down the blue metal drive, straight for the veranda.

Kevin glimpsed behind. The doorway was getting smaller.

~

SHAUN BRACED HIMSELF against the leather seat in front and screamed in pain. Kath unlocked her seat belt and fastened his. Shaun felt feverish as every muscle in his body screamed with panic. He couldn't take his eyes off the beast. Everyone was freaking, he couldn't concentrate, his senses were locked on the entity. He knew he had seen it before in his dreams. It collapsed into a thousand mirrored pieces and headed towards them. Daniel was doing his best to shake it off, but Shaun knew they, he, had no hope of escaping this time. He was no longer an innocent boy. *This is Dad's doing*, he thought. The memory of that night ten years ago came flooding back along with all the bad feelings, as if he was a kid again.

He understood his dad had violated his trust, and the trust of so many people, for some non-existent magical cure for his mom. He had loved his mother more than anything. He had prayed for her day and night to be healed. But what his dad did, whatever it was that he unearthed that night, seemed to be causing the extinction of humanity. The explosion, the plane to Egypt, the drug-induced flight, and the memories returned — the Russian in the palace. Everything had seemed so strange at the time. The dreams, the girl, finally it made some sense. It was her all along: Rachel. If only he could go back and stop his dad.

Shaun quickly turned away and faced front. The Dodge disappeared into thin air, just like Kevin and Tim had vanished at the river. What the hell? The swarm was descending again. Daniel swerved left then right in quick jerks.

A thousand vile angels swarmed behind the tail of the car. The swarm united, forming into one gigantic beast, stopping and sniffing the air as if searching for its prey. Filled with fury it turned from side to side in a rage. Its serrated tail sliced through the buildings and the people behind them on the streets. It shrieked and took off in flight.

The devil was enriched; his army of death was free to hunt. It exploded into a swarm of a thousand micro-beasts again, heading for the car. Sharp claws dragged along the boot of the car. Kath covered her ears, trying to block out the high-pitched screeches. Shaun saw the demons suddenly vanish behind them. The feeling of flying overcame him, and he relaxed. Every muscle, every cell was infused with light and peace. His burning hands cooled, the pain gone. He was in slow motion, gazing over his shoulder through the rear window, searching for the swarm, and saw a horizon of green and blue mountains stretching to the ocean. As suddenly as it had begun, the floating sensation ceased, and the car fell from the sky. Shaun's body became heavy, and he was aware once again of the metal cage around them. The car landed heavily. Shaun's neck whipped back and his head smashed into the side window as the car slid along the gravel slamming into the rear of the Dodge. Hidden under a few layers of dust, the cars became one piece of metal beside the grazing cow.

22

———

LABYRINTH OF DARKNESS: CASEY. ENGLAND

*S**ophia, are you there?*

Casey thought. Lying on the cold dirt floor on his back with his head resting on Terry's leg, Casey stared into the darkness. The chamber was musty. The air was stale. Terry was propped up against the cold stone wall and Amy leant against his shoulder. He could feel Terry playing with his curls; he wouldn't admit it out loud in a million years but Casey actually found it soothing. He shouted louder inside his head, *Sophia, are you there?* and Amy jumped a little. Casey was worried about Sophia because this had been the biggest gap between communications. *Maybe I could dream about her.* After sealing them in, he had tried again and again to break the wall down so they could get back into the house.

Amy had suggested they should just rest a while so he could build up his strength. "It will come when you're ready. You used a lot of energy in the forest beforehand. It might be best that we stay here and not go rushing back upstairs, for a while anyway."

Casey felt pressure building on his bladder. He closed his eyes and tried to sleep, directing his thoughts to his mom, her smile, the sound of her laughter and the smell of her perfume; he inhaled

296

deeply to imagine the scent. Sometimes he felt so lost without her. *She would have liked Sophia — and Terry and Amy.* His bladder was becoming so uncomfortable his eyes flew open and he desperately looked for a place to relieve himself. *How long had they been here? Two hours at least,* he thought, looking back at the wall. He saw a shadow out of the corner of his eye; something was moving towards him. He closed his eyes, ignoring his bladder. He felt the presence getting closer and the darkness behind his eyes became intense. Internally, he tried to move away from the presence, slipping further away from his body, hiding in Terry's aura. He sensed it looking closely into his face, trying to see if he was awake. He kept as still as possible and felt like he was floating out in space. His heart was racing, but his breathing was relaxed as if in sleep. A breath crossed his face, and he nearly yanked himself out of hiding. He heard a voice in his head. His palms were sweaty. He disengaged from the separation of his body, feeling the intensity of the darkness move away. He allowed himself to float closer to the surface and open his stubborn eyes a crack. An apparition of an old man with ginger hair and a scruffy beard down to his chest, wearing a brown robe with a sash had disappeared into the wall. Casey's fear evaporated. He focused on the wall again and it moved like a Chinese block puzzle; he shuffled the bricks, restacking them. Casey slowly sat up, watching them move left-right and up-down. He reached out his hand to hold them and they succumbed to his energy. *I'm back.* Without touching them or moving from Terry's side he laid the bricks on the ground. He could hear the trunks sliding along the wall.

Terry and Amy were up on their feet beside him, motivated to step into the opening and back into the basement.

"What do you think, Terry?" Amy said. "Do you think it's safe? I don't feel the heaviness any more. It feels like a blanket has been lifted."

"Let me go upstairs first," Casey said.

Terry raised his brows and said, "No!"

"I hate to say it, but I think he's right, Terry."

"I'm not letting Casey go up there on his own!"

"Yeah, you should let me. You need to be here for Amy, and I'll know better than both of you if the entities are gone, or are hiding in the walls."

"Entities, is that what you saw? What do they look like, Casey?"

"They were metallic grey liquid like mercury. They had the snout of a dog, the wings of a bat, the tail of a scorpion, and death dripped from their mouths. They didn't have a stable, solid form. They fight for existence and that's why they need us: to possess our body and soul, leaving us only a corner of our mind to reside in. They have no souls, they're from hell. And to answer the questions you want to ask, Amy, I don't know how I know this stuff. Sometimes I feel like I am an old man who has lived a thousand lifetimes. But other times — well, you get the picture. I survived drowning that day for a reason. You found me, Terry, for a reason. This is all connected."

The darkness of the basement hid his face as he climbed the stairs. The golden retriever followed. Casey placed both hands on the door like in a fire and felt the silence.

He slowly pushed the door open and peeked into the dark kitchen. The sun had gone. They had been down there longer than he thought. Night hung over the house and his bladder was about to burst. He couldn't go slow; he had to get to the bathroom before his teeth started to float!

CASEY STEPPED INTO the kitchen and crept into the center of the room. He peeked into the lounge room; the edge of the curtain was possessed by a pre-dawn breeze. A fog drifted through the open window and Casey shivered. The wooden panels that had hung over the window lay by the bookshelf and the side table, lamp, and chair were knocked over. Casey stood with the dog by his side in the middle of the room, testing for a sense of any other presence in the house. It seemed quiet and empty. He flicked off the light switch and waited. Nothing: no lost souls, no apparitions, no emotional memories. Something had taken them away. It had become eerily quiet and empty. He walked cautiously into the foyer and flicked the light up the stairs. Satisfied he was alone, he entered Amy's great-aunt's old room where she had stayed during her final years. He wanted to use the bathroom and closed the door slowly behind him, hoping to reduce the sound of the squeaking hinges. The torch clanged as he laid it on top of the porcelain. He quickly unzipped his pants and sighed in relief as the stream went on forever.

Casey zipped himself up, washed his hands and opened the squeaky door. The sound unnerved him, making him feel silly. The floor was loud, and the room smelt musty, but it felt happy and comfortable, and he imagined this was how Amy's great- aunt was. The thought of frying up eggs and sausages, a Sunday English breakfast, made his stomach rumble. The clock in the room chimed, signaling dawn and the sun's imminent rising. *Where has the night gone? Where is Sophia?*

Casey walked back to the basement passing the dog that patiently waited for him. She stepped in behind as he reached for the door handle. Suddenly the door was pushed inwards. He let go, stumbling backwards over the dog.

"What the ..."

Terry emerged from the darkened doorway. "Why are you on the floor?"

Casey, Terry and Amy laughed nervously.

"What the hell took you so long?" Terry asked.

"I had to go to the bathroom. It's all clear."

"What's clear?" Terry said. "The house or your bladder?"

"Funny! The house. It's just a bit of a mess."

The dog scratched at the back door, so Amy let her out. Five minutes later it scratched at the door, wanting back in. It settled on the kitchen floor and slept for the next few hours while Amy, Terry and Casey cleaned and secured the house. Terry and Casey boarded the windows and Amy tidied up. Light started to shine under the back door. There was no point in going to bed, they were all hungry anyway.

"Let's have breakfast." Terry fired up the stove and Amy pulled out the sausages and egg powder. Casey made the toast. They worked together as a team, not talking but enjoying the ordinariness of preparing breakfast.

IN A LABYRINTH OF darkness Joe watched Sophia glow while she slept restlessly. Stunned, he looked on in silence.

Beads of sweat sparkled on Sophia's forehead like jewels. She was the only source of light in the dark tunnel. Slowly she started to lift off the ground, then gently as a feather floated back down and the glow dimmed. Father McDonald kept murmuring his prayers and Joe joined in and whispered his own. Together, they begged God to give her the strength to do His will.

Father McDonald switched on the torch. Joe covered his eyes to shield them from the artificial light, watching Father McDonald pop a tiny pill into his mouth. Rubbing his chest he said, "It just needs to keep ticking until this is over." Then he leant over to Sophia and whispered, "Sophia, it's time to wake up. We have to get moving."

Joe packed up the rubbish of their snack bars as the torch flickered, unnerving him. It was the last torch. Sophia dusted herself off and silently they continued walking. The tunnels narrowed. Two hours passed before the torch flickered again, and the light was suddenly gone.

Father McDonald pushed the light on his watch and said, "Have trust, Joe, we will be out of here soon. I feel it in my aching bones."

Joe thought he could hear the sound of water drip, drip dripping into a pool. *Pinpointing sound in the tunnels is difficult.* He walked on, took three steps, then dropped into a body of cold water.

"What was —" Father MacDonald said.

It's too late to stop them. They were walking so close. Joe felt the weight of Father McDonald, followed by Sophia, falling on top of him, driving him under. The backpacks weighed them down. Joe started to panic. Father McDonald's head went under the water and he stretched his arms out to Joe, shining the tiny light from his watch. Joe saw the dot and struggled to the surface.

The light went out. Under the water, Father McDonald struggled out of his backpack. He splashed to the surface. "Let go of the bags."

"We won't survive if we let go of the packs," Joe said.

"Joe, let them go. We have no choice."

"Oh God." Joe slipped one arm at a time out of the harness. "Sophia, hold onto my shoulders and don't let go. I'll get us out of here." He didn't want to turn, he didn't want the light, he was afraid of what he might see.

"I'm a good swimmer, I am right behind you," she said. "But Joe, what about your prosthesis?"

"It's an Aqualeg, an amazing invention. I can do everything I did before I lost my leg. Now stay close, hen. Both of you stay close. After this, I think a warm fire with good friends and a whiskey might be in order."

After ten minutes, the water felt as if it was now freezing over. Joe breaststroked slowly in front of them hoping he was not leading them in circles. *We have to get out of here.*

Father McDonald said, "I suppose we could think of this as an extended baptism."

"Or a mikveh," Joe said, shivering.

Sophia's teeth were chattering. If there had been light, Joe would have seen that her lips and under her eyes were purple. "What's a mikveh?" Sophia asked.

"It's an opportunity to cleanse your spirit of any negative energy that you may have collected. The mikveh is a body of water that is connected to the flowing waters of mercy that come out of Eden. The ocean is a perfect place for a mikveh. You meditate on the layers of your spirit, or aura, being cleansed while you bob up and down under the water eleven times or more."

"I love the idea of the ocean but I have never seen it in real life.

One day, Joe, I would like to go to the beach and maybe we can do a mikveh together," Sophia said.

"Ah, shit!" Under the surface of the water Joe hit his leg on something hard.

"Okay, maybe not," Sophia said.

"Ah, no, hen. I hit my knee on a rock." He reached under and felt around, finding a rock ledge. He pulled himself up onto it and crawled on his hands and knees until he slapped dry land. Joe climbed out of the water, then walked back, careful not to slip, and lifted Sophia up. They both fumbled in the dark for Father McDonald's arms. Joe seized Father McDonald's cold skeletal hands and pulled his dead weight up and onto the rock. They all sat on the edge.

Father McDonald pushed the light button on his watch and the chamber's darkness was penetrated by the faintest glow. Using the light, he awkwardly tried to force his hand into his wet pocket.

"What are doing?" Joe said.

"My pills. They're gone."

The roof was invisible beyond the reach of the light. Joe helped him up and they started shuffling over the rock onto solid ground. The cave walls were opening out. Joe felt Sophia, at his back, hook two fingers into his pants belt loop.

"Stay close, hen." Joe walked with his arms outstretched, feeling for obstacles and hit another wall. His heart beat faster; he thought he had reached the end. They had been travelling for days. *This can't be it.* He felt along the walls. "Sophia, let go, and stay where you are." He shuffled his feet a few steps to the left and hit a wall. He then shuffled to the right and there was another wall, a dead end. He wanted to weep, but placed his forehead against the cold rock, his arms outstretched, touching each side. The tips of his fingers on his right hand slipped into a crevice. He moved them deeper into it, not daring to move any other part of his body. He could fit in his fist; he opened his palm, and turned his body towards the gap and measured the space with his hands.

"Father McDonald, turn your watch light back on, please."

Sophia and Father McDonald moved up beside Joe. There was a

gap, hardly big enough for Joe to fit through. Sophia would fit. Side-on, they all might be able to squeeze through. Where would it take them? Joe wondered. He smiled at his two companions. "What do we do?"

"We keep moving forward," Father McDonald said. He let his light fall dim and waited for Joe to lead.

One by one they slid into the suffocating space. The darkness was getting to Joe; frustrated, he wanted to scream out loud. He thought of Sophia and how brave she was. He reached back and searched for her hand and held it tight. He sucked in his belly and kept shuffling to the right.

"You know, Joe, every turn we have made is to the east," Sophia said.

He stopped shuffling, breathing heavily. "Really, I'm going to resist the urge to ask you how you know that."

Time was non-existent and the darkness was making Joe feel a little crazy. He stopped again and looked at his hand against the rock and thought he could see it. He held it up in front of his face and was able to detect a faint outline. He looked back at Sophia and could identify her shape. He shuffled forward, urged on by the possibility the light was just around the next bend. It was getting tighter and the rock scraped against his belly, ripping his clothes. He squeezed around a sharp narrow corner past a protruding boulder into an opening of blinding light. Instinctively, he covered his eyes. "You're going to have to let your wee eyes adjust, hen. It's bright."

Sophia and Father McDonald followed him into the open, shielding their eyes. A stream of light from above shone down into the middle of a domed cavern. Beyond the hole in the ceiling was the sky. Their movement disturbed the wildlife nestled amongst the cracks in the cavern's walls. Hundreds of birds took flight, chirping and squawking, spiraling up and escaping into a clear blue sky. It was a magnificent sight. With their heads tilted back they watched in awe as the birds flew into the streaming light. The cave went silent. Joe reckoned himself to be trapped in the pit of a lion's den. He looked at Father McDonald who was holding his chest trying to catch his breath. He dropped his hand to his side aware of Joe's gaze.

Father McDonald squeezed out a few words. "Smell that? That's the smell of fresh English air."

"How do you know we didn't make our way to the tip of Scotland?" Joe asked, sitting on a boulder. "Don't look at me like that, hen, I'm just resting me peg. I suggest you two do the same."

"Scotland has a sweet fragrance of life that warms your heart in the coldest of winters. That's how I know we must be in England," Father McDonald said.

"Come on, we have to push on. It's not much further," Sophia said. But the men weren't budging. Sophia sat down and wrapped her arms around her legs trying to warm up. "Okay, five minutes." Her clothes were drying slowly, but she knew a warm bed awaited, and a breakfast Joe would die for.

THE AIR THROUGH THE opening in the cave ceiling was sending a chill down Sophia's spine. They had been resting for fifteen minutes, but it seemed to her like ages. She was feeling the cold more and more and just wanted to get going again — they were so close. Off to her far right a shadow moved and she turned her head as slowly as possible. The figure was familiar, an animal. It looked like the deer and it knew she had seen it. It turned down a tunnel on the other side of the cave. Sophia got up. "We have to go now. Joe, help Father McDonald. Follow me," and she ran off after the deer.

"Wait, Sophia, don't run off like that," Joe said.

Sophie walked closer to the deer. Every step she took made noise and she was afraid she would scare it off. She reached out her hand and it was gone. Joe and Father McDonald came up behind her.

"What is it?" Father McDonald asked. The three of them stood waiting for their eyes to adjust to the new darkness. The smell of salty air had penetrated down the musty tunnel.

"It's not far now," she said, looking at Father McDonald. "Casey knows we are coming. The others are together. They are tired and scared but safe for now." They moved in silence. Joe had given up questioning her. *His life, all our lives, have changed so much.* She knew what it was like to lose the people you loved and felt his heartache. *If we could only live within our dreams we would be happy and live a thousand lifetimes in a single night.* He lost his best friend and brother. She reached out and held Joe's larger hand.

"Can you smell that?" Joe said. "That smells good." They walked into another tunnel, another chamber.

"Casey was here," she said, looking at the jug and bones on the ground.

"Who is Casey?" Joe finally asked.

"He's my friend. That's who we are going to see. He's from Utah."

"Utah in the US of A? But, hen, we haven't left the country. At best we are near the Holy Island."

"That's perfect, Joe. I knew you could do it. God sent you for a reason. To be the navigator."

"That smell, it smells like a breakfast bar."

"Is Casey still here?" Father McDonald asked.

"Not in the caves," she said, "but I can feel something else. He was upset, something about a dead girl."

"Oh, shiver me timbers, hen, we'd better get a move on, so we can help."

"No, we can't help. She died a long time ago." They walked on and Father McDonald stepped into another cavern, and into and through another tunnel. "Over there," he said pointing, "up ahead."

"What?" Joe said. "Something smells good."

Sophia could see the ginger-bearded man in medieval robes passing through a wall. "I see him."

"Who is 'he'?" Joe said. "I don't see anything."

"I don't know," Sophia said. "Can you see him too, Father?"

"Yes, yes, I can Sophia."

They moved towards the wall and Joe followed his nose and found the opening into the basement. The smell of fresh eggs and toast drifted down the stairs.

"What if we are in the wrong place and the people on the other side of that door aren't friendly, after all? It could be a base of infected soldiers."

"Have you seen any of the infected eat?"

"At the beginning, yeah. I couldn't tell them apart until they got violent," Joe said.

"Okay, Joe, you go first," Father McDonald said.

"No, it's not necessary," Sophia said.

"If it's not necessary, why are you whispering?" Joe asked.

"I, I don't know. You started whispering first," she said.

CASEY WATCHED TERRY cook. He was currently working at shaking the pan to keep the scrambled eggs from sticking. He had made porridge with stewed rhubarb as well as kippers with fried tomato and toast. He scraped them into a dish then searched for a place on the table. Terry looked at all the food and shuffled a couple of plates around to make room; he realized he'd overdone it.

He looked at Amy. She was looking at him with a smile. "Hope you don't think we three are going to eat all of this?"

Terry was wearing Amy's great-aunt's apron and wiped his hands on it. He scratched his head. "I don't know what I was thinking," he said. "How wasteful. We should be conserving the food. Look at me acting like nothing is happening."

Amy got up and hugged him. "It's okay," she said, picking up a plate and kissing his cheek before spooning scrambled eggs onto it.

Casey felt Terry was tearing up. It was all starting to get to him. "Don't worry, Terry. I promise you all this ..." Casey said, waving his hand over the table like a magician, "will be gone in no time and —" Casey stopped speaking. They froze and looked towards the basement door. The stairs creaked. The dog started to bark. Casey pushed back his chair and stood up.

"Hush," Casey said and tugged at the dog's collar. The dog growled at the door.

Terry stood in front of Amy and looked back at her and Casey. "What now?" Terry whispered. "God, please, give us a break." He turned back to the basement door. *Bang bang bang.* All of them jumped with fright. The dog barked. Nobody headed for the door. Terry turned to Amy and Casey indicating for them to go into the other room and hide, but neither of them budged. He picked up the frying pan. The handle started to turn. A big wet dirty man stood at the threshold. Terry waved the frying pan up in the air, like a batter waiting for the pitcher to throw the next ball. He watched the big fella eyeballing Amy and Casey.

"You Casey?" he said in a thick Scottish accent and nodded to the boy.

"Who wants to know?" Terry said.

"Yes, I'm Casey." He stepped around the table out of Terry's reach.

"Casey, get back. What are you doing?"

"I have someone who wants to meet you," the intruder said, stepping aside.

"Don't you come any closer. Who are you, and how did you get into the house?" Terry didn't take his eyes off the man. "Casey, do you know this man?" Terry was at his wits' end, tired and hungry, endorphins from the last twenty-four hours starting to ache in his muscles, and the frying pan was getting heavy.

"My name is Joe," he said. "I have a strange wee lass who believes you are expecting her."

Terry looked at Casey; they held each other's gaze.

"Where is she?" Casey asked.

"*Sophia.* Come up here."

They could hear a mixture of delicate and shuffled footsteps climbing the stairs. There was more than one person. He couldn't hold the pan up any longer. Amy put her hand on his arm and it collapsed by his side.

Joe said, nodding to the table, "Looks like the lass was right. Looks like you were expecting us. I could smell it for the past five minutes."

Amy stepped around Terry. "Please, sit. Where are my manners?"

Terry kept one eye on the big fella and the door. Coming out of the darkness, Sophia stepped into the kitchen. She was wet, dirty and skinny, in need of a good meal. Despite that, her long wavy golden hair shone like Amy's when caught in a summer's rain. She had rosy lips and cheeks and she was beautiful. Casey had tears welling in his eyes as he looked at Sophia. Together they smiled, and gave a little chuckle. Casey was entranced and slowly walked over to her and she hugged him. Terry couldn't resist; he approached Sophia and squeezed her arm to check she was real.

"I'm real," she said.

He pulled his hand back and looked over to Amy, who was staring at Sophia as well. Suddenly there was a cough from behind her.

"Sorry, Father," Sophia said, moving further into the kitchen and stepping aside. There was a tall, frail man behind her. Terry grabbed a chair and sat him at the table before he collapsed. "Are you okay? You don't look well."

"Please, everyone come in, help yourself. My name is Amy, this is Terry and, well, it seems you know Casey."

Joe and Sophia went to the sink and washed their faces and hands. "Why are you rinsing them three times?" Casey asked Joe.

"My grandfather used to do that," Amy said. "Casey, get the man a clean hand towel from the drawer next to your right leg."

"How did you find us?" Terry said.

"Joe," Father McDonald said.

Joe blushed. Regardless of his size, Casey thought, he seemed harmless.

"Do you mind if we could dry off our clothes?" Joe asked.

Casey ran upstairs and fetched towels for them.

"Thanks son," Father McDonald said, drying his clothes before draping the towel around his shoulders.

Casey couldn't quite believe what was going on. As they sat down to eat, Joe helped himself and began telling them how he had met up with Sophia and Father McDonald. How they escaped the giant hooved creatures; that the evil eye was searching for them. Amy told them about being visited by demons and wandering spirits that were starting to appear more often. She also mentioned what happened in the barn and how he had glowed and used telekinesis to rebuild a wall to protect them. Everyone was talking at a hundred miles a minute, spilling details of every danger they had come face to face with over the past few months.

"These eggs taste so good," Joe said.

Sophia was enjoying the porridge with rhubarb and Father MacDonald had his hands wrapped around a warm cup of tea. The worst, Casey thought, was the shooting at the church. Sophia told the story with such sadness, his heart ached; and she believed it had been her fault. Casey could see Terry on the edge of his seat, wanting to pick her up and protect her from all the evil that she had seen. Sophia was mesmerizing. He supposed he had fallen under her spell over a year ago when he first saw her in his dreams. He was surprised how much she looked like Amy.

Terry started clearing the dirty dishes off the table and Joe stood to help. "No offense," Terry said, "but you guys could focus on a bath."

"Right you are," Joe said, taking a whiff of his armpit.

"The challenge is going to be coming up with some clothes for you," Amy said, leading them out of the kitchen.

Casey started clearing the table. "You go help Amy," Terry said. "Go practice whatever you call it, do your thing. And make a few quick beds."

Casey smiled and headed out of the room, but not before Terry whipped his behind with the wet end of the tea towel.

"Oi, that hurt," Casey said, rubbing his butt.

"*Oi, that hurt,*" Terry mimicked, enjoying their play.

"You must be tired, and dreaming of a warm shower," Amy said.

"You smell like you've been buried alive," Casey said.

"What sort of comment is that?" Amy said. "And how do you know what it smells like to be buried alive — no, don't answer that."

"I just meant they smell of dirt and murky water laced with sweat."

Amy crinkled her nose and shook her head. "Only a boy would

say something like that. Come on, everyone, let's go upstairs and rustle you up some clothes. Then you can shower."

Terry placed a supportive hand on Father McDonald's elbow. "Are you okay with the stairs?"

"I'll be fine. Just need to go slow. I will be much better after a good sleep."

"I'll help you, Father," Sophia said, taking his arm.

23

ORDER AMONGST CHAOS: JADE. AUSTRALIA

Daniel took off his seat belt and asked, "Sally, are you okay?" as he reached back between the two front seats to check on Alex as well. He could feel Sally's arm moving against his, and he could see Kath and Shaun in his peripheral vision. Alex was conscious, and didn't appear to have a mark on him. His little face looked like it was about to crumble into tears. "Did we crash-land in heaven, Daddy? Did nanna and pops ask God for their house to go to heaven, too?"

"No, mate, you can't take things like houses to heaven," Daniel said.

Daniel looked at Kath. "You okay?"

"Freaked. Where did that house come from? Where are we? What happened?" Kath said.

Daniel checked Shaun. His head was flopped over and bleeding. "We are at the foot of Saddleback Mountain at Alex's nanna and pop's house. Isn't that right, Alex?" He wanted to hear him talking to know he was still okay.

"Yes, Daddy."

Shaun was unconscious and had a massive lump on the side of his head.

Kath looked out the window as if they were on Mars.

"Sally, talk to me," Daniel said. "Kath, sweetie, listen to me, can you move okay? Can you check on your mom?"

Kath slowly got out of the car, steadied herself and pulled her mother's door open. "Mom, Mom, you okay? Show me — show me your face. Ah — that's got to hurt."

"My face really hurts. I think the airbag broke my nose."

Daniel pulled himself back between the two seats and took a look at Sally. Her nose was broken. "This is going to hurt, but it will be quick."

Sally screamed as Daniel cupped his hands around her nose and snapped it back into place.

Daniel got out of the car, rechecked Shaun, then gently moved him from the car and laid him on the ground making sure his airways were open. "Watch him," he said to Kath.

Daniel lifted Alex out of the child seat and sat him on the grass next to Shaun. "If he wakes up, Alex, tell him he has to stay still. Can you do that?"

Alex nodded.

Daniel approached the Dodge where he saw Callie slumped over the steering wheel. His stomach tied in knots. "Callie, Kevin, you okay in there? Answer me, Cal." Kevin opened his door and stumbled out, carrying Molly. Tim was close behind. "You all right, mate?" Daniel asked, placing his hands on Kevin's shoulders. He held him at arm's length and looked into his eyes then checked Molly. Satisfied they were fine he scanned Tim's eyes and body; he too was all right. *This is incredible,* Daniel thought. "Go help your mother, Tim. She's okay, just got a bloody broken nose."

"No need to swear, Mr D."

Daniel walked around to Callie's door, staring back at Tim. "You're not squeamish with blood, are you, mate?" he said, opening Callie's door.

"No, I'm good as long as it's not mine," Tim said, getting out of the car.

Callie's and Jade's airbags had been released. Jade's head had been pushed back into her seat and he was afraid that the blow of the exploding bag had snapped her neck. He checked Callie's pulse. She was alive. He reached over and felt for Jade's and she started to stir.

"Don't move, Jade. Don't nod or shake your head, keep still until I come over and check you. Can you do that for me?"

"Yes," she whispered. Her eyelashes glistened. "You need to make sure I haven't snapped my neck, don't you? I can feel my fingers and toes."

"That's great, Jade. Just keep still for me. I'm checking on Cal … she's unconscious. I'm just going to check she is breathing okay."

He carefully moved Callie's head back against the head-rest. No bleeding from the ears. Her left eye and cheek was swollen and the airbag had knocked her out cold. He pushed her hair off her face and lifted her eyelids, checking her pupils. She started to come around.

"How you doing, Jade? Not much longer."

JADE KEPT AS STILL as she could. Everything in front of her was like looking through a kaleidoscope. She wanted to move and wipe away the tears. Even though she was scared she was impressed. She was facing a pretty, blue-grey two-and-a-half-story house. White window frames and a large homely wrap-around veranda. A cane chair hanging on the veranda was swinging slightly. They were in the country! *Kevin has an incredible talent.*

"How are you, Cal?"

"Sore, like I fell on my face."

"Wiggle your fingers and toes for me. Does it hurt anywhere? Look at my finger, any dizziness?"

"I think I'm dreaming. Is this a dream?" "Why do you think you're dreaming, Cal?"

"Because we're butted up against my parent's veranda forty minutes away from Wollongong?" Suddenly she sat up and whipped her head left and right searching for the swarm that had chased them. Her eyes widened, memories flooding in. "The beast, the swarm, where is it? The kids, Daniel, the kids!"

"Keep still. No sudden movements, we're all safe. How did you do it, Callie? How did you get us here?"

"I don't know. I don't know what happened."

"It was Kevin," Jade said, still rigid in her seat, only swiveling her eyes in their direction.

"What? Kevin, how?" Daniel moved around the front of the car yelling back at the others. "Sally, Kath, Alex — how are you guys doing?"

"Shaun woke up, Daddy. Kath said if he moves she's going to sit on him."

"I don't think that's a good idea, Alex. Maybe you should keep an eye on both of them."

Jade tried hard not to laugh, afraid of moving. It was all so absurd. "Okay, Daddy."

Out of the corner of her eye, Jade saw Sally come up on Callie's side of the car holding her nose. "I'm all right, Daniel. How are you, Cal?"

"Could be better."

Daniel opened Jade's door and went through the same procedure he'd probably done a thousand times for car crash victims.

"You seem uninjured," Daniel said. "Although without an X-ray I can't be a hundred per cent sure."

Callie was already getting out of the car, ignoring his protests. "Jade, sweetie, are you okay?"

"I'll be fine," Jade said, slowly moving and rubbing her neck.

Kevin, with Molly in his arms, came up on Jade's side of the car. Callie walked around and hugged Kevin and Molly as one, before taking the baby into her arms. Kevin stood there as if stunned, but automatically reached out his hand to Jade and helped her from the vehicle.

Alex shouted, "I'd give you a hug, Mommy, but I have to watch Shaun."

Callie went to him and affectionately ruffled his hair. Jade saw the way Kath was looking at Shaun. Callie passed Molly over to Kath and said, "Take care of her, will you," as she knelt by Shaun and went through the same procedures as Daniel, making sure there was no bleeding or symptoms of internal damage. He was obviously concussed and had a gash on his head.

"Do you think you can sit up?"

"Yeah ... my hands — they don't hurt." He sat up and started to pull at his bandages with his teeth. "Take them off," he said, in between biting at the bandages. "Take them off."

"Shaun, you need to leave them on. It's going to take a few weeks for them to heal," Daniel shouted.

"TAKE THEM OFF."

Callie frowned and moved away.

"Hey, mate!" Daniel said. "That's no way to talk. If you want them off that badly, okay. But you won't be able to do anything and it's going to hurt like hell if you knock them."

"They don't hurt any more," Shaun said. "They just stopped. One second they were on fire and then they just stopped hurting."

Daniel unwrapped Shaun's right hand and Callie unwrapped his left. They both slowed as they removed the final strands, careful not to rip the wet gauze too fast.

"This is going to hurt a bit," Callie said.

"No, no, it won't. It doesn't hurt any more." Shaun jerked his hands away and the final bandage fell to the ground. His hands were healed. There was no sign of the burns.

"Just like my leg," Tim said. Tim flinched as Kevin nudged him in the ribs.

Callie and Daniel were flipping and rubbing Shaun's hands, over and over. Shaun smiled. Jade thought it was the first time she had seen him smile.

Tim said quietly to Kevin, "Why have his hands healed, but his head is still bleeding, and my mom has a broken —?" Kevin elbowed him hard.

"I can answer that," Jade said. "When we passed through the membrane of the parallel world, he was healed of existing injuries.

But when we were ejected back into this reality we were at the mercy of gravity and he hit his head when the cars crashed. And your mom was probably king-hit by the airbag like Callie and I."

Everyone looked at Jade.

"Don't you know anything about quantum physics? It's the healing part that really confuses me," she said. "And don't look at me for answers," she said, looking directly at Callie. "It's your son who can manipulate time and space."

"How did we get here?" Sally asked Daniel, ignoring Jade as if she found her words baffling.

"Right now, your guess is as good as mine," Daniel said, watching Kevin, Tim and Alex walk up the veranda steps to the house. Kevin fished the spare key out of the hanging flowerpot and opened the front door.

"How about we get our things inside? We also need to separate these cars. We can talk about this when our nerves have calmed, and we can rationally analyze the situation." Daniel lifted the cover off the back of the Dodge and started unloading. Shaun stood next to him. "Why don't you go inside with the others and take it easy? Just don't fall asleep for a few hours."

"No, I want to help. My hands don't hurt. I can't believe it. There is a place where everything can be healed. How did it happen?" He raised his eyes up and looked directly into Daniel's. "My dad believed there was such a place. I thought he was just ..." Shaun looked away.

Daniel saw the pain. "I'm not going to lie to you. I don't know, mate. I'm just as confused as you. I thank God we're alive. What was that thing chasing us? I have never seen anything like it in my life."

"It's from hell," Shaun said.

"Well, it has to have come from somewhere, but I'm not sure that hell is the answer. You want to take this?" Daniel handed over the cardboard box of canned and packet foods.

"It is. I was there — when the gates were opened ten years ago in the Middle East."

Daniel stopped and looked at Shaun, not sure what he was

talking about. Shaun was struggling to reveal something he had kept hidden for a very long time.

"He took me on a dig. He was an archaeologist, my dad. My mom was dying and he believed he had found a cure. A world where there was no pain and suffering. Immortality. He called it heaven on earth. He blew up ten men along with a young girl, Rachel, to have that artefact. But then he sold it to a prince, or a Russian oil tycoon in Egypt, I'm not sure. I am only starting to recall what happened and piece the memories together. I thought he just wanted the money for medicine." *There were two flights, not one,* he remembered. "My dad argued with the buyer about something. I was drugged most of the time, lying on a red and gold silky daybed, but occasionally I woke to hear my dad yelling, begging them to let him use the artefact, to open the door to a place that would heal his dying wife. My father carried me as they escorted us off the premises, shoving us into a limo and driving us to the airport."

Jade couldn't help her curiosity, but now wished she had gone in with the others. Daniel seemed as if he didn't know what to say to Shaun. She felt he was telling the truth. Maybe some of the story was confused in Shaun's mind because he was young and fragile when something extraordinary happened to him and now he believed all of it to be true memories. She watched Shaun pull out a bulging leather pouch and pour the contents into his hand.

"I think they somehow needed these too."

Jade couldn't see.

"They fell out of Dad's backpack to the Jeep's floor and I took them."

Kookaburras laughed, crows cawed and the smell of cow manure suddenly overwhelmed Jade's senses. Shaun tipped the contents back into the pouch and shoved them deep into his front pocket.

"Be careful you don't lose them. They would be worth a fair bit. You shouldn't carry them around."

"Sure." Shaun took the boxes from Daniel and walked up the porch stairs.

NIGHT WAS FALLING by the time they had dinner, cleaned up and were settled for the evening. In the living room, Shaun was playing a game of jacks with Alex on the rug using the stones from his pocket. He scooped them up off the floor as soon as Daniel walked into the room. "Where's Kevin?"

"He went outside to the hangar to show off the plane to Jade. I think he's got a thing for her. Has he really flown it?"

"Yeah, Callie's dad taught him as soon as he could see out the window. He's a pretty awesome dude. Why don't you guys get along?"

"I don't know." Shaun closed up and walked out of the house.

"Come on, little guy, it's past your bedtime." Alex jumped up into Daniel's arms and hugged him tight.

"I don't want to sleep alone. I'm scared the angry giant is going to pull the roof off the house when I'm sleeping, and stick his hand inside and search through the rooms until he finds me. Shaun said that he would sleep with me and stab its hand if it tried to get me. But he just left, where is he going?"

"He's just gone to get some fresh air. How about I stay with you until he comes back?" Daniel carried Alex to bed. He nudged open the bedroom door with his foot and laid him down on the bed.

"No, not this bed! Shaun said he would sleep in this bed in case it comes through the door and he will attack it so I can run away."

"Okay, buddy," he said, laying Alex on the other single bed. He closed the window and the shutters. Alex was making him aware of his own fears. *I suppose we are all going to be a little jumpy and afraid for a while.* Daniel lay on the bed, sharing the pillow with Alex, and started to tell him a story about the time when Alex had visited his nanna and pop in the school holidays with Callie and Kevin. "Early in the morning, Kevin showed you how to milk the cow. When you were finished, he pulled two straws out of his back pocket and gave you one. Together you sat in the barn on the hay drinking the warm milk." Daniel felt Alex's breathing settle into a peaceful rhythm. The door squeaked open and Shaun popped his head in. Daniel waved for him to come in and turned on the bedside light and whispered, "Are you okay?"

"Yeah, tired. I'm going to hit the pillow," Shaun said.

"I'll come in and check on you both later. Thanks for your help today."

"You don't need to check on me," Shaun said, lying on the bed with his back to Daniel.

"Night." Daniel left the bedside light on and quietly walked out.

AT THE FAR END OF the sweeping wooden veranda that stretched around the country home Jade sat in an egg-shaped white cane chair that was hanging from the roof. Jade had her feet tucked up on the seat and she rested her chin on her knees. She studied her toes, thinking of her parents. Her contact lenses were annoying her but she resisted the urge to rub. Kath and Sally had made themselves comfortable sitting on a cane sofa.

"Mobile phones are useless these days," Kath said to Sally. "We can't just stay here, we have to do something."

A warm morning breeze gently lifted Jade's raven hair as she vacated her solitary chair. She went inside and the screen door closed quietly by itself. Jade agreed with Kath, having tried to call her dad six times this morning, without success. She went to the bathroom to dry her eyes and adjust her contact lenses. She thought about Kevin and couldn't help believing that he could help her get back to her dad and find her mom.

It had now been a couple of days since they had arrived and everyone was on edge. Kevin had asked his dad if they could go for a walk up Saddleback Mountain later today, saying it was important, but he didn't know why.

Jade could hear the boys at the back of the house, and Daniel and Callie were in the kitchen cleaning up from breakfast. The house reminded her of her own home, just a lot bigger. She closed the bathroom door. Her eyes were irritated from crying and she fished out her contact lenses. Sitting on the edge of the toilet seat she grabbed her stomach as if in physical pain, then dropped her head forward and cried. Her tears splashed onto the blue and white tiles. Jade hardly moved for ten minutes, letting it all out. She felt her mind becoming distracted, intrigued by the way her tears had landed in between the tiles and falling close enough together to dampen the grout. How random ... but no, it wasn't random, was it? Because her posture and lack of movement created the same pathway for each tear to fall. It gave her some sense of relief to see order amongst the chaos. "S = k log W," she said aloud. "S = k log W."

Bang, bang, bang. "How long are you going to be in there? I've got to do a number two," Alex's muffled voice said.

"Coming out now." She flushed the toilet and washed her face and hands.

"Hurry, I can feel it popping out like a turtle head."

"That's disgusting, Alex." She pulled open the door and held it for him, but he didn't rush in.

"Are you sad?"

"No, just dirt in my eyes."

"That's what Kevin says too."

"I thought you were busting?"

"Is it going to smell? Do I have to hold my breath?"

"Is what going to smell?" Jade said.

"In there," he said, pointing inside the bathroom. "You were in there for such a long time you must have done a number two."

"No, it's not going to smell," she said. A smile crept across her face and she gave him a little push inside the bathroom. Just before the door closed, Alex yelled, "Oh, K's looking for you."

Jade walked down the long hallway towards the back of the house and out to the veranda. It was peaceful and everything looked so ordinary, it was hard to believe the world was falling apart. She had to stop thinking like that; it didn't help anyone. Focus on sifting through the disorder to find order. She leant against the rail and looked out across the fields. The hangar side door boomed as Shaun slammed it behind him.

"And stay away from my brother," Kevin yelled.

Jade watched Shaun turn around and lunge at Kevin and suddenly they were both on the ground wrestling. She jumped over the wooden rail. "Stop it, you two," she said, coming up beside them. Tim came running over and pulled at Kevin. Jade pulled at Shaun's shirt.

"Stop it," she said.

Daniel came up behind her and pulled Jade off Shaun. "What's going on here? All of you over here, park yourselves on the steps."

Kevin dug his elbow into Shaun's ribs as he got up and as he went to the steps Shaun smacked him up the back of the head.

"Enough, you two. Kevin, what's going on? Why don't you two get along?"

"I don't know, Dad."

"Yes, you do, don't give me that."

"Maybe you would like to explain, Shaun?"

"He's a bully," Tim said. "He beats up on anyone who pisses him off and has a fascination for petrol bombs."

"Shut up!" Shaun said, swiping at Tim.

"How do you know this, Tim? Think carefully before you answer. I have only seen Shaun helping out since he has been here with us. He has paid more attention to Alex than you, Kevin. He has just lost his father in a fire and you are accusing him of being a firebug. Did you see him start any fires?"

"Well, no, because —" Tim said.

"So you didn't see him start any. Did he tell you he started any?"

"No, but —"

"But what?"

"I was there."

"You were at the scene of the fire?"

"We were down at the river when we saw Shaun and his entourage leave the area just before it went up," Kevin said. "That's all."

"We need to work together, guys. You both have seen what happens if you give in to urges of violence. Nobody wins, we all lose.

For the rest of the day I want you two to work together. Whatever your differences are, or what you think each other has done, you leave behind now and you start to care for one another. I know it sounds gross, but try it. You understand what I'm saying? Kevin — Shaun?"

Jade watched Kevin and Shaun avoid looking at each other until the tension seemed to ease as Kevin relaxed.

"Sure, Dad. I'm sorry, we all deserve a second chance."

"Shaun?"

"Yeah."

"Okay, pack a couple of backpacks and we will take that hike up the mountain."

Jade stood up and Kevin followed with Tim. "Wait up, guys," Daniel said to Kevin and Shaun, still sitting on the veranda steps. "Together. If one of you is in the toilet I want to see the other one standing outside the door waiting. Got the picture?"

Jade found the image funny and quickly turned away. Shaun stood up and fell into step with them.

"Why do you guys dislike each other?" Jade asked.

"It's nothing," Kevin said.

"Nothing!" Tim said.

"He broke my leg, crushed my knee. He is a maniac," Tim burst out.

"I knew I broke it!" Shaun said, as if a puzzle had just been solved. "I heard it crack, but then when I fell off the roof I saw you standing next to me. I couldn't work it out."

"There, he admitted it," Tim said, looking at Jade. "I told you he broke my leg."

"Is that when you went into the parallel world to escape the fire?" Jade asked. "If it is, that explains why you saw him walking around, Shaun. He had been healed. Isn't that amazing? You could create a space for the sick to walk through — like opening and closing a door — as long as they work out why they are sick in the first place, because everything has a cause and effect. Like what's happening around the world. There has to be a root cause somewhere that we can go back to and correct."

Shaun looked at Tim's leg again and back at Jade and she thought he was going to cry.

Instead, he said, "Well don't give me reason to do it again," and walked off. Kevin followed him and Tim stayed with Jade.

24

SEEDS OF EXISTENCE: CASEY. ENGLAND

Casey waited, sitting at the bottom of the stairs, for one of them to wake up. It was after three in the afternoon and they had been sleeping all day.

He wanted to burst into Sophia's room and check she was still there. Twice Amy caught him trying to quietly open the door to take a peek, and twice she scolded him with just a look, ushering him downstairs to this very spot an hour ago.

"You're going to have to come up with a name for that dog," Amy said. "Come on, let's go for a walk."

"Where to? It's not safe," Casey said.

She held out her hand to him. "Come on." Casey took it and allowed her to lead him through the living room into the kitchen and out the back door. The dog came running out of the woods, glad to see them. The wind had a sharp chill, their breath was frosty. Winter had crept up on the calendar. They approached the edge of the woods and waited for the dog to catch up.

"I was thinking of calling her Lucy," Casey said, dropping to his knees. The dog licked his face and Casey wrapped his right arm around its neck, giving it a rough pat and a scratch along its back.

"After your mom. That would be perfect."

"Why?" Casey asked.

"Because ever since this dog showed up it has done what it could to protect you, just as your mom would."

"I haven't decided yet." Casey looked down at his boots as they walked.

"I'm sorry about the other day," Amy said. "I am so sorry. I don't know what came over me. At first I thought I had the virus and that frightened me so much. I was worrying about you and Terry and the baby."

"Babies! And it's okay, I get it," he said. "I know you're sorry. The twins will make you smile."

She bit her bottom lip, hesitated and in a soft voice she asked, "What do you see?"

"One image, just one image, of you wearing a white summer dress, sitting on your knees on a picnic blanket on green grass trying to control two babies determined to crawl all over you. You are laughing. They are giggling and climbing over you and you nearly lose your balance and have to throw your hands behind you for support, while they continue to keep climbing. One is trying to suck your chin. I can't quite tell if it is two boys, or a boy and a girl. One is definitely a boy. You are very happy."

"What about you and Terry, and everyone else?"

"I don't know, that's all I see," Casey said.

She put her arm around him and gave him a squeeze and kissed his head. "You still need that haircut." He put his arm around her and together they walked to the front of the house.

They came across Father McDonald on his knees on the ground, praying, his eyes closed. *When did he wake up?* Casey approached Father McDonald and knelt beside him. Amy did the same so that they were all side by side. Casey closed his eyes and imagined an angel hovering above, ready to take their prayers up to God.

"May your light shine upon us Lord, and enter our hearts so we may be filled with your mercy and strength. I pray ..."

Casey listened to Father McDonald pray and his body filled with effervescent light. He was unaware the prayer had finished. He was still on his knees, but felt the movement of sand under his feet and between his toes. His mother was walking next to him, pointing to the eastern star in the sky. It was dawn and it was the only star, the sun not quite woken from its slumber. He thought he caught a glimpse of a man wearing robes and a funny nightcap, with a ginger beard. He vanished as soon as Casey tried to focus on him. His mom told him of things to come, and that people needed to dare to dream. She talked of him growing up into a man and how he was to teach the others when he was of age. But not once did he see her lips move or hear her voice. They walked in silence and after watching the gentle rhythm of the whitecaps she was gone, the feeling of the sand was gone, the ocean and the morning star, all gone. His knees started to feel the ground beneath him, his ears heard the sound of Amy's voice. He took in a deep breath and opened his eyes. His face was wet with tears, but he didn't recall crying or why. The images faded as a dream fades, their meaning passing, like the sweet fragrance of flowers in a garden. He looked up to see Father McDonald and Amy talking, waiting patiently for him to come around.

"Sophia is often doing this," Father McDonald said. "You just have to be patient and wait for them to return."

"Return from where?" Amy asked.

Casey cleared his throat and said, "I'm right here, I haven't gone anywhere. I may have dozed off but I can still hear you." He got to his feet. "Why were you out here praying? Couldn't you have done it just as well inside?"

"Casey don't be rude, he can pray wherever he likes."

"No, I didn't mean anything by it."

"It's actually a good question. I was outside for a reason. I was reading paragraphs for protection. We are all in great danger of losing our souls. Our bodies are always destined to return to the earth, but our soul is for eternity. If we lose that we will be outside the gates of heaven forever."

"Great, just when I was starting to feel a little better," Joe said from behind.

Casey spun around and there she was standing next to Joe

wearing Amy's jeans and sweater. Her hair was in a plait that draped over her shoulder.

"You remind me of someone," Amy said to Sophia.

Sophia smiled at Amy as she walked closer to Casey. They fell into step and walked away from the adults.

"Where are you two off to, hen?" Joe asked.

Casey had to wait for his brain to interpret the accent. But before he could reply, Amy said, "Don't go into the woods or past the garage, and don't let the dog out of your sight."

"Lucy, here, girl," Sophia called to the dog and it ran up to her and sat down in front of her. Its tail dusted the ground waiting for praise. Amy and Casey held each other's gaze. Casey pulled away first.

"Why did you call the dog Lucy, Sophia?" Amy asked.

"Isn't that its name?"

Amy looked at Casey, Sophia looked at Casey, they both waited for an answer.

"Yeah, her name is Lucy."

"Okay, then that's settled. Lucy it is," Amy said. "Dinner will be ready in an hour," she said, reaching to touch Joe's shoulder. "Come on, I bet you're famished," she said.

Casey felt a sense of gratitude towards Amy. Father McDonald, Amy and Joe wandered inside the house and the smells of Terry's stew came drifting out as they opened and closed the back door.

"Hmm, that man can cook," was the last thing Casey heard. He was alone with Sophia for the first time since she had arrived. Now that they were together and alone he didn't know what to say or do. He could feel she was feeling a little strange too. He felt her hand brush his and he gently took it.

PIGEONS COOED IN the loft and light streamed through the rafters. Sophia passed an eye over the items in the barn and sat on the motorcycle. She leant forward, holding onto the handlebars and said, "We have to meet up with the others, although I can't see how it's going to happen."

"We can chill and wait a day or two and see what happens," Casey said. "I keep coming back to this one thought: we are all that is, all that was, and ever will be. We carry all the seeds of all existence. From the stars in the sky to the table in the kitchen to the pain in our hearts, we are the light and the darkness."

"You're right. Can you see how we meet the others? I think we will come together when we least expect it, but sometimes I just want to know. It can be so annoying at times not knowing, but sort of knowing, if you get what I mean. Can you start this motorcycle?"

"I get it." He didn't need to be asked twice. He directed his energy smoothly over to the motorcycle and it roared into life.

Sophia's body tensed. She smiled in joy and trepidation. "That's so awesome," she said. "I have never been able to do anything like that. I can feel its power. It would be marvelous to go for a ride." He watched as her energy expanded with joy and excitement.

"Can we take it for a ride?"

"I ... I don't think so."

"Oh, come on. Just out the front and back," Sophia said.

"Okay, why not? We're probably going to die anyway, might as well have fun."

She climbed off the bike and pushed him. "Don't say that. Take it back, right now! We're not going to die Casey." She gently put her hand on the side of his head. "It's all in here, remember. If you think you will be defeated, then that's what you will be — defeated. If you think you will be successful, then you will be successful. Put out negative thoughts, you get negative results. Put out positive thoughts and you get positive results. Simple. If you don't believe me, try it."

"Sorry, I didn't mean it the way it sounded," Casey said, defending himself.

"Nobody does. I know. You have to put consciousness into each thought, otherwise you become a drifter and then you are open to all sorts. That's better, your aura just changed. Now I can see flashes of emerald-green, peachy-orange and violet. You balanced yourself, excellent. Let's go for that ride."

"Do you always see auras? I don't."

"No, not always, and I have worked hard not to see. It's paying off."

"You will have to get off while I push it out."

He wheeled the Bonneville backwards out of the garage and climbed on. He held it steady while Sophia threw her leg over the back. She held onto the passenger side-bars. Casey wished she would hold onto him. He slowly let out the clutch. It revved out in first gear, but it didn't matter. Casey worked out the clutch and how to shift into second. The bike jerked and accelerated a little faster down to the gate. They skidded slightly at the fence. Slowly, Casey maneuvered the motorbike and did a wide U-turn. He saw Terry on the back steps with his hands on his hips. Casey rode slowly up to him.

"My turn!" Terry said.

Casey had been sure Terry was going to be cross. "No worries, she's all yours," he said, putting the motorcycle in neutral.

Terry held the bike still while Casey and Sophia dismounted. Terry popped the stand down with his foot. Climbed on and flicked it back up. He gave the Bonneville a couple of revs and took off. It wasn't long before Joe came out and wanted a turn. Amy sat on the step with Father McDonald and watched. It was Casey's turn again and this time he went solo and felt the freedom, the wind in his hair. He felt alive. Casey settled into the seat and the joy and freedom of riding. He could have headed out the drive and down the road and just kept going.

"You know you have to wear protective gear next time!" Amy yelled.

"What about me?" Sophia called.

Casey circled back. Sophia was grinning with excitement and hopped on as soon as he pulled up. This time she put her arms around his waist. Butterflies danced in his stomach, his face felt like he had stepped into a sauna. Anxious to have the wind cool his face he put the bike into first and turned to ride back to the front gate.

Another great feeling; being on a motorcycle, he thought. *It couldn't get better than this.*

Having fun was energizing. After the adults finished playing with the bike Casey and Sophia had one more turn, then parked it in the garage. Casey kicked an old coaster under the stand after he positioned the bike just right.

Sophia waited and fiddled with the odds and ends in the barn. "While I was on the back of the motorcycle," she said, "I saw us riding again. We weren't alone, and I don't mean Joe and Terry. Those from the other side of the world are going to have a turn on your Bonneville. They are coming to us."

IT HAD BEEN A long day. After spending last night in the basement, Casey was extremely tired. He didn't want to sleep, though, and he was worried that when he woke, Sophia would be gone and it had just been a dream. But his eyes were not going to stay open unless he pinned them to his eyebrows. They were all sitting in the lounge room and he had his legs flung over the arm of the chair next to the bookshelves. Amy and Terry had their legs curled up on the sofa. Father McDonald and Joe sat in the armchairs facing them. Sophia was only an arm's length away, the coffee table with the lamp on it between them; it was the only thing separating the pair. He tried to focus on the conversations. He grew more and more tired. The lights started to flicker, he floated into a restless sleep, and was unaware Amy and Terry were now standing by his side.

THE EMERALD TABLET: CONVERGENCE

PART THREE

25

___

INTRUSION: KEVIN. AUSTRALIA

"Why have you got a backpack on, K?" Alex asked, hanging upside down on the sofa.

"We're hiking up to the lookout," Kevin said, adjusting the straps.

"Can I come, pleeeassse, can I come?"

They were gathered in the front room that overlooked the driveway, waiting for Daniel. The room was filled with light and the house smelled of sage and lemongrass. Kevin missed his nanna. Even though he felt her presence, she was always just out of sight. With his backpack ready and strands of his hair caught in the corner of his mouth, he said, "No. You can't come."

Daniel walked into the room. "Get your hair out of your mouth. You will be coughing up fur balls like a cat." Shaun and Tim laughed at the same time and they both cleared their throats.

"Dad, can I come? *Pleeeease*?" Alex stretched his neck as far back as he could looking up at Daniel. "*Please, please.*"

"No, buddy, it's just the big boys this time. Maybe you can come next time."

"But she's going and she's not a boy. Why does she get to go?"

"That's enough, Alex. We need a man to stay back and look after the girls."

Jade huffed and put her hands on her hips.

"What?" Daniel said, looking at her pose.

"That was two sexist comments in a row."

"Alex, you are getting me into trouble here, buddy," Daniel said.

Jade stepped towards Alex and put her hand on his shoulder, crouching down to his height. "You can't come because we have long legs and you would have to run to catch up with us and that would make you very tired. Then you would have a miserable time and want someone to pick you up. Do you understand?" Jade said.

"Yep, you don't want me to come because I am small," he said, stomping away.

"Don't you think that was a bit harsh?" Daniel asked.

"No, he now knows the truth. It's just logistics; there is nothing emotional about the decision."

Shaun, Tim and Daniel headed out the door with Jade and Kevin bringing up the rear.

They started heading for the green paddock where a couple of cows were grazing. They all jumped over the white fence, ignoring the cows.

"Hold up," Daniel said. "Shaun, take off your pack. Kevin, I want you to carry it."

With a smirk on his face, Shaun dropped a strap off one shoulder and then the other, and handed the pack to Kevin.

"What? *Daaad*, what gives?" Kevin said, taking the straps.

"Take yours off and give it to Shaun to carry."

The smile fell from Shaun's face. Together they all walked in silence until a brush turkey ran in front of them. It did a random dance and then took off into the bushes.

"Why do you always have your hand in your pocket?" Tim asked Shaun. "You playing with yourself?"

"You're disgusting! It's none of your business."

"That's rich, coming from you," Tim said.

Kevin and Jade had a bird's-eye view walking behind them. His dad looked at Shaun as if waiting for an answer too. He handed Tim the binoculars to carry. Shaun was ignoring Tim, but he pulled his hand out of his pocket, adjusted the straps on Kevin's backpack and kept walking. Kevin could feel his dad's tension, Tim's excitement and the sadness in Shaun, plus the cogs in Jade's head were spinning faster than the rest of them put together.

"What are you thinking?" he asked. "You really want to know?"

"Sure."

"About S = k log W. Entropy, it's a mathematical formula for a concept measuring from order to disorder and it can't be reversed because of the arrow of time, which is the direction of events that always moves forward. Like an apple fallen from a tree can never levitate itself back onto the tree, but we could make apple pie. If we take broken colored bottles and, for instance, glued them together they will never be the same, but the fragments can be turned into a stained-glass window creating a beautiful new state of order — perhaps ... to create order from disorder lies within our thoughts. Order is there but our perception only sees the disorder until we create a sense of order. But we can't go back to the original state." *Why not, why can't we go back in time or forward for that matter?* Jade stopped talking, aware she was lost in her own train of thought. She looked at Kevin and smiled, wondering what he thought of her mental rambling.

"And why is this important to you?" he asked.

He had been listening. She felt excited. "Because I believe we can change what is happening to the world. If we know at what point it shattered — I mean, like when the virus first manifested itself, which is the cause, we can create a new reality — order from the disorder, like the broken glass bottles. The world won't be the same after the virus — think of it as humanity's visit to the brink, hopefully no more than that — we will begin to grow and rebuild again."

"What are you talking about back there? Come on. Catch up, ketchup." Tim laughed at himself. "You know the story of the slow turtle ... I suppose you had to be there."

Ignoring Tim's sick joke Kevin immersed himself in Jade's theory, which was hard to grasp. "We can put humpty dumpty together again, he will just be in a different state of being. Okay, so we can somehow change the global mess we are in if we find out how it all started and fix it."

"Well, yes. Simply put, we have to find the pieces that created the disorder. This didn't just happen. This was the effect of something. We have to change it, put it back somehow." They reached the mountain a few minutes behind the others who were leaning casually on the railing and looking outward. No one was moving.

"What is it?" Kevin asked as he approached his dad, although he didn't need any explanation, because he could see everything from the mountains to the ocean. Most of the waterfront apartments were halved and smoldering. Out at sea, coal ships were on fire and three massive giant demons were forming and unforming, breaking down into smaller versions of themselves into what looked like a flock of birds or a swarm of bees. Nobody moved. Kevin felt like he was in a cyclops movie. Instead of dumb and clumsy, these were an intelligent negative life force of death, an abomination. "A fresh southerly wind is blowing north-east. That's why we weren't getting any smoke," his dad said.

"Look over there, ten o'clock." Tim pointed to the west where the lake met the trees. Five figures, all men, stepped from two four-wheel drive vehicles. Tim handed the binoculars to Kevin.

"What do you think they're doing?" Jade asked. "If we wave, do you believe that we can get their attention? I can barely see them."

"We don't want them to see us," Kevin said.

"Why not?"

Shaun took the binoculars from Kevin. "He's right," Shaun said and handed the binoculars to Daniel. In the distance, the car door slammed silently. Daniel peered through the glasses and could see clearly, as if the five men were mere yards away. One reached into the back of the car and dragged someone out, throwing him to the edge of the lake. Seconds later, Jade drew in a sharp breath. Gunfire echoed across the valley.

"Don't look," Daniel said, but it was too late. Shaun pulled the binoculars back off Daniel. Unsure of what they had just seen, not wanting to believe it, they were rooted to the spot and watched the men get back into the vehicle. They drove off, revealing the actual carnage.

"What did you see?" Kevin asked Shaun. Shaun didn't say anything. "What did you see?"

Shaun had his arm outstretched offering the binoculars to Daniel, but Kevin grabbed them.

"No!" Daniel said.

Kevin held the glasses to his eyes. The crimson shoreline was littered with dead bodies. The water gently lapped up against them. Kevin dropped the glasses and doubled over, his hands on his knees. His legs felt shaky, his stomach did a backflip and turned and turned and turned. He couldn't hold it any longer and his breakfast splattered over the ground.

"Tim, Shaun, get away from the edge." The four-wheel drives had stopped. One person stepped out onto the side rim with his own pair of binoculars and was looking in their direction.

"Guys, quickly, get away from the edge and hide," Daniel said, pushing them down. They made their way back to the pathway and lay down on the ground.

"I think they may have seen the glint of the sun on the lenses," Jade said.

Kevin had never seen so many dead people. "Normal people like you and me. Families dead for what? Nothing." He wiped his mouth and felt the blood moving through his veins again.

"Do you think they saw us?" Tim asked.

"I'm not sure. We'll just wait here until they move on," Daniel said.

The binoculars were where Kevin had dropped them and Shaun started to slither across the ground to get them. Daniel yelled at Shaun to get back. He kept going. He handed the binoculars to Daniel and said, "How long do you think it would take them to get to us from over there?"

Daniel carefully moved into the scrub beside the path and peered down, across the valley to the lake. He saw the men were moving again. "If they wanted to get to us they could be here in an hour."

"But it took us that long to walk up here," Jade said.

"Then we'd better run," Shaun said.

They headed down the path, out into the car park and started jogging down the narrow winding road. Kevin kept pace with Jade and Tim. Shaun and Daniel led the way. Jade held her side.

"You okay?" Kevin asked, jogging beside her.

"Just ... just a stitch in my side."

Tim skidded on the gravel as he turned off the road, grazing his leg. Jade and Kevin helped him up. Daniel looked over his shoulder and saw Tim on the ground and ran back. "You okay?"

"Fair dinkum, what did I do? I must have killed a thousand people in a past life."

"Well, actually, "Jade said, panting, "if you believe in karma ... then I would say you must have done something right because you haven't been vaporized, crushed, beaten to death, shot, or even swallowed up by *that*," she said, pointing to the east. "So you're doing pretty well. Wouldn't you say?" Jade stopped talking and rested on her knees trying to catch her breath.

"Dust yourself off, mate, it's just a scratch," Daniel said.

They headed off the road and across the paddock. The house was in sight and looked just as they had left it. The road was clear, no dust in the air. All was quiet.

Shaun came up to the wire fence that stretched across the paddock and held the barbed wire down for them all to climb over. It was his turn and Shaun hesitated; Kevin pulled the barbed wire down as far as he could to show him it was okay and there wasn't going to be a surprise attack.

They jumped the white fence onto his grandparent's property. The house was peaceful. Mixed smells of cooking and laugher filtered from the kitchen window, and waiting to greet them on the back veranda was Alex. His dad sighed with relief as he laid his hand on the screen door and Alex's head before picking him up and opening the door fully. He stopped before stepping across the threshold.

"Okay, guys," Daniel said. "Someone needs to always be at the far corner of the front veranda, it's the best view of the approaching road." Alex put his little hand on Daniel's chin and turned his head towards him. "What's happening, Daddy?"

"Nothing, Alex. Go tell your mother we're back." He put Alex down. He watched him run along the hallway with his hand under his armpit trying to blow out a tune.

"No mention of what was on the shoreline, and tonight we will need to reduce the amount of lights. Go around the outside of the house and take the bulbs out of the sensors. If you see a light on in the house turn it off. Make sure all blinds are closed. Keep the noise down and we should take turns during the night watching the road for approaching lights, just in case. Any questions?"

"Yeah, why don't we just get the hell out of here?" Tim asked.

"There isn't anywhere else to go."

KEVIN COULD HEAR, inside the house, Kath and Molly laughing at Alex who was making sounds from his armpits. The smile on his mother's face disappeared as he walked through the kitchen doorway. She looked at his dad, Shaun, Tim and Jade, then back at Kevin.

"You look like you all ran back. Is everything okay?"

He challenged his own urge to hide and pretend she wasn't seeing their worry. "You're right, mom," he said.

"Oh, God, what happened, who's dead?"

Daniel looked at Callie, and then back to Kevin.

We must look to him as if we're having a silent conversation. But I've said nothing, she just knows.

Her hand went to her mouth and she turned back to the sink. Her voice was a little shaky. "Okay, we have made a jug of lemon juice. There was an old cake packet in the cupboard that was only out of date by three months. It will be out of the oven in five minutes. Clean yourselves up, then we can talk about what you all saw."

Kevin moved to the sink and without turning around she said, "Not here, all of you upstairs."

Kevin waited until everyone had gone upstairs before he looked up and down the hallway. The kitchen smelt wonderful from the fresh chocolate cake baking in the oven, and the sound of laughter mixed with lemongrass and sage. He could see out the front door and out the back door, both leading onto the veranda. A gentle breeze banged the back door, which hadn't quite latched. "Nanna, are you here?" He stood still using his peripheral vision and caught a whisper of light that passed him by.

"I knew you were here keeping a watch. Ask God to send the crows and let us know if anyone approaches, please." He breathed in and closed his eyes, breathed out.

"Kevin, who are you talking to?" Callie asked, stepping into the hallway.

What do I say? Kevin opened his eyes, meeting his mother's. "Nanna."

"I feel her too."

Cautiously, he asked, "Can you smell her?"

"What does she smell like to you?"

"Lemongrass and sage."

"Is that so? I've been smelling sage since we arrived," Callie smiled. The oven beeped, the cake was ready. For a moment, they stood there awkwardly.

She's changing. "I'm going upstairs," Kevin said and walked off after the others. He stopped at the top of the landing and looked out the arched window. The road was clear.

26

EXTRACTION: SHAUN. AUSTRALIA

Shaun could hear Jade in the next room, crying. He tried to ignore it. Something else had woken him. He looked over at Alex and the little fellow was snoring. The bedside digital clock in bright red announced it was 4:44 a.m. Shaun threw back the sheet and sat on the edge of the bed, mopping his brow. He was covered in perspiration again. He had been dreaming of Rachel and they were in a cave. She had grown into a young woman, standing fearlessly before a giant blazing black dog surrounded by a firestorm. It swiped at her, stabbing her with its claws. He could still feel the heat as he had tried to save her. Then something woke him up.

He pulled on his jeans, quietly opened the door and stopped and listened. He went into Kevin and Tim's room. Tim was snoring and Kevin was half hanging out of the bottom bunk. Shaun then looked into Jade and Kath's room, where Kath was fast asleep, oblivious to Jade's sobbing. He gently poked Jade in the shoulder, trying not to startle her awake. Her eyes shot open, and she stared with a lack of recognition. He had seen that look a thousand times in his father's eyes, but it didn't last long with Jade. She looked puzzled.

"You were crying in your sleep," he whispered, as Kath started to stir. Moonlight was streaming into the room.

Jade looked out the window; a crow crashed into the glass and she gave a little shriek. "Crows don't fly at night," she said, alarmed.

Kath woke in fright and screamed. Shaun slapped his hand over Kath's mouth, frightening her. She struggled and bit his hand.

"What the fuck? Shut up or you're going to wake everyone in the house." Then headlights probed the blackness of the room. "Oh, shit! Jade, go wake Kevin and Tim."

"Kath, get your mom and meet us in Kevin's room. You've got about thirty seconds."

His bare feet slapped the wooden floor as he ran down the empty hallway. He ducked into his room, lifted Alex out of bed and carried him as best he could, although the boy's dangling feet kicked him in the groin. He struggled with the door handle. Alex seemed to weigh a ton, but finally the knob turned and he entered Daniel and Callie's room. Shaun gently tossed Alex in the middle of the bed.

"What's going on?" Daniel said, trying to open his eyes, reaching for the side lamp.

"Don't turn it on, we have company. I just saw their headlights coming up the road."

"Shit, go wake everyone."

"I already have and told them to meet us in Kevin's room."

Alex nestled into Callie, peacefully drifting in and out of sleep. She soothed him, keeping him calm. She moved him aside to climb out of bed, quickly dress and slip into her sneakers. Shaun ran back down the hall to Kevin's room. Daniel carried Alex, and Callie had Molly in her arms. Shaun reached out for Kevin's doorknob. He hesitated, listening to the sound of tyres moving along the dirt and stone driveway. It was getting closer and stopped somewhere out front.

Quickly, he slipped into Kevin's room. Alex started to whimper in Daniel's arms. Molly was asleep and Callie gently rocked her willing her to stay that way. The car doors opened ... they all held their breaths.

"Shh, you have to stop crying," Shaun said to Alex. "If they hear you crying they will come and hurt us."

"Don't talk like that to my brother. We don't know who they are," Kevin said.

"Yes, we do. It's those guys we saw pop a cap into that dude by the river yesterday. They are also the same guys who chased you and Tim."

"What, no way. Shouldn't we do something? We can't just hide in here," Kevin whispered.

"You saw what they did to that guy?" Now an inch away from Kevin's nose he said. "Didn't you?"

AT SIX IN THE EVENING Casey was slouched in the armchair and started to toss and turn as he dozed. He was burning up. He called out Sophia's name.

"What's happening, is he sick? Why won't he wake up?" said Amy.

"He's okay. I could go into a trance and help him, but this — he has to do this one on his own. If I was meant to be with him, we wouldn't be having this conversation."

Casey's head hung over the side of the chair at an odd angle. Joe picked him up and laid him on the sofa.

Sophia held Casey's hand and the room around them started to change. "Relax, Casey, just relax. We're with you. Don't be afraid, you are here with us." There was a circle of light forming around them and she saw Amy become alarmed and agitated. Sophia wasn't shocked, she knew what was happening. The ghosts of the past started to appear and the apparitions and emotional memories began to play themselves out for all to see. Sophia couldn't help feeling excited; she was thrilled and touched by the display of memories, and the reality of the promise of the afterlife. She had always felt the gentle touch of a world beyond her sight. Father McDonald pulled out his Bible, and started praying for Casey's protection, just as he had done for Sophia throughout her life.

Amy brushed back Casey's hair and blew a cool breeze onto his brow. The apparitions took stronger physical form than previously.

She became afraid for Casey. "My book," Amy said, "my grandfather's book."

Sophia saw Amy's fear. "Don't be afraid. No matter what happens he will be okay, even if he dies."

"How can you say that?" Amy said.

"Because it's true. There is an angel that only answers to God that keeps watch over Casey. But he won't die again, not today."

Amy knelt on the floor by the sofa and knocked her knee on something; she pulled a book from under the couch. Sophia was in awe of the light radiating from it. Amy opened the book and the letters glittered and danced off the page. Sophia felt jubilant, astonished and totally amazed.

"Amy, you are holding a book of splendor, a channel to the creator. You are blessed." Tears pooled in her eyes as she looked at Amy, who looked as innocent as a child sitting on the floor. The letters circled and expanded to include everyone. It was a spectacular sight.

"How can I be blessed when I am surrounded by such turmoil, and I am filled with anguish for the pain of humanity? I have no family. I have lost children before they were born. I am terrified I will lose Casey and he will fall victim, like so many, to the darkness."

Sophia didn't answer. She had no words to express the love Amy amplified with her words.

"Tell me, how can I possibly be blessed?" Amy asked again.

THE WINDOWS WERE closed, the white blinds were drawn. Shaun saw Callie look at Kevin and Tim sitting on the bottom bunk with Jade in between them. Nobody was doing anything. *What are they waiting for?* Shaun thought. *Why are they just sitting around, don't they get it?* Alex was bravely holding back his sobs and buried his face into Daniel's neck and wrapped his legs tight around his waist. Daniel paced the floor. Molly continued to sleep in Callie's arms, unaware of the commotion. "She's always been a good sleeper. Once darkness falls, she dependably sleeps till sunrise," Callie said to Kath.

"We can sneak out the back to the car, or we could make a run for it into the hills," Daniel said.

"Can't we just hide?" Sally said, pulling Kath close to her.

"They will eventually find us," Callie said. They heard the car doors opening and closing.

"I'm not hiding anywhere," Shaun said. "Those guys won't think twice about offing us."

Callie held Molly close to her chest. "I know, follow me!" She left no room for protests. She opened the door, checked the corridor, and was out of the room and rushing down the hallway.

"What the hell, Callie?"

"Daniel, hurry up," she whispered.

The kids jumped up and squeezed past Daniel and Alex. Shaun, Kevin, Tim and Jade ran down the back stairs after her. She went out the back and onto the veranda. Quietly, in the dark, they slithered along the side wall of the house towards the hangar. There was only fifteen feet between the house and the hangar's side door, but it might as well have been a mile. Callie had stopped. Shaun heard the front door splintering as it yielded to the pressure of heavy boots. He felt a chill rush up his spine. He saw Callie clutch Molly even tighter. Suddenly she ran into the opening making a dash for the hangar. Kevin raced past Callie and he reefed the side door open and they all piled in.

Lastly, Daniel ushered Sally and Kath into the hangar. The door quietly clicked closed behind them. "What are you thinking, Cal?" Daniel whispered.

"We can fly out of here. Isn't it obvious?"

"The plane hasn't been started for over a year — and what about those things in the sky? It's filled with them."

"These guys are going to —"

Before she could finish there was a flash of light streaming from the house. The hangar's only window lit up. Suddenly there was a loud bang. *Gunfire*, Shaun thought.

"Come out, come out, wherever you are." The stranger's voice was loud and sinister.

Callie reached for the plane's keys. Daniel moved Alex onto his hip and stepped up onto the wing. With one hand he held the door open. "Come on, everyone. Quick. It is going to be a tight squeeze," he said.

Callie stopped Kevin before they climbed up onto the wing. "You have to help me. You're the only person who has flown this plane."

"What? Me!" Kevin protested. "Pop only gave me a couple of lessons."

"Just about the same as me," Callie said. "You remember the walk-around checks? Remove the tie-downs, check the fuel, tyres, remove the cover from ... what's it called?"

"The Pitot tube. Shit, Ma."

"I'm not getting in there if he's flying," Shaun said.

Callie raised her eyebrows. "You have to."

"Kevin! Stop underestimating yourself. Now move."

He stood smiling at her positive words, which didn't elude him.

"Why are you smiling? Move."

Kevin hurried to begin the external procedures. Callie jumped up into the cockpit. Shaun climbed in after her and watched her start the pre-flight checklist. *This is going to take forever.*

KEVIN SEARCHED THE empty bench drawers for the clear flask to do the fuel check. "Top drawer, K," he imagined his pop saying. The Piper Cherokee 6-300 had been sitting unused in the hangar for over a year. Kevin wasn't sure that it would even start, but first there had to be fuel and it had to be un-spoilt. He could hear gunshots as the men searched through the house, randomly firing like idiots. He had to relax, he had to concentrate. There was a lot of ifs in front of them. Relax, Kevin told himself, and the image of his first night flight six years ago when he was eight came into his mind. The yellow and white streetlights below had been beautiful. It had looked as if the city was wrapped up in glittery gold and silver tinsel. He fell in love with flying that night. The gunfire brought him back to the present. *What the hell? Daydreaming now, K, is going get you killed.*

He found a torch and a tube and walked over to the plane, draining about an inch of fuel out of each wing. He first smelt it; the potency smacked him in the face. He then checked the color and clarity of the mix and, to his surprise, it was perfect. He checked the tanks: the left wing was full, the right side not so much. He continued the procedure, remembering how much he loved flying. He nearly jumped out of his skin when gunfire echoed through the house. He kicked the tyre blocks out of the way and climbed up onto the wing. It all took no more than couple of minutes, but it felt like an eternity.

"Left wing's up to taps," he said to his mom.

He looked into the back of the small plane; it only had four passenger seats. Next to Jade, Alex was sitting on his dad's lap. Sally was cradling Molly, sitting beside Kath. Tim climbed over the white leather seats into the baggage space and nestled in the rear fuselage behind Jade. Shaun sat on the floor between the four seats. Kevin suddenly felt his eyes well up and his throat tighten with tears, then realized they weren't his tears, weren't his emotions, they were Jade's. He smiled at Jade, then looked at his mom. "There's no room in the back for me," he said.

She patted the co-pilot seat. "I reserved it for you." She resumed going through the pre-flight checklist; he could see the aileron and the flaps on the wings going up and down. He moved to his seat and put on his headset. Callie handed him the laminated checklist and he read out the next instruction.

"Carburetor heat — off."

"Check." His mom's voice came through his speakers loud and clear.

"Annunciator panel — check lights."

"Check."

"Circuit breakers — check in."

"Throttle — ¼ inch open."

"Check."

"Mixture — rich."

"Check."

"Fuel pump — on."

"Check."

"Primer —"

"Callie," Kath said, her face butted up against the small side panel posing as a window. Her voice was quivering. "How much longer is this going to take? I can see them. Do you think they know we are here? The house is lit up like a power plant. They are going to kill us, aren't they? They're going through every room. Three of the men are heading onto the veranda."

Daniel placed his hand on Callie's shoulder, his voice controlled, totally monotone. "I don't think we have time for this, Cal."

Kevin and Callie ignored them, concentrating on the procedures.

"Okay, I don't want to open the hangar until we have started the engine," she said. "We are going for a cold engine start. Sorry for stating the obvious."

Kevin nodded and kept reading the pre-flight checks.

"Magnetos — both."

"CLEAR PROP," Kevin shouted, looking out the side panel window.

"Start engine — set 1000 rpm and confirm oil pressure."

And Callie started the engine. The plane coughed and went silent. Callie started the engine again. It coughed — and pulsed into life.

Kevin checked the oil pressure. "Okay, handbrake off," Kevin said and the plane began to move.

"The door! The hangar door!" Daniel yelled.

"Where's the remote?" Callie fumbled in the side pocket of the door where the pre-flight checklist was kept, and blindly searched with her fingers for the remote control. "Got it." She pushed the button. The hangar door groaned, slowly moving and clunking as it folded back into the roof. She lifted her toes off the brakes and onto the rudder.

"Damn, I forgot the specimens." Callie braked hard. "Handing over control," she said into the mike, "You got it, Kevin?" and started to undo her seat belt.

"I have control," he said robotically just like his pop taught him. But he didn't want control, he wanted his mom to take it back. "Where are you going?"

"Taxi out of here and pick me up at the back paddock fence," she said.

"But, Mom —"

"No buts!" In a softer tone, she said, "You can do this, Kevin." Callie climbed onto the wing and slid off the plane.

Daniel yelled at Callie over the sound of the engine. "Where the hell are you going? What could be more important than your family? For Christ's sake... Cal!"

Kevin saw her shoot out from behind the plane, out the side door and she was gone. The hangar door was wide open, and Kevin steered the plane with his feet. Three men suddenly appeared in front of the aircraft and Kevin slammed on the brakes. He idled just before the threshold.

"Get out of the plane," one of them demanded. Their rifles were raised, ready to fire.

"Dad?"

"Floor it, K," Daniel said.

"But, Dad, what if they don't move?"

"Floor it, K, full throttle."

Kevin released the brake and the plane started rolling. Flashes of light ignited from the gun barrels. The bullets ricocheted off the propeller blades. The men didn't budge. Kevin turned the plane as sharply as he could, trying to avoid them, hoping they would duck under the wing, but he felt the sudden shudder of the propeller. There was a yell from inside the house. Callie screamed. They could see her silhouette fighting, struggling with one of the men by the kitchen window.

"Callie!" Daniel screamed and held Alex's head close to his chest blocking his ears.

Kevin screamed out his window for the men to leave her alone. It was impossible for him to be heard. The two men still standing in their way took off and went back into the house. Kevin rolled the plane out of the hangar, towards the front of the house and the two four-wheel drives.

~

SHAUN WASN'T IN THE best position to see what was going on outside the plane, but his hearing was just fine. He was cramped, but he felt safe. It had been a long time since he had been on a plane and a long time since he felt safe, but now, hearing Callie's screams, anxiety crawled over him. The anguish in Daniel's voice as he shouted to Callie was like nails down a chalkboard.

"Oh, God, please, please no." Daniel sat Alex on Jade's lap and reached for the door.

Shaun watched Daniel. He was ready to jump onto the wing and off the plane, but he hesitated. He looked back at them all and Shaun could see, in his eyes, the pain. Shaun knew then that Daniel wouldn't leave them. He sat back down and gripped the cold metal handle, while Kevin taxied in front of the house. Shaun looked up into Daniel's face and saw the torment. He wriggled out of his tight spot and slipped through the partially open door. He felt Daniel grapple for his shirt before he fell onto the wing. Shaun landed hard, grazing himself on the gravel driveway. He jumped up and hid behind the side of the moving plane. Hunched over, he ran to the back of the house. He was out of sight. He no longer heard Daniel yelling at him to get back on board.

He saw Kevin speed down the drive, into the dark, towards the short runway. Shaun stayed down. He had the advantage of surprise and wanted to keep it that way.

"It's the woman. Hold her still."

Shaun snuck up the back steps. Then he stopped, and remembered the can of petrol under the workbench, below where Callie had found the keys. He crept back down the stairs and ran into the hangar and grabbed the can and some rags. Keeping quiet he headed to the front of the house and crouched beside the first four-wheel drive. He popped open the petrol cap and stuffed in the dripping rag, then did the same with the second four-wheel drive. He could hear Callie screaming and it actually bothered him. *When did I start to care? It hurts too much to care.* He couldn't cut off the sound of her screams. *Why did she go back, anyway? For what, a couple of specimen jars?* The doubt was smothering him. *I should just run and not look back. I don't need them.* Ignoring his thoughts he focused on the lighter in his hand and the soaked rags. This was familiar, making petrol bombs, and the feeling of confidence returned. He knew how to blow shit up. Shaun set each rag alight and ran down the side of the house. The explosion threw him off his feet and he could feel the heat over his back and head. He could smell it singeing his hair. He scrambled to his feet as the men ran out the front door.

Shaun ran up the back stairs and through the back door. He stopped in the hallway and peered into the kitchen. Callie was being held by the neck up against the far wall. There was only one man in the room. Shaun picked up the brick that was acting as a doorstopper and rushed at the man, whacking him hard in the back of the head. It took Callie a few seconds to register Shaun, but as soon as she did she was moving, pulling open the refrigerator for her little blue esky.

Shaun gripped her wrist. "Leave it. We have to get out. Come on."

Callie had what she was looking for and was first out the back, the screen door's spring slowly retracting as the door closed gently behind them. They hurdled over the veranda railing and headed across the paddock. Shaun could just make out the flashing red and green lights on the wings of the plane as it turned off the road speeding across the paddock towards them. It slowed, but didn't stop. The cabin door flung open and Daniel grabbed the esky from Callie. She ran next to the plane, stumbled. Daniel leant out and reached for her hand as bullets whistled past their heads. Daniel lifted Callie up into the plane. The men ran across the paddock closing the gap between them. A bullet hit the tail wing. Shaun heard it first pass his ear and he instinctively ducked. The plane was pulling away. They were going to leave him.

Daniel came back out onto the wing. "Run, Shaun, run. Come on, boy, faster."

Shaun dug his toes into the grass and sprinted to catch up. He reached his hand out to Daniel, missed, and touched the flap. He reached up and felt Daniel's hand around his wrist. Shaun tried to climb, his dirty feet slipping, leaving skid marks along the wing. Daniel held the door with one hand and pulled Shaun towards the cabin with the other. Shaun gripped the side of the cabin, practically crawling in through the door and felt a hot poker in his back. He slipped back out onto the wing. The pain quickly became excruciating and swept over his whole body. Daniel had a strong hold and pulled Shaun screaming, up and inside the plane. Shaun lay slumped over Jade and Daniel's lap.

Alex put his hand on his head. "You'll be okay, Shaun."

Shaun felt Alex's little hand on his head patting him as the plane turned and accelerated away from the house. Kevin pushed the throttle all the way up and the plane thrust forward. It seemed to take forever to get into the air and when the tyres left the ground Shaun's stomach suddenly dropped and they were up.

"You're bleeding! Oh, my god, you're bleeding!" Kath said.

He could see ahead between the two front seats as if he was lying on the back seat of a car. Kevin and Callie were pulling back on the yoke, changing the pitch of the plane, as it went higher and higher into the dark sky. *Molly's ears must be aching*, Shaun thought when she let out a piercing scream. Alex sobbed quietly on Jade's lap. Daniel pushed down harder on Shaun's back trying to stop the bleeding. *I've been shot*, he wanted to say. *The bullet hasn't come out the other side. It must be lodged in an organ or something.* He was dizzy and didn't feel much of anything any more. He looked at Alex and said, "You're alright ... you'll be fine," and Shaun's eyes closed.

Casey lay on the sofa in Amy's house. The windows were boarded up. The chill of the English air was coming under the doors and down the chimney. Casey could hear Sophia and Amy as they tried to wake him up. Their voices seemed to be a long way away. He was too far from his body to go back now.

Casey could feel the other boy's distress and moved closer towards him until he saw him shudder. A cold chill ran down the boy's spine. *I'm the cold chill*, he thought. Casey endeavored to see where he was and to get a look at him, but he could only see out of the boy's eyes. He was in a plane, that much was obvious. The boy was hot, sticky with sweat and he could feel everyone else's emotional pain. He was peering through the cockpit window into the dark, searching the fields for someone. He spotted a woman, his mother, running from the back of the house and steered the plane straight across the field towards her. A wave of relief washed over him once she was on board and could help fly. Casey felt the boy's surge of gratitude for a boy who was with his mother, when suddenly the other boy was shot in the back.

Casey managed to move from the boy's mind, around the cockpit and out through the windshield to look back at him. *This is so incredible — I've totally left my body. Hey, I know that face, I know that guy!* Casey thought. It was the last thing he remembered seeing a year ago, when he fell from the bridge into the floodwaters.

Casey heard the boy's mother telling him to pull up; they pulled on the controls together lifting the nose up and the plane rising into the air. She called him Kevin — his name is Kevin! They were in the air. Behind them, Casey could see dark clouds heading towards the rear of the plane. It wasn't any ordinary storm. The clouds were controlled; a swarm of evil micro-organisms were chasing them. A few surrounded the engine, so it became totally concealed by what looked like a swarm of bees. It ignited into flames and Kevin and the passengers screamed as the flames lit up the sky.

Why am I seeing this? I am about to witness this kid's death. It was terrible, they had no chance, and the engine was gone. The nose bowed to the earth and gravity did the rest. The girl in the back was yelling at Kevin to open a door. *Why would she want him to open the door?* Casey wondered. There was no point in jumping. Casey slipped back inside Kevin. Kevin's desire to save his family was so over-whelming that Casey felt like he was going to explode with energy. Kevin had become a powerhouse.

The girl leant forward and Casey could hear her as if she was in his own head. "Kevin, listen to me," she said. "Relax, you got this."

Next to Kevin, his mother was fighting with the controls and trying to spin a wheel down at the side of her seat. "Trim, trim," she said, trying to get the nose of the falling plane to lift up. "Trim, damn it. I can't hold it."

Then Kevin relaxed. Casey could feel him relax and his own body, lying on the couch with Sophia and Amy around him, relaxed. *Kevin, can you hear me?* Casey asked. He didn't answer. Casey watched as a small hole started to appear in the atmosphere directly in front of the plane as it jolted and dived. Everyone screamed. Lightning slammed into the tail, taking out the rudder along with Kevin's focus.

Kevin? Casey said.

KEVIN STRUGGLED WITH the controls and thought, *I'm a little busy, if you haven't noticed. I hear you, loud and clear. Get the hell out of my head.* Then suddenly they traded places. Kevin was inside Casey's mind seeing Casey's memories. He could feel a cold cloth on his brow. He was lying on a comfy couch. Casey had been with a girl, laughing and riding a motorcycle. She looked familiar too. Kevin didn't have the mental capacity to focus on her, because his family was about to die. He pulled himself out of Casey's head and back into the cockpit.

Casey could feel Kevin's confusion. You know her, Casey said, don't you? Come here, come to us, come to England.

You're about a thousand miles away and three days too late, Kevin replied. The girl was yelling again for Kevin to open the door. *I know who you are.* Kevin's eyes moved over Casey's memory again, seeing him riding down the driveway lined with birch trees on a chilly English afternoon. He focused on the memory and opened the door. The cockpit was filled with sage and lemongrass and his mouth tasted of metal. A soft hum pulsed through the plane. Lightning exploded, revealing a translucent ripple of energy stretched out in front; an opening, a doorway.

The engine stopped and the sky was filled with silence. The plane continued to fall, dropping into the mirage, vanishing from the sky.

CASEY FELT HEAVY, back in his own body on the sofa. He was surrounded by Joe, Terry, Amy, Father McDonald and Sophia. Casey willed his muscles to move; he had to tell Sophia what he had seen. He stirred. It was hard to get control of his own body again, it felt like lead. He started feeling the sofa under his body and Amy changing the wet cloth on his brow. Slowly he opened his eyes. Apparitions in the room were fading as he returned.

"Hey, you," Amy said. "Are you okay?"

Casey tried to slowly prop himself up. His body still felt like it weighed an additional two hundred pounds. He was exhausted, but he needed to talk to Sophia. He needed to tell her before he forgot. He dropped back onto the sofa. His lips were dry and Terry was ready with a glass or water. Casey reached for the glass. Terry held it to Casey's mouth. He took a sip and said. "Sophia, I think it's the others. His name's Kevin."

Father McDonald struggled onto his feet and moved closer to Casey. "Is the boy okay? Who else is with him?"

27

KNIGHTS AT THE LONG TABLE: CASEY. ENGLAND

Boom! The windows rattled. Outside, a high-pitched, teeth-clenching screech of metal could be heard scraping down the driveway.

Joe was first to the door.

Terry, Amy and Father McDonald, already on their feet, followed Joe. "You two stay here," Amy said, looking at Casey and Sophia. Amy's gaze met Sophia's blue eyes. "Look after him, okay." She left the room.

"You guys!" Joe yelled over his shoulder as he ran out. "It's a plane!" He jumped down the steps following the aircraft and waiting for it to stop sliding.

～

JUST SHORT OF CRASHING into the birch trees, the plane lay silent in the twilight. No burst of flames, no smoldering fire. Joe approached with caution. The plane rested, tilted on its side. The left wing had been torn off on impact and lay a yard away from the aircraft. The paint was stripped back, the side sliced open and the tyres had blown out. It was amazing it wasn't a fireball. Joe thought he saw movement

355

from inside the plane. He pushed down and bounced on the right wing testing its stability. Confident it would hold he hoisted himself up. He saw people moving in the darkness of the cabin. He pulled at the door. It wouldn't open, so he dug his nails in between the cracks of the door and the plane and tried to wrench it open. No good. The grass around the belly of the aircraft was starting to smoke a little and he thought he could smell fuel. A baby cried. Someone was kicking at the door. The plane rolled a bit more onto its belly, tilting further to the left and flames ignited in the grass. The banging against the door grew stronger. Joe pulled and pulled at the door. Everything was happening too fast.

Terry came up next to Joe with a crowbar in hand. "Okay, Joe. Together!"

Both men leant their weight against the wedged bar and the door strained and popped open. A baby coughing, choking on its own tears was handed to Joe. He passed the little bundle down to Amy, and she quickly walked away from the plane to safety. Next was a young boy. Terry lowered him to the ground. Father McDonald took the boy's hand and together they rushed to Amy. The plane's tail ignited.

"Mommy, Daddy!" the young boy cried. He was pulling at Father McDonald's hand trying to go back to help.

Joe held his hand out to each person emerging from the plane and guided them off the wing. Two teenage girls, two women, one gripping a white and blue icebox, two boys, and the man who had kicked the door dragged an unconscious young man out onto the wing. Joe's eyes were tearing with smoke.

"Joe, move back," Terry yelled.

Joe jumped off the wing and the man dragged the boy to the edge of the wing and climbed down. He grabbed the young man under his armpits and pulled.

"Grab his legs," he yelled to Joe.

Together they carried and laid him on the ground next to the coughing boys. Joe expected the plane to blow any second. Amy took the two women and children into the house. Joe scrambled after

Terry to grab a hose, and shovels. "We have to get this fire under control before it burns the surrounding trees." Joe dragged the hose across to the plane, passing the passengers taking refuge against the house, and saw the unconscious young man was sitting up. Terry was firing foam onto the burning aircraft.

"Where did you get that from?" Joe asked.

"It was in the boot of the SUV," Terry yelled back.

The man and one of the boys picked up the shovels and tossed dirt from the driveway onto the fuselage. Joe turned the nozzle and a stream of water flowed.

The man yelled at him to stop.

"Not water! It will just spread the fuel." He sat the boy back down against the house and jogged over to Joe. "Let it burn itself out."

Joe turned off the nozzle and Terry finished emptying the fire extinguisher.

A boy with a button nose and auburn hair hanging in his eyes stood next to Joe and said, "Hi, thanks for that. The plane looks like it's ready for a shave, don't you think? Fair dinkum, we're lucky. We've made a hell of a mess of your yard. That will be Kevin's fault," he said, pointing to the athletic-looking chap.

Joe smiled. The odd young man walked off over to his friend and smacked him on the back and side by side they watched the smoldering flames.

Joe, rubbing dirt off his hands, walked up to the man and Terry and said, "Where are you from? Your accents tell me you're not from around here. If I was to take a stab in the dark, I'd say you're from that land down under. Aye, well, you're best to be moving inside."

Terry shook Daniel's hand and said, "I'm Terry. That was Joe. Come in and get yourselves cleaned up."

Joe walked up the back stairs into the kitchen and leant his elbows on the sink. He turned on the tap, and allowed the water to pool in his cupped hands, splashing the water onto his face. He gave the soap to Terry, before pulling paper towels off the wall mount to pat his face and hands dry. He sized up the newcomers who had literally dropped out of the sky.

The woman, late thirties, shoulder-length sandy blonde hair, hiding behind glasses that gave her a dull, slightly old-fashioned look, was clutching a wee icebox under one arm and held the girl baby in the other.

She stood up and moved to the fridge. "Can we put this in your freezer?" she asked, and reluctantly handed over the tiny icebox. Amy smiled and obliged, moving a few items to make space.

"What the hell?" Joe tossed the wet paper towels in the garbage. He moved smoothly, considering his size, around the kitchen table, nearly knocking Amy off her feet as she closed the refrigerator door. The eldest boy from the plane had a large patch of fresh blood on the back of his shirt. It was soaked. His shirt was torn and burnt around the tear, a bullet hole. The boy followed Joe's gaze and tried to crank his neck around to look at himself. Joe pulled up his shirt to find the source of the bleeding. The icebox woman handed the baby to one of the teenagers and joined Joe's search of the boy's back. But there was nothing there.

She held the boy's shoulders and said, "What were you thinking!" She pulled him in for a hug. He had no chance to pull away. "Thank you," she said, "but don't you ever do that again."

The man holding the little lad also embraced the young man.

"Okay, it was nothing. Don't sweat." Embarrassed, he stepped out of the embrace.

The other young lad with the sooty face — who was trying to hide behind his fringe — looked up and said, "Yeah, thanks, man."

"You did it, K. You did it," the girl said softly.

No one seemed badly hurt, a few bumps and bruises. *They can't be all one family.*

"Nice flying, dude. Fair dinkum, I thought we were on our way to meet my dad. I was shitting myself," his button-nosed pal said, patting him on the back.

But what the hell does fair dinkum mean? Joe thought.

Terry cleared his throat and began the introductions. Joe was impressed by his host and hostess who were now unflinchingly welcoming these new people into their home. It was hardly forty-eight hours since they let Sophia, Father McDonald and himself take refuge.

In a strong Aussie accent the man shook Terry's hand and arm and said, "I'm Daniel, thanks a million. I wouldn't have been able to open the door without you and your crowbar. This is my wife Callie, and our baby Molly. This is Sally and her two children, Tim and Kath. That's Jade, Shaun and my two sons, Alex and —"

Joe turned at the utterly unexpected sound of Sophia and Casey's voices in unison saying, "Kevin."

Everyone turned in the direction of the living room. Standing on the threshold, half-hidden by shadows, were Sophia and Casey. Kevin wiped his eyes against his shoulders, pushing his fringe to one side to see clearly. Confused, he stepped forward. *What the hell?*

Casey and Sophia stepped forward into the light and Kevin stopped as if he recognized Casey. He turned to his mother to say something and stopped.

"How do you know my name?" Kevin asked.

The atmosphere in the room had changed. Everyone was mystified and wanted to know.

"Sophia talked about you. You recognize her, don't you?"

Kevin looked nervously at his mother and father and then at his friend, who shrugged his shoulders.

"Yeah, I remember her. She was there that day, when you fell. You fell into the river."

Joe caught glimpses of confusion, affection and shame from Kevin's parents.

"How the hell did you survive?" Kevin said. "How?"

"Yeah?" Tim said, stepping around the table and standing by Kevin. "He got into so much shit trying to help you that day. Everyone thought he was a crazy attention-seeker." Tim raised his hands and made exclamation marks with his fingers. "The boy who cried wolf."

Jade stepped forward too and stood next to Tim. It was starting to look a little like a showdown.

"Okay, people," the young lass said, "I think we should be focusing on why we are all connected? Why are we *all* here?" She moved forward and introduced herself to Casey and Sophia. "I'm Jade."

Then she shifted uncertainly from one foot to the other, looking down at her feet, as if deciding whether to speak further or not. She chose not to speak and stepped back. Kevin looked at her as if he couldn't quite work her out. *She's a strange wee hen,* Joe thought. *One minute she was shy, the next outgoing and taking control.*

"She's right," Father McDonald said. "Sophia has been prepared for …. I don't fully understand what, but the time is now. For these young ones to know each other is a miracle. You just survived a plane crash and that's a miracle, and for none of us to be sick with the virus is another miracle. God has protected us with his armor."

Then, in a faint voice, Kevin heard Shaun say, "And I took a bullet in the back and only have a bloody shirt, is a miracle."

Terry said. "You're welcome to stay as long as you like."

JOE HELPED AMY prepare the house for her new guests. He carried the linen to her great-aunt's old room downstairs, which was for Daniel, his wife and his two young ones.

"This room has an en suite and the bed should be big enough for you all," Amy said, showing Callie the room. "If you'd like a cot, there is one in the basement. The men can bring it up, so just ask."

Joe laid the fresh towels and linen on the bed.

"That won't be necessary, thank you," Callie said.

"The three boys can share with Casey. It's a massive room and is right above you. Upstairs, next to the main bathroom, is Sophia's room and Jade can bunk with her. The room is across and down the hall a little from the boys. Father McDonald and Joe are next to Sophia's room. Sally and her daughter will be further down the hall in the old nursery. Once you've freshened up, please join us in the living room for some tea." Amy left Callie with her little boy and baby. Exhausted, Amy went and sat down in the living room.

Joe followed her. He was struck by her caring nature; he couldn't take his eyes off her. She picked up her black book and held it open in her lap and started to read. He wasn't sure if she knew he was there. He cleared his throat and she closed the book in fright.

"Oh, sorry Joe, you gave me a fright. I didn't hear you come in."

"Amy, I want to thank you."

"For what, Joe? I haven't done anything that you yourself wouldn't have done. Why don't we go and help Terry and you could slice up some of that delicious boiled date cake you made. I think I am going to like this."

"What's that?" Joe asked.

"Two men in the house who love to cook."

It wasn't long before Kevin, Tim and Jade came downstairs, refreshed and hungry. Casey and Sophia sat alone at the far end of the white kitchen table that seated twelve. Terry was at the kitchen bench wiping the side of a teapot with his tea towel, and Joe was slicing up two cakes.

Kevin pulled out a white chair and sat opposite Casey and Sophia. Jade decided to sit at the head of the table in between them like an adjudicator.

"You saw me that day," Kevin said to Casey.

"You were the last thing I saw above the surface of the water, when I was pulled under for the last time."

"What do you mean, pulled under?" Tim asked.

"I felt something. The water went murky and I felt as if a claw had wrapped around my leg. It held me and dug its nails into my calf muscle, and my knee was wedged between the rocks. It was pretty mangled when Terry found me. I was lying on a road a mile away from the creek, in the middle of a freak hurricane."

"That wasn't a creek, that was a raging river," Kevin said.

"It was a creek earlier that morning, a dried-up creek."

"What happened between the time you were being pulled under and when you were found on the road?" Jade asked, resting her chin in her hand, leaning forward as if intrigued with Casey's story. Kevin couldn't help smiling as he watched her.

"I don't know. Suddenly I was on the road in the middle of a storm spewing up muddy water and hearing a panicked voice telling me it's going to be all right. That was Terry, and I have been with them ever since."

"What about your parents?" Jade asked, sitting back.

"Dead." Casey lowered his head and traced the lines on the table before looking back at Jade.

"You worry about your mom," Sophia said to Jade as Joe gave her a piece of cake. "Thanks, Joe."

"How? How do you know that? You don't know me." Jade became defensive.

"No, I don't, but it governs your aura. You care for her; you believe Kevin is the key."

Feeling the emotions and tension escalating between the two girls, Kevin moved in his seat uncomfortably.

"We all have something, a gift, and that's why we are together," Sophia said.

"Okay, peeps, cards on the table," Tim said. "Am I the only non-gifted person here? I suppose that makes me unique — extraordinary, as a matter of fact."

Kevin rolled his eyes, smiled and nudged him in the side. "Chill."

"Dude, really? My ribs are killing me from the last time you elbowed me," Tim said. "And let's not mention the plane crash."

"Guys, if you want to hug, go ahead. They are always like this," Jade said, looking at Joe as he put the cake on the table next to cutlery and plates for everyone.

Joe smiled at her and said, "I was like that with my brother. I would love to have been free enough to just hug him." He walked out into the living room.

"Okay, what do we do? Who goes first?" Kevin could feel a sense of urgency from Casey and Sophia.

Sophia pulled her chair a little closer to the table, leant forward and said in a soft voice, "We need to return something. I have seen images of caves and statues. But I don't know what has to be returned. I'm hoping one of you know."

They looked at each other: Tim at Kevin and Kevin at Jade, Jade at Casey and Sophia. Casey kept looking at Jade.

"What, why are you focused on me?" she said.

"Your energy is connected to whatever it is, and don't ask me how I know, I just see it around you."

"When I touched her …" Kevin ran his fingers through his fringe, pushing back his hair as he moved in his seat, becoming uncomfortable. He worried what he was about to say would be misinterpreted. "What I mean is, when I helped her up, I felt a strong connection, and there was a surge of energy that raced through my body. I felt like it was uniting us. Jade is crucial. Then I find out she knows my mom, and my mom knows her mom, and my mom was the last person to see her mom."

"Think about your mom, Jade," Sophia said and closed her eyes. Sophia's breathing started to slow.

Kevin could sense that Jade was scared and she folded her arms across her chest. "I'm waiting for the crystal ball to appear," she said. "I suppose it's in the cupboard with the shackles and the sheets for a ghost. This is like a carnival sideshow." She was trying hard not to burst into nervous laughter. Sophia spoke, sending shivers down Jade's spine.

"The Indian knows … your mom's not dead … Great Turtle said she's not in the spirit world."

"Stop it!" Jade pushed back her chair and stepped away from the table. She looked at Kevin to back her up.

He could feel her panic. She wanted to believe, but her logic was keeping her suspicious and confused. He gave her the most innocent look of support and kindness. She zeroed in on Tim instead and punched him in the arm.

"Why me? That's it!" Tim said. "No more violence! We are up to our necks in this crappy world because of violence; no more. Next person that hits me is going to get …" Tim chewed his lip, looked up for an answer. "I don't know what, but I'll come up with something non-violent!"

Jade went cherry-red. "Sorry, Tim, I just want it to be true." She started crying and Sophia went to her and hugged her. "I'm sorry."

Jade shoved Sophia into a chair and held her down by the shoulders. "Don't hug me, I don't know you. I want it to be true, I want it to be true so much, please tell me it's true." Jade turned away from the table and leant against the sink.

"It's true. I don't know where she is, but she's not dead." Sophia reached for the tea pot.

Tim picked up the knife and started cutting more cake and passed everyone a second piece. No one spoke. They sipped tea and picked at the cake. Tim was finished within three bites and had a third piece. Kevin watched his friend and could feel his light energy. Tim, unknowingly, had changed the atmosphere, clearing the heaviness that Jade's emotions created in the room. Kevin gave his mate a half smile and raised his eyebrows.

"Well, if we don't know what it is that has to be put back," Kevin said, "how do we find out?"

"Someone will know," Sophia said.

"But none of us know," Casey said.

"Someone knows," Sophia said again.

Joe walked into the kitchen and leant over Kevin to cut a piece of cake, excusing himself as he did. "If she says someone will know, you ought to believe her." Joe scraped a wooden chair over the floor as he pulled it out and sat at the table. "She told me that we would find this place. We were walking underground in the dark, and here we are." He stuffed the piece of cake into his mouth, pushed back the chair, and walked out.

"I like that man," Tim said. "I think we are from the same loaf."

"Okay, then," Casey said, watching Kevin chew his fingernails. "The man's got a point."

Jade pushed off the sink, picked a napkin off the table to wipe her eyes and sat down in her chair, still trying to process the information. She started twisting the napkin. "Is he a Buddhist?" she said softly. "Jewish, Hindu or Kabbalist? The red string? Is it to realign his energy, a symbol of prayer, to bring people together, or is it a sign of protection and goodwill? You have one too, Sophia."

"Are you going to keep guessing the answers to your own questions, or would you like me to jump in?" Sophia asked.

Jade blushed again. "Please, sorry."

Sophia twirled her red string and touched her medallion under her shirt and looked thoughtful, before saying, "You should ask Joe. But it does, it does all those things."

"Tell them what you know," Casey said to Sophia.

Kevin couldn't take his eyes off Casey. He still couldn't believe it was actually him — and he was alive. "Where were you when you drowned?"

"In Utah, USA."

"I thought I recognized your accent, but why do you two sound different?" Tim asked, referring to Jade.

"We are from different parts of the States, approximately two thousand miles apart," Jade said.

"How did you get here?" Kevin asked.

"Amy's great-aunt left her this place. We came over just before the borders closed and flights were grounded. We have been stuck here ever since."

"So how do you know each other?" Kevin said to Casey.

Sophia and Casey looked at each other and Sophia said, "After I saw him drowning, I kept an eye on him."

"How?" Tim asked. "You have an unmistakable Scottish accent."

"I can astral travel."

"You can what?"

"Astral travel. I was, am, a disturbed kid. I miss my dead family and wanted to be with them so much I separated my spirit from my body, and astral traveled. I have to be asleep or in a deep meditative state. Is that how you saw Casey in the river?" she asked Kevin.

"Well, no, I was wide awake when I popped up in the middle of the river."

"We're getting off the subject here," Casey said. He turned to Sophia and expressed in a hushed tone, "If you think we are supposed to be in this together, you'd better tell them what you know."

"Hang on, hang on, everybody," Tim said. "The question is," he said, pointing to Kevin and Jade, "where are we now?"

"What do you mean?" Casey asked.

Father McDonald walked in from outside. "Sophia, it's time. You need to inform the adults."

Sophia stood up and Father McDonald put his arm around her shoulders, more for her help rather than her comfort. The others without a word got out of their chairs and followed them into the living room.

"Where are we?" Tim watched them leave. "I asked one question."

28

———

WINDOWS IN TIME: ENGLAND

S haun opened the door and steam rushed from the en suite.

"You will pass out in there if you have it too hot," Callie said.

"I want Shaun to stay with me," Alex said with a little boy's enthusiasm.

"No, Alex. Shaun will want to go in with the big boys."

"I don't want to go to sleep," Alex said, jumping up on the bed, then jumping onto Shaun's back as he passed. Shaun didn't anticipate the move, and staggered about, then spun around playfully before dropping backwards onto the bed.

"Body slam," Alex said.

Shaun had never had a younger brother and wasn't sure how to behave. He preferred to scare little kids, so they would stay clear. Alex was persistent and wasn't easily scared. "I don't mind," Shaun said. "I'll stay with Alex until he goes to sleep."

"Yeah, yahoo!" Alex was thrilled and jumped up and down on the bed.

"Alex, shh, Molly's asleep. Shaun can only stay if you promise to be quiet and get in bed." He bounced down onto his butt and scrambled under the blankets.

"Move over," Shaun said.

"Okay," Callie said. "Shaun, when he's asleep, come into the living room."

"No worries," Shaun said.

Shaun made himself comfortable and began to tell Alex a story his mother had once told him about a boy with magical balloons tied to the post of his bed. When night fell and everyone else was asleep, he would untie the balloons and they would take him on a magical journey across the world, returning him before sunrise. Alex fell asleep before the balloon boy's journey ended and he returned from the heart of Africa. Shaun slid off the bed and quietly left the room, closing the door gently behind him. He quickly stepped across the foyer, avoiding the others, and headed straight upstairs to his room.

"How did we get here? Your guess is as good as mine," Daniel said to Terry.

Daniel placed his cup of tea on the side table as Sophia and the others entered the room. Tired, they plonked themselves on the floor and leant against the furniture.

"We were going down," Daniel continued. "The engine was on fire and it stalled. Time seemed to stop: everything went quiet, muffled, the plane levelled. Sound returned and again we were falling, the craft screaming with the acceleration. Callie and Kevin pulled the nose up seconds before we nose-dived into the ground. My question is, how did we survive?"

"Over the last week we have seen things that are just not of this world, and we have experienced the absolute impossible," Callie said.

"Miracles ..." Father McDonald cleared his throat. "You're experiencing miracles. You have been chased by the servants of hell. Your cars collided at the front of the farmhouse you escaped to. Next you're in a plane running from some men who wanted to kill you. The young man shot in the back while saving Callie was dying in your lap but now is totally healed after you crash-landed thousands miles away. You all walked away from the wreckage, and then you find out your son knows the people whose yard you have just used as a runway. Sounds like you are experiencing miracles on a regular basis, Daniel."

Everyone sat in silence as Father McDonald's words reverberated around the room. Tim peeled his back off the leather lounge, leaning towards the coffee table to pick up a plate and napkin. As quietly as possible he lifted the knife and sliced a piece of cake. The blade hit the plate as it sliced through and Tim winced at the sound. *You could hear a pin drop*, Sophia thought. She wanted to laugh at Tim with his mouth full of cake and expression of anguish. But instead, to break the silence, she said, "I'll have a piece of cake, please." Tim cut a piece and passed it to her. As she leant forward her medallion slipped out from under her shirt. With one hand, she tried to tuck it back in.

"Miracles," Tim said, between mouthfuls. "Then we really must have done something right to have been able to redeem three miracles."

"That's a lovely necklace. It looks familiar," Amy said.

"Thanks, it's a family heirloom."

"It's more than that," Jade said. Her crossed legs unwound as she pushed herself off the floor and casually stepped over the boys' splayed legs. "It's a symbol, a very powerful medallion of protection. You okay if I touch it?" Jade asked.

"Yes, but I'm not taking it off. My great-grandmother gave it to my mother to give to me. It was always handed down to the seventh daughter of the next generation of seven," Sophia said.

"Wow, seven sisters," Tim said, looking at Kath.

"Shut up, idiot."

"Kath, that's no way to speak to your brother," Sally said.

"This is serious," Kath said, "and he keeps cracking jokes."

"Just leave your brother alone."

"My great-aunt was from a family of seven girls, I think," Amy said.

Jade, still holding the twisted napkin, held out her wrist to Sophia. "My great-grandmother gave me this."

Sophia tenderly touched the bracelet and instantly felt her

internal and external energy centers expanding. She withdrew her fingers, uncertain, as a stream of consciousness tried to communicate with her. Sophia said, "That's a unique bracelet."

Jade reached out and held Sophia's locket between her fingers, turning it around to see it was double-sided. The curved metal was smooth and warm from Sophia's skin. "See this," Jade said, "this symbol is Penelope's web." There was an embossed image of a ten-spoke wheel with stars at the end of each spoke. Each star had twenty sharp outward points. "This is a sign of protection. The stars are also known as the Seal of Solomon, which amplifies your locket's message of protection," she said. "The lines of the wheel and stars are interlaced by two lines joining at the center of the symbol. The symbol is composed of only two lines. It represents unity, the drawing together of people for the preservation of all. It also reflects numerological mysticism. Seventy-two: the primal magical number can be achieved with sacred geometry.

"Sophia, on the other side of your locket," Jade said, turning it over and looking at the symbol's multiple connecting spheres, "is the flower of life. It holds the secrets of the universe. It's a symbol that was created from one sphere, the first seed of life. It multiplied, spiraling out until it contained all the sacred patterns and secrets of the universe. The flower of life can be seen throughout history in religious architecture. It's in the atom, the building blocks of life. It can be found within everything: a piece of fruit, an icicle, a person or an animal. It's geometry, it's Platonic solids, it's everything."

"What are Platonic solids?" Joe asked.

"Shapes. Geometry. Like a tetrahedron — it looks like a pyramid, a hexahedron better known as a cube, and they connect with the different elements of earth like water, air, fire. All of this is within the flower of life." Jade stopped talking, looking around at the faces staring at her. She let go of the locket, smiled at Sophia apologetically then quickly looked down, nervously twisting the napkin in her hand. Her face grew redder by the second. "Anyway, that's all I know." Jade settled back next to Kevin without looking at anyone, and started to chew the ends of her long hair.

"That's all!" Tim said. "What are you, a walking Wiki? I thought K had the smarts, but you, you're good."

"Tim, don't," Kevin said.

Touched by Jade's insights, Sophia was moved and grateful for her knowledge. She herself had never thought to seek that knowledge, which now made so much sense. "Nice, Jade," Sophia said. "I've always been protected. It's a tall order, preservation of all. We might just have to go there, to the center. Where the virus began," Sophia said.

"Do we have to build an ark?" Tim asked.

Callie ignored Tim and said, "What do you mean 'the center'?"

Jade started talking at a hundred miles a minute. "The Middle East, Jerusalem, the spiritual center where it all began. It's also where the virus started, like Sophia said. We have to go back to the beginning."

Sophia sat on the floor quietly, uncrossed her legs, re-crossed them lotus-style, and massaged her toes. "When we left Joe's cafe I was completely freaked; it was so surreal. The monsters we encountered can only be described as demons, stinking of garbage. It was an abomination of earthly creatures, it was beastly and they transformed back and forth into giants, and then into millions of tiny black demons. I have seen them around the heads of the infected too. I think we have been seeing the same thing."

"You're right on the money," Tim said. "We saw the same thing happening with the giants as we fled the city; they were vile. That's what chased us."

Daniel lifted up his cup and took a sip of, probably cold, tea. "You two aren't related?" he said, pointing to her and Amy.

"No," Amy said.

"Is anyone going to eat that last piece of cake?" Kath asked. She looked at Tim. "You've had three."

Amy's attention was fixed on Sophia. "What do you mean? Are you saying we have to go to Israel? That's the last place in the world you want to be right now," she said, looking at Casey. "We don't even know if anyone is still alive over there. The virus infected so many at the very beginning."

"Even if it were true, there is no way of getting there," Terry said.

Joe moved his large frame in his seat and pulled a pillow from behind his back, tucking it by his side. "I have to say, if we are supposed to walk there, we will find a road. One will open up for us. If we have to fly, then we will find a plane, and the same if we need to sail. You have to be certain it's a journey you're willing to take."

Sophia smiled at Joe, and looked deep into the energy of the room. It wasn't well lit, which highlighted each person's iridescent aura. She could feel her energy changing. Casey was looking at her strangely. Amy's book was resting in her lap and it had a soft pulsation and Sophia's vision started to blur. Everyone began to fade. Her body felt heavy, a tickle formed in her throat. Her face was itchy, crawling with hair; she felt six-feet tall and smelt of fur and ale. Stars filled her eyes. Her mouth moved and a deep, raspy male voice, distant and foreign to her ears, said from her lips: "Disease seeped through the bowels of Gehenna. You have the key now find the lock, and lay it to rest upon the golden rock, the heart of the gatekeeper, the guardian of the underworld. No end or beginning to face the heavens and the emerald heart will glow and light will be returned. The Emerald Tablet must be returned."

Sophia's throat was sore and dry and she needed water. She could feel the spirit backing away. The sensation of her face and the smallness of her head and body returned; her arms felt light. Sophia strained to open her eyes. They were glued shut. "Water, please," she said between tingling lips, happy to hear her own voice.

Casey was on his feet and soon held a glass to her mouth. "What was all that about? There was the spirit of a hooded man with a ginger beard enveloping you. I have seen him before, like when we went through the basement wall, but there was something else. What was it? I know, it was one of those canvas paintings, Amy. His portrait is in one of the old trunks in the basement."

"He could be my great, great, great-something grandfather, the owner of the book of Splendor?" Amy said.

Sophia waited for her eyes to open, and listened to the adults murmuring around her. Fresh smells of sage filled her senses, and her chest rose as she drew a breath into her belly. The familiar sound of Father McDonald praying was soothing. Everyone talked amongst themselves, eager to know what was happening.

Jade spoke up. "Trance mediumship."

"Have you seen it before?" Amy asked.

"I have seen it once, a shaman channeling the spirits of my great-grandmother's tribe. I have seen shadow dancers getting in touch with the inner wolf to tame it and I have seen coming-of-age ceremonies where the participants consumed potions to induce a trance state. But they were all controlled by a gifted elder. No offence, Sophia, but you are what, fourteen, fifteen?"

Casey hadn't moved from Sophia's side. "How are you feeling?"

Her eyes fluttered open. "Heavy, like I have been in a deep sleep."

Callie raised her voice slightly over the others. "What happened to you? Are you, or were you, in any pain?"

"No, no pain, just really weak and distant."

"Has this happened before?"

"No, nothing like this."

"Did you hear what was said?"

"Yes."

"Do you understand what it means?"

"Yes and no. Something was taken off a statue that has to be returned. Behind my eyes, I watched a slideshow of images while the man spoke."

"How do you know it was a man?" Callie asked.

"I could feel the size of his body, and I could smell his fur coat. He had a beard that made my face itch. He seemed kind, but firm and ancient."

"What were the images you saw, can you tell us?"

"I saw a picture of a statue deep underground, in a cave, I think. Over its chest was a cavity where a breastplate of armor belonged, and on it was dusty gemstone of different shapes. Then a beautiful huge old door with many locks, all closed. There was a rotten stench, a whirlpool of dark matter. It was the same as Joe's cafe. There was a sense of sand, lots of it, with thousands of people in white standing in silence holding candles as a horn was blown. The plate must be returned before the last horn blows. I think *we* have to return the breastplate. Each image was charged emotionally with either agony and anguish, or hope and joy."

"Do you have the tablet?" Kevin asked.

"No, I have no idea what or where it is." Sophia looked at Jade. "Tell me what you're thinking."

"Oh, nothing."

"Yes, you are. I can see your cogs turning," Kevin said.

"Please tell me," Sophia said.

"There is a tablet called the Emerald Tablet. It contains text that is thought to give those that possess it the ability to move between different dimensions, different worlds. It was believed to contain the knowledge from Abraham, and it was passed onto Moses and so on. Egyptian mythology puts it in the hands of Thoth. In Greek mythology, Hermes — thought to be the reincarnation of Thoth — was called 'Thrice Great' because of the three parts of his ability: the wisdom of the whole universe, alchemy, and astrology and divine influence in humanity. The mention of the Emerald Tablet pops up and appears in numerous cultures and was apparently studied by Isaac Newton, I think, who thought it to be pure ancient doctrine so he studied the scribe to understand this physical world. He believed the writings revealed secret techniques to influence the stars and the forces of nature. I'm not sure, but I think I read that his translation is housed in King's College Library, Cambridge University. But if that's the case, how can it have been removed from a statue in the Middle East. I can definitely jumble up things I have read, but —"

"Do unto others as you would have them do unto you," Father McDonald said.

"I'm lost," Tim said.

"Well," Jade told him, "basically, it means it's instrumental in maintaining the balance and structure of the universe, and the removal of it, from wherever it was, has caused the virus and an unbalance within our society. Thoth was thought to stand between good and evil. If he was, the statue that you saw, Sophia, could be his. He kept the balance between this world and the underworld and had the power to heal."

Sophia witnessed Jade's aura pulse with excitement. Everyone else seemed confused.

"Also, I have been thinking about an equation: $S = k \log W$."

"What does it mean?" Sophia asked.

"Entropy," Jade said.

"Speak English, people. We're not all intels," Tim said. "My head's hurting."

"Entropy," Callie interrupted, "is a measurement of disorder or randomness. Order to disorder. Move from an ordered state to disordered states. Life is filled with entropy." Callie took a breath.

And Jade jumped in. "Making order from chaos; it's exhilarating. Entropy is a measure of molecular randomness, or disorder. The second law of thermodynamics, any spontaneous process increases the disorder of the universe and —"

"There she goes again," Tim said, rolling his eyes.

"Sorry, it's just stimulating," Jade said and stopped talking.

"Never apologize for who you are, Jade. It is exciting. Where are you going with this?" Kevin said.

Sophia saw Jade physically start to fatigue. Her brain had used up so much energy, she needed more. Sophia nudged Casey and whispered, "Give her a zap, she's exhausted."

Casey, wide-eyed, said, "No, I'll hurt her."

"No, you won't," she whispered back. "I promise."

Casey looked into Jade's ethereal body and rubbed his hands together. He clapped and coughed, thinking it would somehow disguise his intentions.

"What the hell are you clapping at?" Tim said. "You scared the shit out me. You've got a sonic boom for a clap, mate."

Kevin cracked up, Casey smiled and Sophia had to turn her head, to disguise her laughter. Jade stretched and her aura expanded, rippling into Tim's, giving him a static shock.

"What is the reactive state?" Jade continued with a surge of energy. "It is a state of being. A person's actions or thoughts without pause. A negative thought while in a negative state can trigger natural disasters – like when someone gossips or is jealous – a reactive state is a negative state of being that creates a reaction upon the collective human soul and the planet. We can change a negative effect into a positive state — sort of like the butterfly effect — we have a negative right now, so how do we change that negative to a positive one? By being proactive and actively changing the effect; that is, by reversing the negative action or creating order from the disorder. This doesn't make any sense to you, does it?"

Callie continued, so Jade could catch her breath and slow down. "Yes, it does. But you can't eliminate chaos. The Big Bang is the most ordered state and entropy was at its lowest. We can't go back to the seed. You can't reverse a butterfly flapping its wings."

Jade jumped back in again. "Well, why not? We can go back to the chain of events that started this current mess and create a better outcome for humanity. Or at least put back what was removed, making the statue whole again — order from chaos. K may be able to create windows in time," Jade said.

"K, enlighten me, buddy. What are they talking about?" Tim said.

"Return the missing artefact that unleashed hell. Change undesirable to a desirable," Kevin said.

"I'm tired," Tim said.

"I'm sorry, you're losing me too. Windows in time?" Father McDonald said.

"The way I see it," Joe said, "is that we have lots of chaos and we can choose how we will shuffle the broken pieces to create balance and harmony. Forgetting science for a moment, we need to bring back the smile on people's faces, the love in their eyes, the gentle touch of the wind and to see the crystal colors of the light. As Sophia said, we need to have certainty." Joe looked up to the ceiling and said, "We beseech you, God, with the power of your greatness help us undo this entanglement."

"Amen," said Father McDonald.

"I'm way too tired to keep this conversation going," said Terry. "How about we get some sleep and maybe we will find some answers in the morning."

"That sounds like a good idea," Amy said.

"Jade," Sophia said as everyone started to move, "you're right, we have to make a change. Your thinking has been the reason why you're here. You have been searching in your mind for a way to find your mother and she has a burning desire to heal the world of this virus."

"Thanks, Sophia," Jade said. The floodgates opened and Jade's eyes were shiny with tears, but she didn't let a drop spill.

Sophia tasted a change in the air and sat down on the edge of the lounge. She screwed up her nose in concentration and watched everyone stretch and yawn, agreeing it was time for bed. Joe was already on his feet helping Father McDonald, and Tim was telling Kevin his head hurt from all the thinking. Sophia stood up next to Casey. Suddenly the lights began to flicker, pulsating. She looked at Casey and he wanted to take her hand.

"It's not me," he said.

They were all drawn together, reducing the space between them and found themselves standing still in the middle of the room. Amy still had hold of her book and it became illuminated. Sophia saw Kevin's head turn towards Amy. *He must be sensing it too*, she thought. Sophia's necklace, hidden by the depth of radiance from Amy's book, now surged with light. She hadn't noticed it ever come alive before. It felt buzzy, effervescent, against her skin. The room became animated, filled with whispers and fogged images.

Father McDonald said in a soft voice, "The dead. The fragile curtain between the living and the dead is dissolving."

The power in the room intensified. Shadowy phantoms appeared. The energy of the ghostly forms was compressing, and they almost looked solid, physically alive, although with the absence of consciousness. No different from the infected, the only difference being that these bodies were long dead. Nobody spoke and Sophia felt confused, vulnerable and alarmed, almost stunned by the apparitions. The distance and aloofness she had felt in her visions had turned into foreboding; she felt mortal amongst the ghosts and became aware of her love of life. *The smell of a flower, the touch of the wind, sun on her face, and laughter — they are heaven,* she thought and looped her pinkie with Casey's. Slowly, the energy dropped and the phantoms and shadows faded and so, too, the circle of light that united and protected them vanished. *The world is dying, becoming the promised living hell. Since the removal of the Emerald Tablet the veil has been lifted and the dead must be rising.*

"This is the third time this has happened," Casey said, "and it's getting stronger."

"Are we safe?" Sally asked. "Why has God forsaken us?"

Father McDonald took Sally's hands in his. "He hasn't forsaken us, Sally. He brought us together to help one another."

"We will be safe," Sophia said. "There is an angel watching over us, battling on a higher realm for our victory. Down here, this is our battle to overcome."

Terry yawned, rubbed his eyes and put his arm around Amy's shoulders. "Let's get a few hours' sleep and talk about this in the morning."

Callie hugged Kevin, Tim and Jade. "Look after each other," she said.

"I can't go to sleep after that!" Tim protested as Callie let him go.

Kevin headed up the stairs with Jade and Tim, watching his mom and dad walk across the foyer to their room saying their good nights. The door closed quietly behind them. Sophia heard the faintest click as Joe helped Father McDonald wearily up the stairs.

THE GHOSTS HAD TRIED to touch him. He was burning up so much his shirt clung to his body. Shaun lay still on the bottom bunk listening to squeaky old stairs as everyone ascended to their rooms. He rolled over on his side, facing away from the bedroom door and listened to Kevin, Casey and Tim enter the room. Without turning on the light, they changed, ready for bed. Shaun was glad he was no longer alone.

Casey was talking about caves, green armor and flying creatures. Shaun was feeling shaky, anxious. Their jabbering about caves and statues frustrated him. His stomach tightened, aching. "Will you assholes shut up?" he said, with clenched teeth. The sound in the room was reduced to whispers and shuffling, and ruffling of sheets as they climbed into bed. Shaun searched his mind for something to focus on and the image he conjured was a good day at the beach with his parents. They had built a sandcastle and they were creating a moat and tunnels around it.

His eyes darted back and forth as he drifted into sleep and dreams of falling into one of the tunnels around the sandcastle, and the sand starting to collapse around him. The ocean was rising and streaming into the moat; he ran, looking for a way in and found an entrance under the castle. He climbed some stairs and reached the top expecting to see the ocean and his parents, but he saw a barren landscape with mountains of sand in the dead of night. One single light was shining in the distance. He looked back down the stairs and could see the frothy ocean water rising up. He couldn't go back, only forward. He walked across the sand towards the light and it never seemed to get any closer. It was moving from side to side. It was a lantern, held by somebody, guiding him. It appeared to take hours, but the sun didn't rise. There was movement under the sand and occasionally, if he stopped moving forward, he started to sink. *Where am I? It feels familiar.*

He was getting excited as he continued to approach the light and he felt the warmth of the sun on his back, but there was no sun or moon in the sky. A shapely woman stood behind the lantern calling out his name and he wanted to run towards her. Tears were trapped in his throat, hope teased his heart. She called out his name, urging him to hurry. Shaun ran. His legs were getting heavy and he lifted each leg higher and higher. The sand was wet, the foaming water of the ocean had followed him to this place. It was getting harder to move; he was sinking in the wet sand. She called out to him again. "Hurry, we have to go back." He was immobilized in the sand — it had become thick like ice, holding him around the waist. He knew that voice, laced with the maturity of a woman and the pleading of a child. He could hear the beauty of her soul, the rhythm of each word touched his heart. It was Rachel. As soon as he said her name, there was an explosion of light behind her. He sank down into the sand, struggling to be free as it buried him alive.

The smell of freshly cooked food aroused his olfactory senses and his body was filled with sounds. His shoulders were pressed into the mattress and he heard giggling. It was Alex. Tim told Alex it was okay to go ahead and body-slam Shaun, and Casey said it wasn't okay because he was dreaming. How did Casey know he was dreaming? A cold little finger touched his eye, lifting up his eyelid. Shaun lunged at his neck playfully like a rabid dog going for the kill. Alex squealed and fell to the floor. Shaun watched Alex's face turn into a smile then a serious knot appeared on his tiny brow.

"Are you crying? Are you sad?" Alex asked. He pushed himself up off the carpet.

Tim hung his head over the side of the bunk.

"No, buddy, I'm not crying," Shaun said, reaching out to slap Tim's head and caught a handful of hair. He pushed Tim's face away.

"Breakfast is ready," Alex said. "Mommy said I could wake you."

Shaun pulled up the sheet and wiped his face quickly before tossing them back and stepping into his jeans.

"Morning," Casey said.

"Morning," Shaun grumbled. He kept his head low, avoiding eye contact. He collected the clean blue t-shirt Terry had given him and said to Alex, "Lead the way, dude." He pulled the shirt over his head, walking out the door.

Shaun and Alex went past the bathroom. Shaun stepped back, feeling the urge to go to the toilet. Alex continued to follow him into the bathroom. "No, buddy, you wait here." Shaun closed the door and Alex slid down the wall and squatted against it, waiting.

Shaun leant on the washbasin, looking at his reflection in the mirror. He splashed water over his eyes and cheeks, washing away traces of tears. The cool water felt refreshing in his hands and on his face. He was quite sticky from the night and couldn't resist having a shower. He let the water cascade over his head, trying to erase the images from the dream. There was a knock and Alex's muffled voice asking him how much longer he was going to be, because he was alone and scared in the dark hall. Shaun turned off the water, quickly toweled himself dry and dressed. He left the room feeling lighter and maybe even a little invigorated.

"Now are you ready?" Alex asked as the bathroom light flooded into the hallway. Alex pushed against the wall and stood up.

The odd pair walked along the short corridor to the stairs. Shaun's foot was poised ready to step down, but he stopped, and looked back towards the bedroom and down to the end of the hall. The boards covering the end window made the corridor appear dark and mistrusting, creating a creepy feeling. Shaun had a sense of being watched.

29

MELTING POT: ENGLAND

Daniel reached for the tea towel to help Terry dry the dishes after lunch. Joe was already cooking a stew for dinner. "That smells great, Joe."

Shaun came in through the back door. "There's a motorcycle in the barn. Can I take Alex for a ride?"

Terry looked at Daniel and shrugged his shoulders. "It's up to you. They're your boys."

Daniel was going to correct him, but then turned to Shaun. "Have you ever ridden a motorcycle before?"

"Sure, heaps of times. My mate had a dirt bike and we used to churn up the school grounds."

"You did what?" Terry said. "You can't take it out if you're going to wreak havoc around the place."

"No, that's not what I meant. I just meant I know how to handle a motorcycle."

Daniel looked at Shaun and said nothing.

"I won't let anything happen to him, I promise," Shaun said.

"How many promises have you made in your life? Ten, twenty, a hundred?" Daniel asked.

"Two," Shaun said.

Daniel shifted his weight to his right leg and put a dry plate into the overhead cupboard. "I think I'll go take a look. I have my own motorcycle back home," Daniel said to Terry. He draped the tea towel on the edge of the bench to dry.

"The keys are on the hook over there by the door."

Daniel unhooked the keys. "Come on then, let's have some fun." Daniel and Shaun walked over to the shed together to find Alex sitting stretched out on the seat. He was trying to reach the handlebars pretending he was speeding down a racetrack.

Daniel lifted Alex off, and wheeled the bike outside. He climbed on, started the bike, and kicked up the stand. "Get on," he said to Shaun.

Shaun hesitated.

"Get on."

Shaun threw his leg over and hung onto the back of the bike. Daniel put it into gear and took off. They cruised on the Bonnie down the driveway, past the plane wreckage, and turned around heading towards the hedges at the back of the house. They slid a little on the wet grass and Daniel stretched his leg forward for balance. The other kids watched them until they were out of sight.

Alex was jumping up and down on the spot waiting for his turn. Daniel stopped in front of Alex. Daniel swapped with Shaun, jumping on the back. Once Daniel felt Shaun was confident with a pillion passenger, he tapped him on the shoulder and pointed to Alex. Shaun turned the motorcycle and headed for the kid. Daniel jumped off and put Alex on the back. "Now you hold on to Shaun tight with your arms, and squeeze his hips with your legs, okay? Shaun, don't go above second gear, alright?"

Shaun slowly let out the clutch and accelerated. He stayed in first gear down to the fence and did a wide U-turn at the bottom of the driveway. He did this about four times to Alex's delight. The other kids were perched on a log looking out into the silver birch trees.

Tim got up and walked over to Daniel. "Can I have a turn?"

"No, mate."

"Why not? You let Shaun ride it."

"He's a little older than you. When you're his age you can ride it."

"He's not that much older."

"He's old enough to have a license. You're not. Don't argue, you cheeky monkey." Daniel ruffled his hair. "You can get on the back."

"No, I'm good."

Shaun was coming back up the driveway and Daniel walked over towards him. Shaun stopped. "Listen, the others aren't allowed to ride it on their own. You can take them for a ride on the back. The sky is really overcast. I don't suppose the rain will stay away for too long. When you're done, put it back in the shed and put the key where it belongs, okay?"

"Sure, no sweat, will do."

Kevin, Casey, Jade and Sophia were walking towards Tim. They stopped and watched Shaun and Alex for a minute before heading to the house as if they were carrying the weight of the world on their shoulders.

"Where are you guys headed?" Daniel asked Kevin.

"Inside. It looks terrible out here, and the air feels strange," he said.

"Is Father McDonald alright over there?" he asked Sophia.

"Yes, he will pray until he feels the evil is pushed back."

Daniel looked out over to Father McDonald sitting on the ground on his knees, unwavering. "He hasn't slept much. He looks a little pale."

"He never does. He is always pale these days. It's his heart, it's physically weak but he pretends it's okay. He doesn't want me to know."

Daniel held the door open for them to pass, taking a glimpse over his shoulder at his son and Shaun. He could hear Alex shouting, "Slow, slow, slow." And Shaun went very slow. Then Alex yelled, "Faster, faster, faster." And Shaun would speed up. They were having a ball of a time just going up and down the driveway. Kevin was exceptional with amazing gifts, but so was Alex. He had the biggest heart that melted the toughest characters.

ON THE RUG BY THE bookshelves Shaun handed Alex the gemstones from his pouch. He focused on listening, watching Amy and Father McDonald out of the corner of his eye, while teaching Alex a game. Amy closed her book gently in her lap and moved out of the high-backed leather chair under the stained-glass lamp, which bathed the lounge room with a soft glow of color. She offered her seat to Father McDonald. "Come and make yourself comfortable," she said. "This chair is extremely comfortable."

"What are you reading?" Father McDonald asked, nodding towards her book. "It's a book of light. It's filled with the mysteries of the universe." She handed the book to him and he accepted. It felt light even though it was as thick as an old encyclopedia. He opened the book, surprised it was in Aramaic. "Can you read this?" he said, looking at Amy excitedly.

"Unfortunately, no, I can't. The letters, they look like symbols to me, and I remember when I was a child I would watch my grandfather run his finger under the letters as if reading from right to left and then turn the pages in the same direction. I scan over the pages and don't comprehend a single sentence. It was passed down through the generations to my grandfather and I feel him and I feel closer to God every time I open the book. I was always intrigued and would watch his face reflecting the light from the book in his hands."

"If you can't read the words, how do you know it holds the mysteries of the universe?"

"I just do," and with that said, she placed the book on the side table under the glow of the lamp, and a rainbow of colors shone across its cover.

"It's bedtime, Alex," Callie called from the other room.

Amy walked past Shaun and Alex, and as she did Shaun scooped up the gems to play another game with Alex.

She tapped on Callie's door. "You have beautiful children," she said, standing at the threshold. "Molly is a gorgeous happy little girl."

"Do you plan to have any more children?" Callie asked, stepping from the room.

"We want a big family. My great-aunt was from a large family of girls, who spread out across the world, eventually losing contact with one another. My great-aunt was my only surviving relative, although we didn't know of her until she had passed away. This was her place, which she left to me."

"That's sad," Callie said.

"What happened to Casey that day?" Amy asked.

"What do you mean?"

"Kevin said he was there, that he saw Casey. At first we believed him when he came home crying, swearing he saw a boy drown in the river, so we called the police. They were searching for days but there was nothing. They started to say Kevin had made it up. We too thought he was seeking attention. I had been overseas and soon after I got back my parents were killed in a car accident. He had told me to tell them not to come, but it was too late, they were already on their way."

"Oh, I'm sorry to hear that."

"He was very close to them. He blames himself and thinks I blame him too."

Molly was sucking on her bottle, drifting off to sleep in Callie's arms.

"May I?" Amy said, reaching out for Molly.

Callie carefully passed Molly over and Amy walked back into the living room and sat down.

"You look as if you're a natural," Callie said, following her.

"I hope so. I'm about four months," Amy said.

She's pregnant, Shaun thought. Why would she let us stay knowing she is pregnant? Wouldn't she want to protect her unborn baby?

"How exciting. Congratulations!" Callie said.

"It's ironic how in times of such despair life continues. If we listen to Casey, I'm having twins."

"What do you mean, if you listen to Casey?"

"He sometimes senses the future."

Shaun was intrigued and tried to move closer without Alex noticing.

"Really? Kevin's a bit like that." Callie turned towards the door and Amy followed her gaze. There was no one there. The boys came down the stairs and into the room seconds after her stare.

"I can see where he gets it from," Amy said.

"What me? No, I don't think so." Amy sat back, ignoring her numb arm from the impossible weight of someone so tiny, and watched Molly sleep.

The boys walked past Shaun and Alex. Kevin stopped, curious. "What are they?"

Shaun didn't answer, but scooped up the stones, tucking them into his pouch. Casey, Tim and Kevin continued into the kitchen.

"Shaun, why don't you go with Kevin? Alex, it's time for bed."

"Oh Mom, no, one more game."

"I'm sorry, Alex, it's way past your bedtime, and besides Shaun has played with you all day."

"Can I fall asleep with Molly and Amy, on the lounge? And you put me to bed later?"

Amy watched Tim and Kevin come out of the kitchen with snacks for the rest of the gang upstairs in Casey's room. Kevin tossed a packet of crisps to Shaun and handed him a coke.

"Come on," Casey said.

Shaun reluctantly got up and followed the boys upstairs.

CASEY TOOK THE OLD stairs two at a time, trying to figure out what he could say to Shaun to help him be more trusting and open up. Casey could feel things were going to get worse. Shaun tripped on the carpet at the top of the stairs. Tim laughed and Casey reached out for Shaun's arm. Casey felt like he had been tasered and stabbed in the heart all at once; life and joy vanished, leaving feelings of guilt and abandonment. Casey felt emotionally bankrupt and suddenly alone. The image of Shaun lying across his mother's chest, crying so hard he had to be forcefully removed from the sterile room by a man Casey assumed was his father. Shaun shook off Casey's hold and the scene in his mind faded. Casey became aware of his own emotions and felt vulnerable. The images had aroused a sense of loss.

"What the hell are you staring at?" Shaun snapped.

"Your mom died when you were a kid. It wasn't your fault. You're carrying a shitload of guilt. Let it go, you're not the cause of her illness."

"Who told you that? Who told you about my mom? One of your stupid new friends?"

Tim had been laughing at Shaun when he tripped; Casey saw he was straight-faced now, with a look of caution. He walked into the bedroom, leaving Casey and Shaun alone in the dark hallway.

"You told me, just then, when I helped you up. I pick up shit and you've got a truckload."

"You're weird."

"I lost my mom last year. She was crushed during a freak tornado. I didn't get a chance to say goodbye, but you did and you should cherish that."

"Who are you to tell me what I should do?"

"There was nothing more important to her than you," Casey said to him. "She saw the gift you had brought for her." Casey looked down at the ground, then up to the ceiling, then stared at Shaun's face searching for a connection. "You took something extremely valuable, priceless."

Shaun instinctively touched his pocket. "I don't know what you're talking about," he said. He walked into the bedroom, chucked the packet of chips at Tim and threw himself onto the bed. Casey watched him: *You know exactly what I was talking about.*

"I LOVE THIS ROOM," said Sophia. "I thought my room at the convent was special because I had a window. This, this is such a beautiful blue. It's endless, like the sky, and the bunk beds built into the wall with the archways is just magical. The lower beds are practically the size of a double bed. Look at these little nooks for bookshelves cut out of the bedheads. And a little portal that must look onto the lawn. If it wasn't covered up I'm sure it would look lovely. This is a beautiful home, Casey. I would pick this for my bedroom and all my friends could come for a slumber party." Sophia's shoulders drooped and the enthusiasm trickled away as she remembered her friends Gemma and Lisa lying face down in the car park with blood pooling around them.

"Give it a rest. What century are you from? And did you say you live in a convent?" Shaun said, lying on his bed flicking his shoes off. They just missed hitting her.

"Pretty much," Sophia said, sitting on the edge of his bed.

Casey watched her effervescent aura change to darker tones. "This wasn't the original design, of course. The real estate agent said Amy's great-aunt redesigned it as a B&B. That's why there are four beds and a sitting area in this room," Casey said.

"It looks like a studio. The layout is a great use of the space," Jade said, sitting at the writing desk nestled amongst more bookshelves.

"If you girls talk about the curtains," Tim said, "I'm going to puke."

"Where's Kath?" Sophia asked.

"She won't hang with us. We're too immature for her," Tim said.

"I think you spoke too soon," Kevin said.

"What?" Tim said.

"Wait for it, " said Sophia. There was a gentle knock on the door and Kath walked in and everyone laughed.

"What's the joke?" Kath asked, looking down at her clothes.

Kevin, Casey and Sophia looked at each other with understanding.

Jade and Tim looked at them as if they had lost their minds.

"It's nothing," Jade said. "Synchronicity I presume. Your timing is impeccable. They were just wondering why you weren't here."

Kath walked across the room and plunked herself down onto the two-seater. She stretched her legs out towards the beds and with her back to Jade snatched the packet of open chips off the table and took a handful.

Sophia watched her munch on the chips, trying to get Shaun's attention. *She was going about it the wrong way. But then what do I know about boys?* Sophia thought.

"How're your hands, Shaun?" Jade asked.

"Why? They're fine, you know that," Shaun said.

"Look, we need to cut the crap and get down to why we were all brought here. I don't know about you guys, but I want to go home," Jade said.

She's right, Sophia thought. No more procrastination, it was time. Sophia climbed up on the bed above Shaun.

"Sophia," Jade said, "there are things you said last night, the message. *We have the key, now find the lock.* We know the lock is the Emerald Tablet."

Sophia and Casey's intuition heightened. Shaun sat himself up on the bed and leant against the boarded window.

"The second thing was, we need to get to a cave somewhere in the Middle East, and the third —"

She was interrupted by Shaun. "What the hell are you on about? For an intel, you are thick. Who told you? How do you know?"

"Know what?" Jade said.

"He wasn't with us last night, he'll have no idea what we're talking about," Kevin said.

Shaun's aura expanded and he was covered in reds and oranges. He wanted to know what was going on, but he was angry.

"Sophia believes — we all believe—" Casey said, looking around at everyone in the room, "we have survived and united to right a wrong that has caused the world to go haywire and the virus to magnify."

Shaun blurted out, "What makes you guys so unique? We are all going to die anyway. The world is getting smaller and smaller if you haven't noticed. We are all stuck in one house."

"You should believe more than anyone!" Jade said. "The flesh was falling off your burnt hands, you were shot in the back. What more do you need to see that you are a vital cog in a bigger picture? Like I was saying, we need to place the Emerald Tablet back where it came from, but we don't know where that is."

Kevin interjected. "What about the rest of the message? That was just the first line."

"We'll have to work it out as we go," Casey said.

"That's it in a nutshell," Tim said. "I know how we can get there!"

Sophia looked at Tim and saw Kevin was becoming restless and nearly jumped off the bed when Jade shouted out, "Of course! Kevin!"

"That was my moment," Tim said, throwing up his hands and smacking them down into his lap spilling his chips in frustration.

"Whatever," Jade said, raising her eyebrows. "He can take us anywhere in the world."

"I can't," Kevin said. "I have never been to the Middle East. I wouldn't know how to begin."

"Just like the plane crash. We passed through some window in time that Kevin opened. Do you know how we met? He found me lying on the forest floor about to be mauled by a wolf. Where? On the south coast of the United States! We escaped into something similar to a plasma energy field that shimmered and sparkled like a mirage. When we stepped through, it was magnificent. We emerged a few hours later. Where, you ask? Get this — on the other side of the world in Australia. It was so intense. When we arrived at his home, what seemed like a typical day to Kevin and Tim was actually three days later. The cops were looking for them." Jade had her hands on her hips for emphasis.

"I saw those cops from my roof," Shaun said, "and I saw Kevin and Tim on their bikes in the bush vanish into thin air. I waited for hours. I even fell asleep and that was two days before the cops started casing the streets."

"You were watching us?" Tim said.

"Get over yourself," Shaun said and threw the pillow at him.

"Anyway," Jade said, feasting her eyes on Sophia, "when we were being chased, he opened a portal that was paper-thin and we practically landed on his grandmother's porch within seconds and we had been miles away. The adults still seemed to be clueless. It must be their defense mechanism."

"Kilometers," Tim corrected.

"And that's how we got here. When the plane was going down he opened a doorway. He can get us there, even if he thinks he doesn't know how."

"The image," Kevin said, rubbing the back of his head, "needs to be emotionally charged. The picture of Casey and Sophia riding the motorbike was emotionally charged. We have to focus on the message."

Casey, his cheeks on fire, said, "What about a demo?"

"Yeah, retard, give us a demo. Idiots."

"Why are you being so mean?" Kath asked.

"Mean? You should have seen what your golden boyfriend did to some dumb fuck on the train," Shaun said.

"What?" Kath said.

"I saw him across the road from our place smashing up the neighbor's car. He's infected," Tim said. "Sorry, Kath."

"Can we get back on topic?" Jade said.

"Who died and made you queen?" Shaun said to Jade.

"Why are we so agitated all of a sudden?" Casey asked.

"Enough, guys!" Kevin said. "If I open up a doorway, I don't know how to calculate the time. Our parents will freak if we disappear on them again."

"I was thinking about that," Jade said. "Kath, you stated that they were gone for three days, and the boys thought it was only a day. That would break down to ..."

Sophia saw Jade's mind ticking over. "We need to keep continuity, and not over-complicate things with facts," Sophia said.

"I'm not doing it," Kevin said.

"Go on, K. Show them what you can do. What about just from one room to another?" Tim said.

"That's a good idea, Tim," Jade said.

"Thanks."

"I don't know."

"Come on, creep, show us how you do it," Shaun said.

"Don't call me that."

"Why? What are you going to do?"

"Nothing, it just makes you look stupid, that's all. It doesn't bother me."

Sophia watched Kevin take in a deep breath, rub his hands on his knees and walk towards the center of the room.

"Okay, off the beds and come stand behind me." They did as he said. Except for Shaun.

"You missed some," Sophia said, pointing to Tim's shirt. Tim looked down and finished picking off the chip crumbs before brushing himself down. He made her smile; he wasn't bothered about what others thought. Tim was true to himself.

"Wait," shouted Shaun. "You got a knife?" he asked Casey.

"Sure, a pocket knife. Why?"

"Can I have it?"

Casey opened the desk door and fished out the knife and gave it to Shaun. He flicked it open and sliced into his own leg. Blood started to soak into his jeans. He hobbled in behind Kevin.

"What did you do that for?" Tim asked.

"He wants to see if it heals. Isn't that right?" Jade said, watching him wipe the blade clean on his other leg and place the knife in his pocket.

"You're not just a pretty face, are you?"

"Okay, K," Tim said. "Let's go."

"Relax as much as you can," Jade said softly. Sophia waited beside Casey and Tim. Kevin's hands rested by his side. His pinkie reached out, finding Jade, and she responded. Their auras began to pulse with light. She watched as a fluid spiral of energy came from Kevin's forehead, chest and abdomen, joining into one swirl and the molecules in space retracted, opening a shimmering waterfall of light in front of them. He let go of Jade's finger, stepped forward, merged into the light and disappeared.

"Doesn't it look like embryonic fluid?" Jade said, moving up and touching it with her hand. Light rippled across its surface as if it was alive and sensitive to her touch.

"It looks like thin jelly to me," Tim said, "and it feels just as cool and smooth." He stepped away from Sophia and Casey. Arms elevated at chest height, like a zombie, he walked straight through.

Casey and Shaun, a little more cautiously, followed. "You're not coming, Kath?" Sophia asked.

"No, thanks, I'll wait right here and hold down the fort."

Sophia stepped through feeling alive and at peace. Every moment that was, is, or will be, seemed to be one moment in time. She felt like the seed. The freshness was cleansing. *What an amazing world*, she thought, *it is so blissful*. Someone touched her hand and tugged and she fell onto the cold tiles. Sophia looked up and saw Shaun sitting on the toilet. Tim looked like he was waiting for a bus, and Jade was sucking on the ends of her hair blocking the bathroom door. Casey was down on one knee peering into her face. Kevin was standing over her. "You have to stay focused and keep moving through," Kevin said to her.

"Why? What will happen?" she asked.

"I don't know, but we were all in this room within seconds of each other," he said. "Except you."

Jade pushed off the door and said, "You, awesomely, have been gone for twenty-two minutes."

"But it only seemed like a few," Sophia said, getting up from the cold tiles.

"Exactly!"

They piled out of the bathroom and into the bedroom.

Kath was pacing the floor. "What the hell happened to just popping into the next room and back?" she said, looking at Tim and Kevin.

"We had to wait for Sophia. She was — she got — stuck," Tim said, bouncing onto the bed. Sophia sat next to him and he quickly jumped off.

Energized, Jade plonked herself down onto the bed next to

Sophia, and Casey joined them. Tim and Kevin sat on the floor and swung their legs up onto the side of the bed.

Shaun walked in and Kath ran to check his leg. It was healed.

SHAUN COULDN'T BELIEVE what had just happened. His dad was right, but how could Kevin open a doorway without the artefact.

"How is your leg?" Kath asked.

He lifted himself up onto the edge of the bay window. "Not a scratch," he said, sticking his finger in the hole of the pants. He rested his chin on his knees and wished he could see out the window.

"How do we find the tablet?" Kevin asked.

"It has to be in the Middle East somewhere. It's the center," Sophia said.

"Kevin's got it," Shaun said.

"What?" Kevin said, sitting up and pushing his hair out of his eye. "Are you mad? Why would you say that?"

Shaun kept quiet, not sure how far to go. It was agony. He wanted to tell them, he wanted to trust them. He looked at Casey and felt vulnerable, then figured what the hell.

"I know what it can do. I've seen it and what you just did. You need the breastplate of Thoth. The tablet, you've got to know where it is."

"I swear I don't have it. I don't know how I can do what I do. I swear, I never heard of it until the other day."

"What? How do you know?" Jade said, amazed.

"My dad was an archaeologist and he was part of a dig in the desert in Israel. I was only young, seven years old. It was rumored that they found a cave with lost artefacts and a statue of an Egyptian god. He possessed the key to other worlds, and the cure for all ailments."

"Who is the intel now?" Jade said, trying to lighten the mood.

"But how do you know all this?" Casey asked.

"I was there. My mother was in hospital and she begged my dad to take me. He left me outside the cave for hours with the head archaeologist's daughter, Rachel. We were both young and frightened. They found the tablet and my father destroyed everyone who could finger him, including Rachel. He got me to shove the tablet into the bottom of the suitcase; it was green, extremely heavy. We boarded a plane. He drugged me soon after so I am only starting to remember bits and pieces. We delivered it to some Russian oil tycoon in Egypt who promised my dad he would pay him millions, and allow him to use it the once to heal my mother. He received the money and flew back for her. It was a week before she was able to fly. Egyptian Customs denied us entrance. My father told them we were expected. They took him away and brought him back bruised and bloody. They allowed him to clean himself up, then put us on the next flight out. My mother died soon after."

Everyone was quiet. The boys still lay on the floor, looking everywhere but at Shaun, except Casey who was resting his head in his hands and turned towards Sophia, then Shaun, and smiled.

"Do you know who the Russian was, and where he took it?" Sophia asked.

"No, all I remember is seeing Egyptian passports — I was lying on a red and gold couch and a woman put a pillow under my head — then hearing an argument and the promise. There was a little boy playing on the ground, making sounds of airplanes and gunfire. The next I remember we were landing in Australia and I was throwing up. I vowed never to trust my dad again."

Kevin sat next to him on the bed and said, "Well, that's why you're here. To help right your dad's wrong and return the artefact."

"Rachel and I saw those tiny winged demons, the ones now saturating the atmosphere, fight each other to get out of the cave. That was ten years ago. If you guys think they were the virus, the beginning, why didn't I get sick back then?"

30

THE SHE-DEVIL: ENGLAND

Kevin, upstairs in Casey's bedroom, felt a roller coaster of emotions emanating from downstairs — and it wasn't a barrel of laughs. His mom was becoming aware of him, so he pulled back. But something wasn't right and he felt long dirty nails drag down his face to his stomach. His internal alarm screamed.

Next to him lying on the floor, legs perched over the edge of the bed, were Tim and Casey. *When did the room go quiet? When did they stop talking?* he wondered. It was like the day before his nanna and pop died. Bile suddenly rose in his throat, the color draining from his cheeks. His eyes focused on Shaun nestled in the window frame, squeezing his leather pouch. Something was wrong.

"Something's wrong downstairs. I don't feel good," Kevin said and swung his legs off the bed and sat up.

"What's wrong?" Jade asked.

Kevin stood up listening, the silence distressing. Casey also stood, straining to see beyond the shadows. Kevin went for the door, Tim and Casey on his heels. They stormed down the hallway towards the front of the house and slid down the banister.

Kevin jumped clear and heaved opened the massive double doors to the lounge room. The light of the log fire danced hypnotically, casting a field of shadows across the adult faces, and the chill crept into the room.

Molly and Alex were asleep on the lounge. Simultaneously, they started making noises in their sleep. Alex was the first to let out a little giggle and then Molly.

Callie looked at Kevin. "Why the dramatic entrance?" She tried to see his eyes. "What's wrong?"

CASEY RAN INTO THE room, stopping beside Kevin, and froze. He could see the fiery red vapors of a she-devil. Her long, poisonous yellow nails were trailing down Alex's sleeping face. Three menacing phantom spirits, her entourage, toyed with Molly, and looked back at the she-devil like dogs on a leash seeking approval.

"Casey, Kevin, you're scaring us," Amy said.

"Wake them up," Casey said.

"What do you see?" Kevin asked, his voice full of anguish. "I can feel it, but I can't see it."

Casey didn't have time to explain. He shot out a bolt of energy at the phantoms around Molly.

Tim's mom, whispering, said, "Shh, there's no harm. They could be having a beautiful dream of sliding down rainbows, just like those care bears you guys used to love."

"Wake them up!" Casey said. "You have to wake them up now!"

Callie stood up and went to Alex. "Kevin, what's going on?"

"I'm not sure, but you have to listen to him. There's something terrible happening."

Amy was sitting close to Molly, when her little face suddenly turned red and she was holding her breath. Amy quickly picked Molly up, turned her over and hit her on the back. Amy stopped and placed her hand on Molly's little back and smiled. "I can feel her little heartbeat." Molly gasped for air, coughed and screamed, as if in extreme pain. Her milk and dinner gushed from her mouth all over

Amy. Her rosy cheeks were changing back to normal as she continued to wail.

Daniel took Molly and kissed her face. She was burning up. "Thank you," he said to Amy. He held his baby girl to his chest, blowing air on her head, and her crying turned into hiccoughs and sobs.

Casey could see the spirits concentrating on Alex as Father McDonald crouched on the floor praying loudly and flicking the pages of his Bible. "First they play with them, making them laugh, next they take their souls," Father McDonald said.

"Who are they?" Daniel asked. "I am so over this shit." He patted Molly and gently bounced her, trying to soothe her.

Watching his mom trying to waken Alex was agonizing. Kevin clapped and yelled, "Alex, buddy, wake up!"

Molly's crying and Alex's giggling mixed together was haunting. *What can I do? What can I do?* Casey searched his mind for answers when Shaun walked into the room and stood beside him.

"What's happening?"

Casey didn't answer. He was fixed on the evil spirits, pushing them with his energy, away from Molly and Daniel. They backed off and moved slightly, guarding the she-devil.

"Come on, little man," Kevin said to his brother, "or it's body-slam time for you."

Shaun walked straight to Alex and held onto his foot as if trying to keep him in this world and said, "Why won't he wake up? Alex, one more game. Wake up, Alex, we can play one more game! Come on, Alex, you're my pal."

Alex was laughing like he was being tickled to death, before he went quiet, his body went limp, and he collapsed in Callie's arms.

Everything was happening too fast. Casey expanded his energy force, driving the she-devil's entourage aside and began covering Alex with a shield of energy. He pushed and pushed, focusing streams of energy into the spirit world; his head pounded, his nose started to bleed. He wasn't powerful enough. His energy was like a punch underwater and merely stunned the she-devil. It turned its evil eyes to him and hissed, its mouth dropping open to its chest. It expelled a high-pitched shriek that vibrated through everything and everyone. The room shook like an earthquake. Its tentacles of energy, a hundred times more powerful, swatted Casey across the room. He slammed hard against the wall. His chest felt crushed, he couldn't breathe.

Sophia stumbled into the room holding her ears, protecting herself from the sound of the she-devil's high-pitched scream. Casey's skin crawled. Sophia could see and feel what he saw, and the malevolent spirit saw her too. It hissed in her direction. Sophia expelled a bolt of golden energy that mushroomed, flared and forged a violent shock wave, throwing the she-devil off guard. Its entourage stepped back, confused.

"Cowards," it hissed at its companions.

The she-devil drew all the energy in the room into herself and pushed it back at Sophia's. To Casey it all appeared to happen in slow motion. Its putrid smell, the screaming, its stretched mouth was closing. It thrust its claws forward and Sophia was lifted off her feet high into the air and slammed into the bookshelves. With its hand still extended towards her, as if to hold her back, it sucked Alex's spirit from his body, ingesting him. Sophia struggled against its force, rising up, and her necklace fell outside her shirt, catching the light: a blue laser beam magnificently struck the entity in its chest. It vanished from the room, taking Alex's spirit with it, leaving his little lifeless body behind. Casey, out of breath, helped Sophia to her feet. Daniel held Molly close to his chest.

Callie lowered Alex to the floor. Daniel checked his airways and felt for a pulse before commencing CPR. His face was beaded with sweat but he kept massaging Alex's chest for at least twenty minutes. He stopped and checked again for a pulse.

Kevin was crying, pleading with them to let him help, but his entreaties went unheard.

Daniel, emotionally and physically exhausted, stopped CPR. Callie got down on her knees and cradled Alex in her arms and cried out in pain. Casey didn't know what to do. He sent a bolt of energy at Alex's chest. His body jolted, but his tiny heart did not beat again.

Sophia leant into Casey and said, "We have to go. Tell Jade to get Kevin and Tim and meet us upstairs. I'll get Shaun."

Everyone was heading upstairs, giving Callie and Daniel privacy in their grief. Sophia whispered in Jade's ear to get Kevin and come upstairs.

Kevin lovingly held Molly. Casey's heart was aching for him. He knew what it was like to lose someone you loved. Daniel pried Alex from Callie's arms and lifted him up. He clutched him tight and buried his head in his chest and sobbed, walking listlessly into their bedroom.

Callie stroked Molly's cheek. "I'm afraid she'll fall asleep," she said to Amy through tears.

"If you like I can sit with her awhile," Amy said.

"No." Callie took Molly from Kevin's arms and hugged them both tight. She let go of Kevin and followed Daniel into their room.

Casey went up to Kevin and watched as his parents closed the door behind them. "Come on."

Sophia was holding onto his elbow. "Father." He had stopped praying and the crackling fire seemed intrusive and unwelcoming.

He pushed down on his knee to rise.

Sophia softly said, "We have to go."

He turned around and looked at her. He didn't want to leave, he wanted to pray and comfort the family.

"Come up to Casey's room when you're ready."

CASEY SAW THE DOOR handle turn. Father McDonald was breathing heavily. He saw Shaun slip his knife into his pocket. Casey busied himself packing his haversack and pretended he didn't see him, or Father McDonald come in to the room. Kevin was putting on boots and turned towards the door. They must have looked strange to Father McDonald, dressed in the middle of the night, ready to leave after what had just happened. They stopped when Father McDonald stepped into the room and cleared his throat.

Shaun was the first to speak. "Why is he here?"

"Why are any of us here?" Father McDonald said. "What's going on, Sophia?"

Sophia walked towards him and said, "We know how to get there."

"Now is not the time, whether you know how to get to Israel or not," Father McDonald said.

"Father, you have been with me from the beginning, and I can't do this now without you."

"He's right, I'm not going," Kevin said.

"We need to go now," Sophia said.

"Why now?" Kevin yelled. "My brother just died in his sleep for Christ's sake!" His faced screwed up with grief. The tears tumbled from the side of his eyes and he swallowed back the sobs. "Don't you care?"

"We have to go now, because of Alex," Sophia said. "The curtain between the two worlds is so thin we are losing our hold on this world. We will disappear and become the dead."

Very softly, Jade rubbed Kevin's back and Tim rested his hand on his shoulder. Kevin looked flustered; he pushed his hair back and wiped his face with his forearm. Casey continued to pack.

Father McDonald looked confused, puzzled. "You can't leave your families in their time of need."

Casey finished packing and watched Jade softly talking to Kevin. Whatever she said, it worked. Kevin brushed his hair out of his eyes as a ball of green energy expanded from his chest, pushing his shoulders back. Kevin stood tall, drew in a deep breath, widened his arms and exploded into life. Casey watched speechless as the room hummed and the floor vibrated under their feet. It sounded like a hole was ripping through the fabric of the universe.

"In God's name, what is that?" Father McDonald said.

A doorway began to open. The space before Kevin began to ripple. The atoms in the air ignited with light, creating a hole, separating time and space. The bay window could hardly be seen behind the transparent wall of light.

"Let's go, then!" Kevin said and ran into the wall. Tim, Jade and Shaun followed behind.

Casey threw his bag over his shoulder. "We have to go, Father," he said and gently held his elbow.

The priest walked up to the wall and touched it, quickly pulling away. "God help us."

"Have faith, Father. See the continuity," Casey said, guiding him forward.

Father McDonald stepped into the liquid light. He turned and looked back and Casey saw a rainbow bending around Father McDonald as if he were traveling at great speeds, then he disappeared from Casey's sight.

As Casey began to step into the liquid light, he heard the bedroom door open and saw Daniel walk in. It must have been a shock for Daniel to see half of Casey's body, then to see him completely disappear into the rippling mirage. Casey could feel hands reaching for him, pulling him into the parallel world.

They stood in silence. Father McDonald appeared to be enthralled by the luminous surroundings: an enchanted forest, everything pulsing with life. Casey couldn't help but watch Father McDonald gaze with awe into a clearing towards a garden and a sparkling pond. Scholars from different denominations were huddled together as if studying the secrets of heaven. A rabbi nodded towards Father McDonald, and a monk inclined his head before turning back to the other spiritual scholars.

"Are we in the Garden of Eden?" Father McDonald asked.

"I don't think so," Casey said. "I don't know where we are. We could be?"

"I feel no pain." Father McDonald flexed his hands, bent his knees. "My arthritis, it's gone!" He smiled widely, breathed deeply, drinking in the healing energy of the world. "It's a miracle, a place of miracles. We must be in heaven."

"We should call this place Athanasia," Jade said.

"What does that mean?" Casey asked.

"Timelessness. Everlasting life," Father McDonald said.

"Which way?" Shaun turned and faced Kevin.

Kevin looked around and saw the deer that had led him to Jade standing behind Shaun off in the distance. He stepped towards it and it disappeared.

"What?" Shaun turned, and looked behind him. It reappeared, standing with one foot forward. Shaun took a step, and the deer took a step.

Isn't she a beautiful translucent white? Kevin said in his mind.

Get out of my head, retard, Shaun thought, freaking out.

Sorry, I can't. It goes with the territory. They looked at each other with thoughts flying.

That's so weird, Shaun said, I feel like I'm buzzing.

"The deer's here for you, Shaun," Sophia said out loud.

"Me, why me?"

"You're the key to finding the Emerald Tablet. The deer came to me in the mountains," Sophia said.

"And when Jade needed help, the deer came to me," Kevin said.

"The deer is a symbol of my great-grandmother's spiritual path," Jade explained. "It represents mercy, certainty, and gentleness. My great-grandmother used to tell me the story about the deer. Sadly, today the deer is culled to prevent further damage to the environment; the skins are salvaged. To honor the deer's spirit Great Turtle made medicine drums with the skin and one day we made a drum together. On the pulse of the drum, she travelled through the sacred world to find and heal a person's ailments. She told me the deer can hear Great Spirit calling from the heights of Sacred Mountain. Great Turtle said the deer walked lovingly into the mist as a horrible demon blocked its way, trying to prevent it from connecting with Great Spirit; it told the deer to flee, that Great Spirit didn't want to be disturbed. But the deer felt no fear and graciously sought permission to pass, announcing its intention to journey to see Great Spirit. The deer was filled with love, gentleness and compassion for the monster that knew nothing other than to be a demon. The demon was curious how the deer lacked fear, trying and trying to frighten the deer, but could not. The deer's love pierced the demon's ugly heart, breaking the shell of its armor, and its heart thawed; evil shriveled up, turning into a pebble that lay in the dust at its feet. The beast stepped aside. The pathway was now clear for the deer to proceed up Sacred Mountain to Great Spirit."

The deer in front of Shaun turned and started to walk further into the forest. The foliage parted, creating a pathway as it walked. Shaun, enthralled, followed, and his companions followed him.

They walked deeper and deeper into the wondrous forest. In the aromatic air flew rainbow-colored birds with long tail feathers, and butterflies danced over the ferns. A variety of colorful fluorescent plants parted for them to pass. The light above beamed through the luscious canopy. *We're no longer under Earth's yellow sun, and here the sky is an endless electric blue,* Shaun thought. *My father was right.* The rich brown soil turned magenta as he walked, changing color with his personal heat signature. Petite yellow and blue, and some purple-winged, insects zipped in every direction.

"The Seal of Solomon!" Jade said excitedly. "That's it. That's the picture I've painted and have seen in my dreams for as long as I can remember. A green gate and a golden star; it's the Seal of Solomon. How could I not have seen it before?" The image flashed into everyone's minds.

"What does it mean?" Casey asked.

"We are bound to come across it. It is a key," she said.

A wall shimmered, just yards away, ahead of them and the deer walked straight into it, Shaun following, and one by one they all passed from the safety of the parallel world, the world of Athanasia, and into solid darkness.

Shaun dug in his pocket and pulled out his mini-torch and the small blue LED light. The atmosphere was suddenly hot and humid, the air thick and muggy. He heard Jade coughing. Beetles the size of a fist were scattered over the walls behind her. He decided not to tell her and tried ignoring the snakes that were slithering into the cracks in the walls. Shaun cast the light at the ground. They were standing on a dirt floor and there were iron rings bolted to the walls, chains hung loosely from them.

"This looks like a dungeon," Tim said. "Where the hell are we?"

"I don't know. Shh, someone's coming," Shaun said. They pressed themselves against the wall. There was nowhere for them to hide.

"Down here," whispered Father McDonald.

He looks pretty chuffed, Shaun thought. The old guy was holding up a heavy metal grille covering a hole, big enough for them to fit through. He had a grin across his faced that openly displayed his amazement.

"A gift from Athanasia," he said, jumping in, making a soft splash below. Father McDonald poked his head out of the hole. Sophia sat on the edge and jumped after him. Jade, not needing it, instinctively checked her pocket for her asthma puffer before following her. When they were all together, Shaun pulled the grating across, just as someone flicked on the lights.

Shaun heard a scuffle and a woman's moan, then a blow to a body and a thud to the ground. He twisted his head to see between the metal grates. He was just in time to see a leg and a boot lift up and pull back, swinging forward to kick the woman in the back. Shaun flinched, imagining her pain. It reminded him of his own actions, and the pain he must have caused others. He felt ashamed; a karmic mirror was being held up. *I'm looking at myself.* The woman curled and pressed herself against the wall protecting her head.

A deep voice, in heavily accented English, rumbled through the dungeon, saying, "You Americans are all the same." There was a third man standing on the stairs, his head hidden in shadows. His clothes were clean and stylish. He didn't walk down the final two stairs.

The voice was hauntingly familiar. "You have her blood. When you give us the formula, we will let you die quickly. You have wasted a whole year. If my family dies, your family dies!" He started to walk away, and then spun around, his fists clenched by his sides. "We found the woman, she is dead. Your serum is gone. My men saw her plane fall from the sky. You are stalling. No more. Tonight. It must be tonight. You give me the formula tonight, or tomorrow you die. No more games!"

He mumbled to the two guards in what Shaun thought could be Russian. Before the thug left, he turned back towards the woman and spat at her. Shaun recognized the men as the same guys who had arrived at the farmhouse, and had chased Kevin and Tim at the river. He was sure of it. Shaun signaled to Kevin to look and stepped aside. Shocked, Kevin held his breath, his eyebrows raised and his mouth open, confirmation to Shaun that Kevin recognized them too.

Kevin mouthed. *But how?* He stepped aside, letting Shaun back in. Kevin whispered into Tim's ear, "It's the guys from the house."

The guards picked up the woman by the legs and arms like a lamb to the slaughter, and carried her down one of the many tunnels and out of sight. A loud metal door banged closed and echoed back to them. Keys jiggled, a click: the door was locked. Father McDonald had quietly moved through the water towards the next grate to see. The men suddenly stopped and looked in their direction. Shaun put a finger to his mouth and Father McDonald stopped. The men's elongated shadows disappeared with a flick of the industrial light switch. The dungeon was in darkness. The keys clanged again as the outer door was locked.

Jade whispered, "This tunnel system, canals from early irrigation, probably runs under the ancient buildings of the city. But what's a Russian doing in the Middle East?"

"What's anybody doing in the Middle East? Oil, probably," Shaun said. "I think I've met that man before."

"What the ..." Daniel ran across the bedroom and reached for Casey as he disappeared. Daniel was shocked, gingerly reaching his hand into the flickering light. It was a pleasant sensation, firing his neurons and stimulating his body. Daniel was spellbound. He could hardly see the far wall and boarded window. *Kevin, where are you, where have you gone?* Daniel thought and took a few steps backwards. He rocked on his heels and, then, like a long-jump athlete, sprinted into the membrane, jumping clear of the room and reality. He felt like an excited ten-year-old boy at a fairground, but also nervous like a weary old soul. *Take me to Kevin, take me to Kevin. Where are you, son?* Daniel saw within his mind's eye an image of Kevin surrounded by darkness and he could feel the pull of Kevin's energy. Daniel tumbled out of the comfort of the wall of light into the same darkness he had seen Kevin in. He felt cold and shivered. It was musty and he could taste dirt and sand in the air. He looked back in the direction of where he began, but there was no bedroom, no shimmering wall. He knew he was not in the house.

"Kevin," he whispered. "Kevin." A little louder. "Casey? Kevin? Shaun?" Shining up between his legs into his face was a blue laser beam. Blinded, he stepped back, covering his eyes. He could hear the sound of scraping metal. He backed up a little further and hit a wall. He put his hands out behind him and something crawled over them. He pulled his hands away and lost his balance, falling against the wall. Crunching the crawling things against his back. He jumped away from the wall, vigorously shaking his shoulders and arms, making sure nothing was crawling over him.

"Dad," Kevin cautiously whispered. "Dad, is that you?"

Shaun moved the torchlight up to the ceiling.

A woman's voice echoed in the dungeon. "Hello? Hello?" The silence made it sound as if she was shouting.

Shaun and Kevin climbed out of the sewer.

"Kevin," Daniel said. "Where are we?"

"Shh, if she hears us, maybe they can too," Shaun said. "We have to go."

"Who is she?" Daniel asked. "Where are we? What's going on?"

"Hello?

Help me — they'll kill me — don't leave me here."

"We have to go," Shaun said and headed back to the tunnel. Kevin grabbed his arm and stopped him from moving.

"We can't leave her," Kevin said. "I don't know what's going on, but we can't leave her crying for help."

Daniel could hear a commotion: Casey and Sophia were preventing Jade from climbing out of the sewer tunnel.

"Where is she, Kevin? Where's the woman?" Daniel said.

Shaun shone the torch, illuminating the tunnel's entrance. "Down that way."

Daniel scanned the area. There was little light. An explosion outside rocked the area and sand and rocks were dislodged from the ceiling, hitting them on the head.

"What the heck is going on up there?" Daniel said.

"Hurry, this way quickly." Shaun led them down the tunnel the woman had been carried.

They held their arms up, shielding their eyes and heads from the falling sand and rocks, past rows of empty cells. Shaun waved the light back and forth, searching for the woman. In the second last cell, crouched, hiding in the far corner, was the woman. Her face was buried in her arms. Shaun focused the light on her face, but she didn't move.

"Point it up, Shaun," Daniel said. He pulled on the bars. The door was sealed with an old chain, a shiny new lock. "Do you know where the keys are?" he said to Kevin and Shaun.

"They took them," Shaun said.

Daniel looked around for something to bash against the lock. He picked up a rock, holding it above his head.

"Wait! They'll hear," Shaun said. "I think I can ... I think I can do this. Here, hold this." He gave Kevin the torch. Shaun pulled out Casey's pocket knife and used it to start working on the lock.

"Come on, hurry up," Kevin said.

"Shut up," Shaun said. A click broke the silence. The woman's hair had been hacked off, leaving uneven chunks. She lifted her head, and her face was a swollen bloody mess.

Someone was running towards them down the dark tunnel. Shaun, Kevin and Daniel turned to see who was coming. Kevin swung the touch around. It was Jade. Casey was close behind, trying to stop her, grabbing her shoulder. She shook him off.

"Get off me, get off me."

Daniel caught Jade. "What's going on?" Daniel said.

"That's my mom."

"Jade." The woman had turned towards them, trying to see through her swollen eyes. "Jade! Jade! Is that you? Jade?"

"Mom!" Jade cried. Shaun finished picking the lock and removed the chain as fast as he could. Jade pushed him out of the way and burst into the cell.

Daniel stepped in, watching them cry in each other's arms. Her mother's dirty, bloody hands were running over Jade's body, hardly believing she was real. Daniel helped them up. "We have to go. Ellen, can you walk?"

"Who are you?" the woman said. "How do you know my name?"

"Don't be frightened, Ellen. It's Daniel, Callie's husband." "They said she was dead. I am so sorry, it's my fault."

"She's not dead. She's fine," Shaun said. "Can you walk?"

"Who's that?"

"Ellen, I am going to help you up," Daniel said. 'Help me, Shaun." Together they got Ellen to her feet and Daniel put her arm around his neck.

"Guys, how do we get out of here?" Daniel said.

"This way." Shaun led them back to the grille leading underground.

"No, I mean, home. How do we get home?"

"We can't leave for home yet. In here," Shaun said, letting Casey jump into the sewer first, followed by Kevin. "Get in, Jade." Shaun jumped in after her and Daniel lowered Ellen gently down to the others in the sewer. Father McDonald was at Shaun's side, helping him ease Ellen into the murky water.

Shaun searched his pockets for his lighter. "Give me your knife?" he said to Casey. "Forget that, I've got it." Shaun ran the flame over the blade and placed his hand on Ellen's head to hold it still.

"What are you doing?" Ellen asked.

"Relax. Courtesy of my dear old dad, I have had to do this to myself a dozen times." Quickly, he made a little slit in Ellen's swollen eyelids and the built-up blood spilt out.

"Thanks, I can see a little better now. How did you find me, Jade?"

"By accident. We're here for an artefact," Shaun said. "And we have to get moving."

Jade wrapped her arms around her mom. "I'm sorry, Mom."

"We are searching for the Emerald Tablet. What formula do they want?" Sophia said.

"Callie and I stumbled across a protein that allows metastasizing cancerous cells to revert back to healthy cells, as if there was no cancer at all. We found it by accident. We tested the virus with the samples and it too reversed, transforming into healthy cells. We watched the virus battle and we thought it was going to win, but it didn't, hence the protein's usefulness as a vaccine for the virus. Somehow, that Russian upstairs, who thinks he is a god, found out within days. I can only presume a government leak. And then I was kidnapped. He set up a lab here for me to replicate the experiment, but I couldn't make it work. There was a key element I can't replicate, but he wouldn't believe me. He wanted the vaccination for his family, and for blackmail purposes. He is greedy and is going to hold what's left of the world, hostage. He said all those who had worked in my lab at home were killed. I thought Callie was dead. Over the months I gave them what I could to stay alive. They brought in two pints of blood, saying it was Jade's. At first, I didn't believe them, but they said they would drain her whole body if I didn't do what they wanted. The blood was proof of life. I asked them to let me test it. If it was your blood, I would know. I'm sorry they did that to you. They didn't know how close they had actually come to the missing ingredient. He sold a vial of the experimental vaccine a few days ago for fifty million dollars, but it didn't work. The buyer's family died, hence the bombing, I think, and probably the twenty-four hour deadline." She coughed and choked on the words, wiping blood from her mouth. "He has the Emerald Tablet. He is missing pieces, though, and can only enter the underworld, the world of the dead. He can't find the missing pieces to activate the door to al-mawet."

"What does that mean?" Sophia said.

"No death," Shaun finished for her.

"It's from the Book of Proverbs," Ellen said. "The spelling varies within different religious texts, but they all have the same meaning. *Mawet* means death, *al- mawet* is 'no death'." Ellen held Jade close to her and said, "I am so glad you are safe. I would never have told him what the missing element is, never." She looked into her daughter's eyes.

"My blood — that's the missing element, isn't it. But how? Is that what you wanted to tell me the day before you were kidnapped?"

"You *were* listening," Ellen said.

"I'm sorry, Mom."

"I hate to break up the family reunion but, seriously, we have to get that tablet. Do you know where he keeps it?" Shaun said.

"I'm with Shaun on this one," Tim said. "I really want to get out of this hellhole."

"I think so. It is in his private rooms," Ellen said.

"Is there a sofa, like a daybed, in the foyer outside four rooms with enormous wooden double doors?"

"Yes, that's right, but how —" she said. "Never mind, you can tell me later. We should go that way." She pointed into the darkness of the sewer tunnel.

The canal shook and Sophia fell into the water. Tim helped her up. Jade screamed as more explosions came closer and closer. They ran down the tunnel covering their heads. Daniel supported Ellen and she leant heavily on him. Her ankle was the size of a softball, but she didn't complain.

31

DESTITUTE: ENGLAND

It had been two days since they last saw Daniel, Father McDonald and the children. Joe tossed mixed powdered eggs into the pan, while Terry opened a can of breakfast juice. Amy handed Callie the baby's bottle and sat between Callie and Sally at the kitchen table. Kath stroked the golden retriever's head; Lucy was guarding the back door, preventing anyone from leaving. They had searched the grounds for two days, until the iron-cloud hung low, covering the sky above them for miles, forcing them to stay indoors. The wind began to howl and the trees were moaning, starting to splinter. The outside shutters clapped against the walls and the gale wailed through the seams of the house, but she was a solid old girl and was holding her own.

It's hard trying to attend to basic needs with the wee hen and her pals gone. She must have found a way, Joe thought. The timing was bad, with the young lad taken from them by the she-devil. They had laid Alex in Father McDonald's room.

Terry, Amy, Callie, Sally and Kath sat around, waiting to be picked off. Joe poured the eggs into the big dish for everyone to share. "Come on, people," he said, "you must keep up your strength. They are going to be okay. You said, Callie, that Kevin and Tim had done a disappearing act before. Look on the bright side: this time Daniel is with them. We have to be prepared for —"

"Prepared for what?" Callie said. "Prepared to die, is that it? We are all going to die? The last time the dead showed themselves, we were trapped in limbo for over four hours, Joe. They roamed freely for over four hours. The dead will walk the earth and we will fade into nothingness."

"Come on, Callie," Amy said.

"Don't 'come on Callie' me. I have lost both my sons and my husband. What do you know about loss?" Joe could see the hurt in Amy's eyes, telling him she knew only too well about loss.

"You're right, I don't know," Amy said.

Callie's raised voice frightened baby Molly and she started to cry. Callie jiggled Molly in her arms and said, "I'm sorry, Amy. I am so tired. I miss Alex, I miss Daniel and Kevin."

The dog scrambled to her feet and howled. Joe heard the outside shutters being ripped off and flying, crashing onto the roof. The windows shook violently. The boards split and pushed from the windows into the living room. It sounded like a jumbo jet was landing. The ceiling cracked above them, collapsing.

"Quickly, into the basement," Terry said.

Joe, the last one out, pulled the door closed just as the gas stove ignited into flames. He was thrown down the stairs backwards, landing hard on the ground with the wind knocked out of him. He pushed the door off himself, and crawled over to Terry.

"This way," Terry said, grabbing the torches and pushing Sally and Kath through the hole in the wall. "Come on, Joe." Terry helped him to his feet and gave him a torch.

Joe didn't want to be back in the tunnels. He knew what lay ahead: darkness. He didn't want to be buried alive, but he needed to protect the others and he followed as they all moved deeper and deeper into the tunnels and the sounds of the evil storm faded.

32

DELIVERANCE: EGYPT

The smell wasn't too bad. The sound of dripping water in the sewer tunnels increased, signaling they had arrived at a junction and the main tunnel stopped. Four openings drizzled water into the main chamber.

"Where to now?" Shaun asked.

"I think it's that tunnel there," Ellen said, pointing.

"Really?" Tim said. "There's hardly any room in there."

"Stop complaining," Shaun said and climbed into the narrow space. One by one they followed with Daniel coming at the end.

Muffled voices could be heard up ahead. Everyone stopped. Shaun whispered to Casey. "Tell everyone to back up to the last opening and wait there."

"What?" Jade said.

"Back up, go back," Casey said.

"Don't have to tell me twice to vacate this entombing space." Tim said.

Alone, Shaun pushed his index finger against his nostril and blew the accumulated dirt from his nose. Slithering on his belly, his elbows and forearms became raw and tender. He kept moving closer to the muffled voices up ahead, and saw an air vent. Sound and air filtered between the copper slats. He peered out and looked straight into the head honcho's private suite, sparkling with gold, silk and other elegant materials. A spectacular room, in the center was a golden stand with an angled tabletop. An old familiar slab of rock was displayed upon it: the Emerald Tablet. It extended over the edges of the stand and exuded a green glow.

Boom! The tunnel around him shook, dislodging dirt over Shaun. He coughed and held his hand tight against his mouth, smothering the sound. He was scared he was going to be buried alive just like Rachel. The man was yelling in Russian and waving his arms around. His eyes were black shadows set deep into their sockets. His skin had yellowed. *He looks like a raving lunatic.*

"You! In one hour bring me the American woman, and you bring me the girl, the thief, now! This night of judgement I *will* sit beside the prince of darkness and rule this world."

Shaun wriggled backwards, to join the others.

"It's him, your kidnapper," he said. Ellen moaned. She looked worse than he even had after one of his dad's drunken rage attacks, but she didn't complain. "We don't have much time. He has sent for you, Ellen. The tablet is there, too. It's on a golden stand. The vent is way too small for us to fit through. We have to get into that room now."

"K, we have to get my mom out of here. She needs healing."

"No one is going anywhere till we get that artefact."

"I can do it," Kevin said.

"Do what?" Daniel asked.

"Get us into the room."

"How?"

Jade piped up to say, "He can bend space and time. That's how. How do you think you got here?"

"I can't bend time. I don't understand what it is that I can do. I don't create it, I think I just connect to it."

Daniel shook his head. "Connect to what? Forget it, there is no time. I'll go."

Sophia whispered, "No, no, you can't. Shaun has to."

The bombing had stopped again. Shaun was feeling really strange and edgy. The energy was exasperatingly itchy and he wanted to disappear. The confined space started to intensify everything. He saw Kevin nudge Tim. They were getting on each other's nerves. There was something in the air in the tunnel affecting them.

"I'll go with him," Kevin said.

Jade stood next to Kevin. Controlling her breathing, she grabbed his hand. Their combined energy encapsulated them, they sparkled and lit the tunnel like a swarm of fireflies. Shaun nearly had to shield his eyes. "What the hell?"

Kevin pulled away from Jade's grip, and the light went out. Kevin looked embarrassed and crawled into the tunnel. Shaun followed closely behind making sure he didn't cough and blow it. He waited while Kevin peered between the slats and studied the room before signaling to back up. They wormed their way back. Kevin stood and looked at him. "There is a window with drapes in the far corner on the other side of the room. We will enter there. The curtains will conceal us."

A low hum pulsed in the canal under his feet and up his legs. Shaun thought he could hear the sound of rustling trees. A transparent mercury window appeared. It completely covered the side tunnel entrance he had just wormed out of. Kevin looked at him with raised eyebrows, inviting him to go first.

He climbed through Kevin's window into the suite. The stale smell of cigar smoke was the first thing to hit him. He instantaneously felt a burning deep in his bowels. He was shocked at his own vulnerability and wanted to piss himself to cool down. The memories came flooding back. He felt weak at the knees: the smell, the nauseating cigars, the alcohol and laughter of that night; the tycoon, the buyer of the tablet victoriously slapping his dad on the back, praising him for the successful delivery. Shaun wanted to jump out from behind the drapes and beat the guy senseless. Kevin put a restraining arm across Shaun's chest as if he was aware of his urge, and shook his head and mouthed, *No!* Shaun stepped back and they continued to hide, waiting for their opportunity to snatch the Emerald Tablet.

The enormous doors to the suite were thrown open. A young woman was shoved into the room. She fell on her knees at the edge of a gold and black tapestry. Her veiled head hung low, eyes fixed on the rug beneath her. Her satin, lavender robe barely covered her body. Shaun wanted to grab the tablet and get out. He didn't know how much longer he could restrain himself. He wanted to kill the man. Clouds of anger burst into his mind; his head was aching, throbbing. A remote part of him knew he must wait. His temples felt so tight he was afraid his skull would rupture.

The man turned his back to the tablet and to the young woman. He appeared to glide across the room. He locked the doors and like a lion stalking its prey advanced on her and tore off her veil. Her hands went to her face. She kept her head down, her long wavy, dark hair concealing her features. Her movements somehow felt familiar and Shaun felt a jolt of déjà vu. The man put his hand on the young woman's chin and lifted her head up for a kiss. She avoided his lips and turned her head in Shaun's direction. Shaun stepped back in disbelief, holding his breath. He nearly fell into the shimmering waves and back into the tunnel. The man grabbed the young woman by the arm and pulled her roughly to her feet. He slapped her, knocking her down on the bed. The girl screamed and pulled out a knife from behind her. He slapped it away and laughed. She fell to the floor as the knife slid away. The tycoon dragged her up on her feet by the hair. She screamed, slapping at his arms. He pushed her face down onto the bed and seized her hips.

Shaun's mind and heart raced. It couldn't be, she looked the same as in his dreams. *It couldn't be. Is this all a dream? Another nightmare.* The man stretched out her arms, used her silk belt from around her waist to tie her wrists to the bed. She continued fighting and scream-ing, as her captor knelt on her to hold her leg still, but she still tried to kick against him. *Boom!* The building violently rocked and swayed on its foundations. He rose up and roared, yelled with each giant step he took towards the locked doors.

Shaun saw his opportunity and he knew it might be his only chance to save her. He ran out full of rage and jumped for the man's back. He felt Kevin grapple for his arm just before he went beyond the curtains. Shaun hoped the element of surprise was enough and leapt onto the man's back, pounding his fist into his neck and head and pushing him into the door. Shaun's bottled emotions thundered through his fists. The man turned and twisted trying to shake him off and Shaun saw Jade bolt out from behind the curtains. Her bracelet glowed. Shaun would have sworn he saw strange patterns spiraling from the bracelet like a holographic image projected towards the tablet as she grabbed it. Underestimating its weight, she nearly dropped it.

Shaun dug his fingers into the man's eyes. Kevin raced across the room, picked up the knife and hacked at the silk binding, giving it back to the young woman to tie around her waist. Shaun felt the tycoon's firm hands pulling him over his shoulder and slamming Shaun to the marble floor. Shaun felt happy. He couldn't remember the last time he actually felt this good. He smiled. Kevin opened the drapes for Rachel; she was safe. It took seconds, and that's all they needed. Jade clutched the Emerald Tablet to her chest and jumped straight into the translucent waves. Shaun could see that Kevin was waiting for him, keeping the doorway open. *He had left this kid for dead, and he still cared,* Shaun thought, as he elbowed the tycoon's face and watched the man's nose shift across his face in an odd way. He screamed and stumbled backwards. Shaun peeled himself off the floor and lunged for him, wrapping his arms around his neck from behind. The bloodied man ran backwards, smashing Shaun against the wall. Shaun let go and slid off the tycoon's back onto the floor, gasping for air. He felt like a goldfish out of water. The man's eyes had turned liquid black; Shaun knew he was about to die. He was okay with that — he was ready to die knowing Rachel was safe.

Rachel, he said in his mind, and smiled as she appeared from between the drapes. The room and the violence disappeared as he locked with her beautiful green eyes. Kevin pulled her backwards into the shimmering liquid and she was gone.

The man smashed Shaun in the face again and again, but Shaun didn't feel a thing. Seeing Rachel's smile instantly took him back to that day his father had stolen the tablet. He was a lifetime away, staring into her beautiful green eyes for the first time, and seeing her in her dress and boots sliding under the truck. He remembered the tablet and how heavy it felt. He started to come back to the present. He had flipped over onto his stomach and could feel the gemstones in his pocket digging into his side bringing him all the way back to the present and the pain. He was being kicked, stomped, and screamed at in Russian, Egyptian or Arabic, Shaun didn't know any more. What he did know was the tycoon was releasing his unbridled fury to break every bone in his body. He didn't care. Rachel was safe.

He felt consciousness slipping away. The kicking stopped, his head stopped hurting, he couldn't hear anything. It was quiet. Six wings unfolded before him. They opened up from the feet, the torso and then the face, an angel moving closer, his mother by its side. She too had the beckoning light of an angel. She reached out to him and he reached for her. Suddenly he was drifting; she was getting further and further away. He spiraled out of control, falling, her voice softly whispering in his ear, "I love you, I am so proud of you." And then she was gone.

A blast of pain erupted behind his eyes. His whole body screamed. Daniel was carrying him over his shoulders. The tycoon was struggling to his feet. Shaun, unaware of what had happened, found himself dangling over Daniel heading for the drapes. He tried to open his eyes. The man was on his feet, rushing in their direction. Shaun could taste the filth of the sewer mixed with the blood in his mouth, but his body no longer ached. The room had disappeared. Kevin closed the portal and the tycoon smacked hard into the stone wall, knocked unconscious. Daniel eased him off his shoulder as if he would still be riddled with broken bones, but he didn't feel a thing. He was healed again. He was starting to feel like the cat with nine lives. Rachel was standing with Jade's mom, fussing over her. *They apparently knew each other,* he thought as he watched her crying and laughing.

Ellen told her not to fuss and said, "So this is the knight in shining armor you said one day would come for you?"

Rachel turned to Shaun. "Yes, yes it's him," she said smiling.

Shaun looked at Daniel and offered his hand and Daniel shook it. "Thank you."

"I wasn't going to leave you behind."

"We need him," Sophia said.

Shaun ignored her and walked over to Rachel. She embraced him so tightly, he couldn't remember the last time he was truly hugged.

"We have to go back to the cave," she said in his ear.

"I know. You told me in a dream."

Kevin cleared his throat and said, "Which way to the cave?" Kevin moved next to Shaun and said, "It won't hurt," and placed his hands on either side of his head.

"How do you know it won't hurt?" he said, feeling awkward.

"I don't know, I've never tried this before. What else I am going to say? I am learning as we go."

And before Shaun could react, Kevin pulled his head slightly down to his and they touched foreheads. They looked like two Eskimos touching noses in greeting. The energy abruptly stimulated Shaun's forehead sending a weird sensation into his skull. It gave him a buzz before setting his nerves on fire. He felt his brain smoking like a motherboard with a burnt-out chip.

"Think of the cave, Shaun, not frying computers."

Shaun focused, letting Kevin hijack the image and then he let go.

"I think I've got it," Kevin said.

Shaun wanted to see if the tycoon was actually dead. While everyone was focused on Kevin, he crawled up the tunnel and peered through the slats of the vent. The man was alone in the room, lying unconscious on the floor by the window. The doors burst open and guards ran into the chamber. The window exploded, glass rained upon them and the side of the building started to fall. The tunnel was caving in. Gravity pulled Shaun over the edge into the room, but he felt hands latch onto his lower legs, holding him back, pulling him into the tunnel.

"We have to go," Casey yelled over the noise.

"What gives you that idea?" Shaun shouted.

Casey and Daniel helped Ellen to her feet. Father McDonald had been scanning the letters etched onto the Emerald Tablet. He flipped it over and there was an image of ten circles joined together by lines.

Shaun took it from him and shoved it into Kevin's backpack. "You can study it later. This place is going to come down."

"K," Jade said, "send my mom back. Get her out of here."

"She's right, Kevin," Daniel said. "Let's go home, all of us."

"Okay, Dad. Stand over there and imagine Casey's bedroom." Shaun watched Kevin create an opening big enough for Daniel and Ellen.

The ceiling started to crumble around them and Kevin yelled. "Go, Dad, go now." Daniel and Ellen had no time to react as Kevin pushed them into the portal and closed it behind them.

THE TUNNEL WAS FALLING apart. Kevin put his arm protectively above his head and focused his attention on creating another portal to the cave of Shaun's memory. He was having trouble opening a doorway. He was tired; he needed to feel the sun's rays. He remembered the day riding on his bike basking in the summer sun; it seemed so long ago, and it had recharged him as if he was a solar panel. Over the past few days he had used up so much energy and now it was catching up. He felt depleted, and desired to be full again, to be illuminated by the light, energized. He sensed Sophia looking at him and he shrugged and managed a stupid smirk and said, "I can't." She turned away and looked at Casey. *Sometimes those two seem to communicate without opening their mouths,* Kevin thought. He felt Jade touch his fingers and clutch his hand; he felt sparks fly between them. Casey snatched up his other hand, then he reached for Sophia's, and she reached out to Father McDonald who joined hands with Rachel. Shaun reluctantly reached out to Tim. They united in a circle and the energy raced into Kevin. They were all illuminated in a brilliant radiant warm light. The tunnels collapsed around them as they disappeared and they descended into darkness.

Shaun felt the hard ground beneath his feet and let go of Tim's sweaty hand. He reached into his pocket and pulled out his torch. "It's darker than I remember," he said to Rachel. It was hot and musty with a terrible stench. His skin crawled, he couldn't help scratching. He moved cautiously, thinking the caves might be saturated with the virus. He preferred to think of it as a virus, rather than the horrifying memory that was pushing into his mind. The thought was making him queasy and he felt flushed. He pulled off his sweatshirt and gave it to Rachel to wear.

Rachel took the jumper, turned it the right way and pulled it on.

"It's darker and the smell is stronger," Shaun said.

"Because the entrance is blocked. Your father blew it up remember?"

"I remember."

"There is a story of a secret entrance," she said and slipped the satin gown down around her waist to create a skirt.

Shivers raced up his spine. "It's the same as last time." A faint haunting sound of a bellowing horn could be heard from above. "That sound," he said.

"It's ten years to the day," Rachel said. "It is not coincidence. The master was complaining much about the thousands flocking to Israel, despite his attack. That sound is calling to the terrestrial courts: the lights of Earth are now hidden, and the gates of heaven have been closed. Today is the day of judgement for all mankind."

Shaun saw Father McDonald eyeballing the Emerald Tablet, and asked, "What are you staring at?"

"The writing looks Aramaic, an ancient language." He looked at Rachel and said, "They pass like sheep, one by one. The Lord looks from heaven; he beholds all the sons of men. From the place of his habitation he looks upon all the inhabitants of the earth. He fashions their hearts alike; he considers all their works. God understands all of our actions and today will make judgement upon us."

"What are you talking about?" Shaun said, agitated.

"Yes, you're right, holy man." Rachel stepped closer to him and said, loud enough for them all to hear, "Above ground, the people are meditating on the sound. It's the sound of the shofar; that was the first of one hundred and one blowings, so we maybe only have a little over an hour until the final sounding of the horn. It will reach the heavens and awaken the highest patriarchs this world has ever been blessed with in life and death, so they may bestow good judgement on mankind. The war between the good and bad angels has ceased and if the court is in session the heavenly angels and the prince of darkness are reading from the Book of Life. All our actions have been recorded from this life and past lives. Satan is rubbing his fire sticks together, counting our souls, ready to take control of what's left of Earth."

Shaun nervously moved his feet as she searched his eyes.

"Shaun, we must close the gate that our fathers opened before the last sound is blown. Then mankind will be blessed by God. He will send his mercy and give us the strength and courage to heal the world, to live in a state of immortality. The negative angels are winning so we must move fast. We don't have much time."

Shaun could see Tim shuffling closer and listening as everyone did. Tim cleared his throat.

"That reminds me," Tim said. "It reminds me of a 'Doctor Who' episode — when the world needed to think the same thing to bring his consciousness back. They need to reach a critical mass."

"This is no TV show — this is reality, the world is dying."

"Okay, keep your bra on! I get that. But because I saw that episode I sort of get what you're saying, and I am just saying that I get what you mean."

"I'm tired, sorry." She struggled to remember the boy's name.

"Tim," Shaun said for her.

Shaun had an epiphany, realizing in that moment that they were all meant to be here together. He knew that now.

"Certainty," Sophia said. "We need to be certain. Rachel, you said they were meditating, not praying?"

Rachel respectfully bowed her head slightly to Father McDonald. "Sorry Father, forgive me. Most prayers are like a shopping list of what people want. We hear our own voices. Meditating is listening for the voice of God."

Sophia was leaning against the wall and pushed herself off. "This time there is no second chance. We can do this. We need to have trust and certainty. We can imagine a new reality, take action and live it."

"It's all in the mind," Jade added. "Everything starts with a single thought. Nothing can exist, unless someone thought of it first. We create our futures, good and bad, and we have the power to change it. Free will."

Tim said, "K can do that. Can't you, K?"

FATHER MCDONALD studied the tablet and the ten scripted points. Rachel propped herself against the wall and sat watching the holy man. Sophia and Casey were sitting beside her. The priest did not wear his sacred garments or a cross around his neck, but everyone called him Father. The tablet was obviously hefty for his ageing arms. The metal side of the breastplate glowed upon his face. She looked closer and saw the images on the emerald side. *Channels like pathways joining at circular junctions; the Tree of Life.* Rachel stood and dusted herself off and knelt in front of the holy man. She studied the partly concealed markings: three columns. The two outside columns had three circles each, and the inner column had four. They were connected by parallel lines, like pathways, and she counted twenty-two. Rachel saw the image as two kites end to end and a square in the middle separating them. It looked like an elaborate highway system.

"What are you doing?" Father McDonald asked. "I have been trying to focus on understanding the writings and relate them to the scriptures, but Rachel, your intensity was so acute I couldn't concentrate on anything but your presence."

"I am looking at the drawing on the back," she said, opening up her hands waiting for him to give her the tablet. "May I see it? I risked my life to find that."

He looked at the script one last time and passed the tablet to her. It weighed heavily in her hands and quickly she lowered it to the floor of the cave. *This is what my father died for,* she thought, tracing her fingers over the images. Rachel felt Kevin and Jade move closer, watching her dig away some of the dirt with her fingernail to reveal deep etchings as wide as her small finger. They weren't simply parallel lines, because in between them were symbols. "This symbol," she said tapping the Emerald Tablet with her finger, "is the letter (א) Aleph," she said. "It's —"

"I know what it is," Father McDonald said, irritated. "It's the first letter of the ancient language of the Aramaic and Hebrew alphabet, and that one on the left side is (ב) Bet."

"Who has water?" she said.

"I do," Tim said. "I was saving it." Tim wiped the dirt off his face that was being irrigated by his own sticky sweat. "It's hot and I really wanted to drink it." He pulled it out of the backpack and handed it over to Rachel reluctantly. "You can have it."

Rachel swished the crystal clear water, assessing the amount, and saw Tim lick his lips waiting for her to take a sip, anticipating it. He was probably imagining it hitting the back of her mouth and sliding down her throat. She could imagine he would have pumped it between his cheeks first and just before the coolness subsided swallowed it. He was going to be sadly disappointed.

Rachel pulled her sleeve over her hand and used it as a rag. She scrubbed away the dirt that concealed parts of the image. She twisted off the lid and poured a little over the back of the Emerald Tablet.

Tim yelled. "What the hell? I thought you wanted to drink it. Fair dinkum, there was no way I would have given it to you if I had known you weren't going to drink it!"

Ignoring him, Rachel poured the rest over her sleeve and continued to clean the tablet. She moved from the top circle across to the one on the right and then left, and continued until she had cleaned every circle and line to reveal letters and symbols. Satisfied they were as clean as she was going to get them under the circumstances, she went back to the first and tried to read the markings.

Her eyes lit up. She remembered when her father was alive she would hear him rise in the middle of the night, and sit with a pale light that might as well have been a candle, to study a book that had this very image on the front cover. He would rock back and forth as if to the rhythm of a song only he could hear. Just before dawn, he would close the book and turn off the light. Sometimes she would fall asleep outside the room and he would gently lift her, hoping not to wake her, but even with his gentle touch he did. She kept her eyes shut tight, pretending, as he carried her back to her bed. Neither of them spoke about it. Each time he found her, he would put her back into bed.

"Look, Shaun, look," she said, excited.

Shaun looked at her fingers covered in dirt and blood and he looked into her eyes and back at her hands. A few of her nails had broken, exposing tender flesh. He couldn't help wondering at the struggle for freedom she must have endured. She was so beautiful she should be dancing in the sun, not crawling around dark, evil caves.

"Do you understand the symbols?" he asked.

"Yes, I think so, this means keter — the crown or divine spark." She traced over the three arches above the first circle, keter, and said, "I think it means limitless light: infinite or endless. I can't be sure."

"The two pillars — on the right and down the bottom it reads jachin, the pillar of mercy. The left says boaz, the column or pillar of severity, judgement."

"Doesn't jachin relate to King Solomon and boaz to King David? Tell us what you can in chronological order," Father McDonald said. "Go back to the top and start again, Rachel."

She breathed out heavily. "Um, um um um ..."

"Just relax." Father McDonald said.

Rachel started to cry.

"Why are you crying?" he asked.

"I don't know." Jade rubbed her back and Casey and Sophia moved closer and placed a hand on each of her knees and balanced her energy. She started to relax, took in a deep breath, sniffed back the tears, and breathed out and said, "Okay."

"This one is Keter," she said and trailed her finger down along the right pathway to "Chochmah" and moved her fingers across the inner line, creating the first circle on the left. "Binah." She moved back to right column circle and called out "Chesed" and back to the left. "Gevurah", then back to the right, but this time there was a circle dipped in the middle. "Tiferet." She continued to move from right to left. "Netzach and Hod," and passed down to a third inner column circle, "Yesod, righteousness." Quickly, she moved down to the final inner circle, tapped it and said, exhausted, "Malchut manifestation. It's the Tree of Life, the three-column system, the balance between mercy and judgement."

Father McDonald said, "The channels of the descending divine light and the ascending returning light."

Jade knelt behind Rachel, nearly placing her chin on Sophia's shoulder so she could follow Rachel's finger across the tablet.

"The pathway," Jade said, reaching over and touching it, "has three symbols. I gather from what you said before, Rachel, that this one is an Aramaic or Hebrew letter. I can tell you that this symbol represents a planet, and this squiggle represents an astrological house. Look at the second circle on the middle column. What did you call it?"

"Tiferet," Rachel said.

"Tiferet has the symbol of the sun, a planet. And this symbol," Jade said, tapping the tablet, "represents east, and this symbol represents air."

Rachel jumped in then. "And this says Uriel, the angel. And this one, Chesed. This says Michael. It must be the Archangel Michael."

Jade said, "In the circle you called Chesed is the symbol for Jupiter, water and south."

"It means mercy," Rachel said. "Chesed is mercy."

Father McDonald held his hand over his chest as if in pain and looked at Rachel. "We have ten understandings, starting with the divine spark, right? Then wisdom, understanding, mercy, judgement, harmony, victory, splendor, righteousness and manifestation, and there are twenty-two pathways, twenty-two letters. Ten circles, four directions, four angels — Michael, Gabriel, Rafael and Uriel — twelve planets and twelve astrological signs. What does it mean? It's all mystical and meaningless."

"Why are you being so negative?" Sophia asked.

They all sat quietly. The cave was suffocating. The excitement of their new discovery was quickly disappearing. They struggled to decide what to do next. They lost interest in their quest and sat lethargically, separated, until they stopped communicating.

Father McDonald took the tablet off Rachel. He wasn't interested in the circles and lines, and flipped it over and continued searching for the meaning of the words on the shiny side. Rachel watched him for a while, then closed her eyes to sleep.

CASEY UNFOLDED HIS legs to stand up and move away from Rachel. His body shivered. Images hurried across the walls of the cave. He tried to focus, but all he could see were two children crying, and heading in their direction was a swarm of evil. The swarm scraped like metal against the walls and felt like thunder. Men screaming in pain echoed around the cave. Casey doubled over, squeezing his eyes shut, trying to block the raw images. His stomach somersaulted. He felt faint, and opened his eyes, and the cave spun anticlockwise. He held his hand out to balance against the wall. The coolness was welcoming on the palm of his hand, a single moment of relief — until every muscle in his body spasmed and cramped with fiery bolts of pain. He was frozen, unable to control his body. His mind plummeted into the darkness of the cave, and the vortex that was sucking the life out of the world was here, it was everywhere. He didn't know how to separate himself from it. He could feel the devil on his back and the internal heat was unbearable. He struggled to scream, but like in so many of his nightmares, he was powerless to escape. Casey's body was thrown into convulsions.

"Don't touch him," he heard Kevin yell.

"Sophia, is he epileptic?"

"No. I think he has connected to the cave."

"What? Connected to the cave. What does that mean?" Father McDonald followed all the first-aid procedures, but Casey's body jerked out of control on the ground. Kevin scrambled down to lie beside Casey and hold his convulsing body. Casey felt Kevin holding him as tightly as he could. Sophia sat by his head and closed her eyes. He was watching everything from a distance.

"That's enough!" Father McDonald screamed. He was losing his cool. "It's time we all went home. This has to end." But no one listened, except Casey. He could hear him as if he was far, far away. Father McDonald began to pray.

Warmth surrounded him. He didn't know where he was; all he could feel was warmth. A rhythmic, calm breeze of words passed through his psyche, becoming louder. He focused on the sounds. He knew that voice. *I've got it*, he said to himself, *it's Kevin*. He felt an overwhelming sensation and saw a wash of psychedelic colors behind him; it was Sophia. Sounds of more voices flowed into his ears and his back began to hurt and suddenly a blinding light exploded behind his eyes. An angel took flight, and he tried to remember where he had seen it before.

33

MAZE OF MACHPELAH CAVE: HEBRON

Casey's eyelids sprang open, startling Jade, and he blinked repeatedly as he tried to see. He could only move his arms slightly because Kevin still had him in a bear hug.

"K, you can let go," Jade said.

Casey was eyeballing Shaun who had flicked on his torch. "I saw what happened when you two were kids," he said to Shaun and Rachel as he sat up. "You had nothing at all to do with what happened. You had no idea and you have protected the world ever since without even knowing it."

"I don't know what you're on about, idiot." Shaun moved away and searched for a way out.

"We can't go that way, Shaun," Sophia said, helping Casey up. "We will all die before we even get close. It's waiting for us. This battle has been foretold. We just didn't get the text. I think they have already begun to attack us. We have to leave or we'll die."

Shaun spun around and faced Sophia. He had a haunting smile. "You think you have all the answers."

"I don't know what you mean."

"Stop talking like you're some prophet. You're not a prophet! You're just some kid that has lost her family too. Attention seeker."

Jade looked at Kevin and said, "I don't feel so good."

Jade slid down the wall and cried.

"What's wrong?" Kevin asked, crouching beside her.

"I don't want to be here." Her head started to spin, the vertigo returned.

"None of us want to be here," Shaun shouted. "Don't you think I'd prefer to be at home? You think I've enjoyed being stuck with you retards. You think I want to be crawling around in this cesspool?" He spat on the ground.

Jade started to sob. Shaun walked away rubbing his head, looking confused.

"What the hell? Why are you crying?" Tim asked Jade.

"Back off, Tim," Kevin said.

"Piss off, Kevin. I'm sick of you telling me what to do. She's a pain in the ass."

"Oh, the lovers are having a falling out," Shaun said. "Could he be bi, after all? Oh Tim, what are you going to do? He doesn't love you any more."

"Shaun, don't be a dick," Kevin said, standing up.

Jade stopped crying and was looking around at everyone. Rachel was backing away from Shaun, as if she didn't know him. Sophia and Casey were still sitting on the ground and everyone was arguing. It was only a matter of seconds before they started to get physical with each other.

Sophia looked at Casey and said, "We have to get out of this cave."

All hell broke loose. Tim jumped on Shaun, screaming for vengeance, knocked him to the ground and slammed his fists into his face. Shaun flicked him off; Tim tripped over his own feet and fell onto Rachel.

Jade covered her ears and closed her eyes. She started to cry, feeling helpless. *They're all going to kill each other,* Jade thought. One, two, three, breathe in, one, two, three, breathe out ... she continued to count, chasing away the anxiety, hiding behind her hands, pressing them hard into the sockets of her eyes until she saw sparks of light. Images flashed in her mind: Sophia's necklace, then a swimming turtle, her bracelet, her great-grandmother's face and then her drawing of a door with a star, the Seal of Solomon, her green iron gate — *that's it!*

Jade slowly lifted her head trying not to vomit. She felt drunk, her speech was slurred. "I know." Tears streamed down her face. *Maybe I'm having a stroke,* she thought. This was a dream she had had all her life and now she could act on it, but she was about to blow a fuse. All her life the universe knew this day would come. The idea was profound; it wasn't logical, a paradox. "I know," she whispered a little louder, tilting her head towards Sophia and Casey. She couldn't be heard over the shouting. Jade dragged her leg from under her and stretched it out slowly towards Casey and touched his foot, trying not to move her heard, afraid she would vomit.

CASEY WAS FROZEN TO the spot, watching the rage unfolding amongst them. Emanating from within the walls of the cave were dark angels. *I can feel them.* They were being smothered by the evil that was surrounding them. Suddenly he felt something brush against his foot and instantaneously Jade's emotions merged with his. The nausea was overwhelming and he vomited, his head spinning, Jade pulled her foot away and the spinning sensation stopped. He moved towards Jade. She was trying to say something, but he couldn't hear her. The energy was becoming thick like soup, it was hard for him to move. With all his strength he clapped his hands together and it was like releasing a mini atom bomb. The cave was momentarily filled with light and everyone was thrown back against the wall, winded and struggling for breath. They all looked at each other, shocked and embarrassed. Father McDonald dropped the tablet and Casey scooped it up and stuffed it in Kevin's backpack.

"What?" Casey asked Jade.

"I know where the secret entrance is."

Sophia shuffled on her backside closer to Jade and touched her knees.

"Don't move me or I'll be sick," Jade said.

Sophia crawled over and started rubbing her back.

"Stop." It was too late. She dry retched.

Jade moved her hand towards Kevin. Casey watched him slide his hand forward till their fingertips touched; liquid energy travelled between them, embracing them as one. He balanced her out. She looked up at him with an exhausted look. Sophia stood up and Kevin sat in her spot facing Jade. He closed his eyes and she opened her mind to him. They looked like one soul. Casey was in awe and he felt amazed and privileged to be seeing this. He looked at Sophia and smiled, knowing she too could see. Casey was a mixed bag of emotions right now and grateful for his new friends; they all seemed overwhelmed.

EVERYONE HAD THEIR eyes on Kevin as he sat behind Jade, cradling her in his arms and crossing his legs over hers. Casey could see ripples in space opening up behind Kevin. He tilted backwards holding onto her like a scuba diver dropping off the side of a boat. They merged into the membrane, out of the cave, disappearing into the coolness of the rippling mirage.

Casey was the first to follow, practically landing on top of Kevin and Jade who were still huddled together on the ground. Kevin looked up just in time to see Casey hitting his nose on a green iron gate with a golden star. Kevin was still holding Jade, and Casey believed they wanted to stay in the embrace longer than was strictly necessary.

It was night and hard to see. The air tasted salty as if near the ocean. Casey looked to see what was beyond the green bars and the stone courtyard opposite a window. On the left wall was an ancient carving of a maze. He picked up the shiny new padlock that was nearly as golden as the star: the Seal of Solomon. Kevin and Jade began standing up, patting the dirt off themselves. He noticed the gentleness Kevin had towards her. He pushed stray strands of hair off her face, and gently rubbed the side of her arm. Casey smiled, turning away to focus on the maze that was beyond the gate. He saw something move in the shadows behind the window. A loud male voice, not far from them said, "Ti ... kee .. ah!" followed by a bellowing that pierced into the dark of the night. Casey jerked, the horn was blown again, and it ignited every molecule of light in the atmosphere. It cut deep into his soul, and it echoed far into the sky. He spun around towards the horn and saw hundreds of lit candles being held towards the heavens. Tim crashed into Casey, twisting him at an odd angle, pushing his face back into the gate. He saw a shadow moving out of the corner of his eye again. Everyone poured through the opening, piling up against him and the green gate. He wanted to laugh at the situation. *This is probably what it's like in a mosh pit.* Casey's face was pressed against the smooth cool star, and he felt centered. There was none of the frenzy of a music concert. He had a sense of wellbeing, peace and harmony within the world. *Maybe I should become a spiritual teacher.* He wanted to remain like that forever. If anyone was watching, it might have appeared quite funny to see them all piled up together. Rachel was the first to step aside.

"I know this place," she said. "This is the Cave of Machpelah. This is the gateway for the light to enter into our world. It's the resting place of the world's greatest sages."

"We cannot enter!" Father McDonald said.

"I agree with the holy man," said Rachel. "This gate, the one with the star, is Jacob's resting place."

Jade put her hand on the star, and started to weep again. Her emotions were in overdrive. *She wasn't sad*, Casey thought, she was the complete opposite; she was full of joy and excitement as if she had drunk ten red energy drinks.

"This is my door," Jade said. "I have been dreaming of this door all my life."

"That's incredible," Kevin said. "And you have never been here before?"

"No, never," said Jade. "It's been a frustrating enigma. See over there," she said, pointing to the far right-hand side where a three-dimensional maze was carved into the wall. "That is the key to unlocking the passage that will take us directly where we need to go, I am sure."

"Did you dream of it too?" Sophia asked.

"No, but I just know it is. I have no logical understanding as to why or how I know, but I just know. Oh shit, I'm sounding like you guys."

"This is a holy place," said Father McDonald. "We can't desecrate it. God wouldn't want this." He held the bars in his hands and began to pray. "Forgive our trespasses ..."

Most of the people holding the candles, behind them, were facing away from them and concentrating on their connection to the light of God. Casey was in awe of the proceedings. He didn't think he had ever seen a mass of people so peacefully uniting for a common cause. There must be thousands of uninfected people. Casey could only see a small portion of one side, but it felt as if he was in the middle of a packed stadium. He turned back to the gate to see Shaun take the padlock in his left hand and start to pick it with his right. Father McDonald put his hand over his and said, "You can't, son. This is the way of thieves. There must be another way."

THE WIND PICKED UP Rachel's hair and moved it across her shoulder. The golden candlelight, the symbols of peace, saturated the desolate terrain. Buildings were missing chunks of their walls. *My mother might be in the crowd,* she thought. Rachel stood on her tiptoes, searching. All the men were dressed in white, while the women were on the opposite side and strangely dressed in what could only be described as their "best". She couldn't remember the last time she had seen her mother or brother. She figured they must have given up searching for her a long time ago. She had told her brother her intentions and made him promise not to tell their mother that one day she would return with the artefact their father gave his life for.

Rachel saw Kevin out of the corner of her eye as he dropped his head. She turned to watch as he closed his eyes, breathing deeply in. The stone wall protecting the tomb of Jacob became concealed with a vapor-like mirage. Kevin opened his eyes and stepped through. Tim, Shaun and Casey followed one by one, disappearing into the moving liquid. This was fantastic; she couldn't believe what Kevin could do. She had never seen it before.

It was strange seeing Shaun after all this time. He was more handsome than she had imagined. She had never stopped believing he would come back for her. *There was something magical woven tightly within the tragedy, for he has become so hardened and filled with pain, but still he fights*, she thought.

The moonlight was reflected in Jade's eyes. Rachel was mesmerized by Jade's bracelet — it was glowing. The etchings were rising up from the bracelet and the shapes were like letters from the Emerald Tablet. Father McDonald hesitated in front of her before going through the mirage, and he crossed himself, asking for forgiveness as he stepped across the threshold, followed by Jade. Rachel couldn't take her eyes off the bracelet. *Am I the only one seeing this?* She stood there for a few seconds watching the bracelet disappear and reappear on the other side of the locked gate. Rachel stepped into the membrane and followed. She turned back to peer through the gate, looking at the mass of people. Nobody seemed to notice them moving inside Jacob's tomb.

The maze looks a lot bigger on this side.

"Maybe we just need to find the right pathway and push it in, to activate a door," Tim said.

"It would have to be more complicated than that," Jade replied. "Otherwise it would have been discovered lifetimes ago."

Tim and Kevin slid down the wall and sat on the ancient stones and patiently waited. Rachel and Jade got closer to the maze. Both of them started running their fingers over the patterns.

"The markings were rising up out of the stone. They were geometrically at specific points representing the four elements," Jade said.

"It looks very much like Hebrew, but it's not," Rachel said. "I think it is, like on the tablet, the Aramaic language." She studied each letter and interpreted as best she could. "These represent the beginning and the division. There are twelve lines in the maze."

"What is the beginning and the division?" Kevin asked.

Father McDonald was flicking through his Bible and stopped. "In the Book of Numbers, Chapter Two talks about how the twelve tribe were broken into four groups of three from the center of the tabernacle into the east towards the rising sun; south, west and north."

Rachel ran her fingers over the lines and said, "The twelve tribes, the twelve houses of the zodiac, the four angels. Like the tablet, if this is a puzzle to be solved there are hundreds of combinations."

"What I see," said Jade, "is the squaring of the circle."

"There is no circle, Jade," Rachel said.

"If you put a compass in the center of the maze," she said, drawing it with her finger, "and line it up with the east, you can draw a circle touching each of these markings." She tapped the points. "Imagine all the lines are removed, leaving the four points. You have a circle inside a square. Sacred geometry, the drawing of the squaring of the circle, fits within this maze."

"Why is it significant?" Kevin asked.

"She isn't really talking to us, she is thinking out loud," Father McDonald said.

Jade ran her fingers along a line, out from the center square to the east. "Down to the south-east corner and followed back into the center, and out to the west and up to the north-west corner. Back into the center and out along the eastern line and up to the north corner, and back into the center out along the western line and down to the south. Now draw the outer line from the south to the east up to the north and around to the west, ending in the south, completing twelve movements," she said.

The rock face of the maze grinded like giant teeth as the stones started to move. It was coming to life. Inner sections moved back into the wall, and the lines Jade had drawn along scraped forward, and began to spin in a clockwise direction. The center point protruded about four inches from the rest of the structure. Jade reached out and pushed it back in. After the passing of the centuries, the long rectangular stone slab under their feet, as if on a spring, recoiled into life just like its designers intended on the day it had been created long ago.

Suddenly, like a rug pulled from under them, the stones parted and they tumbled into the dark shaft, screaming. The stone slab sprang back into position, silencing the sounds of their descent. Rachel dragged her nails along the stone wall, trying to slow her fall. They were jumbled together as they fell, hitting one another. Rachel felt her head connect with someone's shoe and was knocked unconscious just before she hit the bottom of the shaft.

34

TOMB OF THOTH

Kevin couldn't catch his breath, his lungs wouldn't expand. Finally, he drew in a breath and dirt filled his nostrils. Kevin coughed. The dirt went down into his throat; he started coughing harder, and then spitting. Not a stream of moonlight or starlight above; the darkness was absolute. Jade coughed in his face and Kevin reactively raised his hand. He sat still and listened. He could hear her coughing, and smelt her sweet odor. He reached out, and there she was. He let loose a sigh of relief. He felt her leg and left his hand upon it to comfort her. A hand gently lay upon his. At first he thought it was Jade, as it was soft, but also a little too big. It was Tim. "Tim, are you okay?"

"I'll be right. Look after Jade."

"Jade?" Kevin whispered. He thought it was best not to talk too loud. He could hear someone or something start to move.

"Sophia? Casey?" They didn't answer.

He reached for the strap of his backpack and lifted one side off. *Please don't be smashed, please don't be smashed,* he thought, as he slowly reached into the bag. The tablet was cold and rough around the edges, but it seemed to be intact. He tightened the straps again and opened up the front pocket, looking for a torch. It was gone, then suddenly a blue light lit up the area and it was Shaun with his little blue LED light. He was sitting against the opposite wall about four yards away. Next to him, Rachel lay unconscious and partly hidden underneath Father McDonald, who was himself bent at odd and hideous angles. Casey and Sophia tried to stand, wobbling as they did. Sophia's hair, which usually looked like golden silk, was matted with dirt and blood. Kevin watched as Jade strained to catch her breath. He put his hand on her shoulder and she held up her finger for a minute, reassuring him she would be okay while she continued to control her wheezing. Over her shoulder he saw that Tim, washed by the glow of blue light, had crawled over to Rachel. Together with Shaun, Tim gently moved Father McDonald off her. Father McDonald screamed in pain, then passed out. Rachel still wasn't moving. Shaun squeezed her shoulders gently, quietly saying her name.

Kevin went to Father McDonald's side. Rachel coughed. Kevin looked up and noticed Tim had left Rachel in Shaun's care as soon as she started to talk. He was by Sophia and Casey, trying to help them. Tim was moving from one person to another, quickly and deliberately, caring for everyone. He was totally in his element. He reminded Kevin of his dad. Tim ripped off his shoe and a sock and then put his shoe back on. *What's he doing,* Kevin wondered. Tim tied the sock around Sophia's head to stop the bleeding. *If the bleeding didn't kill her, the smell would*, he thought.

They were all a mess. Father McDonald's leg was twisted at the hip and his head was slumped to the side. His ear was bleeding, the blood dripping off his shoulder and onto the dirt floor. His hip and leg were broken.

Kevin scanned around for a doorway, an exit. It seemed they were in an alcove no bigger than a small shipping container, but beyond the entrance to their small space was a vast chamber that Shaun shone his pocket torch into.

Tim crouched on one leg beside Sophia, making sure the sock was doing its job and softly spoke to Casey. He pushed himself up and headed in Kevin's direction. *Who is this guy?* Kevin thought, watching Tim make his way over. "Need some help, K?"

"You can tell me where my mate Tim's gone for starters?"

Tim didn't answer. He scanned Father McDonald's body. "His leg is definitely broken. I know that angle," Tim said. "His hip reminds me of my grandma's when she missed the chair and fell. He is going to be in a lot of pain when he comes around."

A scream echoed through the chamber; Father McDonald was conscious. Jade squeezed her hands over her ears. The sound reverberated in the small space and the outer chamber erupted into life. Kevin felt his stomach churn. He began to sweat profusely and his breath became rapid. A three-tiered ancient platform, each level protected by a ring of molten flames, filled the chamber and his eyes. The sudden heat was scorching, and they tried to back away. Orange and yellow flames guarded the first set of twelve ancient steps that led to the first platform. The second level glowed with purple and blue flames, protecting the next set of twelve stairs that led to the third tier. At the top of the thirty-two steps, on the third tier, was a platform surrounded by white molten flames. Upon the platform four cubed columns stood in each corner, like centurions guarding an altar where a golden statue lay. The statue's head was odd and had a pointy, long arched nose like a beak. At the chest was a cavity. Something had been removed; a breastplate, the Emerald Tablet.

"It's a statue of Thoth," Jade said. She stood beside Kevin, each of them breathing shallow and rapid. "It's a bit like a sarcophagus."

Over on the far side of the chamber, a black whirlpool of expanding dark matter began to zap away Kevin's energy. He felt he was looking into the emptiness of the universe and felt overwhelming sadness. He could see something within the swirling darkness accelerating towards them. It started as a dense shape and broke free into the light of the cave. Translucent, it flapped and fluttered like a giant butterfly. As it got closer, Kevin thought, *that's no butterfly.* The translucent entity had razor-sharp teeth, the head of a bat and the tail of a scorpion. It flew over the flames, straight for them.

"Come to me!" Father McDonald yelled with sudden strength.

The entity separated into hundreds of micro parts and went straight up Father McDonald's nose and in through his mouth. His eyes pooled with black tar and he gagged and choked. How he was even conscious Kevin didn't know, but the old man was fighting to stay in control of his body and soul.

Kevin couldn't help him. The dense whirlpool of negative matter had accelerated, drawing everything in towards it. Everything that contained a spark of light was being pulled into the stream of blackness. Kevin could feel the drag. The first and second set of flames violently stretched up to the ceiling. The orange and yellow flames seared the ancient stone without yielding to the strength of the dark force.

He was pulled up onto his toes, but he resisted the compulsion to step forward. The blue-white flames atop the third tier were hypnotic. They too rose into the air, ascending and concealing the statue. A few seconds passed before the flames parted, upon the altar stood a beast made from the blistering flames. The monster was six feet high, six feet wide, and six feet long. The pull of the vortex stabilized, but there was no way they could get the Emerald Tablet to the statue. The beast covered it, owned it. *How can we fix the Emerald Tablet upon the chest of Thoth?* Kevin thought. The fiery beast was blocking the gate to the underworld, preventing the world of darkness from being closed. It pulled back its mouth, snarling, exposing its sharp teeth, daring anyone to move. Fiery wings extended from its back and flapped, fanning the white flames.

Casey moved closer and it growled. Orange flames danced upon its jagged teeth and its scorpion tail slithered back and forth behind it, ready to play. *But nothing is impossible,* Kevin thought. He remembered his bike, his grandmother, the crash, and the day he saw Casey drown. *Nothing is impossible, nothing.*

Rachel was moving forward and started fiddling with Kevin's backpack, feeling for the tablet. He thought she was going to take it out, but she was making sure it was secure. She scrunched her hair into a bun, patted him on the back and walked past him into the open, resisting the pull of the black hole. She turned and looked back at him and said, "It needs a sacrifice and I will be it, for my father. The flames won't hurt if you are of pure heart; you will feel no heat. Remember, mind over matter. Don't give up, we can do this."

Shaun grabbed Rachel by the wrist. "No, I will go!" He stepped in front of her, blocking her way. They stood face to face. Shaun loosened his grip and picked up her other hand, and gently said, "It was my father, he was the cause. I won't lose you again."

Kevin was seeing another person. Shaun was different from the one he had known; he was actually showing concern for another human being. He had been kind to Alex too. Kevin had forgotten Alex was gone; the shocking memory kicked him in the stomach and he doubled over in pain and swallowed back the emotions. As if from underwater, he could just make out Shaun's voice pleading with Rachel not to go. Kevin moved his hands from his knees to his hips and regained control.

"I'll go," Tim said.

"What the hell, has everyone gone mad? This is all a dream, it has to be a dream. I have to wake up. I have too," Kevin said.

Instantly, Kevin felt calm. Sophia had placed her delicate hand on his arm. He could feel her peaceful energy rush through him. "Rachel has to be the one, she has the heart. This is for her soul," Sophia said, still not removing her hand. "We shouldn't take this away from her. Through all her lives she has waited for this moment. Her children and the world will be blessed."

Shaun stormed at Sophia. "Shut up, you're a fucked-up psycho," he screamed. "How can her children, that she doesn't have, be blessed if she's *dead*?" he yelled in Sophia's face.

Sophia, without flinching, said, "She is a gift to her children."

Casey stepped up, trying to calm Shaun and said, "It might seem like a load of crap, but you seriously have to listen to her."

Father McDonald's eyes changed continuously from normal to black pools as he dragged himself towards the flames. Knowing he was witnessing an internal demonic battle, Kevin felt scared and sorry for the priest. Everyone was totally freaking out. Father McDonald had very little strength left; the entity had just about consumed every drop of his light. But he didn't stop fighting. He was trying to speak. Kevin moved closer.

"I must go," he said. "I am the only holy man here. I must be the sacrifice. Stop her."

Kevin had no time to react, because while they argued, Rachel stepped into the flames. She looked calm, as if held in suspended animation, unaffected by the fire or the swirling dark matter.

Shaun stopped yelling at Sophia and turned towards Rachel; she was gone. He ran after her, but the flames drove him back. He couldn't get close enough to reach her. He shielded his face from the flames and screamed Rachel's name. Rachel didn't flinch, or make a sound, just walked on through the orange-yellow flames. She emerged unscathed and climbed up the first twelve steps. Without turning back, she entered the purple-blue flames untouched, and walked up the next set of steps and into the white molten flames. The cave was filled with a sweet smell as if fresh flowers had suddenly bloomed. Kevin moved as close as he dared and saw Rachel exit the blue-white flames. *She is unharmed, not a hair out of place,* Kevin thought. He had expected to see her clothes smoldering at least. She stopped in front of the huge snarling hound, its fiery wings fanning a heatwave, and its tail moved as if it was a separate entity.

It sniffed at her boldness, perhaps intrigued that she dared to enter the flames and stare into its evil eyes. It stepped forward to the edge of the sarcophagus. She didn't flinch. The beast looked behind itself and suddenly two more heads appeared from the rear and faced forward fixing on Rachel. The two heads had been enjoying sniffing its own filth, and were angry at the interruption and the sickening stench of Rachel's unwavering beauty that now filled the cave. The three snouts dripped fiery white mucus. *She looks so small. Why didn't she take the tablet with her?* Kevin thought. *How the hell is she going to get out?* The heads moved inquisitively, seeming to find Rachel of interest and no threat. The beast maintained its stance on top of the statue. The vortex was growing, the cave wall behind the vast ancient steps was collapsing into the black hole. Rachel took another step closer. Saliva the color of coffee dripped from three mouths.

"Do something," Shaun shouted and wrestled with Kevin for the backpack. He took out the Emerald Tablet and ran towards the flames. The intensity of the heat pushed him back again. He tripped forward. Kevin ran to help him, Tim right beside him. The heat of the flames scorched Kevin's face. It was like nothing he had ever experienced. He was worried Shaun was hurt. Tim got to Shaun and started pulling him to safety.

"Get the tablet," Tim yelled.

Kevin snatched up the tablet and turned his back on the flames.

The flames sucked the air from the cave. Kevin had started to feel drowsy, he was slow to think and that's when it happened. A paw surrounded with fire, the size of Rachel's whole body, was extended to her as its claws sprung out and in one swoop sliced the air in front of her. The middle head lifted up and roared. The one on the left bent down and in one motion licked Rachel from her feet to her head. She was covered in brown-black goo that looked like black oil.

We have to do something. Kevin was desperate. We can't just stand here and watch. Shaun and Tim were trying to find another way to get to Rachel. Shaun started to scale the side wall, climbing up and over the flames, but he wasn't going to make it in time.

Just like the day he saw Casey drown, he felt impotent and worthless and didn't understand why God gave him gifts if he couldn't save people from dying. But he had: he had saved Tim, he had saved his dad and Ellen. The hound's wings flapped faster and faster, its paw sliced the air and connected with Rachel. She fell to the ground. Shaun screamed from above, as the beast stomped its paw on her stomach. A second set of claws sprang free and pierced into her abdomen. The monster's massive wings lifted it up and off the sarcophagus. It shoveled Rachel up into its mouth, where she dangled like a puppet with broken strings. Kevin could do nothing but watch in horror.

Shaun pulled himself up onto a ledge, threw rocks at the back of the beast's head screaming, *"Rachel, Rachel."*

A beacon of light, a prism of color, filled the chamber. Rachel was illuminated from the inside out, her entire being glowed. The light travelled from her into the hound's mouth and down into its gut. The beast drew back its snout in disgust and spat her out as if she was diseased. She went flying through the air, over the top of the three sets of flame. The ground cracked open and the orange flames dropped into the belly of the Earth. Rachel hit and bounced off the fallen rocks like a pebble across a still lake. The dirt puffed up around her as she hit the ground for the final time at the bottom of the stairs and slid to a stop. The beast let out a terrifying howl. The heatwave and stench from its mouth was cyclonic, driving everyone back. Kevin sailed backwards and held the Emerald Tablet tight to his chest. He watched as one of its heads desperately snapped blindly at the air. The light went up its snout and surrounded its torso; it roared in agony. Its pain magnified; the heads bubbled and boiled. Rachel's light swamped the hound's entire being, squeezing out the darkness and turning it into falling effervescent lights that fell from the air into the first row of flames. Explosions erupted from deep in the crevasse, rising up into a massive fiery ball and the first row of flames died. The black hole expanded, more of the cave turned to rubble, and fell away into the nothingness. What seemed to Kevin to be an eternity was over in minutes. Rachel lay limp on the dirt, her visible light diminishing; shadows danced on the walls. The vortex was growing and they were all closer to the edge of extinction. The ledge broke from under Shaun.

"Hang on," Kevin yelled.

Shaun struggled to hold on to the rock face; he searched for a foothold and slipped. He fell down to the stone steps and landed on his back.

Sophia kissed Father McDonald on the cheek, despite the demon inside him. "Please don't stop praying. I love you." She felt her hands shaking as she reached into his jacket and pulled his Bible out of his inside pocket, gently placing it in his hands. Mentally and spiritually he was strong. He had continued to fight the physical pain, fighting to stay conscious. She could see the demon swarm to the surface wanting to reach out with Father McDonald's hands and crush her. He wouldn't let it. It was trapped inside him and she could only imagine his pain. "I am so sorry," she said, choking back tears. He was her family; he was the one who cradled her when she wept.

"I won't stop praying. I relish the pain," he said. "This is my gift. We all have a gift. I thought it was to watch over you, but you can look after yourself now. The end of my life is my life's purpose. Look, look at us — all different with different beliefs. Certainty is the glue. I have been a fool." He stopped as his neck swelled. He gritted his teeth in pain, coughed dark blood and moaned. The tension around his throat relaxed. Sophia dropped to her knee to get closer to him to hear him speak.

Panting, he said, "See your spiritual self in all things, Sophia. I'm not going to give up, I'm not done yet. I'll be here for you. End this."

Afraid her voice would tremble she said nothing and untucked her shirt to wipe the blood from his face and kissed him softly again.

Determined, she rose up and shouted, "Kevin."

Kevin had gone to Rachel. He was staring at her, watching her blood quickly spreading, soaking into Terry's sweatshirt, the one Shaun had valiantly given her. Shaun was still on the other side of the deep crevasse, staggering to his feet. He steadied himself, ran down the stairs and on the second-last step, he leapt into the air, swinging his arms and legs and landed inches away from Rachel. Frantically, he tried to stop the bleeding. His hands were covered in her blood; he pressed against her stomach and the blood pooled around his hands. Shaun ripped off his shirt and pressed it down on her stomach to prevent the flow of blood. Tim tore off his hoodie, looped it like a skipping rope and tied it around Rachel's waist. Together they managed to suppress the bleeding; Rachel was very still. Shaun gave a loud, agonized scream.

Kevin stood motionless, hypnotized by the loss of blood and didn't hear Sophia. She felt bad, not wishing to be insensitive, but she knew they had to push on and finish what they started. She spoke a little louder to Kevin, then Tim suddenly slapped him hard in the face. Kevin snapped out of his trance. Sophia seized Kevin's shoulder and sent waves of energy, calming, balancing his emotions, and said in a controlled voice, "Kevin, we have to do what we came here for, or the pain and suffering will never end."

Tim and Sophia looked intently at Kevin. His eyes were darting left, right, up and down; he was searching his mind for something. Tim slapped him again, this time gently.

"Don't say it, K. I know what you're thinking," Tim said. "Believe in yourself, K, believe in the light. It's in you, man. You've got to trust. I've seen you manifest whatever you put your mind to. It's just like it says on the Emerald Tablet: that which is above is like that which is below. The miracle, I know what it is — manifesting — the ability to create your thoughts and desires in the here and now. You know the saying, be careful of what you wish for because you just might get it. You know this shit, this is in you. It's all up in here," Tim said, tapping his temple. "You think and so be it. Sophia's right. We have to undo what was done. Let's do Jade's entropy thingy and create something new from the madness. No space or time. Now."

"Who are you?" Kevin's eyebrows knotted together and he inhaled.

Sophia untied the sock from around her head and left Kevin with Tim. Kevin had to take responsibility for his abilities and act on his own. She couldn't force him into action. She breathed deeply, and could smell the golden fields at home. She wasted no more time. She ran past the boys, tucked in her locket and like a ballerina, leapt high into the air, gliding over the first crevasse to land on the first step. She continued and ran up the stairs to the second tier. With legs fully extended, her toes pointed forward, she leapt directly into the flames, landing at the foot of the next set of stairs, racing up them towards the white ring of flames. She didn't stop there, or leap over the fire. She ran around it, heading straight for the black hole. Sophia stumbled, fell to her knees. Resisting the pull of the vortex she got to her feet. Balancing on the edge of darkness she looked into the silky black whirlpool. It was silent. Rocks and stones floated in the slipstreams, spiraling anticlockwise, disappearing into its evil eye, into oblivion. Sophia closed her eyes. Her hair violently lashed her cheeks. She ignored the desire to look down, the urge to fall into the vortex. *Focus, damn it!* Her aura, a rainbow of colors, glittered; she channeled all the energy deep into the Earth, anchoring her to the edge. Slightly wavering, she reached into her shirt for her locket and held it in her palms. She squeezed it in her hand like she had done a million times. This time, the Penelope's web face disengaged from the rest of the amulet and sat in the palm of her hand. Sophia stretched her arms above her head, and magenta liquid energy poured from the center of the amulet. Twelve channels of curved magenta light emanated from the stars of Solomon like lasers weaving a web, a barricade that held the swirling vortex at bay. Everything behind her went quiet as if they were in the eye of a storm. Sophia looked over her shoulder and could see Casey, Jade, Kevin and Tim. Shaun was pressing down on Rachel's abdomen. She couldn't see if Father McDonald had continued to struggle or was dead. She prayed he was alive. The second blue ring of fire extinguished. Casey and Kevin looked as if they had prepared themselves to jump before the blue flames had died; motionless they gazed down into the crevasse's infinite space.

UPON THE LAST TIER, the flickering white flames momentarily allowed Jade to catch a glimpse of the statue's full beauty. "Look at that! It's amazing," Jade shouted.

"She is, isn't she," Casey replied.

"No. Yes. Not Sophia, the statue. It reminds me of an Egyptian anthropoid coffin," Jade said, shaking her head in amazement. "They were made of gold and inlaid with semi-precious stones." Jade stepped backwards, away from the others, giving her room to jump. "What are you two waiting for? Jump!" she yelled at Kevin and Casey.

Jade sprinted past them and jumped, mimicking Sophia's action without the grace. Arms flailing, she fought her way through the atmosphere, searching for leverage, for that extra inch. Jade started to descend. *Oh shit, my angle of velocity is all wrong.* She came close, but not close enough; her toes skimmed the lip of the fissure and it gave way. She dug her fingers into the dirt, sliding, searching for purchase. Jade screamed. The sound of the billowing horn above had penetrated the depths of the cave as if it had been in the chamber with them.

Kevin yelled at the top of his lungs. "Hang on, Jade, we're coming."

Jade's fingers had latched onto two protruding stones, her feet frantically searching for anything to take the weight off her arms. She dangled like a rock climber and felt the moisture in the palm of her hands. *They're not going to make it, and I'm not worth them dying for.* Jade saw Kevin and Casey clear the edge. Together, they hung over the side and wrapped their strong hands around her wrists and pulled her up to safety.

Sophia held her position. The amulet was doing all the work; the laser light web was arching over the abyss like security sensors. It was wavering slightly and she wasn't sure how long it would hold. They had to hurry. Sophia slowly moved, bent down and placed the amulet between her feet. It shook and vibrated on the spot and started to spin on one of the points. She pushed it back down onto the edge of the pit and it held its ground. She walked backwards, away from the black whirlpool with its swirling demons of death. Sophia turned towards the others and headed to the last barrier of flames behind the four cubed columns, the last ring of fire that surrounded the sleeping statue.

Sophia ran up the twelve steps to where Jade was trying to decipher the symbols on the columns between the dancing flames. Out of breath, she said, "We have to go into it. We have to step into the fire, Jade. You can see the symbols better on the other side. We have to keep moving. I don't know how much time we have left."

"We can't just step into the flames," Jade said. "That is just not logical. I can see no evidence suggesting we have to walk into a blue-white flame which is, like, at least nine thousand and ten degrees." Kevin took Jade's hand and Casey took the other.

"You're serious. We are really going to do this. Oh, God."

Sophia took Casey's hand and said to Jade, "Now you're getting it. Certainty, we can do this. Let go and it will be okay. Close your eyes."

Jade closed her eyes and saw Great Turtle beckoning her forward. Jade let go and together they stepped into the flames.

35

JEWELS OF GOD

The absent heat of the blue-white flames returned as soon as they stepped upon the final tier. Casey quickly pulled everyone away from the roasting temperature at their backs. They struggled against a magnetic force emanating from the golden statue of Thoth that was preventing them from moving forward. Casey felt the force was curved, circular to the touch. He ran along the outside looking for a way to get closer, but he could not go beyond the surrounding four columns.

"Look over here." Jade waved her arms in the air. "The cavity on the chest, it's the second and third part of the message, Sophia. That statue is the golden rock representing the guardian of the under-world and the empty cavity is at its heart. That must be where the Emerald Tablet belongs. We have to somehow get over there.

These columns must have something to do with the force field. They are common symbols: earth, wind, fire and water," Jade said. "Give me your water, K," and she poured it over the pillar that had the sign for water carved into it. Nothing happened.

"The number twelve has come up a lot," Kevin said. "The maze —"

453

"The stairs," said Casey.

"So how can these four columns relate to the number twelve? Besides the obvious divisions," Kevin said.

"The twelve signs of the zodiac," Sophia said.

"Who's a Scorpio?" Jade asked.

"Me," Casey said.

"Is anyone Taurus?"

"I am," Kevin replied.

"You're an Aries?" Jade said, raising her eyebrows at Sophia.

Sophia shrugged her shoulders. "I might be. I was born on the twenty fourth of March. Would that make me an Aries?"

"You have to be. I am an Aquarius," Jade said.

"Find the column with the element that represents your star sign: Taurus earth, Aquarius wind, Scorpio water, and Aires fire. Go."

Casey stopped at the column at the bottom of the statue's carving of squiggled lines that represented water. Sophia was opposite at the head, Kevin was on the east side, and Jade took up her place on the west aspect of the statue.

Kevin grabbed a handful of dirt from the cave floor. Casey was ready with the last drops of his water.

"I don't have a flame," Sophia yelled as she tried to get close to the white flames to steal a little of its fire.

"Wait, I think I have a box of matches in my backpack," Kevin said. He rummaged around before pulling out a box of redheads. Grinning, he ran over to Sophia, then back to his pillar and grabbed another handful of dirt.

Sophia took out a match, and left another one sticking halfway out. She placed the box on top of the column ready to light up the whole pack at once.

"Ready?" Jade yelled. "Everyone on my count: one, two, three, now!"

Casey slowly poured the water over the top of the column, watching Sophia strike her match and drop it in the box, which ignited straight away. The columns began to moan, slowly descending into the ground and a large stone in the wall was slowly pushed out. Water gushed from its opening into the crevasse. The final ring of fire behind them was extinguished by the rising water, but the magnetic force did not wane.

They still couldn't get any closer to the statue. It continued to repel them.

"Damn it," Casey said. Jade watched him as he shuffled his feet, changed his stance, stuck his neck out slightly and lowered his head. He concentrated on Kevin's backpack.

"I can feel that!" Kevin said. "My stomach is doing a backflip."

Casey guided the breastplate out of the haversack and into the air, levitating it above Kevin's head. He stabilized the tablet and slowly walked as close as he could to the statue. *If we can't go around or through the force field, maybe Casey can go over it*, she thought. He raised it up, up, high in the air and gently brought it down to hover over the chest of Thoth.

"We're in! Go, Casey." Jade stood at his side cheering him on as he flipped it in the air, searching for the right angle, trying to place it like a piece of a jigsaw puzzle. It wasn't locking onto the golden statue.

"What is the rest of the message?" Jade asked.

"No end and no beginning —" Kevin said.

"To face the heavens and the emerald light will glow, the light will be returned," Jade said.

SHAUN COULD NOT stop the flood of emotions flowing any more than a pebble could hold back the gallons of water flowing in the surrounding crevasse, Rachel thought, feeling Shaun's despair radiating into the cave around them. Tim stood by Shaun's side, helpless, unable to help as she slipped in and out of consciousness. Rachel felt sorry for them both: Shaun having to witness her death, and Tim the reluctant spectator to Shaun's torment. Rachel opened her eyes and tried to speak. *Oh, God, that hurts.* "You have to ..." she said. Blood trickled from the side of her mouth and she tried to wipe it away. She drew two short quick breaths and had a fit of coughing, spraying blood. Her lungs were filling up.

"Oh, dear God, take me, not her," Shaun said, cradling her head. "Please not now, please, I just found her. Oh God, no, please."

Rachel's vision was fractured as she looked up, following Shaun's gaze, and saw the others passing through the flames and moving towards Thoth.

Shaun looked back at her. She stared into his beautiful eyes. His strong arms held her against his chest. To die in his arms is enough. It would be so easy to just close my eyes and let go. He had come back for me, he had found me.

"Casey ..." she said.

The horn above cried out again to the heavens, silencing her words. The beast had pierced her lung and abdomen, the pain not to be endured. She could feel the warmth of the pooling blood as she shivered with the cold, aware her life was slipping away. She was glad she had sacrificed her life to destroy the beast, having fulfilled her purpose. *No regrets,* she thought. She tilted her head back, reached for Shaun's face and he moved closer to her lips. She could smell his sweet breath. "Casey ..." she whispered again. "Tell Casey to flip it. Writing down, circles up, face to heaven." Her breathing labored; she waited, still couldn't catch a breath. She was drowning and couldn't stop it. "The Emerald Tablet ... once it is on the statue ... only you can activate it, Shaun, only you."

"Shh, quiet, save your strength," Shaun pleaded with her.

"You must ... before the final blowing, before the last sound of the horn ... lay the stones in first formation: mercy, strength, harmony and ..." Before Rachel could finish, she folded within herself and crossed the threshold of her inner door out into the vastness of the universe, free of her body, free of pain.

SHAUN FELT THE STONES digging into his thigh as he drew in a jagged emotional breath, then thought, *Could these be the stones?* Rachel filled his senses; she touched his soul and made him know what love was. Her eyes glazed over and closed. "Rachel, no, Rachel, no, you can't die. I won't let you die." He laid her flat on the ground and started compressions.

Shaun wiped the sweat and tears from his eyes on his shoulder. He stopped and quickly fished the leather pouch from his pocket and tossed the stones to Tim, and said, "I'm sorry. I'm so sorry for what I did to you. Give those to Casey and tell him what she said." He breathed for Rachel and pressed down on her chest again resuming the compressions.

"She said only you can," Tim said.

Shaun ignored him, focusing on counting, breathing for Rachel, trying to keep her heart alive. He felt a sudden emptiness and his soul screamed; he believed he would explode into a billion pieces. "Rachel, come back, please God, don't take her from me. I promise to love her for all eternity. Please God, not Rachel, please!"

Shaun was blinded to everything around him and he no longer cared for the world; everything he wanted was slipping through his fingers. He didn't want to live if Rachel died. Tired, he stopped, pulled her to him and cradled her body. He rocked back and forth, then laid her down, recommencing the compressions and yelled at Tim, "GO!"

Tim picked up the pouch and jumped over the crevasses, raced up the steps onto the platform and handed Casey the stones.

"You're going to need these."

Sophia took the stones and Jade crowed with excitement and said, "Oh my God, can this get any more complicated? Wow! They are Platonic solids. They have different elements. This one, for instance, represents fire, and has six edges and four faces so it's a tetrahedron. This one represents earth and is a hexahedron having twelve edges and six faces."

Tim took it out of her hand. "It's a cube!"

Jade dismissed him and continued twirling a twelve-edged

gemstone that looked like two pyramids joined together and said, "This one is an octahedron; its element is air." Her finger tingled as she touched the tip of the next one that was blue and its shape resembled a pointy transparent soccer ball. "This one is, I think, an icosahedron, element water, and it has thirty edges and twenty faces. It reminds me of what Rachel said about the one of the circles on the tablet. Chesed, mercy, which is blue and represents air, has the same properties as this solid. Maybe that's where this gem belongs, in that circle; maybe the stones are formed to connect all the elements. By laying each stone in the right circle, the energy will flow along the pathways."

"Slow down," Casey said, trying to secure the tablet. "That's a lot of maybes. I haven't even got the tablet in place yet and you want me to position the stones."

Sophia touched the emerald gemstone. "And what's this one?"

"The dodecahedron, the universe, and that one is a tetrahedron. This one is my favorite," she said. "It looks like two stars merged into one. It is named merkaba and this one is Metatron's cube, which has the element of earth."

Tim immediately picked up the transparent cubed stone and Jade could see inside it were thirteen suspended spheres. Twelve small crystallized rods came from the centers of the twelve spheres into the middle sphere, connecting them all. "Check this out. It's like the drawing on the Emerald Tablet and on Sophia's medallion," she said.

Tim, pointing at the dodecahedron, said, "It reminds me of a flower and — what do you call it? One of those superfood fruits ... a pomegranate. What about the three marbles, Jade?"

Jade dismissed Tim's reference to marbles. "This is what Shaun had in his pouch; they were so much more than gemstones." She examined the remaining gems. "All spheres. A sphere contains all forms and all measurement is equal." The sphere took her breath away. "This is beautiful." She felt connected to them and couldn't quite find the right words to express how they made her feel. She held it up to look into its content: she beheld a tiny universe floating inside it. Quickly she studied the other two and saw wisps of colored clouds, like gases, continuously moving, folding, fusing together; creating sparks of light. "Continual potential. It's like the birth of a star," Jade said. "This is incredible. This is absolutely mind-blowing. These are phenomenal and they are the key to the lock." She looked over at Shaun. He sat on his heels by Rachel. *We did have the keys all along*, she realized.

"What about this last one?" Kevin picked up the clear quartz sphere and stared into its depths. He dropped it back into Sophia's hands, as if it had given him a shock. "Wow!"

"What?" Jade picked it up and turned it around and around. "What did you see?"

"My ... me ... looking back at myself ... as if I was inside the crystal, looking out."

"What does it all mean?" Tim said.

Jade's eyes moved from right to left and up and down, thinking, constructing ideas and thoughts before she spoke. "$S = K \log W$. Entropy, a measure of disorder," she mumbled. "Life is filled with entropy. This whole situation reeks of disorder, it's totally dysfunctional." She held up the sphere with the spiraling gasses. "These gemstones will help us to close the gate to go back to the seed level perhaps. Back to the past maybe. I'm not sure, but certainly back to a state where we can create a new future within this reality, the element of earth. It's a paradox. Life is a paradox."

Tim took in a deep breath, loudly exhaled and said, "She's lost it."

CASEY BLOCKED OUT the chatter around him and the images of the ever-expanding silent vortex. The others seemed to be forgetting about their purpose. It was as if all the logical thinking was actually the darkness stalling for time. Casey focused on the Emerald Tablet and following Rachel's instructions. He jerked his head as if he was shaking the hair off his face and immediately the breastplate flipped over with the circles facing the dark roof of the cave. It floated down, feather-slow, as Casey placed it on the statue.

It locked into place.

"K, look at that," Tim said, hitting Kevin in the arm. Everyone's attention zapped to Casey. They held their breaths, expecting an explosion of light, something miraculous, anything to swallow the darkness and consume the power of the vortex. Nothing happened.

Nothing at all.

36

LIGHT OF THE ENDLESSNESS

He's doing it, Sophia thought. The stones vibrated and moved in their hands, lifting off from their palms.

"Now to lay the stones." Casey held them suspended with his mind. They spun in the air three feet above the statue. The markings on the Emerald Tablet cast a faint glow. Casey's intensity increased. Like an orchestra conductor his hands moved in all directions and the stones darted in the air under his command. Sophia felt the pulse of the repelling force around the statue. It was unyielding. The black hole expanded, stretching the force field. The amulet was shaking violently, losing control. She had to do something, but what?

"There must be a way," Casey said. "Which circle and which stone. It was created by the light of God. How are we going to come up with the correct formation? We need more time."

"We have to go back to the seed level, return to the beginning," Jade said.

"Back to where? Where's the starting point? Where do we start, Jade?" he said anxiously.

"Earth, we have to start with the Platonic solid that represents earth, the hexahedron, the cube, and ascend to ..."

There is only one seed level I know and that's the oneness of the universe. Sophia sat down and closed her eyes, ignoring Jade, and opened up her mind to the heavens: she stepped through her internal door into the endlessness of the universe, no limitations, all desires waiting to be realized. She could have floated forever; it was like soaking in a lukewarm bath. She wanted to stay. *I must find the solution of the stones.* She accelerated along her timeline, searching for the telling moment in the future, forgetting to anchor herself to the present.

Sophia levitated off the ground and the gems gravitated towards her, gliding through the air away from the statue and tablet to hover around her.

"Sophia, what are doing? Sophia," Casey yelled as he lost control of the stones.

Sophia felt her aura swelling — the essence of each color changing from warm reds and oranges to cool blues and violets as it continued unfolding — and she recognized her soul expanding, ready to receive the abundant wisdom of the universe. Her aura turned to a shimmering magenta light, a beacon to the darkness. She felt her sense of self melting away; her connection with physical reality was disappearing as she searched along her timeline. Like an untethered cosmonaut, she floated in space, waiting in the silence of the universe. She was in love and wished to stay.

Cloaked by inner peace, her sense of self drifted away.

CASEY HEADED FOR Sophia's floating body, she was almost transparent, like a ghost. "Sophia!"

Father McDonald's body contorted in pain, fighting against the demons inside him for control. He yelled, "Don't touch her!"

Kevin could do nothing to stop Casey. He reached out and touched Sophia's dangling foot and was thrown into the air like he had touched an electric fence. Casey sailed backwards, passing Shaun, Rachel and Tim as he tumbled down the set of stairs and over the edge into the second-tier crevasse. Kevin sprinted after him, and could see Father McDonald crawling on all fours, bent out of shape like a dog. *He's going to maul him*, Kevin thought, and that's when Father McDonald stretched his arm out to Casey.

"Ahhhhhhh," Father McDonald screamed as Casey let go of the edge and latched onto his arm pulling it out of its socket.

Kevin didn't want to begin to imagine the pain Father McDonald was in. He could have sworn he heard tendons and bones snapping. Casey was frozen, glaring into Father McDonald's black eyes.

"Climb," Kevin yelled, looking down at them from the top of the stairs.

Casey used Father McDonald's arm like a rope and quickly climbed up and over his body. "Thank you," Casey said and ran to Sophia. She had floated higher and soon she would be out of his reach.

Casey ran faster than Kevin had seen anyone run before — up the stairs two, three steps at a time, to the third tier and hurdled over the crevasse. *He looks like he's flying*, Kevin thought. He glimpsed Father McDonald on all fours tip over the edge, as if in slow motion, and without a sound, disappear into the crevasse.

"Sophia," Casey yelled. "Sophia. Come back, Sophia."

Sophia was flickering.

She reminded Kevin of a light bulb about to explode. Casey reached for her foot again. Kevin knew Casey would be electrified and maybe even injure Sophia. He fixed his eyes at the ground, imagining millions of tiny particles of golden light weaving a rubber mat under Casey's feet before he touched Sophia. *The mat will ground Casey's energy*, he thought, *soaking it up like a sponge and sending it into the belly of the Earth.* Casey touched Sophia's foot and, as he did, her amulet, on the edge of the vortex, lost its hold. It was flung into the air and skipped like a pebble, hitting Casey on the side of the face, slicing open an old scar. Suddenly it was like being in the middle of a storm.

The magenta force field disappeared. The repelling magnetic energy of the statue receded. Sophia's aura started to turn inward, creating an up-draught, repelling against the darkness. She was imploding.

The sound of the two forces is like being caught between two massive jet turbine blades, Kevin thought.

Sophia looked out at the expansion of the universe, and watched a dot on the horizon moving closer and closer, growing into myriad shapes and colors. Something was forming: a blur, an image, a memory. It's Shaun. This wasn't the future, this was the past: he was a child playing on his bedroom floor with the gemstones, making different patterns. Then it changed, and Shaun was no longer a child but a troubled young man who was out of control, devastated by the loss of his mother and Rachel. Then the images changed again to the present day. His shoulders were slumped, tears rolled down his face, his grief splashing over Rachel's lifeless body as he willed her to live.

Shaun knows the combination! she yelled inside her head. She turned and looked right, then turned again and looked left. Her excitement vanished. The endlessness of the universe was magnified and that's when she noticed she had forgotten her lifeline — she was a lonely astronaut floating in the silence of space. She squashed the panic, allowing the peace to spread within. Free of chaos, her surroundings took over. Her aura continued to expand, brighter and more colorful than any nebula in the galaxy. Sophia was merging back into the endlessness from which she came when from a far, far away corner of the universe Sophia thought she heard a whisper. There it was. She started to feel again, to remember her physical being, the sensation of being inside her body. She listened, moving her thoughts towards the sound. She searched her mind and again heard a whisper. She knew this sound and saw a flash of an image, then suddenly she felt heaviness, as if rising from an ocean pool.

"Come back, Sophia, come back." Casey held fast to Sophia's foot, screaming over the noise of the two repelling forces. "Sophia, come back, we need you, come back."

A flash burst into her solace as her consciousness fully awoke. She screamed inside her head, *Casey, I hear you. I'm lost. Is Kevin still with you? Kevin, are you there? Can you hear me?*

~

Yes, I hear you. How are you doing that? Sweat dripped from Kevin's temples. It had taken intense concentration to manifest something as simple as an industrial rubber mat, and it barely held together, the atoms jumping as if they would pull apart at any moment. Casey and Sophia had an enormous amount of energy pulsing between them.

"Show me the way back."

Casey held onto her ankle determined not to let her disappear. Kevin could see his fingers through her leg.

"Let go, Casey, you need to move back," Kevin said.

"No, I'm not moving. I'm not leaving her like this, she needs to be grounded."

"We don't have time! You have to let go or we will all die. Trust me, I've got her," he said, tapping himself on the temple.

Casey looked up at Sophia. Then he let go.

Kevin concentrated on creating a pathway to Sophia and the image of the mat evaporated. He sat on the ground, his pulse racing. He was so nervous he wanted to scream, or run. He clenched and unclenched his jaw, breathing in through his nostrils and out of his mouth. He shook out his arms and rubbed his hands on his knees, and tried to relax. Involuntarily, he inched across the cave floor, pulled by the expanding swirling black hole. He ignored the external mayhem as Sophia had and went inside himself. He stood before the old door he kept locked. The feeling of the ground beneath him disappeared as he too began to rise. Kevin could only imagine the look on Casey's face.

All his life he had avoided the door, but now he touched the tough hardwood. It was inviting, warm. He reached up and felt the cold metal of the first bolt and slid it back. He imagined he wiped his sweaty palms on his pants, and reached out for the second latch and pulled it back quickly. He lingered, braced himself and took hold of the third bolt and pulled it all the way back. The door unlocked, opened, and he was looking out into the expansion of the universe. Kevin stepped over his sacred threshold into nothing and everything, imagining a carpet of glittering golden light unrolling towards the essence of what he thought was Sophia. He stepped upon the carpet and ran towards her.

A REMOTE MEMORY OF lemon soda came into her mind. Sophia felt something. Searching her expanded mind she knew someone was coming. Her nose was tingling, as if she had one, and it smelt a sweet smell: *a memory of soda pop*. No, it was sweet-smelling and it tingled in her nose like effervescent bubbles. *Nose — I have a nose again*, she thought, and then she tasted the essences of life popping on her tongue like pop rocks. The connection grew stronger. Ahead, a conveyor belt of sparking golden light appeared. She moved her mind towards it, finding Kevin. An awareness of someone else was also behind her, and she felt goosebumps along her arms and wanted to shiver. Kevin was nearly in sight. The sensation behind her grew. She turned, dreading what was there. Sophia decided to move to Kevin.

"Sophia, wait!" It was Rachel. "I have seen the concealed light. It is greater than any light you have ever seen or felt. It will be as bright as the birth of the universe, and you will all be incinerated. Only the purest of souls, the greatest of sages, can merit this sight. You are all key to the survival of the world, and Kevin is the final key."

"Yes, he's coming. That's him, Rachel, come with us."

"No, you don't understand."

"Yes, I do. Come with me. Please."

"My fate is in Tim's hands. Tell Shaun he must do it. Go now. Seal the gate, Sophia. There are only two more sets of blowing. Can you still hear them?"

Sophia listened. "No." She looked again, back at Kevin. He wasn't getting any closer, he seemed to be running on the spot.

Rachel said, "He can't come any closer. If he does, he won't be able to return to his body. He will die, and you will die, everyone will die. You have to meet him halfway."

"Go! Go now, Sophia!" Rachel screamed.

The urgency became overwhelmingly real and Sophia felt like she was in a nightmare, climbing stairs that turned to quicksand. She willed herself to run, imagining one complete step after another. She visualized her legs moving, seeing her knees lifting up, higher and higher as she ran. She saw the image in her mind of running in shallow water, until she was flying towards Kevin as if zooming above the water. Then suddenly she found herself skimming the surface of the golden pathway Kevin had created.

Sophia began to feel the millions of atoms that formed her body being drawn from across the universe, aiming for the spiritual essence of Kevin. Sophia yelled out to him, "It's Shaun! He knows the combination of the stones." She flew above the golden carpet Kevin had unfolded in the astral plane for her.

"Hurry, Sophia, we have to get back. My body is going to combust," Kevin said, just as the impact of Sophia's spiritual essences sent his physical body into convulsions. He could feel his nose dripping with blood.

Shaun and Tim took turns and did what they could to keep the blood circulating through Rachel's body. It was Shaun's turn. He knew they all thought it was pointless, but he didn't care. *I won't stop.* Tim was a big help and didn't ask questions.

He could see the others on the altar. Casey was transfixed, watching Sophia's body flare. It sparkled and flickered, infused with light, and solidified. Her energy was drawing into herself, causing the gemstones orbiting in her aura to start falling away. Kevin's body trembled. Casey tried to reach out for him when simultaneously everything was tumbling down: Sophia, Kevin and the stones. Jade scrambled to catch the gems, throwing herself towards the swirling dark matter with her arms outstretched as if she was an outfielder catching a fly ball. She missed one and it rushed towards the vortex. Kevin's limp body hit the ground hard on top of the stone. Casey, the true knight in shining armor, was there to break Sophia's fall. Dazed, Sophia and Casey clumsily got to their feet and pulled away from the vortex.

"Shaun!" *Is she calling me? Why would she be calling out to me?* He had been doing compressions for so long his body was acting purely on muscle memory now. Sophia, as if she carried a heavy burden, tucked her head down and quickly descended the flights of stairs, yelling his name. "Shaun! It's you. Only you know the sequence."

What now? he thought, seeing them all coming his way, except for Kevin, who stood by the altar watching, holding his head. Sophia's silky hair was flying everywhere as she jumped down the last few steps and rushed to his side. Out of breath, she said, "I saw Rachel. Shaun, she said you are the only one who knows the sequence of the Platonic stones."

He looked down at his bloody hands. "I don't know any combination," he yelled, resuming the compressions.

Sophia put her hand on his shoulder. It was soft and delicate, cool on his hot, bare skin.

"She's gone, Shaun."

He shook off her hand. "No, I won't give up. In the past ten years she never gave up on me." Tears dripped off his chin.

"It's okay," Tim said. "I'll do it. I promise I won't stop till you say. It was my turn anyway. Do it, Shaun." Tim knelt on the opposite side and slowly, as if unrolling dough, slid his hands onto Rachel's chest. The tips of his fingers gently nudged Shaun's away.

Jade's face was flushed. She was more than a little freaked out. "Shaun, move, damn it!"

Shaun couldn't move. A soft blanket was draped around him. He had an image of Rachel as he remembered her, but she had turned into the woman who lay beside him now. He saw, as if looking through a keyhole, everything moving away from him. Jade pulled back her hand and slapped him in the face. *Whack!* Rachel's image was gone, replaced with a burning sensation on his cheek.

"You fake," Jade screamed. "You don't care about her. If you cared, you would fight her fight. She guided you here for a reason, she needed your help. So what the fuck are you waiting for? Get up and put those stones in order and finish this."

Something snapped and Shaun's face burned, his fists clenched. He wanted to punch her. "You bitch." He stood as Tim kept up the compressions. "A swift kick in the face would shut you up and send you back to wherever you came from. How dare you, who the fuck do you think you are?" The desire to hit her was compelling, growing, boiling up inside him. He should beat her like he had wanted to beat his drunken father for letting his mother die and killing Rachel. *Rachel, he didn't kill Rachel. She was here. I killed her. I couldn't keep her safe.* The shadows of doubt were prowling around Shaun's head. *I'm just like my father. He couldn't keep the one he loved from dying and I couldn't keep Rachel from dying.* For the first time in Shaun's life he felt sorrow for his dad. He now understood. It must have been hell for him to live without her. The guilt his father must have felt. Shaun looked at Tim. He looked exhausted, pumping away on Rachel's lifeless body. "Let her go," Shaun said. His voice was shaky and barely audible. He cleared his throat and said a little louder, "Let her go, she's not there. You can stop." He got down on his knees and kissed her cheek and whispered in her ear. "I love you. I'll finish this. I will see you in my dreams."

Tim looked up and said, "Not yet. You go. I know what I'm doing."

Jade flung her arms across her face, ready to block his blows as he reached out for her. He pulled her arms down and pulled her close to him. Her nostrils flared, he could feel her breath; his own tasted sour. His cheeks were salty, sticky with sweat and tears as he hugged Jade and said into her ear, "Thank you."

Shaun hadn't even noticed Kevin until his friend vomited. It splashed on his runners and was sucked weirdly backwards by the growing vortex. Soon they weren't going to be able to resist its pull. The guy looked like he was going to drop.

Jade helped Kevin down and propped him up against the step. She grabbed his face and stared into his eyes, checked his ears and head. "You look concussed."

The vortex had stretched above the statue and was building momentum. It was the biggest, darkest cloud Shaun had ever seen. This was going to be the mother of all storms.

"Shaun, let's do it," Sophia said, climbing the steps, and she jumped. No — she flew from the pull of the vortex up onto the third tier and tumbled and somersaulted to a stop at the base of the golden statue.

At the top of the last tier he could see the devastation. The second half of the cave was disappearing into nothingness. He concentrated on the stones, not knowing what to do with them. Sophia was in his peripheral vision. "Please, hurry," she said. Her hair and clothes were flapping all over the place. It was incredible that her small frame hadn't been sucked into the darkness like everything else. Sophia urged him on gently. She was always gentle. *Rachel was fiery and forceful, absolutely amazing, fun, beautiful, full of life.* He wished he had jumped from the Jeep that night and stayed with her. He hadn't known she survived. He had been nothing but a little kid. Shaun glanced into Sophia's soulful eyes and her eyes very slightly squinted, and at that moment they both knew, as if cymbals had clashed, that things were about to change forever.

Sophia called, "Jade! Jade! Jade, tell Kevin. Tell Kevin to get ready, we need a way out."

"What?" Jade yelled back, running halfway up the stairs.

Shaun, seeking protection, sat with his back against the dazzling statue, thinking that it was really just a coffin. All its magnetic propulsion had changed into a tiny hum. Casey and Sophia gathered around him as if Shaun was the last burning flame. They huddled over him, guarding the stones and him from the vortex. Shaun tossed the stones on the ground between his legs. He didn't know what to do. He had never given any thought to patterns and formations. He picked them up again, closed his hands around them, and tossed the gems, watching them tumble and roll on the dirt like he was some high roller in a casino. But he wasn't, he was just some punk kid with a shitty life. The image of playing a game with Alex came into his mind.

Shaun scooped up the gems and got to his feet, stretching to his full height, completely exposed to the vortex, allowing the energy to drag him across the floor. *What is the world going to be like without Rachel, anyway? Maybe this is humanity's destiny and who am I to get in the way?* He felt light as a feather as he glided across, to the edge, closer to the point of no return. The sound was deafening, his mind went silent, and that's when he saw Jade leaning over the statue, touching the tablet now set in its chest, and saw her bracelet and the Emerald Tablet come to life. A radiance of white-blue light came from the bracelet, the markings lifting from it, spiraling into a 3D hologram, entwining together as the hologram traveled around the tablet. Alex appeared in Shaun's silent mind. He watched as Alex showed him the last game he had taught him at Casey's house in England and Shaun saw the order in which he had laid them before he began. *That must be the pattern ... well, it's a pattern,* he thought. All of a sudden, a wave of clarity rushed over him and he felt hope. Rachel lived to correct the mistake his father had made. She wanted to heal the world. He had to destroy the vile creatures that escaped that day; he had to eliminate the dark angels and close the doorway.

Shaun realized he had foolishly allowed himself to be dragged nearly to the edge of the swirling black hole. Spellbound, he saw Rachel's dark, long curls in the outer rim of the whirlpool, like leaves down a drain, swirling and swirling. Shaun was sinking.

Maybe none of this is real; maybe I have a brain tumor, just like Mom, and I'm delusional. For a second, he nearly believed it was Rachel. He felt like he was in a rip. His mom had suffered. She had taught him to swim before he could walk, and surf as soon as he could stand. Always warning him about the undertow and rips. Your board goes where your eyes go, she had said. He started to panic, his eyes glued to the slipstream of evil. He pulled back, away from the darkness. *Not now, oh, please God, not now. I know what to do. I can do this, I know my purpose.* He fought to gain control of his mind and body: he pulled and inched away, shuffling like a crab back towards Sophia and Casey. His chest, back and arms felt like his skin was being ripped off as if it were a shirt and his jeans were giving him the biggest wedgie ever.

Casey held onto the statue, while Sophia, Jade and Kevin made a human chain. Kevin held out his hand. Shaun took hold. They made a human shield around him, protecting him. Quickly, he ran his hand over the cold breastplate of Thoth and began laying the stones. There was no force field now. The 3D hologram of glittering letters swirled and danced and twisted above the statue, blocking the negative vacuum.

I hear you little buddy. One more game, Alex. Shaun got to work on placing the stones. Starting in the bottom circle of the middle column — the suspended thirteen circles that looked like a reflection of all that was below it — he placed the first stone, Metatron's cube. Moving up to the next circle, he placed the octahedron and he kept moving up, placing the merkaba in the circle Rachel had called harmony. Swiftly, he positioned the remaining stones on the outer columns, leaving the top three in the shape of a triangle till last. He was moving back and forth, right to left, up and down, checking the order. Shaun stopped as if he had all the time in the world, reviewing his handiwork. He focused intently on the last three spheres, not quite sure which one went where. The noise around him intensified. *Think, damn it.* The sphere that Jade said reminded her of swirling gases — the formation of stars —definitely belonged at the top right, he decided, and the other at top left. He held it tight, rubbing it like an Aladdin's lamp between his hands. He held it up to his mouth and kissed it like he had done as a kid and placed it at the pinnacle of the Emerald Tablet's design. Shaun looked over his shoulder to where Rachel lay. Tim had kept his word. They weren't the only souls he could see. An angel, twelve feet high, stood over Casey, Sophia, Kevin and Jade.

The walls of the cave disappeared and were replaced with the blackness that was moving in on them. The noise was so great his own thoughts sounded like they were a long way away. Shaun looked at the Emerald Tablet; still it had not come to life. Kevin, Casey, Sophia and Jade stared at him with anticipation as the stones locked into place, but again nothing happened. Shaun reached down into his pocket and pulled out the last of his memories of the first day he met Rachel: a black onyx stone, and placed it face down between the top three spheres. The Emerald Tablet of Thoth radiated blinding light, while, above, the last bellowing horn cut unnervingly through the dense energy. A brilliant shaft of light was cast down from the sky, towards the Emerald Tablet.

The circles and gemstones turned to liquid light that flowed along each pathway, crisscrossing between the circles in a predetermined formation. Sophia pulled the group back as the light joined forces with the Earth circle and Metatron's cube, the hexahedron. All the gemstones were oscillating, and the light was returning, rising up the pathways to the pinnacle.

"We have to go!" Sophia screamed. No one moved. They stood united, rooted to the spot. She yanked on Casey's and Jade's hands and leant towards Kevin, shouting, "You're up, Kevin!"

"What!"

"She said you're on, K."

"You have to get us out of here." Sophia glanced in the direction she last saw Father McDonald and began to cry. His life was her life, she couldn't remember being without him. She closed her eyes and felt his spirit all around her, and she turned. He was with her. He would always be with her. The lock and key, the emerald-green tablet, had been returned to Thoth. *Go, Sophia,* she heard him say in her mind. *Go now!*

HIS FIVE FRIENDS looked like warriors. He imagined Kevin couldn't concentrate with the high piercing scream. The light and the darkness was clashing, making it impossible to focus. Tim smiled, Jade reached out and took Kevin's hand and yelled something, and that's when Tim saw the vibrant colors, the rippling wall that had come to life under Kevin's persuasion. There wasn't too much of a harmonious hum, or the sound of the tear in the universe as the doorway opened. There was only the battle, the vortex losing control.

Jade and Sophia stepped forward into Kevin's gleaming curtain of light and were absorbed into the gentle flowing wall, free from the darkness.

Casey corralled Shaun. He must have been afraid he might run back to die with Rachel. But before they entered, Shaun turned back to Tim. It was too late to say or do anything as Casey pushed him into the soothing wall. Tim remembered how it had cooled his sunburn and healed his broken leg.

"Come on," Kevin yelled.

Reluctantly, he stopped the compressions. "I'm right behind you." He jumped up, ran. The black hole was imploding and the ceiling vanished. The column of light passed through the third center circle and grew so bright it was becoming hard to keep his eyes open.

"It's just us," Kevin yelled to Tim. "You go and I will close it behind us."

They both went to jump, but Tim stopped. He could see Shaun on his knees behind the sea of animated color. Sophia put her hand on Shaun's shoulder as if to console him. Tim turned back for Rachel; he wasn't going to leave her. He hadn't performed CPR for the last twenty minutes for nothing. *Focus, Tim, it could still work. His original idea could still work. There is no reason why not.*

Tim sprinted to where Rachel lay. He quickly dragged her into a sitting position, put his head under her arm, and lifted her over his shoulder. He had underestimated her weight and staggered slightly. He was close to the wall and could see Kevin about to step back through. The light ascended to the Emerald Tablet's second last circle. Tim no longer felt Rachel's weight, or felt his own limbs for that matter. The light penetrated and vaporized every dark corner of the chamber, pushing him into the air as flashes of brilliant light exploded in a fireworks display that moved across his eyelids. But just before he closed his eyes, he had seen the horrors of the underworld trying to escape from the vortex, screeching and howling in pain in the all-consuming light.

Tim closed his eyes tight, imagined his legs were still there, and walked blindly with Rachel over his shoulder, in what he hoped was the direction of the world Jade called Athanasia, the parallel world.

A SONIC BOOM PULSATED through the membrane as the cave exploded. Sophia, sheltered from the blast, couldn't help reacting and covered her eyes. The wall sparkled and bowed, arching under the force, creating a cocoon protecting them. Light, color and sound rippled and flashed like a cosmic storm. The cave disappeared. Tim and Rachel were propelled by the blast through the closing doorway. The darkness consumed everything, the evil falling into oblivion as the vortex of dark matter collapsed in on itself and a final atomic explosion erupted: the birth of a star.

Sophia sent a thought message to everyone to turn away from the wall, to walk into the luscious forest before them, and not to look back. Above them, outside the membrane, a darkened sky filled with streaks of silver and golden sparks of light like a magnificent meteor shower. The dark angels fell from the sky consumed by the light. They watched in awe.

Sophia sent out another guiding message, gently urging them on. We need to move forward into the future. Don't look back. There is no existence beyond this moment. We have to step into the future.

They all knew what each other was thinking. There wasn't a thought amongst them that was hidden; there was no space between them. Kevin wanted to turn back for Tim. Shaun wanted to run back for Rachel, but he believed this time she was truly gone and he was glad that she wasn't alone. Tim had been with her to the end. Sophia longed for Father McDonald's comforting prayer. There were other thoughts, some of which Kevin had imagined sounded like Tim and Rachel. Shaun heard them, too, and he couldn't contain himself any longer. He started to cry, wanting so very badly to turn around.

Don't turn, he heard Sophia think.

Had they made it through? Shaun wondered. How could they have survived the blast?

Tim was mesmerized by Rachel's fluttering eyelids. Her beautiful, emerald- green eyes were opening and looking up at him. She was confused and dazed.

Tim helped her to her feet. Kevin had so much belief that he heard Tim's thoughts, he wanted to turn back and see if what he was hearing was real. Rachel went to look over his shoulder. Tim grabbed her face to stop her. He had heard Sophia tell them not to look back and quickly covered Rachel's eyes. Her lashes tickled his palm. He remembered how he felt after seeing his leg broken one minute and healed the next. He wondered what Rachel might be feeling. He walked on.

Kevin could hear them both inside his mind. Rachel felt very strange and confused as she too had heard Sophia's words inside her head. Facing into the forest she opened her eyes and saw Sophia, Casey, Kevin and Jade, plus her handsome knight in shining armor, Shaun. Rachel hugged Tim and the sides of their faces were lit by the exploding light as she whispered in his ear, "I never doubted you for a minute." She let go of his hand and drew the air into her lungs. She felt so fresh and alive and started walking towards Shaun.

Shaun had stepped forward with a heavy heart into the future. He could feel Rachel was still with him, her spirit strong, when suddenly he thought he felt her touch, a soft hand interlocking with his. He knew it was Rachel, but how could it be? He didn't want to look to his side in case it wasn't her. He rubbed where the bullet in his back had been. Tim had continued CPR right up till the last minute, but how — ? Then he heard Tim's thought: *I don't remember you telling me to stop, so I brought her with me.*

This must be what a mental breakdown is like, Shaun thought. It was all too much. The hand squeezing his was soft. He had to look, he had to. It was Rachel.

"You and Tim kept my heart pumping," she said, not realizing all she needed to do was think it and they all would know what she wanted to say. "You kept my body alive and my soul reclaimed it. Shaun, you told me the first day we met, you would come back for me. Not once did I doubt you."

37

BECOME THE CREATOR

The seven friends walked through the majestic rainforest. Kevin had tried to open a doorway home, again and again, but it just wasn't happening.

"Let's just sit for a while," Sophia said.

Kevin sat amongst the fluorescent green leaves watching the tiny blue insects.

Each time they stopped, he would look beyond the surrounding membrane, and his eyes would feast upon the universe as if they were a part of it, as if they were floating amongst the Milky Way.

"What do you think is happening out there?" Jade asked.

They all sat around and seriously gave it thought. It was like listening to multiple radio frequencies and Kevin was learning to dull out the others' voices in order to hear his own thoughts. "Maybe there are still some rescue teams helping people somewhere. People have to pick themselves up. They have to pull themselves together and get through this."

"Come on," Sophia said. "Let's keep moving."

Jade quickened her pace to catch up with Kevin and Sophia. "You know, when everything gets back to normal, or close to it, you can travel anywhere in the world, K. Can you imagine the enormity of your skill in the world? I wouldn't mind paying a visit to the Big Apple."

"I don't think we should tell anyone about Athanasia. We need to protect it." Kevin saw images from Jade's mind of New York and she was biting into a big slice of pizza. Kevin imagined what New York might be like now. Jade's colorful image dissolved. Kevin remembered that awful day, so long ago. So much sadness, fear and anger and he had been unable to understand or process the emotions he felt from the adults and the world around him. It made his heart ache even now, thinking about the pain and suffering. Suddenly, before he finished the thought, they came upon an outer wall and beyond the membrane was a dusty grey New York street, as he had just imagined. The sky above the street curved like the dome of a snow globe and sparkles of light danced upon a long velvet sash of time unrolling from the heavens. The street was the center of Kevin's giant snow dome. Energy was falling from the heavens to the street, scintillating, coming together as one compound; a building formed, glowing with color. It was Jade's pizza restaurant. The rest of the street remained grey and congested with fallen bricks and mortar, nothing but rubble. There wasn't a bird in sight. There were lifeless bodies; so many, the debris beneath them could barely be seen. Kevin started moving away from the horrific scene. How long had it been? Time had little meaning for them in Athanasia and this was the first time they had seen the outer world. Glittering light floated down from the heavens settling as gently as snowflakes upon the bodies. "If only one person would move, just one." Kevin said. "We have to go help them."

"Wait," Casey said reaching out for Kevin holding him back. "Something is about to happen."

They all stopped, waiting, watching as time continued to unfold in front of them and beyond. Holding his breath, Kevin paused. *Just one person. Come on, one person.* They shared the thought, willing it to happen. A brick moved, an arm moved amongst the rubble. An ashen face lifted and looked out at the vastness of destruction around them. The seven ran forward to the wall to cross over and help, but for the first time the wall was impenetrable. They looked on. It was a woman. She stood and looked into the sky before she reached down to the person next to her, pulling them up. Then another person stood and helped the person next to them. A chain reaction was occurring among the people the sparks of golden light had touched. They were rising; color was returning to the world one hue at a time. Not everyone rose. Only a third of the fallen had stirred; the others remained lifeless, lost to the darkness forever. The people who had risen tried selflessly to help those unmoving. They dropped back to their knees and cried for the strangers who were gone.

Tim put his arm around Kevin. "Let's go home, K."

KEVIN EFFORTLESSLY OPENED a doorway back to his family, back to Casey's bedroom where he had sent his dad and Ellen only hours ago. It seemed like forever.

It was morbidly quiet back in Casey's room. No one spoke. The sunshine was streaming through a hole in the roof, highlighting the broken wooden beams littering the polished floor. Worried that Daniel and Ellen lay pinned beneath, Jade and Kevin quickly leapt into action, climbing over the beams like it was some wacky obstacle course searching for them. Without asking, the others helped lift the planks of wood when, abruptly, everything floated up to the ceiling. Casey smiled with his arms raised in the air like the conductor of an orchestra.

Casey saw Daniel's ashen face, his lips dry and cracked like a riverbed in the outback. Ellen started to stir.

"Mom!" Jade said, and slowly helped her to a sitting position.

"Dad," Kevin said.

He looked afraid to touch his dad. *Maybe he wasn't breathing,* Casey thought. Then dirt puffed around his nostrils slightly.

"Dad," Kevin said again. Daniel's eyes moved behind the lids and his eyebrows rose as if trying to pull the eyelids open.

Tim spat on the edge of his shirt and wiped Daniel's lashes clean before Daniel tried opening his eyes again.

Casey was standing next to them with his arms raised to the ceiling. "Guys, my arms are getting a little tired," Casey said, slowly backing out of the room.

"Dad, can you stand?"

His dad's voice was harsh and raspy, nearly unrecognizable. "Kevin. Ellen?"

"I think she's okay. Can you stand?" Kevin asked again.

"Water."

Tim ducked into the bathroom and came back with two soaking wet face cloths. He gave one to Ellen and one to Daniel. "Suck the water out of the cloth and let's get you out of here."

Ellen was grateful and sucked deeply.

Daniel did the same, then wiped his face and put the cloth around his neck. He held onto his left leg and lifted it out straight and cringed. "It's okay. Oh, my throat. Everything is stiff," his dad said, massaging his calf muscles. "It's been at least a few days. As soon as we came through the ... the ... portal, the ceiling collapsed. We yelled and yelled but no one came. I'm worried about the rest of them. I haven't heard any sounds, K. Where's Father McDonald?"

"He didn't make it."

His dad searched his eyes for answers.

Kevin and Tim each put their shoulders under Daniel's armpits and helped him to his feet.

The wood hovered in the air. Daniel ogled it. "Marvelous, absolutely marvelous," he said to Casey.

Jade and Shaun aided Ellen into the hallway. "How long has it been?" Ellen asked.

Jade answered for Kevin. "Actually, it probably hasn't even been twenty-four hours for us. Let's get you out of here before Casey's arms drop."

"What?" Ellen said. "It's been at least two days, maybe three."

"Casey?" Sophia said. "You don't have to raise your arms. You know that, don't you? It's your mind that controls the wood."

They went from room to room and still hadn't found anyone in the house. In the kitchen, Casey said, "This whole place has been cleaned."

"It looks pretty messed up to me," Kevin said, looking around.

"No, I mean there are no lost souls. Not a flicker of residual energy. Everything feels new somehow." Outside, a dog barked. Casey opened the back door and Lucy jumped all over him.

"Hey girl." The dog pulled away and ran down the basement stairs.

The basement door was missing from its frame. "Wait," Daniel said, but it was too late. Casey was on the dog's tail.

One by one they stepped over the door that was lying in a wonky position at the bottom of the stairs. Lucy had stopped at the entrance of the tunnel and looked back and waited. Casey took the lead. He cautiously made his way to the place they had stashed their supplies, passing where he had found the young girl's bone. *Come on, Amy, make a noise, anything.* He stopped and touched the limestone walls searching for Amy and Terry.

"This way," Casey said, rushing down the next tunnel. "I can feel them, down this way."

He raced through the tunnel afraid of what he might find. Scared, Casey moved carefully, as if not to disturb the dead. He stepped into the opening. The air felt fresh. It should have been musty; it puzzled him, because it actually smelt fresh and vibrant. The tunnel opened up ahead and in his mind he saw the red-bearded man, Amy's great-great-something-grandfather, was looking over his shoulder at them before he disappeared leaving them with the silence.

Shortly, they found the group huddled together lying on the ground as if asleep: Amy, Terry, Callie, Kath and Sally. Somewhere amongst them were Joe and Molly, and the Book of Splendor, which was twinkling.

Daniel rushed past him and felt the nearest body for a pulse.

Casey felt the presence of life and expelled a breath when he realized he had been holding it. *But are they all alive?* They lay as lifeless as rag dolls.

Shaun and Kevin moved to Callie, stepping into the radiance of the fluttering lights from the book. Casey knelt by Amy, scared to touch her. Ellen came and knelt beside him and checked her pulse and pupils and smiled.

"She's alive, Casey. She's alive."

Sophia found Joe, the red string still tied to his wrist, his arms outstretched around Sally and Kath, protecting them. "Joe is alive too," she said excitedly.

Casey held onto Terry and Amy's hands, watching Rachel reach for the edge of a pink blanket sticking out from under Callie's arm. It was Molly. Rachel tightened the tiny blanket around Molly and picked her up, holding her close. Rachel softly spoke and rocked Molly in her arms and kissed the crown of her head. Molly's sudden scream shattered their fears. There was no room for silence as she continued to cry. Callie stirred, searching for her crying baby. Amy and Terry began coughing, and reached for each other. The dog licked Kath on the face, until she pushed it away. Sophia wedged herself behind Kath to reach Joe.

"Sophia," Casey said. "Is he okay?" He knew Sophia had only known Joe for a short time, but had grown very fond of him, and having lost Father McDonald, Casey was afraid she had lost Joe too.

Lovingly, Sophia put her hands on Joe's big face. "Hey you," she said as Joe blinked and smiled at her. She hugged him tight and cried.

"Whoa, hen, why the tears? I knew you'd be back. Where's the Father?" He looked around and painfully pushed himself into a sitting position. Sophia sat down and lifted his arm up over her head and nestled into him. Joe squeezed her shoulder. "When was the last time you ate? You're wafer thin."

"He sacrificed himself for us." Tears filled her eyes. "Are you hurt?"

"Not hurt, just very stiff, lass. We've been here perhaps a few weeks. There was an awful crash and that's the last I remember."

Casey closed the book of light and smiled. Terry and Amy were locked in a hug. They opened up their embrace for him to join them.

"This is incredible," Ellen said. A smile burst through her tears of joy and she tasted the salt that lingered on the edge of her lips. "Callie, my dear friend Callie."

Callie looked towards the voice, perhaps waiting for her eyes to adjust, not believing her ears. She leant heavily against Daniel and gradually stood. She didn't bother brushing the dirt off her face or reining in her joy and relief. "Ellen, is that really you?"

Ellen held her arms out and walked forward. They stood in a tearful embrace. Jade twirled her bracelet on her wrist. *It now looks like any other bracelet,* Casey thought, watching Kevin move closer to Jade, smiling. Casey looked from one person to another; everyone was shaken, but would be okay. Rachel handed Molly to Daniel and without hesitation, kissed Shaun, before tightly embracing him.

Callie had pulled back and wiped her tears. "I have your specimens." And nodded her head to the little blue esky half buried in the dirt.

"What's in the esky?" Casey asked.

"My life's work," Ellen said. "The reason I was kidnapped. The cure for cancer, the vaccine. You name it, I think I can cure it," Ellen said.

*** The End ***

GLOSSARY

Al-mawet – Mawet means death, al-mawet is no death. The spelling varies within different religious text, but they all have the same meaning.

Arrow of time – the direction of events; movement in time is generally forward.

Athanasia – means timelessness, everlasting life. Athanasia is referred to as the parallel world/dimension.

Dark matter – a negative energy force. In this story the dark matter also contains micro shapeshifting demons.

Dovesti zhenshchinu – pronunciation for Russian довести женщину. English translation: bring the woman.

Dunny – toilet.

Fair dinkum – an expression in Australian slang proclaiming a truth about a statement.

Intel – slang for intelligent person. As in geek. (Created by the author)

Merkaba – two tetrahedrons combined. Mystically it is a channel for the descending energy of the universe and the ascending energy of Earth. Spiritual tool of transformation.

Metatron's Cube – a geometric shape/solid. It has thirteen equal circles. Lines from the center of each circle extend out to the centers of the other 12 circles.

Outback – A remote area of the country.

Platonic Solids – shapes with equal sides. The five platonic solids are; tetrahedron hexahedron, octahedron, dodecahedron and icosahedron.

S=k log W – the second law of thermodynamics. Entropy – a mathematical formula that represents the lack of order or predictability. A slow decline into disorder or randomness. (Our characters want to reverse this state of being or create a new one from the disorder the negative thoughts of man and the micro beasts have created.)

Sphere – a round solid with equal distance from its center.

Stickybeak – an overly inquisitive person.

Talking stick – a ceremonial stick that is passed around a group of people giving the holder the right to speak.

The devil's puppets – the people controlled by the micro demons. Those infected by the virus which is the dark matter.

The Tree of Life – a spiritual concept that has been used and referred to throughout the centuries in mythology, religion and philosophy to name but a few. It refers to the interconnection of life and its evolution.

Vremaya dlya distsipliny – Russian pronunciation for Время для дисциплины. English translation: time for discipline (a good whipping in this story).

If you enjoyed The Emerald Tablet Series, feel free to email the author by visiting www.jmhartwriter.com or by email author@jmhartwriter.com

Enjoy this book? You can make a big difference

Reviews are the most powerful tools in my arsenal when it comes getting attention for my books. Much as I'd like to, I don't have the financial muscle of a New York publisher. I can't take out full page ads in the newspaper or put posters on the subway. (Not yet, anyway).

But I do have something much more powerful and effective. A committed and loyal bunch of readers.

Honest reviews of my books help bring them to the attention of other readers.

If you've enjoyed The Emerald Tablet I would be very grateful if you could spend a few minutes leaving a review on your favorite online bookstore.

And If you've enjoyed The Emerald Tablet you can access BOOK TWO REALM OF LOST SOULS at: https://jmhartwriter.com/buy-now/

Thank you very much.

ACKNOWLEDGMENT

With gratitude, I would like to thank my high school English teacher and my supportive family and friends for their encouragements. Thank you, to the invaluable editors, Linda Funnell and Stephanie Smith who have been a tremendous support, and Creativindi Cover designers. No book is complete without the vital service of editors, proofreaders and great book cover designers. Finally, I would like to acknowledge the professional project management services of Joel Naoum from Critical Mass, who made it possible to share my story with you.

ABOUT THE AUTHOR

About JM Hart

Now semi-retired, JM moved to a peaceful county town south of Sydney, to focus on her grandchildren and writing.

JM Hart is the author of the Chronicles of the Supernatural. She makes her online home at http://jmhartwriter.com

You can also connect with JM Hart (Jeanette) on social media, and you should send her an email at author@jmhartwriter.com if the mood strikes you.